Judith Lennox was born in Salisbury, Wiltshire. She read English at Lancaster University and now lives in Cambridgeshire with her husband and three sons. She is the author of eight highly praised and bestselling novels, including most recently *The Dark-Eyed Girls*, *Written on Glass* and *Middlemere*

ALL MY SISTERS

In the years before the First World War, sisters Iris, Marianne, Eva and Clemency seek to follow their dreams. Marianne meets handsome Arthur Leighton, the love of her life, but Iris finds her ambition of a grand marriage dashed. Eva falls in love with a Bohemian, Gabriel Bellamy, whilst Clemency remains tied to the family home. Marianne finds herself trapped in an outpost of the empire. Only her beloved son and the memory of her sisters give her the strength to survive. As the clouds darken and war changes the lives of all the sisters, Iris, Marianne, Eva and Clemency must free themselves of the bonds that confine them and discover love at last.

Books by Judith Lennox
Published by The House of Ulverscroft:

SOME OLD LOVER'S GHOST
THE DARK-EYED GIRLS
WRITTEN ON GLASS
FOOTPRINTS ON THE SAND
THE WINTER HOUSE
THE SHADOW CHILD
MIDDLEMERE

JUDITH LENNOX

ALL MY SISTERS

Complete and Unabridged

CHARNWOOD
Leicester

First published in Great Britain in 2005 by
Macmillan
an imprint of Pan Macmillan Limited
London

First Charnwood Edition
published 2006
by arrangement with
Macmillan Publishers Limited
London

The moral right of the author has been asserted

British Library CIP Data

Lennox, Judith
    All my sisters.—Large print ed.—
Charnwood library series
1. Sisters—Fiction 2. Domestic fiction
3. Large type books
I. Title
823.9′14 [F]

ISBN 1–84617–121–0

Published by
F. A. Thorpe (Publishing)
Anstey, Leicestershire

Set by Words & Graphics Ltd.
Anstey, Leicestershire
Printed and bound in Great Britain by
T. J. International Ltd., Padstow, Cornwall

This book is printed on acid-free paper

To my sisters-in-law,
Frances and Sam

Acknowledgements

Grateful thanks are due to my son, Ewen, for his help with the medical issues in this book.

Thanks and appreciation also to the many kind people I met in Sri Lanka, who gave their time and shared their memories and expertise so generously. Special thanks to Susantha for making my stay in Sri Lanka so memorable and informative.

And, as always, thanks to my agent, Maggie Hanbury, and my husband, Iain, for their unflagging support.

Prologue

Nights she couldn't sleep, she soothed herself by making lists. Lists of the counties of Great Britain, her manufacturing cities and the principal exports of the empire. Lists of the kings and queens of England and the works of William Shakespeare. Every now and then something sparked a memory. *The Winter's Tale, Cymbeline, The Tempest*, she muttered to herself in the small hours of a hot January night, and she found herself remembering an evening at the theatre. Sitting beside her in the darkness, Arthur took her hand in his. His thumb stroked her palm; she remembered that small, insistent touch, recalled how desire had uncoiled inside her as she listened to the voices on stage. *Nothing of him that doth fade, but doth suffer a sea-change . . .*

Yet he had faded. There were gaps, pieces missing. Whole days — weeks, even — whose events she had forgotten. She could not recall, she realized with a pang, the events of ordinary, unremarkable days. Just as she could no longer really remember the precise shade of his eyes, the exact planes and angles of his face.

Her lists became an attempt to seal and solidify the past. She remembered picnics in the hills, holidays by the seaside. Here, in this desert place, she recalled the tang of the sea and the slippery rubberiness of a flail of brown seaweed. She heard the groan and clank of the bathing machine as it descended the beach, and remembered how, in the dim, stuffy interior of the hut, she had held her breath, anticipating the shock of the ice-cold water of the North Sea. She and her sisters had worn bathing costumes of black serge. The heavy material of the costumes, when wet, scratched the skin. On another part of the beach the poorer women bathed

1

in the sea in their summer frocks: she and Eva had watched, had seen how their pale skirts floated and billowed around them, giving them the look of strange, transparent sea creatures. *Like jellyfish, Marianne,* Eva had cried, her hand shading her narrowed eyes. *Like great big jellyfish!*

Had they watched them at Filey or at Scarborough, those women who had bobbed, fully dressed, in the surf, their tired faces rapt with delight? It troubled her now that she could not be sure. Waking in the early hours, her head full of nightmares, she was afraid of the future and haunted by the past. On the worst nights a voice echoed. *Four in the morning. The devil's hour.*

More memories to drive away the dark. She remembered the city of Sheffield, in which she had been born and brought up. She remembered the great shops and hotels in the centre, and the slur of grey smoke that hung like a shroud over the industrial district. She remembered the roar of the furnaces, the incessant clatter and crash of hammers and machinery. The crush of people, the smell of smoke and rain.

One airless, sleepless night, she recalled the drawing room at Summerleigh, with its four low armchairs upholstered in rust-coloured velvet, and Great-aunt Hannah's chair by the fire. On top of the piano were framed photographs of Mother and Father in their wedding finery, and a picture of Grandmother Maclise, as monumental as Queen Victoria, with her bun and jowls and steely glare. And a snapshot of the three boys — James was wearing a blazer and boater, Aidan and Philip were in sailor suits.

And a photograph of the four Maclise girls. She and her sisters were wearing their white muslin dresses. In the photograph the silk sashes around their waists had turned to shades of umber. But in Marianne's memory the sashes were coloured: Iris's sash was the same bright blue as her eyes, Eva's was apple green, Clemency's

2

butter yellow. Her own was the pale pink of Albertine roses. Iris — golden-haired, pink-and-white Iris — leant against the branch of a tree, laughing as she turned towards the camera. Tiny, shapely Eva stared fearlessly ahead. Clemency wore her dress awkwardly, as if ill at ease in muslin and silk. Marianne remembered that she herself had looked away, that the photographer had thought her shy of the lens.

He had been wrong, though. It was not that she was afraid to look, rather that she had always disliked to be looked at. She hated to walk into a crowded room; she never paused, as Iris did as she made her entrance, waiting for men's glances to turn to her, never managed that artful flick of a heel to reveal an alluring few inches of petticoat frilled with lace. She was both contemptuous of flirtation and incapable of it. Love, she had then believed, should be a meeting of hearts and minds, sealed by a glance, capable of surviving absence, change and death. Love, thought Marianne, came once in a lifetime.

In the distance an engine hooted, jolting her. She started, her eyes wide open in the darkness, her concentration wobbling and splitting, darting down all the familiar nightmarish byways.

The things she had seen, the things she had done. Things she would not then have believed herself capable of. Was anything left of the girl she had once been, the girl who had shied away from a camera lens, the girl who had fled when she felt a man's gaze on her? Was it possible to mutate into a completely different person?

Tell me about your family, Arthur had said to her the first time they met. *Your three brothers and your three sisters.* What would she reply if he could ask her the same question now? That she no longer knew them, those people she had once loved most in the world. And that if they had changed as much as she, then they must

3

be unrecognizable to each other.

Or that she missed them so much she sometimes thought that her grief must ooze with the sweat through her pores. Her sisters, all her sisters, whom she must never see again.

1

Glued to the wall as she made her slow, solitary circuit around the ballroom, Marianne overheard one of the chaperones make the remark to Mrs Catherwood, who had taken the Maclise girls, along with her own daughter, Charlotte, to the ball. The chaperones sat together in a room next to the ballroom, the door open so that they could keep an eye on their charges. The *tricoteuses*, Iris called them, in that gently sarcastic way of hers. Mrs Palmer said, 'The second Maclise girl is such a beanpole!' and kind Mrs Catherwood replied, 'Marianne will be very striking in a year or two, when she has grown into her looks.' Yet it was the first sentence that stayed with Marianne as she retreated into the shadow of a heavy purple velvet curtain. *Such a beanpole . . . such a beanpole . . .* The familiar doubts began to creep over her. It was hard not to stoop as some tall girls did to make themselves smaller, hard not to twist the ribbon of her dance programme round its empty pages.

She wished she were at home with Eva and Clemency. Lucky, lucky Eva, to have a cold, and lucky Clemmie, not to be out yet, not to have to endure this horrible ball. She wished she was curled up on the window seat of the bedroom that she shared with Iris, having taken *Three Weeks* from its hiding place beneath bundles of stockings in her chest of drawers. Reading, Marianne found herself turning the pages in a fever. Sometimes Paul Verdayne, pursuing his mysterious beauty in a Swiss hotel, seemed more real and vivid to her than her home and family.

She longed for mystery and romance, for new sights and faces, for something — someone — to speed the

5

beat of her heart. But what mystery, she thought, as she scornfully surveyed the room, was there to be had in Sheffield? There was Ellen Hutchinson, in a perfectly dreadful pink satin frock, dancing with James. A poor look-out when one's own brother was the bestlooking man at a ball. And there was Iris, being steered clumsily round the floor by Ronnie Catherwood. Marianne sighed. Every face was familiar to her. How could she possibly marry one of these boys she had known since childhood, whose faces sported patchy moustaches or, worse, a scattering of scarlet pimples? There was something unfinished about them, something slightly ridiculous. The thought of leaving her family to spend the rest of her life with one of these awkward, commonplace young men was distasteful.

Yet she must marry because, if she did not, then what would she do? Her life would go on, she supposed, in much the same way as it did now. Because her mother never seemed to keep a maid for more than a year, the house did not run as smoothly as it should. And because her mother's health was poor, and because Iris had the knack of avoiding such things, she, Marianne, took responsibility for much of the housekeeping. It occurred to her that she might end up like Great-aunt Hannah, a spinster aunt. She would wear enormous stays like Great-aunt Hannah's and possibly a wig. Imagining herself in black bombazine with whiskers on her chin, Marianne giggled.

And then she became aware that someone was looking at her. Later she could not have said how she knew. You couldn't *feel* the direction of a man's eyes, could you?

He was standing on the far side of the room. As their eyes met, he smiled and inclined his head in a small bow. She was aware of an odd feeling of recognition. She must know him, she thought, she must have met him at some interminable At Home or dull concert. Yet if they had met before, she would surely have remembered him.

His gaze seemed to burn into her; she felt a sudden need to escape. Darting between portly ladies with ostrich feathers in their hair and middle-aged, moustachioed men, who ogled her as she passed, she hurried out of the ballroom. She reached a long, ill-lit passageway, from which rooms led off to either side. She could hear the clank and hiss of the kitchens. Maids bustled along the corridor carrying trays of glasses; in the distance a manservant in shirt sleeves and apron struck a match to light a cigarette.

Opening a door, Marianne found herself in a small room. Inside, there were a couple of chairs, their upholstery worn and sagging, a music stand, and a piano, a battered upright. Marianne unbuttoned her gloves and ran her fingers over the keys. Then she shuffled through the music. Sitting down, she played softly at first, not wanting to be discovered, but then she lost herself in the music, gave herself up to it.

The door opened; she saw the man from the ballroom. She lifted her hands from the piano. They shook, hovering a few inches above the keys.

'I beg your pardon,' he said. 'I didn't mean to startle you.'

Quickly she closed the music book. 'I should go back.'

'Why did you run away? Do you prefer playing the piano to dancing?'

'But I wasn't dancing.'

'Did you wish that you were?'

She shook her head. 'I wished I was at home with my sisters.'

His thick, wavy, golden-brown hair was clipped short, and his blue eyes were several shades lighter than her own. His even features and firm jaw gave an impression of solidity and strength. She guessed that he was some

7

years older than her and several inches taller. Beside him she would not have to stoop or bow her head.

He asked her, 'How many sisters do you have?'

'Three.'

'Any brothers?'

'Three.'

'Seven of you! I'm an only child. I've always found it hard to imagine what it must be like to be part of a large family.'

'Only children often seem to envy large families.'

'Do they? I'm afraid I've always rather enjoyed my solitary state. In a large family one must fear being overlooked.' His gaze rested on her. 'Though I don't suppose you are ever overlooked.'

'I wouldn't mind being overlooked. It's people looking at me — judging me — that I can't bear.' She fell silent, horrified to have spoken so frankly.

'Perhaps they're not judging you. Perhaps they're admiring you.'

The second Maclise girl is such a beanpole. Marianne half-rose from the piano stool. 'I should go back.'

'Why? You don't wish to dance. The company bores you. So why go back? Unless, of course, I bore you more.'

She should return to the ballroom because the proximity of him, enclosed in this small room, unsettled her. But she could not say that. Instead, she sank back into her seat.

'Well, then, that's splendid, Miss . . . ?'

'Maclise,' she murmured. 'Marianne Maclise.'

'Arthur Leighton.' He took her hand. 'Tell me about your family. Your three brothers and your three sisters. Where do you fit in?'

'James is the oldest and then there's Iris. Iris is here tonight. You must have seen her in the ballroom. She has golden hair and blue eyes. She's beautiful.'

8

'Was she wearing a white gown? Diamonds in her ears and a white gardenia in her hair?'

'You *did* notice her.' She was aware of a stab of envy: Iris was always the favourite.

But he said, 'I like to observe. There's often a greater pleasure to be found in observation than in conversation.'

'Oh, do you think so? So do I. Conversation often seems so . . . so *forced*. So *false*.' The words rushed out, a gasp of recognition.

'Though not always,' he said gently. 'Our conversation doesn't feel false, does it?' He went on, 'So there's James and Iris. And then . . . ?'

'And then me, and then Eva. Eva's dark, like me. Though she's not like me at all, really. She's not nearly so tall, and she's more . . . more *certain*, more sure of herself.' Marianne pleated the folds of her silk skirt. 'I seem to see two sides to everything.'

'Some would say that was an asset — a sign of maturity.'

'But how do you choose? When you have to decide something important, how do you know?'

'Sometimes you have to take a chance. That's what I find, anyway.'

She said bitterly, 'I expect the decisions you make are a little more important than mine. I seem to spend an age racking my brains as to whether I should wear my pink dress or my white, or whether I should tell the cook to make blancmange or jam roly-poly.'

'Oh, jam roly-poly,' he said seriously. 'Much nicer than blancmange. And you should wear white rather than pink. Leave pink to pretty blondes like your sister Iris. Though I should love to see you in more dramatic shades. Violet, perhaps, like your flowers — they're just the colour of your eyes.'

Marianne was speechless. No man, neither her father nor her brothers nor her friends' brothers, had ever

9

commented on her clothing in such a way. She was afraid that there was something improper about it.

He went on, 'Who's next? A sister or a brother?'

'Clemency,' she said. 'My sister Clemency's next. And then there's Aidan and Philip. Aidan's thirteen and Phil's just eleven. I'm not sure I know what they're really like. They're just the boys, and they're there at the end of the family. Only Clemmie seems to have time for them. The rest of us just let them get on.'

'It must be a very busy household. You must never be lonely.'

She should go back to the ballroom, she thought. An unmarried girl should never be alone with a man, it was an inviolable rule. Yet she stayed where she was, sitting on the piano stool. The hidden, rebellious part of her, the part that she so rarely allowed a voice, told her to throw caution to the wind and ignore convention. Just now she felt alive; she could almost feel the blood coursing through her veins. For once she did not want to be anywhere else, or be with anyone else.

She gave herself a little shake, as if to drive away such unsuitable thoughts, and said, 'Please tell me about your family, Mr Leighton.'

'I haven't much of one, I'm afraid. My mother died when I was an infant and I lost my father when I was in my twenties. I have an uncle and a cousin or two. But you mustn't feel sorry for me. I have a great many friends.'

'Here? In Sheffield?'

'I've been staying with the Palmers for the past week. I rather like this city. There are some fine sights.' The corners of his mouth curled.

If she were Iris, she would simper now and make some remark that pretended to discourage him, yet which inspired him to further compliments. For the first time, it occurred to her that he might merely be flirting with her. Her spirits sank, her disappointment heavier

10

than she would have thought possible after such a brief acquaintance.

Then he said, 'When I saw you in the ballroom you were laughing. You looked so serious and then suddenly you laughed. And I wondered why you were laughing.'

'I was imagining,' she said, 'that I was a very old, fat spinster.'

His mouth twitched. 'That doesn't seem a likely fate for you.'

'It seems to me perfectly possible.'

'You can't really think that.'

'I know that I disconcert people. They don't say anything, of course, but I know that I do. I say the wrong things.' She looked up at him. 'Our conversation has been full of wrong things, Mr Leighton. We've talked about things we shouldn't have talked about. Things that aren't quite proper.'

'What should we have talked about?'

'Oh . . . the weather . . . and how splendid the Hutchinsons' ballroom looks.'

'I see — '

'And how well the band played.'

'The violinist was out of key. Would it be proper for me to mention that?'

She smiled. 'Well, he was. Quite dreadfully.'

After a silence, he said, 'Would it be proper for me to tell you, then, that you were mistaken earlier?'

'Mistaken?'

'When you told me that your sister, Iris, was beautiful.'

She repeated, startled, 'But everyone thinks Iris is beautiful!'

'Iris is very pretty,' he said. 'But she is not beautiful. You, Miss Maclise, are beautiful.'

She had the odd habit, when she was embarrassed, of losing what little colour she had rather than blushing.

11

Now, she felt herself pale, the surface of her skin chilling.

He sat back in his chair, watching her. 'Well then,' he said, 'you should know the truth.'

★　★　★

After the ball, in her bedroom at home, Marianne unpinned the posy of violets she wore at her waist and laid them carefully on her dressing table. Then she unhooked her gown and hung it in the closet and untied her layers of petticoats: they whispered as she shed them, falling to the floor in a pool of silk. She unlaced her stays and peeled off her silk stockings, camisole and knickers. Then she reached up and pulled the pins from her hair. It fell, long and dark, down her back. Naked, she studied her reflection in the mirror. He had told her that she was beautiful and, for the first time in her life, she believed that she was.

She remembered that Arthur Leighton had asked her to play for him and she had played a piece by Rameau. Now, as she hummed the melody under her breath, she recalled how, halfway through the piece, she had reached up to turn the page just as he had reached down to do likewise, and their hands had touched. And with that touch, in that single moment, she had moved through the thicket of disguises that surrounded men and women, and all that confused her, all she had been contemptuous of — the artifice of appearance, the falseness of flirtation, and all the cold marital calculations of wealth and class — had become unimportant. She had desired him, and she had known, though he had not said, that he had desired her.

She put on her nightgown, and then she took out her diary. *May 20th, 1909*, she wrote. *A magical evening. Tonight, my life has truly begun.*

★　★　★

Clemency reached the top of the attic stairs and peered into the darkness. 'Philip?' she called. 'Philip, are you in here?' Shapes loomed in the light of the oil lamp she was gripping in her hand, revealing themselves after a moment as a three-legged chair or a tower of books, spines hanging from their crumbling backs.

'Philip?' she called again. Philip had a habit of going into hiding the day before he had to return to boarding school, but the attics had been a long shot: he was unlikely to have hidden there because he was afraid of the dark.

As she went back down the corridor, a flicker of movement beneath a bed in an empty room caught her eye. Clemency knelt down by the bed. 'Philip?' she said softly.

No reply. But she could hear his slightly laboured breathing. 'Philip?' she said again. 'Do come out, please. No one's going to be cross with you, I promise.'

There was a shuffling and then he emerged head first from beneath the bed. There were dust balls in his hair and his clothes were filthy.

She sat down on the bed and took him on her knee. 'Dear old Phil,' she said, hugging him, 'I'm so glad to have found you. I've been looking for you since breakfast.' He was wheezing slightly. 'You shouldn't get so dusty. You know it makes you unwell.'

They went downstairs. It was half-term; Philip's bag lay open in the bedroom he shared with Aidan. Clemency thought: *Six weeks, six whole weeks till I see him again. Don't you dare blub*, she scolded herself, and said briskly, 'Your crayons, Philip. You haven't packed your crayons.'

He looked round. The crayons were in an old biscuit tin on top of the chest of drawers. Philip's vague blue

13

gaze turned in their direction, washed over them, moved on.

'On the drawers,' she prompted and watched him squint, struggling to focus.

Clemency went to see her mother. Lilian Maclise was sitting at her dressing table. As always, the room was in semi-darkness, the curtains drawn to shut out the sunlight. Though the day was warm, a fire flickered in the grate.

'Are you feeling better, Mother?'

'I'm afraid not, Clemency.' Lilian sat back in the chair, her eyes closed. Her fair hair fell around her face, framing delicate features. Her hands, rearranging the bottles and jars on the dressing table, were small and pale and slender.

Beside her mother, Clemency always felt big-boned and clumsy. She said, 'I'm worried about Philip, Mother. I think he has trouble with his eyes.'

'Nonsense,' said Lilian. 'No one in the family has poor eyesight.'

Clemency persisted. 'I don't think he can see very well at all. I thought perhaps he should wear spectacles.'

'*Spectacles?*' Lilian glanced at her reflection in the mirror and gave her silk shawl a forceful twitch. 'What an extraordinary idea. If Philip's eyesight is poor — which I dispute, Clemency — then wearing spectacles would be the worst thing for him. It's well known that wearing spectacles weakens the eyes.'

A trickle of sweat ran down Clemency's back and she moved away from the fire. 'But Mother, he can't see — '

'If you could speak a little less loudly, dear. My poor head.' Lilian closed her eyes.

Alarmed, Clemency said, 'Mother?'

'I'm so sorry, darling.' Lilian pressed her fingertips against her forehead. 'I feel exhausted. And the pain . . . '

Clemency's stomach swooped unpleasantly. Mother's

14

health had been so much better recently that for the last month she had been able to join the family downstairs at mealtimes. Clemency had begun to hope that her mother was recovering at last. Not that Clemency could remember Mother ever having been really well — she had taken to her bed shortly after Philip had been born, when Clemency herself had been only five. Philip was eleven now, and the mood of the Maclise household rose and fell according to the state of Lilian's health.

Lilian whispered, 'Oh dear. This really is too tiresome. You must be so fed up with me, darling. I should think you've had just about enough of your hopeless old mother.'

'Of course not! You mustn't ever think that, Mother. I only want you to be well. That's the only thing that matters.'

Lilian smiled bravely. 'Perhaps you'd ask Marianne to bring me a small glass of port wine. And if you would make sure my letters go by the next post . . . '

As Clemency took the letters and left the room, she thought with a sudden rush of joy, five days, just five days till the beginning of term. Unlike Philip, she loved school. She bounded down the stairs three at a time, her plait bouncing against her back.

Iris caught her at the bottom of the stairs. 'Where are you going?'

'Mother wants a glass of wine and I have to post these.'

Iris, the mean thing, snatched the letters from her. 'I'll take them,' she said and, seizing her hat from the stand, left the house.

★ ★ ★

Iris's bicycle had a puncture so she took Clemency's. One advantage of Mother's aversion to the telephone, Iris thought, as she pedalled out of the drive, was that it

15

necessitated a great deal of letter writing and consequently a great many excursions to the postbox.

Sometimes, escaping from the house on her bicycle, she glanced in shop windows or just looked at other ladies to get new ideas for trimming hats. Occasionally, breaking the rule that an unmarried girl should never be alone in the company of men, she met the Catherwood brothers for a walk in the park.

In the four years since she had left school, Iris had received more than a dozen proposals of marriage. She had accepted none of them. One or two of her suitors would have been a very good match, the sort of advantageous marriage Iris expected eventually to make, but still she had turned them down. She simply hadn't wanted to marry any of them. It wasn't that there was anything wrong with them, just that she didn't love them. Recently her inability to find a husband had begun to trouble her. She was twenty-two years old and most of her contemporaries were married or engaged. Some had children. She had begun to doubt whether she was capable of falling in love — other girls seemed to do it all the time, but not once had Iris's heart been touched. Sometimes she found herself staring in the mirror as she brushed out her hair before going to bed and thinking: *Perhaps I am losing my touch*. She had to look at her reflection to reassure herself, to see how her hair, her greatest beauty, fell almost to her waist like a golden veil. Yet it remained with her, that moth of disquiet, stirring now and then, a small, dry flutter in the back of her mind.

The bicycle began to gather speed as she headed downhill. Houses and trees rushed by; Iris's hat threatened to fly from its anchorage of pins and her skirts billowed up, showing rather a lot of ankle.

Then, without warning, the front wheel suddenly bit into the tarmac and Iris lost her grip on the handlebars as she was thrown forward. A split second later and she was sprawled face down on the road. She couldn't move because the bicycle had fallen on top of her. She wailed, 'My *frock*!' and someone scooped the bicycle off her and said anxiously, 'Are you all right?'

Looking up, she saw that her rescuer was young and not at all bad-looking. He wasn't wearing a hat and his fair, untidy hair, which was lightened in places by the sun to the colour of straw, curled slightly.

The frill which Iris had sewn onto her dress only the previous day was now a ribbon of pink cloth snaking across the tarmac. She said, furiously this time, 'My *frock*. It's *new*.'

He offered her his hand to help her up. 'I think it was the frock that did for you. That bit — ' he pointed to the frill — 'got caught in the chain. I say, you *are* hurt.'

Iris's gloves were ripped and her palms were bleeding from where she had put out her hands to break her fall. 'It's nothing much.'

He dug in his pocket and found a handkerchief. 'If you'd let me help.'

She sat on a low wall while he peeled off her gloves and picked out grit from the deep grazes in her hands. Though he was very careful, she had to bite her lip to stop herself crying out. As he tied a handkerchief round each hand, she said politely, 'You've been most kind, Mr — '

'Ash,' he said. 'Just Ash.'

'Ash?'

'Ashleigh Aurelian Wentworth. It's a bit of a mouthful, isn't it? I prefer Ash.'

Iris told him her name. Then, looking round, she said, 'I was supposed to be posting my mother's letters.'

He found them in the gutter, the envelopes crumpled and smeared with mud. 'Perhaps you'd better take them home. Your mother may want to re-address them.'

'Oh dear.' Iris sighed. 'I'm afraid there's going to be a dreadful fuss.'

17

'It was an accident. I'm sure your mother will understand.'

'Clemency won't,' said Iris ruefully. 'It was her bicycle.'

Ash picked up the bicycle. The front wheel was buckled. 'Where do you live?'

She told him and he said, 'I'll push it home for you, then.'

'I don't want to put you to any trouble. I'm sure you have things to do.'

'It's no trouble. And no, I don't really have anything to do just now.'

'Nothing at all? Where were you going?'

'Nowhere in particular.' He was unpicking a remnant of pink cloth from the bicycle chain. 'I like to wander, don't you?' He flashed her a smile. 'You never know who you might run into.'

They were heading up the hill. She said, 'That's what I was doing, actually. Just wandering. I'm not supposed to, of course.'

'Why on earth not?' She noticed that his eyes were a warm hazel — so much nicer, Iris thought, than the cold blue Maclise eyes. She realized also that he didn't understand at all. So she explained.

'Because I should be chaperoned, naturally. I'm not meant to go out on my own. My mother or my aunt or my sisters or one of the maids is supposed to come with me. But all that's so tiresome.' She shrugged. 'And, anyway, I like to break the rules.' Glancing at him, she asked, 'Haven't you any sisters?'

'Not one, I'm afraid.'

'And you're not married?' It was always best to establish that sort of thing early on.

'Married? Oh, no.'

'Do you come from Sheffield?'

He shook his head. 'Cambridgeshire. I graduated from university a couple of years ago.'

'And since then?'

'I suppose I've just been *wandering*. And you, Miss Maclise? What do you do?'

'Oh, the usual things,' she said vaguely. 'Tennis and bridge and dancing . . . '

He was looking at her as though he expected her to say something more. She racked her brains, trying to think how she passed the time, and added weakly, 'And I sew . . . '

'Do you like to read?'

'Sometimes. My sister Marianne always has her nose in a book.'

After a short silence he said, 'Tennis . . . dancing . . . Doesn't all that get rather . . . rather *dull*?'

'Not at all! I love playing tennis — and I adore dancing.' She felt disconcerted, forced to defend a way of life she had not previously questioned. 'What do *you* do, Ash? Apart from wandering, that is.'

'Oh, this and that. I was in London after I left university.'

'*London*. Lucky you.'

'I was working at a university settlement — that's an association which brings university students and the poor together. And then I travelled for six months on the Continent. And since then I've done various things — some journalism, some photography . . . and I did a bit of climbing in the Highlands of Scotland. Oh, and I've been helping my guardian with his book.'

'Your guardian's writing a book? What kind of book? Is it a novel?'

He shook his head. 'It's a compendium of all the knowledge there is in the world. History and science and mythology — everything.'

'Goodness,' she said faintly.

'He'll never finish it, of course.' Ash grinned. 'People keep coming up with new discoveries and poor old Emlyn has to rewrite an entire section.'

19

'That must be rather depressing.'

'I don't think Emlyn finds it so. He always says that it's the journey that matters, not the destination.' He glanced at her. 'You don't agree with that?'

'I'd never really thought about it.' She thought of her so far fruitless efforts to find a husband: she had loved the dancing, the flirtations, the stolen kisses, yet if, heaven forbid, she never married, then what was the point of it all? She said, 'Journeys must have an end, surely? And it may as well be a nice end.'

'But then,' he pointed out, 'when you reached the end, you'd have to start all over again and think of something else to do.'

'Dear me, how exhausting you make it all sound!' But, looking at him, she saw a glint of mischief in his eyes and, piqued, she cried out, 'You're teasing me!'

'Just a little. How are your hands?'

'Fine,' she said. 'Absolutely fine.'

'You're very stout-hearted, Miss Maclise.'

No one had ever described her as stout-hearted before. She was afraid that there was something unflattering about it.

They turned the corner of the road. 'This is where I live,' Iris said.

Ash looked up to where Summerleigh was scrawled in wrought-iron across the gates. As they headed down the drive, the front door opened and Eva peered out. 'Iris,' she called out as she ran down the steps. 'Mother's been looking for you for ages.' She stopped, her eyes wide. 'Your *dress*. And your *hands*!'

Iris turned to Ash. 'If I were you, I'd go. There's going to be a bit of a row. But you've been so kind and I'm very grateful. And you must promise to call again so that I can introduce you to my family.'

★ ★ ★

20

Eva was painting Great-aunt Hannah. She placed the stoneware vase with the peacock feathers to one side of her, and had the spaniel, Winnie, lie on the rug at her feet. Great-aunt Hannah was wearing a gown of shiny black stuff. The folds and wrinkles of her neck drooped around the high collar of the gown, and the stiffly boned bodice encased her body like armour. Eva had often wondered whether Great-aunt Hannah possessed one shiny black dress or twenty dresses all the same. It seemed to Eva that a great many mysteries surrounded Great-aunt Hannah: how old she was, how she passed the time during the long hours she spent alone in her room, why she always smelt of camphor, and whether she ever released her hair from the tight knot on the back of her head — whether it *could* be released, in fact, or whether, as Eva suspected, it had been twisted into a knot for so many years that it had long ago adhered into a solid lump.

The portrait was almost finished. Eva put a white highlight on the stoneware vase and a smaller touch of white in Hannah's eyes. Then she stood back from the easel and thought: *There, even if you are a hundred years old and you die tomorrow, now I shall have something to remember you by.*

After she had left school the previous summer Eva had continued to have fortnightly lessons with her art teacher, Miss Garnett. Miss Garnett's lodgings were in Plumpton Street, above a yeast merchant's. She had chosen the attic rooms, Miss Garnett explained to Eva, because of the light. The sitting room looked out onto the soot-blackened rear of a carriage maker's. On the window sill, a bowl with an opalescent glaze caught the coral rays of the late afternoon sun. The heavy aromas of linseed oil and paint mingled with the Bovril smell of the yeast. Eva loved Miss Garnett's studio. One day, she promised herself, she, too, would have a place of her own.

At the end of May Miss Garnett invited Eva to a women's suffrage meeting. The meeting took place in the overfurnished, overheated drawing room of a house in Fulwood. Their hostess, a buxom matron in electric blue cretonne, peered at Eva through her lorgnette and said in a carrying voice, 'Sweet little thing, but she has a wilful look. Are you wilful, Miss Maclise?'

Miss Garnett rescued Eva and introduced her to two young women standing in a corner of the room. One of the women, Miss Jackson, wore the purple, green and white ribbon of Mrs Pankhurst's Women's Social and Political Union pinned to her loose dress of chequered blue and white cotton. The second woman, Miss Bowen, had straight, shiny black hair cut level with her shoulders and tied at the nape of her neck. Her mouth was a slash of scarlet. She wore a square-necked dress of mint-green linen and her ankles were bare. Eva bitterly envied Miss Garnett and her friends. A recent attempt to imitate Miss Garnett's simple clothing had ended with her being banned from the breakfast table by her mother and banished to her room until she was decently dressed. Now she was sweltering in a jacket, blouse and skirt, petticoat, stockings, camisole and stays, her heavy brown hair piled on top of her head, her body wrapped up like a parcel, concealed beneath layers of material, trapped, breathless, gasping for air.

Miss Bowen studied Eva. 'Is she talented, Rowena?'

'Talented enough,' said Miss Garnett, and smiled at Eva.

'High praise indeed. Rowena isn't usually so generous with her compliments, Miss Maclise. You must be terribly clever.'

Someone rang a bell, calling the meeting to order. A grey-haired woman stood up and began, in a low monotone, to read the minutes of the previous meeting. Miss Bowen yawned and offered Eva her cigarette case. Miss Garnett whispered, 'Lydia, I didn't bring Eva here to corrupt her,' and Lydia pouted.

'What did you bring her here for? To galvanize her? To stir her to revolutionary zeal through the eloquence of our oratory?'

Miss Jackson sniggered.

'I brought Eva here to *inform* her, perhaps,' said Miss Garnett mildly. 'But she must make up her own mind.'

'Didn't that school of yours teach her anything, Rowena?' Miss Jackson accepted one of Miss Bowen's cigarettes. 'How old are you, Miss Maclise? Eighteen? I should have thought that you would have come to an opinion on the subject of women's suffrage by now. There can hardly be a matter of greater importance.'

'Oh, come now, May.' Miss Bowen fitted a cigarette into an elegant onyx holder. Her green eyes sparkled. 'There are dozens of matters of equal importance. Such as what should one wear, and how one should do one's hair, and whether one can be bothered to attend whichever dreary party one has been invited to.'

Miss Jackson had gone rather pink. 'Really, Lydia, if you're going to be flippant — '

'Don't take any notice, May,' said Miss Garnett gently. 'Lydia's just teasing you.'

'Not at all,' said Miss Bowen. 'I stand by what I say. It often seems just as much trouble to choose one's frock as to march through Hyde Park. More, perhaps.' She smiled at Eva. 'But then I'm hopelessly lazy, I'm afraid.'

'Lydia, you're being ridiculous. You work so hard.' Miss Garnett explained to Eva, 'Lydia owns a gallery in London.'

'In Charlotte Street, actually.'

Miss Jackson gestured wildly with her cigarette, spraying ash over the Aubusson rug. 'Here we are, independent, responsible women with careers and homes of our own, and yet we have no say in who represents us in parliament or in the laws that bind us. It's quite outrageous, isn't it?'

'Absolutely preposterous,' said Miss Bowen. 'And I can't see anything changing for some considerable time. Women have been fighting for the vote for more than forty years. If we're good girls and behave ourselves and write nice letters to our MPs, then we're told that we don't care strongly enough to be given the vote. So we've marched and filled Hyde Park with women demanding the vote, and we've thrown eggs at politicians and we've been sent to prison for our pains. And what has been the response of our lords and masters? Well, they shake their heads and say tut-tut, we've proved that they were right all along, we're far too silly and hysterical to be allowed to vote.' She turned to Eva. 'Will you go to art school, my dear? If you're as talented as Rowena says you are, then you should study painting. Miss Maclise should go to art school, shouldn't she, Rowena?'

'Well,' said Miss Garnett slowly, 'since the subject has come up . . . I've been meaning to talk to you, Eva. If you're to develop as an artist you must broaden your horizons. You could continue to study in Sheffield, of course, or you could try for a college in Manchester. But I'd like you to consider the Slade in London. I studied there, and I know that you'd learn so much. Women students are allowed to draw from life at the Slade. Some of the other colleges are rather old-fashioned about such things.'

'Art school . . . ' Eva felt a thrill of excitement.

'Yes, why not?'

Eva imagined herself escaping the routine of home, a routine which, during the year since she had left school, had settled around her like a smothering blanket. She imagined herself in London, surrounded by daring, fashionable friends.

Miss Garnett said, 'Or would your father object, do you think?'

Eva's dreams punctured, fizzed, fell to earth. But she

24

stuck out her chin. 'I'm sure Father will see that I should go to art school. I'm sure I can *make* him see.'

'Bravo, Miss Maclise,' cried Miss Bowen. 'Spoken like a trooper.' She clapped her hands.

★　★　★

A few days later Eva went to see her father.

He was in his study. His desk was covered in paperwork, but he held out his arms. 'Give me a hug, kitten.' He smelt of tobacco and sandalwood soap, scents Eva had always associated with security and affection. 'How's my girl, then?'

'I'm very well.'

'Splendid,' said Joshua and picked up his pen.

Eva said quickly, 'When you were young, what were you good at, Father?'

He considered. 'Arithmetic. I've always been good at arithmetic. And I understand machinery, of course. And I was the one to see when we should invest and when we should get rid of a line that wasn't making money. If I hadn't had the knack of it, the business wouldn't have grown.'

Eva said cunningly, 'And if your father had told you that you must do something else . . . if he'd told you that you must — oh, go into the Church or become a schoolteacher — '

Joshua snorted. 'Fine schoolteacher I'd be. Haven't the patience.'

'But if he had?' she persisted. 'Would you have been happy, do you think?'

He looked at her sharply. 'This isn't to do with your painting nonsense, is it?'

His casual dismissal of what she most cared about angered Eva and she cried, 'Painting isn't nonsense!'

'Oh, it's a nice enough hobby for a girl to have.' He was sorting through the heap of letters; Eva sensed that

25

his mind was only half on the conversation. 'It's refined and ladylike to be able to paint a nice watercolour, I suppose.'

Eva marshalled her thoughts and tried to recall her most persuasive arguments, arguments which, when planning this conversation, she had been certain must sway her father.

'The Bible tells us we shouldn't waste our talents. You didn't waste yours did you, Father?'

'It's different for girls,' he said. 'I wouldn't want you mixing with some of the people I've had to mix with, Eva, or putting up with the muck and noise I have to work in each day. My grandmother made bone handles for knives. She had a hard life. I'm proud that none of you girls have to live as she did. Everything I've done has been so you could have a better start in life.'

'Painting's not like working in a cutler's shop. It's not noisy or dirty.' Eva hid her hands in the folds of her skirt so that her father would not see that her fingers were black with charcoal. 'You can paint sitting in a studio. Or in a field. You can paint anywhere.'

'If you can paint anywhere, then why do you have to go to London?'

She began to feel cornered. She said desperately, 'How can I do good work if I've not been taught?'

'You don't *need* to work. And that's the truth of it, Eva. You're lucky enough to have me to keep you in pretty frocks.'

'I don't care about frocks,' she muttered.

'You'd care soon enough if you had to earn your daily bread,' he said sharply. 'That sort of talk is nonsense. You haven't seen what I've seen — lasses your age with hardly a rag to cover their backs. Kiddies with no shoes on their feet in the middle of winter — and in this city. You should be thankful for what you've got.'

She wanted to say to him: I haven't seen what you've seen because you won't let me see. I *long* to see the world. Instead, she took a deep breath and said, 'Please don't think I'm not grateful for everything you've done for me, Father.'

'You're very young, Eva. Just a lass. How could I let you go to London on your own? How could I cast you loose in a place like that? Anything could happen to you.'

Anticipating this objection, Eva had come forearmed. 'Miss Garnett told me that there are boarding houses for ladies in London. Ladies from good families.'

She could see him teetering on the brink of changing his mind. Her heart pounded with excitement. Then he said slowly, 'It's only . . . *London*. I can't abide the place myself.' His face lightened and he said suddenly, 'What if we split our differences, Eva, you and I? I could pay for you to have lessons with some fancy teacher up here. Someone better than your Miss Garnett. In Sheffield — or Manchester, even.'

'But I need to go to London!' she wailed. 'I need to learn to draw from life!'

'There's plenty of *life* in Sheffield.'

'I need,' she explained, 'to learn to draw from the human body.'

As soon as she had said it, she wanted to bite the words back.

She saw the shock in his eyes. 'The human body?' he repeated. 'You're not saying what I think you're saying, are you, Eva?'

She found herself gabbling, 'There's nothing wrong in it — it's not improper — artists have always drawn from life.'

'That's as maybe, but no daughter of mine will!' Joshua's mood had always been quick to change; now he lurched from conciliation to outrage in the space of a moment. 'And '*not improper*'! If that isn't improper, then I'd like to know what is in your book!'

'But I have to go to art school, Father!' she wailed. 'I

27

have to. Other women do — respectable women — '

'No, Eva,' he said sharply. 'Enough of all this fuss. You're giving me a sore head. I'll hear no more of it. Be off with you, I've important work to do.'

'But this is important to *me*! This is the most important thing to me!'

'Aye,' he said. 'Too important, perhaps.' His dark blue eyes, the twins of her own, narrowed as he looked at her closely. 'What's that?'

He was staring at the ribbon she had pinned to her lapel. 'It's the colours of the Women's Social and Political Union,' Eva said proudly. 'Miss Garnett's friend, Miss Jackson — '

'Miss Garnett this, Miss Garnett that!' cried Joshua. 'That Miss Garnett's putting ideas into your head. Maybe I should have a word with her, tell her you won't be taking any more lessons!'

She gasped. 'Father, you mustn't — '

'Mustn't I? How dare you question me? You'll do what you're told, young lady! You'll forget about this painting nonsense, Eva, and you'll do your duty at home!'

'But I *hate* being at home!'

He had gone crimson. 'How can you be so stubborn? How can you be so . . . so . . . *unladylike?*'

The words tumbled from her unchecked. 'And how can you be so narrow-minded — so old-fashioned — so *cruel* — '

As Joshua rose, he thumped the desk so hard that the cup jumped in the saucer. Alarmed, Eva took a step backwards, and then she turned and ran out of the door.

★　★　★

After the quarrel with her father, Eva cried so much that she felt lightheaded and rather sick. Though she

28

went to her art lesson, Miss Garnett, noticing her red eyes and trembling hand, sent her home early. On her way back to Summerleigh she wheeled her bicycle into a small park. Clouds were gathering overhead, blotting out the sun, casting shadows on the lawns and gravel paths. Eva sat down on a bench. She knew that her dream was over before it had even begun. Her father would never change his mind; if there had been a way of persuading him to let her go to art school, then she had not found it. She had lost her temper and had screamed like a fishwife. And how could she have been so foolish as to let slip that she needed to learn to draw from life? Nothing could have been more designed to antagonize him.

Only her father could reduce her to tears and temper, yet her feelings for him were unmixed and always had been. She might never articulate her love for him, but it was there, a golden thread that ran through her life. She admired his energy, his confidence, his strength. Part of her recognized that they quarrelled because they were in some ways the same. They shared the same stubbornness, had the same knack of making up their minds and refusing to change. They neither drifted with the wind like Marianne nor used subtlety to achieve their ends like Iris. They were incapable of manipula- tiveness — incapable, often, of tact.

They had never quarrelled like this, though. Her father had never before been so angry with her. The memory of what she had said to him made her feel hot with shame. *How can you be so narrow-minded, so old-fashioned, so cruel?* She had recognized shock in her father's eyes and, worse, hurt. She knew that she had crossed a line and she longed to put things right.

A church clock chimed. Eva had a sudden inspiration. She would cycle to the works and ask Father to forgive her. Instead of going home to Summerleigh, she headed for the city centre. Cycling past the big hotels and department stores, she made her way to the industrial district. Here flames from the foundry chimneys gouged orange scars through a turbulent sky. She could hear the gasp and crash and roar of the steam engines and hammers; she could taste the soot in the raindrops. The warehouses were reflected in the soupy, discoloured waters of the river; ships unloaded coal and loaded up with steel girders and machine parts. Eva imagined those ships heading out to sea, crossing oceans, making their way to the far distant countries of the empire. Enveloped by noise and crowds, she felt as if she were coming alive, waking after a long sleep, charged as though with electricity.

Looming through the smog, she caught sight of her father's name, *J. Maclise*, painted white in letters four foot high across the blackened brick of a warehouse. Pausing in the gateway, Eva looked round. The buildings — warehouse, foundries, workshops and offices — formed a rough square around a courtyard. Coal and used crucibles from the furnaces lay in heaps in the cobbled yard. Workmen stared at Eva as she walked through the gates, and a girl wearing a brown-paper apron giggled until her neighbour, nudging her in the ribs, muttered to her and she fell silent.

In the office, Mr Foley looked up as Eva came in. Mr Foley was Father's assistant. Father invited Mr Foley to Summerleigh once a year at Christmas. Iris delighted in mimicking Mr Foley, making fun of his serious expression and his brief, careful phrases. So *gloomy*, said Iris, so *dull*. And he isn't even old. But Eva thought that he had an interesting, almost handsome, face, with strong cheekbones and jaw, and eyes and hair of a matching brown-black.

Now his eyes widened in surprise. 'Miss Eva,' he said, standing up. 'Are you looking for your father? I'm afraid he left early today, about ten minutes ago.'

30

Eva felt a great wash of disappointment. All the exhilaration of her journey dissolved.

Mr Foley asked, 'Is there anything I can do?'

Eva shook her head. 'No, thank you, Mr Foley.' She had only made things worse by coming here. She would be late home and her father would be angry with her all over again.

As she turned to leave, Mr Foley asked, 'Did you come here on your own?' Eva nodded. 'I'll see you home, then.'

'There's no need. I cycled here.' She smiled at him. 'It's quite all right.'

It began to rain as Eva made her way back through the city. As she headed into the suburbs, the stone villas became larger, their gardens bounded by wrought-iron gates and leathery leaved shrubs. It seemed to Eva that her future was as drearily predictable as the streets which surrounded her. Father would stop her having lessons with Miss Garnett. Soon, stifled by lack of stimulation and aware of her own limitations, she would give up, marry the first passable man who asked her and spend the rest of her life immured in Sheffield.

There was a crack of thunder and the rain turned to hail. Balls of ice gathered in the gutters and in shop doorways. Schoolgirls shrieked and ran through the crowds, delivery boys cursed and cycled faster. The hailstones stung Eva's face and rattled on the brim of her hat. She had to narrow her eyes to see her way through the traffic.

And then her heart lifted as, hurrying along Ecclesall Road, she caught sight of her father among a sea of black frockcoats and umbrellas. Tall and strongly made, Joshua Maclise towered head and shoulders over most of the other men. Eva called out to him, but her voice was lost in the rattle of the hailstones and the clamour of traffic.

A cart had shed its load, scattering turnips across the

31

street, and she had to jump off her bicycle and weave through the debris. When she looked up, she could no longer see him. Trying to run, she slipped on the swirls of hailstones. Then, as the hail eased, she caught sight of her father again, turning off the main road into a side street.

Following him, she eventually spotted his umbrella propped outside a house. Eva recalled that the house belonged to Mrs Carver, whose husband had died the previous year. Eva had visited the Carvers to offer her condolences. She remembered that the two Carver girls, who were a few years younger than Eva, had been sullen and silent, and that their flame-red hair had sat ill at ease with their black dresses.

Now she stared at the house's closed doors and lowered blinds, and the house stared unblinkingly back at her. Then she looked down at herself. There were black smuts on her blouse, and at some point on her long cycle ride she had snagged the hem of her skirt so that it drooped unevenly. Her wet hair trailed in a straggling untamed mass around her shoulders. Her father had accused her of being unladylike, and she was, she thought miserably.

She climbed back on her bicycle and headed home. No one noticed that she was late. And her father seemed to have forgotten their quarrel: arriving home an hour later, his mood had altered. He ruffled Eva's hair, coaxed a smile from Marianne and complimented Iris on her frock. Then he kissed Mother's cheek and apologized for being late. He had had to stay behind at the works, he explained. They were late with an order.

Eva opened her mouth to speak, thought better of it and folded the lie away. She would forget what she had seen, she decided; she would not think about the way it niggled at her, like a burr caught in a glove.

★　★　★

When, four weeks earlier, Marianne had met Arthur Leighton, she had believed that something magical had taken place, something that happened only once in a lifetime. Yet she had not seen Mr Leighton since then. Recalling that he had told her he was staying with the Palmers, she spoke to sallow, squint-eyed Alice Palmer and discovered that Mr Leighton had left the Palmers' house the day after the ball. He had given no reason for his sudden departure.

'Mr Leighton asked Mama about your family,' Alice said. 'Mama saw you dancing together. She wondered whether you'd made a conquest. You'd be aiming very high if you were sweet on Mr Leighton, Marianne. He's quite a catch. He's related to an earl.' Alice bit at a hangnail. 'Or maybe it's a viscount.'

Marianne's conviction, so unshakeable in the immediate aftermath of the ball, that something extraordinary had happened, faltered. Perhaps Mr Leighton had asked Mrs Palmer about her family and Mrs Palmer had told him the truth: that Joshua Maclise was a manufacturer of edge tools, and that Marianne's grandmother had made bone handles for knives. Perhaps Mr Leighton had found her passable enough company to get through a dull evening at a provincial ball, but, realizing that Marianne Maclise was far beneath him socially, had decided not to pursue the acquaintance any further.

Now, when she looked in the mirror, she saw nothing but her faults: her Roman nose, her pallor, her solemnity. She had glimpsed something marvellous, only to have it snatched away from her. Nothing had changed except that she now held herself in greater contempt. How ridiculous, how pathetic, to have set such store on the events of a few hours. A cleverer, more sophisticated woman, she told herself savagely, would have known that he was only flirting with her.

And then, one evening, when Joshua had taken Iris

and Marianne to a dinner at a house in Fulwood, and Marianne was contemplating with utter lack of enthusiasm the hors d'œuvres Russes on her plate, she looked up to the end of the long table and saw Arthur Leighton. Her heart jumped into her throat. She was afraid that she might faint in front of all thirty other guests and the ranks of servants. Ostrich feathers swayed, diamonds caught the light. She breathed deeply, took a hold of herself and looked along the table once more. It *was* Mr Leighton. When he turned in her direction, Marianne looked quickly away. She wasn't going to embarrass either of them by staring doe-eyed at him, like some silly schoolgirl.

White-gloved footmen served the food. Candles and crystal glittered. Even the simplest things seemed beyond her: the glass trembled in her grasp so that she was afraid of breaking it; she dropped her napkin. Conversation rose and fell around her, dreamlike and unreal. She noticed the impatience in her neighbour's eyes at her lack of response, and was angry at herself. *You are a fool, Marianne Maclise,* she thought, *a clumsy, cowardly fool.* Pride made her draw herself erect, paste a smile on her face and begin to talk. *Tell me what sort of steel you use, Mr Hawthorne. How fascinating. And your padlocks are shipped to America! I should love to travel to America . . .* As she talked, she became aware of a power she had hardly known she possessed. She sparkled.

The meal ended and the ladies left the men to their port and cigars. Sitting in the drawing room, the fleeting elation left her and she felt chilled and tremulous. No one seemed to notice her discomfort.

Then the men came to join them. When Marianne saw that Arthur Leighton was crossing the room to her, her heart lurched.

'Miss Maclise. I hoped you might be here.'

She murmured, 'I thought you had abandoned

Sheffield, Mr Leighton.'

'The evening we met — I was called back to Town unexpectedly the next day.' He made a quick, impatient gesture. 'Business, I'm afraid.'

'Your hostesses must despair of you, Mr Leighton,' Marianne said, with sudden sharpness. 'Such an uncertain guest. The Palmers were disappointed at your departure.'

'Only the Palmers?'

Marianne felt a stab of despair — she would leave, and they would have said nothing important, and she might never see him again.

Then he said, 'I'm in Sheffield for the next few days. I wondered whether I might call on you.' When she did not speak, he said more insistently, 'May I?'

She knew, suddenly, how much depended on her reply. 'Yes, Mr Leighton, please do,' she said calmly.

But by the following morning her confidence had deserted her once more. Stubbornly convinced that he would not come, she took no special care over her dress or hair. When he called, she was in her old dark blue dress and her head full of grocer's orders and Mother's prescriptions still to be fetched. She felt disadvantaged. Alice Palmer's voice echoed, sly and disparaging, coldly estimating her worth. *You'd be aiming very high if you were sweet on Mr Leighton, Marianne.*

On her way to the drawing room she swept up her sisters: Iris, Eva, even Clemency, off sick from school with a summer cold. 'I *need* you,' she hissed, and they rose and followed her.

Whenever she was in the same room as him, she seemed to notice things more. The green of the fern, the gold leaf on the plates. The sweet, beguiling scent of the honeysuckle, wafting through the open window.

Her sisters' voices and Mr Leighton's plaited together in the hot, heavy air. Talk drifted to the weather. *Such a glorious June . . . almost too warm . . .*

35

Iris nudged Marianne. She made herself speak. 'The heat makes one long for the countryside. Cities can be so — so — ' She couldn't think of the word: her gaze darted from one sister to another, seeking assistance.

'Muggy?' said Eva.

'Close?' suggested Clemency.

'Enervating,' said Mr Leighton, and Marianne gave a relieved outward breath, and said, 'Yes, of course. Enervating. Don't you find it so?'

'I lived in India for three years. This seems delightfully cool in comparison.'

'India!' exclaimed Marianne and had a sudden, jolting view of a different Arthur Leighton, in tropical whites and a pith hat, standing by a verandaed house on a hill top. She knew nothing about him, she thought wildly. Why, he might have been married and widowed. He might have travelled the world, a mistress in every port.

Yet when he looked at her she was aware of that feeling once more, the feeling she had almost forgotten — or had almost persuaded herself to forget. Inside her something seemed to uncurl, to flower. She pressed the tips of her fingers against her palms, astonished by the ease with which she, cool, serious Marianne Maclise, seemed to be losing control.

The quarter of an hour passed and he left. Marianne had to fold back the edge of the curtain to watch him walk out of the drive. When he was out of sight, the day seemed duller.

'He's in love with you,' said Iris at her shoulder.

Marianne pressed her palms against her face and shook her head.

'It's true.' For once, Iris did not sound flippant. 'He's in love with you.'

2

In church, Eva studied the Carvers. The Carver daughters were white and freckled and they wore their ginger hair in long, springy plaits. Mrs Carver's hair was a shiny tawny-brown like a fox's coat; it escaped at several points from beneath the confines of her hat, as though it had a life of its own. Eva took a stub of pencil from her pocket and began to draw in the back of her prayer book. She was halfway through the complicated arrangement of ribbons on Mrs Carver's hat when the service ended.

The congregation trailed from the church in twos and threes. Eva lingered, pencil and prayer book in hand. The ginger-headed Carver girls pushed past her. Hidden in the shadowy porch, Eva looked back. There were only two people left inside the church, Mrs Carver and her father. As Eva raised her pencil to finish the hat, her father's fingers coiled through Mrs Carver's. Then he pressed her hand to his lips. Eva's pencil stabbed, tearing a hole in the prayer book's thin paper. Black and white, Eva saw them with relentless clarity. Mrs Carver's black gloves, her father's paler hand. She saw how her father closed his eyes as he kissed Mrs Carver's fingers. A muttered word or two, then a falling apart. Eva ran out of the church.

She couldn't get the image out of her head, though. The church, the kiss. It preyed on her, coming into her mind when she was sitting at the dinner table, or when she was taking Great-aunt Hannah to the shops. Though the shops were only a short distance from Summerleigh, the trip required the preparation and forethought of a Polar expedition. There was always a bonnet to be righted or a dog collar for Hannah's spaniel, Winnie, to be extracted from the heaps of shawls and prayer books in Great-aunt Hannah's bedroom. Pushing the heavy, cumbersome bathchair up the hill took all Eva's strength.

Great-aunt Hannah's purchases never varied: lavender-scented soap and lozenges in Gimpson's, stockings or handkerchieves in the draper's, writing paper and envelopes at the stationer's. Last of all, Great-aunt Hannah always gave Eva tuppence to buy macaroons at the baker's. They ate them in a nearby park, where nannies pushed perambulators between clumps of lilac and laurel.

Eva let Winnie off the leash and offered the last macaroon to Great-aunt Hannah.

'No, Eva dear, you must have it.'

She shook her head. 'I'm not very hungry.'

'I expect it's the heat,' said Great-aunt Hannah kindly. She patted Eva's hand. 'You do look rather peaky. So selfish of me, dragging you out in such weather.'

'It's not that. I like going shopping with you.'

'What is it then, dear?' Crumbs dotted Hannah's shiny black front and clung to the whiskers on her chin. She brushed at them ineffectually. 'Are you worried about your mother?'

'Not especially.'

'Perhaps you're still disappointed that your father won't let you go to art school.'

'Yes,' said Eva. It was the easiest thing to say.

'Your father's a good man, Eva, one of the best. I've been most fortunate. Joshua could not have been a more generous nephew.'

Eva wanted to say: *Good men don't tell lies. Good men don't lecture you about propriety one day and kiss that horrible woman's hand in church on another.*

'Joshua dislikes change,' Hannah added. 'It takes him time to accustom himself to a new idea. You must try to

38

be patient. He may yet change his mind.'

'He'll never change his mind!' said Eva vehemently. 'He doesn't think art college is proper.' Her lip curled.

'Please try not to despair, Eva. God works in mysterious ways.' Hannah glanced from beneath the black peak of her bonnet at Eva. 'We should go home. This heat . . . '

Eva wheeled the bathchair down the steep path. She let the heavy chair gather speed as she ran, keeping hold of the handles. The ribbons of her hat streamed out behind her and the folds of Great-aunt Hannah's dress billowed like a black-sailed yacht. Winnie ran alongside, yapping, and a smile of delight spread across Hannah Maclise's lined face.

Eva wondered whether, if she ran fast enough, she might forget all the things that troubled her. An umbrella outside a door, a pointless lie. And her father's closed eyes — closed in ecstasy, it seemed to Eva — as he kissed a black-gloved hand.

★ ★ ★

Ash had become a frequent visitor to Summerleigh. He visited at any time of day and always stayed longer than the unspoken but mandatory limit of a quarter of an hour. When Ash called, the sisters never seemed to sit in the drawing room as they were supposed to, but drifted into the garden or, when the weather was bad, sat in other, less formal, rooms. Within a short time they were calling each other by their Christian names — far too longwinded, Ash said practically, to specify continually which Miss Maclise he was addressing. No one halted these transgressions. Mother was still poorly and Father was late home from work most days, so there was every opportunity to break the rules. Ash taught Iris how to use his camera, a hefty thing of mahogany and brass. One, two, three, four, five: there was a flash, and the sisters in their white muslin dresses, sitting in the orchard, were frozen in time forever.

Ash's parents were both dead. Since the age of eight he had spent the school holidays with his guardian in Grantchester, near Cambridge. He was currently staying with an old university friend in Sheffield and was engaged, Iris registered uninterestedly, in some sort of good works. It always surprised Iris that she enjoyed Ash's company. They weren't in the least alike. They didn't share any of the same interests or tastes. And he dressed appallingly — Iris suspected that in the mornings he put on the first clothes that came to hand. He would turn up at Summerleigh in an old Norfolk jacket with cricket whites, or in some dreadful musty tweed thing that was going through at the elbows. When Iris, who took great care over her appearance, pointed out to him his errors, he nodded vaguely.

Iris had been aware of her power over men since her midteens. She never doubted that, if she chose to, she could make almost any man fall in love with her. Only the dullest, stuffiest men were immune to her considerable charms — and Ash was certainly neither dull nor stuffy. Yet the unease she had felt recently at her continuing lack of a husband had deepened. For as long as she could remember she had been accustomed to being the centre of attention. The second oldest in the family, and the oldest — and prettiest — girl, she had long experience of being made a fuss of by friends and relatives. Yet, though she enjoyed Ash's company — found, if she was honest with herself, that the days seemed long when he didn't call — he never made a special fuss of her. If anything, he was nicer to her sisters. Every now and then he would say something to her that made her suspect he was making fun of her. It wasn't as though she never teased him about his various obsessions — politics and poverty and his dreary university settlement — and it was refreshing, in a way,

40

to talk to a man who didn't choose his words to please her. But it troubled her that he didn't make any overt attempt to win her favour. He rarely complimented her, had never tried to kiss her.

That summer they played tennis together and went on long cycle rides. Sometimes they just wandered, discovering parts of the city Iris had never seen before. Often they argued. He had a way of provoking her, a way of querying long-held assumptions that she had never before questioned.

One day, they were walking when there was a sudden rain shower. 'My *hat*,' said Iris crossly. The straw brim was rapidly wilting. 'Why does seeing you so often seem to involve ruining a hat, Ash?'

He grinned. 'My guardian, Emlyn, doesn't believe in wearing hats. He thinks they overheat the head and are bad for the brain.'

Iris snorted. 'My mother thinks loud noises, fresh air and the company of more than one person at once is bad for her. Oh,' she cried, exasperated. 'This weather!'

She had not taken a jacket, and was wearing only a muslin blouse and cotton skirt. Ash said, 'Here. So you don't drown,' and took off his jacket and wrapped it round her. He asked, 'Has your mother been unwell for a long time?'

'Decades,' said Iris.

He gave her a questioning glance. She said, 'I'm sorry if I sound unsympathetic. I don't mean to be. But it's very wearing.' She wondered how to make someone who had no family understand the shifts of power between parents, brothers, sisters. 'I used to try to cheer Mother up,' she explained. 'I'd go to her room and talk to her, tell her what I'd done that day, perhaps. But I could tell she wasn't interested and that it made no difference, so I stopped. And now Mother is the same as she always was, but I'm happier because I'm not sitting in a dark room, struggling to think of cheerful conversation to make to someone who hardly answers.'

The rain fell harder, bouncing on the pavement. Ash drew Iris beneath the shelter of a tree. Motor cars and carts passed them, their wheels sending up curls of water. Iris was aware of the rain trickling down the back of her neck and Ash, standing beside her, his hand resting lightly on her shoulder. Glancing up at him, she said, 'You think I'm selfish, don't you, begrudging the time I spend with my sick mother?'

'I didn't say that.'

'I'm only being practical. My mother's been ill for eleven years. The doctors have never agreed on what's wrong with her — one tells us she has an inflammation of the spine, another says she has a weak heart, another is convinced that something's wrong with her blood. And so on. This morning Mother got out of bed, came down to breakfast and announced that we were to give a summer party. It was as though she'd never been ill at all. But it won't last, Ash. It never does. Nothing I did made her any better. Nothing Marianne or Clemency does makes her any better, either, but they can't see that.'

'Perhaps simply having her daughters near her is a comfort to your mother, even if you can't make her well again.'

'Perhaps. But one of us will be trapped, I'm sure of it. One of us won't marry, but will stay at home for the rest of her life looking after Mother. And I'm determined that won't be me.'

He looked at her sharply. 'I hadn't realized that was a possibility.'

'Why should you? You're a man. James, Aidan and Philip won't have to give up their lives to look after Mother. Men may do as they please.'

The rain had eased a little. He said, 'Come on. Let's run for it.'

'*Run?* I can't run. My shoes — '

But he seized her hand and they dashed up the street. Iris's hat flew off; ruined anyway, she let it fly. Reaching Summerleigh, she collapsed against him, laughing, gasping for breath. And as they went into the house, she said, 'You see, Ash, I won't be the spinster daughter, running errands for Mother.' Her eyes narrowed. 'I'd do anything rather than that. Anything at all.'

★   ★   ★

During his stay in Sheffield Ash had befriended two families, the Maclises and the Browns. The contrast between the families could not have been more glaring. The Browns lived in a grim single-room dwelling in High Street Lane in the Park district of the city, the family of six — mother, father, a ten-year-old girl, Lizzie, and Lizzie's three younger brothers — all eating and sleeping in the same room.

The summer that Ash had spent working for the university settlement in Whitechapel had changed him. He, who had never wanted for food, had seen children suffering from malnutrition; he, who had always had warm clothes to wear and a roof over his head, discovered that there were a great many people who had neither. He had been unable to forget what he had seen. The squalor and misery and, most of all, the unfairness of it all had outraged him. He had left Whitechapel knowing that he must do *something*.

Though many slum-dwellers had far too much pride to let him into their houses — they pasted brown paper to their window panes so that passers-by could not see the degradation inside — the Browns had eventually given him permission. They had reached such a level of destitution, he concluded, that they were forced to sell even their pride. Over the summer he had taken a series of photographs showing how the Browns lived; he had come to know the family quite well. Recently he had become concerned about the youngest child, a baby of a few months old. Surely babies should cry? Surely babies should not be so pale, so unresponsive?

Often, after visiting the Browns, he went to see Iris, needing to shake off the hopelessness and lack of spirit that hung over the slums like a dark cloud. Iris's bright liveliness almost made him forget what he had seen. Almost. Increasingly the contrast between the two families troubled him. He couldn't help thinking that the wealth of the one was in some way dependent on the poverty of the other.

In July he went with the Maclises and their friends for a picnic in the Peak District. Leaving Sheffield, the motor cars and charabancs climbed steadily into the clearer air of the hills. Huge boulders littered the high escarpment and the hillside curved sharply down. On the far side of the valley the crags brooded, making a stark silhouette against a shimmering sky. In twos and threes they dispersed across the rocky plateau. The midday heat gathered, warming the stones.

After the picnic Ash wandered away towards the clutter of gigantic stones that lay, like a vast cairn, on the highest land. Hearing footsteps, he turned and saw Iris hurrying to catch up with him.

'Where are you going?'

'Somewhere,' he said. 'Anywhere.'

He began to climb the heap of boulders. Iris followed him. He gave her his hand to help her scramble up the stones. From the top of the cairn, the picnickers below them were small, colourful insects, the ladies' parasols like thistledown.

Iris sat beside him on the highest boulder. 'Aren't you enjoying yourself, Ash?'

'I was too hot.'

'You didn't have any strawberries.' She produced a tied handkerchief. Strawberries nestled like rubies in the

44

folds of fabric; she offered them to him. Then she said, 'What's wrong?'

He threw a pebble down the incline and watched it bounce from stone to stone. 'Does it ever worry you that you'll never work out quite what to do with your life?'

'Not at all.' She ate a strawberry. 'I know exactly what I'm going to do. I'm going to marry a very rich man and live in a lovely house with lots of servants and have simply masses of new dresses and hats.'

He lay back on the flat stone, watching her. 'And you think that'll make you happy?'

'Of course. Perfectly happy.'

'Rot,' he said. 'You'd be bored stiff in a week.'

Her eyebrows raised. 'Such nonsense. Why should I be bored?'

'Because it wouldn't be enough for you. What would you do all day, Iris? Arrange the flowers?'

'Why not? And why do I have to do anything at all?'

He said calmly, 'You like to break the rules. You said so yourself. You wouldn't be content.'

She glared at him. 'You may be terribly clever, Ash, much cleverer than me, but you don't really understand, do you? Girls like me aren't supposed to use their brains or to bother about things. We're supposed to look pretty and marry well. That's what we're for.'

Sometimes she infuriated him. Her lack of awareness of the outside world; her lack of self-knowledge. He said, 'And you just . . . accept that? You accept a lifetime of — of *uselessness?*'

He saw her flush. 'You could say that I was doing my duty. That I'm being a good daughter.'

'So you'll settle for being purely decorative — when in reality you're as tough as old boots?'

'*As tough as old boots!*' Iris looked outraged. '*Ash!* That's not true — what a dreadful thing to say!'

45

'Just look at the way you scrambled up these rocks. And that time you fell off your bicycle — '

'What of it?'

'You let me pick the grit out of your hands, but you didn't cry out once. Not once. And it must have hurt like hell. I noticed that.'

She looked away. After a silence, she said, 'All this . . . the way I look, the way I behave . . . that's how I'm supposed to be. Don't you understand, Ash, that's how I'm *supposed* to be.'

He said flatly, 'But it's not how you are.'

'Maybe not. It's rather . . . rather ungentlemanly of you to notice.'

He realized he had upset her and felt ashamed of himself. He touched her arm. 'I'm sorry, Iris. Let's not quarrel.'

She turned to him. '"Tough as old boots"!' she repeated. 'No man's ever said that to me before.'

'Then no man has ever appreciated your finer qualities as I have.' He saw her smile reluctantly. He ate another strawberry. 'And besides,' he went on, 'times are changing, surely. There are women doctors, and women read for the law and study at the universities. And just look at the suffragettes — '

'If you think I'm going to wear a hideous purple, white and green hat and march through the streets carrying a banner, then you're quite wrong!'

They glared at each other. 'There, we're quarrelling again!' she cried. 'Why do you delight in making me cross?'

Rising to his feet, he looked out over the valley. 'Wear whatever colour hat you wish, Iris, but let's not argue any more.' He sighed. 'It's two years since I left university and I still haven't settled to anything. I need to make up my mind. I feel I'm just . . . treading water.'

'What's wrong with treading water? What's wrong with enjoying yourself?'

'I want to make a difference, you see. And you can't do that if you're constantly flitting from one thing to another.'

When she did not reply, he looked back at her and said, 'You don't approve of me wanting to make a difference? Perhaps you think me arrogant. Or naive.'

'It always seems to me that it's impossible to change other people's lives. People can only change their own. And very often, they can't even do that.'

'But we should try, surely.'

She stood up. 'Tell me what you're thinking of, Ash, and I'll choose for you.'

'Medicine . . . or journalism. Or the law, perhaps.'

She had begun to saunter back down the slope towards the other picnickers. 'Oh, that's easy,' she said. 'The law, obviously.'

'Why?'

She was some way below him; she looked up. She was smiling mischievously. 'Because then you could argue to your heart's content, couldn't you?'

She disappeared out of sight, behind a boulder. Standing above, he waited for her to reappear, and then he watched her, a flicker of white muslin and golden hair, as she ran back to her friends.

★　★　★

Marianne had looked forward to the picnic, had expected that away from the house and the constant possibility of Arthur Leighton calling she would feel calmer. Instead, she felt restless and out of sorts. Knowing that she would not see him, the day had no spark.

She went for a walk, heading away from the rest of the party, back towards the road. Around her, the landscape seemed to glitter, blue-black shadows gathering in the hollows, the sunlight flashing on the

47

rocks, as though there were diamonds embedded in the gritstone.

In the distance a motor car followed the curve of the road. Stabs of silver refracted off the glass and metal. As it approached the bridge, the motor car slowed, then came to a halt. The driver climbed out. Recognizing Arthur Leighton, Marianne's heart began to thud. She saw him pause, look in her direction, pinpoint her and walk towards her.

He said, 'I have to speak to you alone.'

'Mr Leighton — '

'I don't doubt your sisters are scattered like lizards among the rocks, but nevertheless you'll allow me to speak to you.'

He led her down the narrow path to the stream, where ferns gleamed emerald in the dark crevices between the stones and the water arched and spat.

He said, 'The first time I saw you, at the ball, I was struck by your beauty. I couldn't stop looking at you. And then, when we talked, it seemed to me that there was a meeting of minds as well.' He raised her chin, making her look at him. 'Speak to me, Marianne.' His voice was low and urgent. 'Tell me what you're thinking.'

'I don't know,' she whispered.

'You don't know what?'

'I don't know what you want of me.'

'It's quite simple. I want *you*.'

She gave a little gasp. He pressed his lips against the back of her hand. She closed her eyes and felt herself sway slightly. She heard him whisper, 'Poor thing, your skin will burn in this sun. Such white, white skin.'

When he kissed the hollow of her elbow, she shivered. He drew her to him, and through her thin summer blouse and skirt she was aware of the warmth and strength of his body. His mouth brushed against the curve of her neck. When, at last, their lips touched, she felt as though she were drowning, dissolving, as though she, Marianne Maclise, who always seemed so separate, so apart from everyone else, had begun to blur, to melt into him. The chatter of the stream magnified to a roar, the sun beat down, and she was burning, on fire.

Something made Marianne open her eyes and look up. She became a part of the world again; she heard the clatter of shoes on rock and glimpsed a green-and-white striped parasol dancing against a blue sky.

She pulled away. 'There's Mrs Catherwood,' she hissed.

Mrs Catherwood, red-faced in the heat, was trotting along the path towards them. 'Marianne, dear, we couldn't find you anywhere. We're serving tea.' A beady eye alighted on Mr Leighton, paused, then glared. 'Will you join us, sir?'

'Thank you, no.'

He would go again, Marianne thought, he would leave her alone again. It was unbearable. '*Please* — ' she whispered.

'You will excuse me, Marianne. I endured this ritual years ago, when I was younger, and I would prefer not to repeat it now.' He seized her hands. 'But, my love, I must know — '

Mrs Catherwood was watching them. It was intolerable, thought Marianne, that her most private emotions should be so publicly paraded. She said quickly, 'My mother has decided to give a summer party. You will come, won't you, Mr Leighton?'

Marianne watched him walk back to his motor car. As she followed Mrs Catherwood back along the path, she noticed that one of her buttons was undone. With shaking hands she refastened it. She remembered the heat of his skin on her skin, the pressure of his tongue on the inside of her lip, the way his hands had discovered the contours of her body. And she had not tried to stop him. An hour ago she would not have believed it possible that she would permit a man to touch her in such a way. An hour ago she would not have believed that she would long for Arthur Leighton to touch her like that again and again.

★   ★   ★

Iris wasn't enjoying the picnic as much as she had expected to. The food had dried out in the heat, the champagne was warm, and the conversation flat and aimless, spiked with the occasional barb of malice.

Alice Palmer drew Iris aside. 'Mrs Catherwood found Marianne and Mr Leighton together,' she whispered. 'They were *kissing*!' Alice had a squint; her wandering eye struggled to focus on Iris. 'What a surprise it would be if Marianne were to be married before you. I remember when you came out everyone thought you'd be snapped up in your first season. I should hate Louisa to be married before me. Imagine having to be your younger sister's bridesmaid! How I should detest it.' She tapped Iris's arm playfully with her fan. 'We all thought you'd be the first Maclise sister to marry. Better not leave it too late, Iris.'

Remembering how Mr Leighton had looked at Marianne, Iris realized with a sinking heart that it was all too probable that one of her sisters might marry before her. Previously she had always discounted the possibility — Marianne was too quiet, too solemn, Eva was too uninterested and Clemency too young. And, besides, she herself was the eldest and also the prettiest. It would be quite ridiculous — and utterly, utterly humiliating — for any of her sisters to marry first. It couldn't — it must not — happen.

After tea, Charlotte Catherwood, Iris's best friend, led her away from the crowd. 'I need to talk to you, Iris. I need to tell you something.' Charlotte took a deep breath. 'I've decided to become a nurse.'

Iris stared at her. If Charlotte had said: *I've decided to become an African explorer*, or, *I've decided to become a nun*, she could not have been more shocked.

'A nurse?' she repeated. 'Lottie, don't be ridiculous!'

'I mean to begin my training at the end of the year.'

'Lottie, you *can't*.' Seeing that Charlotte was serious, Iris cried out, 'But *why?*'

'Because I don't think I'll ever marry,' said Charlotte calmly. 'I'm twenty-two, Iris. I've been out for four years. No one fell in love with me when I was eighteen, so why should they fall in love with me now? Especially as younger, prettier girls are coming out all the time.'

'But . . . nursing. So *tiring* . . . so *dreadful* . . . '

'Nurses can travel. Nurses can see the world. I'll have independence and money of my own. I won't have to stay here, getting older, everything always the same. *That* would be truly dreadful.' Charlotte looked round. 'Mother's woken up. I'd better go and see if she needs help with the tea things.' Before she walked away, she said, 'You should think about nursing too.'

'*Me?*'

'Why not? Think what fun we could have, the two of us.'

When Charlotte had gone, Iris picked up her parasol and headed away from the rest of the party. Inside she had begun to feel something close to panic. To reassure herself, she ran through the list of her male acquaintances. Surely one of them would do as a husband? They were all kind, pleasant boys from well-off, respectable families. Every few months, Gerald Catherwood asked her to marry him and even Ronnie had once stammered out a proposal. But she realized with a sudden jolt that it must be six months since Gerald had last proposed to her. Perhaps he had given up. Perhaps he didn't love her any more.

Well, then, she told herself, what about the Hutchinson girls' brother, Oswald? She dismissed the

51

idea immediately; Oswald was nice enough, but he was dull, dull, *dull*. Or Alfred Palmer. *Ridiculous*, thought Iris, appalled at the thought of herself walking down the aisle beside stout, pompous Alfred Palmer.

Or Ash, she thought suddenly. What would it be like to be married to Ash? It would be impossible. They would argue all the time. But it would not be dull, and it would not be ridiculous.

She paused and looked back. She saw that Ash was heading down the cairn back to the picnickers. She watched him, her eyes narrowed, noting his height and the easy grace of his movements. *Ash*, she thought again. Why shouldn't she marry Ash? Because she must marry someone, and soon. Or she ran the risk of leaving it too late and ending up an old maid.

She had always had the knack of making any man she chose fall in love with her. Iris found herself smiling and, for the first time, she began to look forward to the Maclises' summer party with a sense of lively anticipation.

★   ★   ★

Eva waited in the narrow alleyway opposite J. Maclise & Sons, her bicycle propped against the wall. At one end of the street was a boy selling baskets and horsewhips; a hansom cab, its curtains closed, stood at the far end.

Rain slid down the waxed cloth of Eva's mackintosh and made glassy puddles on the cobbles. Father's employees had begun to pour out through the iron gates. Eva watched for a top hat, an umbrella. She would follow her father, she decided, and if he walked to Mrs Carver's house, then she would hail him before he started down the front path. She would tell him that she had taken a wrong turning cycling home from her art lesson and had got lost. She had seen him in the street and, relieved, had caught up with him at Mrs Carver's house.

She couldn't decide what she should say next. *I didn't know that Mrs Carver was a particular friend of yours, Father. Or, Poor Mrs Carver, she must be terribly lonely. How kind of you to keep her company.* Everything seemed too intrusive or too vague. The right words would come to her, she told herself. From the expression on her father's face and the look in his eye, she would know whether her suspicions had any foundation.

Shortly after the last of Maclise's workers went out of sight her father came out through the gates. He paused on the pavement, looking to left and right. Then, instead of turning towards the city centre, he walked to the parked hansom cab. There was a flurry of movement, the horse shifted in the traces and the curtain fell open. Eva caught a glimpse of the woman waiting inside the cab and saw how her father leaned across to kiss her as he stepped into the dark interior. There was a gleam of coiled hair, red-brown like a fox's coat, and then a black-gloved hand reached up and drew the curtain.

The cab drove down the road and was swallowed up by the rain and the high brick buildings. For several minutes after it had gone Eva was unable to move. Then she gave herself a violent shake, as if to eject from her mind the image of her father kissing Mrs Carver in the hansom cab.

She began to cycle blindly away, choosing her direction at random. She found herself borne along by the press of the crowds towards the Shambles, the meat market, where every morning short, stocky men wearing leather aprons sharpened their knives and beef cattle destined for slaughter bellowed as they were funnelled through the narrow streets. The smell of blood and cattle dung was still sweet and heavy; Eva's stomach rose. Soon she was skirting around railway sidings; there was the shriek of steam and the clatter of trucks and engines. As the rain fell, it bore with it through the gutters a jumble of spent matchsticks and straw and left a dark film over the flaking whitewash on the brick buildings.

The streets and houses that surrounded her were now small and mean; she felt her heart beat faster as she realized that she was in the slums, an area forbidden to her. Defiantly she walked on, dismounting from her bicycle and pushing it into the maze of narrow alleyways and dark courtyards. She wanted to see, she wanted to *know*.

She found herself in a different world. Even the shops were different. Cuts of meat hung from hooks in a butcher's unglazed window and flies buzzed in a black cloud around a carcass suspended from the canopy. Outside a pawn shop the queue tailed along the road. A few objects were displayed in the window: a man's jacket with patches on the elbows, a cheap calico petticoat yellowed with age. In a cramped square bounded by high tenements, an old woman sat on an upturned box, ragged clothes arrayed for sale on the cobbles in front of her.

Tiny children played in puddles; they stared at Eva as she passed. On the doorsteps, hollow-eyed women sat nursing their babies. Nappies and sheets, grey with smuts and worn thin with use, dripped from lines strung between the houses. Eva walked on, transfixed. That so many people should be crushed into such a small space, where all was dirty and dark and where the colours came from a restricted palette of blacks and greys and browns, and where even the blue of the sky was masked by a pall of smoke and soot, appalled her.

In the midst of the squalor she heard music. Following it to its source, she threaded through a narrow passageway, where mangy dogs fought over a gnawed bone and an old sofa, horsehair gouting through its torn plush cover, stood next to a run of stone steps. The passageway funnelled into a square, where children were dancing to the music of a barrel organ. Girls in patched pinafores skipped and pirouetted, their expressions serious and concentrated. As the organ grinder cranked the handle and his monkey capered, an infant with blonde pigtails clenched her fists and swayed from one foot to the other.

Eva, too, would have liked to lose herself in the music, to waltz alone. Instead she began to walk slowly out of the square, her thoughts turning continually to her father. She had always admired his energy, strength and vitality, just as she had always shrunk from her mother's ill health. Squeamish by nature, she spent as little time as possible in her mother's overheated, darkened room. Yet to her just now Eva Maclise, who felt faint at the sight of blood, seemed every bit as contemptible as Joshua Maclise, who so casually betrayed his wife. She herself displayed the visible signs of her father's wealth in the soft whiteness of her hands, in the silks and fine woollens she wore. A heaviness washed over her, an awareness of her own complicity in the creation of these mean streets, and she knew that she could no more have joined in the dance than she could have borne to dress herself in the old woman's rags.

The image of her father bending down to kiss Mrs Carver in the hansom cab remained with her. With sudden, crushing clarity she realized that she must tell no one what she had seen. If her mother were to find out about Mrs Carver then the shock might kill her. She, who wore her heart on her sleeve, must learn to dissemble.

Looking around, Eva realized with rising panic that she was lost. The high brick walls of the buildings excluded the remaining daylight. Men sat on the front steps of the houses, smoking or playing dice or cards, their eyes intent, spitting on their palms for luck. Their gaze followed her as she walked by. One called out to her, 'Fancy a drink, love?' and she quickened her pace. His voice followed her as she rushed down a cinder ginnel. 'What're yer in such a hurry for, darlin'? I said, pet, what're yer in such a hurry for?'

Someone ran past her; she had to shrink against the wall to let him pass. Another man tore after him, shouting curses. Where the ginnel widened, forming a shabby area behind a row of shops, the two men fought, fists and elbows jabbing, hobnailed boots kicking. Eva let fall her bicycle and ran blindly out of the alleyway. Her heart drummed in her ears and her lungs seemed about to burst.

As the alleyway opened out into a wider street, she cannoned into someone warm and resilient and came to a sudden, breathtaking stop. A voice said, 'Miss Eva.'

Looking up, she saw Mr Foley. He was holding her shoulders to steady her. Her fingers gripped the sleeves of his jacket, as if only by doing so would she be safe. It took an effort of will to disentangle herself and step back.

'Are you all right?' He looked concerned.

She gave a gasp of relief. 'Yes. Yes, of course.' She would never have believed she would be so glad to see dull, dour Mr Foley. 'But my bicycle! I've lost my bicycle!'

'Where is it?'

'Down there.' Fearfully she peered back down the alleyway.

'I'll get it. Wait here.'

He disappeared into the gloom. Alone, she searched through her pockets for a handkerchief. Unable to find one, she wiped her wet face on the back of her sleeve.

After a few minutes, Mr Foley reappeared, wheeling

the bicycle. He said, 'I'll see you home,' and this time she did not argue.

She sensed his unasked questions as they walked through the city. Her mind felt empty, wrung out, and she could think of neither excuses nor deceptions. After a while he began to talk to her about his sister, a schoolteacher, to tell stories about her pupils. Once or twice she managed to smile.

They were in sight of Summerleigh when she said, 'I think I'd better go the rest of the way by myself, Mr Foley.'

'Of course,' he said, and handed her the bicycle.

'And — if you please . . .' she began, and faltered.

'We never met,' he said. 'If it helps.'

At the top of the driveway, she looked back, and saw that he had waited, watching until she had reached the safety of the house. Then he raised a hand in salute and, turning away, walked back down the hill.

★　★　★

On the evening of the Maclises' summer party, shortly before the first guests were due to arrive, the family assembled in the hallway. Great-aunt Hannah wore black, as usual, a black jet brooch her sole concession to the evening's festivities. Lilian's gown was a froth of mauve silk crêpe de chine. The diamonds at her throat and in her ears emphasized her fragile beauty. Marianne, Iris and Clemency were dressed in white. When the women moved, their layers of petticoats whispered, a frou-frou of lace and baby ribbon, and their long trains rustled behind them. Corsets constricted their waists and thrust out their breasts and hips. The air was heavy with the scents of violet, carnation and tuberose.

'Where's Eva?' asked Marianne.

There was a movement at the top of the stairs. James

glanced up. 'Sweet Jesus,' he muttered under his breath. Joshua Maclise let out a wordless roar and Hannah, Iris, Marianne and Lilian looked up to where Eva, wearing a loose white frock, her dark hair unbound and hacked off short at her shoulders, was descending the stairs.

★ ★ ★

The dinner was interminable; Marianne saw faults in every course. Every now and then her gaze would slide down to the far end of the table to where Arthur Leighton was seated next to Mother. When he caught her glance, she found herself fixed, her sentence to her neighbour unfinished as the room stilled, the other guests fading away until there were only the two of them. Did he love her? she wondered. Did she haunt him as he haunted her? A soaring happiness welled up inside her, a mixture of excitement and elation and a sudden conviction that she teetered on the verge of a wonderful adventure.

★ ★ ★

Iris caught sight of Ash by the French windows, standing a little apart from the other guests.

'Ash,' she said. 'Aren't you dancing?'

Which was meant to produce the usual reply: *Only if you'll dance with me, Iris*, but Ash merely shook his head and said, 'Not just now.'

'The dinner was rather indigestible, wasn't it?'

'Eight courses . . .'

'I know. Quite a task to wade through it all.'

'I meant, that anyone should need *eight* courses — '

'It's not a question of *need*.'

'No,' he said. 'Plainly not.'

'Oh, Ash, don't be so *disapproving*!'

He did not, as she had half-expected, smile and

apologize. Instead he said abruptly, 'If you'd excuse me, Iris,' and walked away.

Iris's annoyance deepened — that he should just leave her! Coupled with her bad humour was a sudden anxiety. She stared at her reflection in the window. Was her hair less bright? she wondered. Had her complexion begun to fade?

Well, she thought angrily, as she turned back into the room, she'd soon make him sorry that he'd left her alone. *She* knew how to make a man notice her.

She made a show of studying her dance programme as she crossed the room to the group of young men who stood by the fireplace. 'Oh dear,' she pouted. 'I haven't a partner for the next dance.'

'You'd better dance with me, Iris,' said Oswald Hutchinson eagerly. 'All the rest of 'em have two left feet.'

'What rot,' Ronnie Catherwood protested. 'Dance with me — I won't bore you with the price of coal, like Oswald will.'

'You'll bore her with cricket,' said Gerald Catherwood. 'You know you can't talk about anything but cricket, Ronnie. Dance with me, Iris. My conversation's more interesting than Ronnie's and I'm a better dancer than Oswald.'

A streak of mischief made Iris cut through the chatter and say, 'I shall dance with Mr Summerbee.' Tom Summerbee was a friend of the Catherwoods'.

Ronnie Catherwood groaned. Gerald protested, 'You can't possibly dance with Summerbee. He can't dance for toffee.'

Gerald was right: Mr Summerbee couldn't dance for toffee. Neither did he bore her with cricket or coal — in fact, red-faced and with a sheen of sweat on his forehead, he said nothing at all. They were halfway through the dance, when, out of the corner of her eye, Iris noticed Ash come back into the room. Leaning

59

closer to Tom, she smiled at him seductively.

'I haven't seen you for ages, Tom. Where on earth have you been?'

'Oxford.'

'*Oxford*. Are you terribly clever, then?'

'Not r-really.'

Iris gave a little sigh. 'I'm not in the least clever. I was awfully stupid at school.'

He gasped. 'I c-can't imagine that. I should think you're good at everything, Miss M-Maclise.'

'Should you, Tom?' She waited for him to tell her that he was in love with the blue of her eyes, or that he would sell his soul for a lock of her hair. When he said nothing (though he had gone much the same shade of crimson as the curtains), she said sadly, 'Sometimes I'm afraid that you don't like me very much.'

'D-don't l-like you?'

'You hardly ever ask me to dance.'

He stumbled and Iris had to move quickly to save her toes. 'I'm not much of a d-dancer,' he said apologetically.

There was another, much longer, silence. Iris began to feel bored: she wondered whether it was more trouble than it was worth, flirting with Tom Summerbee to make Ash jealous.

He said suddenly, 'And they are such asses!'

'Oswald and the Catherwoods? Yes, I suppose they are. But they can be good fun.'

'You won't m-marry any of them, will you?'

She said soothingly, 'I shouldn't think so.'

★ ★ ★

That afternoon Ash had lugged his camera round to the Browns' house in High Street Lane. The parents had gone out, leaving Lizzie in charge of her younger brothers. After a while Ash had noticed that the baby,

60

sleeping in a cardboard box, was very still. He touched the infant's face; it was cold. It must have faded away in its sleep, he realized, and no one had noticed the moment of its passing. But then it had always been so quiet.

He had sent Lizzie to find her parents, and had taken the little boys outside so that they did not have to stay in with *that*. When the parents came home, he had given them what money he had to help pay for the burial. And then he had gone back to his friend's house, drunk a couple of stiff Scotches in a vain attempt to erase the horror of the afternoon, and then changed into evening dress before going to the Maclises' summer party.

The two families he had got to know: the Browns and the Maclises. Never had the contrast between them seemed so sharp. Images from the afternoon lingered as he choked down his dinner and watched the matrons of Fulwood and Abbeydale flaunt their husbands' wealth and their daughters' marriageability. He watched Iris, too, watched her move from the arms of one man to another, dazzling in white, nestling in their embrace. His gaze lingered on the small, red pout of her mouth, the pale curve of her neck and shoulders. He saw how, as she danced, she moved teasingly closer to her partner, and how he, poor fool, looked down at her, open-mouthed, slack-eyed.

Then, sickened, he left the ballroom and walked out of the French doors into the garden, where he stood, his arms outstretched and his face raised to the sky, letting the rain fall on him.

★   ★   ★

In the conservatory heat had gathered and ferns cast lacy shadows on the terracotta tiles. The rain beat down on the glass roof.

61

Mr Leighton said, 'You must know why I wanted to speak to you, Marianne.'

Marianne remembered the picnic: the stream rushing beneath the bridge, and Arthur Leighton's lips brushing against her skin. The strength of her longing shook her.

He said gently, 'I don't mean to frighten you.'

She said, 'After the Hutchinsons' ball — when I didn't see you — I thought that perhaps you thought — '

'What did you think, Marianne?'

'That I wasn't good enough for you. Alice Palmer said — '

'What? What did Miss Palmer say?'

'That you're related to a viscount. Or an earl.'

'Did she now?' He looked amused. 'Well, I have a great-uncle who's a baronet. We never speak — he quarrelled with his brother, my grandfather, long before I was born.' His smile died. 'You thought I looked down on you?'

She jutted out her chin. 'Didn't you?'

'No. Your father is a manufacturer and I'm in shipping. I can't see a great difference. We're both by and large self-made men. But there are things you need to consider. The disparity in our ages, for instance. You are twenty and I'm thirty-eight.'

'I don't care about that.'

'Don't you? I'm glad to hear it. Though you should think about it, at least. When you are forty-five and in your prime, I'll be in my sixties, an old man. And there's also the more difficult question of how fair it would be for me to take you away from your family. And if we were to marry — '

If we were to marry . . . The drum roll of rain seemed to announce her sudden rapture.

'If we were to marry, I'd have to ask you to leave Sheffield. I'll be honest with you, I detest the provinces. It seems a lot to ask of one so young, to take you away from all that's familiar. Of course, you would be able to visit your family and they'd be able to stay with us for as long as you wished. But there wouldn't be that everyday proximity that you're used to.'

'Sometimes I long to be by myself,' she said. 'Sometimes my head seems to jangle with everyone's news and quarrels.'

'You wouldn't be by yourself, though. You'd be with me.'

'*You* are part of me.' There was a glorious liberation in saying it at last. 'When I'm with you, Arthur, I like myself better.'

He opened the glass doors to let in cooler air. 'Dearest Marianne,' he said softly, 'that first time we met I felt such a bond between us. And then — I suppose I was afraid. Afraid that history might repeat itself. I was engaged, you see, a long time ago, when I was much younger. I'd gone through all the rigmarole of a couple of London seasons, and then I met a girl and asked her to marry me. She broke off the engagement a fortnight before the wedding. She'd met someone else. You told me once that you found it hard to make decisions, that you can always see two sides to everything. I don't want to persuade you into marrying me if you have doubts. I can offer you all the advantages that wealth can buy, and perhaps I can give you a fuller, richer life than you have at present. I can give you a beautiful home and interesting company and we could travel, too. But that may not be what you want. And if that's so then I'd prefer you to tell me now. I'll accept your decision, and I'll go away and never trouble you again.'

'Travel and company and houses . . . I don't care about any of *that*,' she said vehemently. 'Did you love her? That girl you almost married — did you love her?'

'I thought I did.' He cradled her face in his palms. 'But I was wrong. I love you, Marianne. I've never loved

63

anyone the way I love you.'

She was drowning in happiness, drunk with it. Yet she drew back, suddenly wary, afraid of the traps that love created, the possibilities of pain it opened up. 'Don't ever leave me,' she said fiercely. 'You must promise me never, ever, to leave me.'

He took from his pocket a small blue leather box. When he opened it, she saw the diamond ring inside. 'Always and forever,' he said, as he slid the ring onto her finger. 'I'll love you always and forever, Marianne. Beyond death, if need be.' The rain crashed against the roof and rolled down the gutters as he kissed her.

★　★　★

She would *make* Ash dance with her, Iris decided. It wasn't fair that he should treat her so. She tapped him on the shoulder. 'You can't come to our party and ignore us all. It's impolite.'

'I haven't ignored you all. I've spoken to your mother and Marianne and to Great-aunt Hannah. Oh, and James tried to cadge some money off me — couldn't help there, I'm afraid. Where's Eva, by the way? No one will tell me.'

'She's indisposed. Or that's the official story. Actually she's in disgrace. She cut off her hair — she looks like a shorn lamb. Father's sent her to her room.' She looked at him sharply. 'Do you mean that you're only ignoring *me*?'

He blinked. 'You've seemed rather busy.'

'I'm not busy at all just now. In fact, I've kept this dance just for you, Ash.'

'I'm not really,' he said, 'in the mood for dancing.'

His hair was tousled and darkened by the rain: he must have walked in the garden for some time, she realized. And there was a hard brightness in his eyes that she had never seen before and that should have

64

warned her. But she gave a little laugh and said, 'Ill temper's no excuse. I order you to dance with me, Ash.'

She thought for a moment that he was actually going to refuse, which would have been intolerable, but then he led her onto the dance floor. 'I wasn't sure,' she said, 'that you'd be able to dance.'

'I've a great many hidden talents.'

'I've never doubted it.'

'For instance, I've worked out what all this is for. It's not as though many people are enjoying themselves, is it?'

'I don't know how you can say that. It's all going splendidly.'

He looked down at her. There was a calculating expression in his eyes that she found she did not care for. He said, 'The men are making deals and the women are making alliances. This isn't about *pleasure*. It's about money. And power.'

He steered her round a corner; he was a perfectly competent dancer, yet she, who loved to dance, wasn't enjoying herself as much as she had expected. Something in the tone of his voice, the glint in his eye, unsettled her.

He said, 'You have an eight-course dinner because you can have an eight-course dinner. You can afford the food and wine and the servants. It's easy for you. And then there are the clothes you wear.'

'My gown? Don't you like my gown, Ash?'

'I don't know. I hadn't really thought about it.' His gaze slid down her, studying her from head to toe. 'Actually I think I preferred you in that outfit you wore when we went to the picnic.'

'I could hardly wear a simple muslin frock tonight!'

'So you wear diamonds and ostrich feathers because you *can* wear diamonds and ostrich feathers. You might look nicer in something plainer, but your clothes aren't chosen for their beauty, they're chosen to show what you're worth. And those flowers on your dress . . . ' His fingers brushed against the white silk roses Iris had sewn to her neckline. 'Do you know how much the women who make these are paid?'

She began to feel annoyed with him. 'I've no earthly idea.'

'They work for fourteen hours a day. They earn one and three for a gross of roses — that's a hundred and forty-four flowers — '

'I know what a gross is,' she said stiffly. '*I* don't decide what people are paid for things. It's all very hard, I'm sure. But it's not my fault.'

'People like your father decide,' he said, with sudden bitterness.

'Then you can hardly blame *me*. I haven't a penny of my own, Ash. We're not *heiresses*. Really, I haven't a penny.'

Again, that measuring look. 'There are other sorts of power, though, aren't there?' She saw his gaze drift to the fireplace, where the Catherwood boys, Oswald Hutchinson and Tom Summerbee stood. 'For instance, there's your puppy dogs over there. Just look at them. Their tongues are hanging out, waiting for a kind word from you.'

'You're not being very nice tonight, Ash.'

'And you're not very *kind*.' He stopped so suddenly she jolted against him. 'If you don't care for them you should tell them so.'

'That's nonsense!' she said furiously. 'They don't take any of it seriously. They know it's just a game.'

'It isn't a game to Tom Summerbee.'

She flushed. 'How can you say that?'

'Because he collared me in a corridor and insisted I share a bottle of champagne with him. And when he was drunk enough he told me how he felt about you.'

He had drunk too much too, she realized. Ash had drunk too much. That was the cause of his over-bright

66

eyes and the scarcely contained anger in his voice. She was surprised at him; she wouldn't have thought he was the sort of man to take his drink badly.

The music stopped and the dance came to an end. 'You're mistaken,' she said coldly, just before she walked away from him. 'You're not used to this sort of thing. You've been shut away too long in your dusty old schools and colleges. I told you, it's just a game.'

But to Iris's immense irritation, Tom Summerbee pounced on her as she left the ballroom and insisted on talking to her alone. They went to the conservatory and there, among palm and ficus, he knelt down in front of her and asked her to marry him.

She murmured the usual formula about being terribly honoured but unable to accept, assuming that would put an end to it and she could go back to the ballroom and dance the last waltz and maybe, just maybe, if she couldn't resist it, tell Gerald about Tom Summerbee. She was a good mimic and she could always make Gerald laugh.

But then Tom leapt to his feet and flung himself at her, kissing her. He was surprisingly strong and far more forceful than she would have guessed from his meek exterior. In the end, she had to give him a shove and he lost his balance, stumbling against a plant pot and tipping it over, showering the floor with earth and leaves.

She said, 'Really, Mr Summerbee, I wouldn't have thought this of you,' in her most crushing tones.

Instead of apologizing and clearing up the mess, he sat down on the tiles, his head in his hands, sobbing. Then he whimpered, 'But I love you, Iris.'

'No, you don't,' she said crisply. 'Don't be ridiculous. Of course you don't.'

He looked up at her, wet-eyed. 'Yes, I do. I want to marry you. I thought you felt the same way about me. I thought that was why you wanted to dance with me.'

A button had come off her glove and there was soil on the hem of her dress. 'Of course I won't marry you,' she said icily. 'How could you even think that I might?'

He flinched and then he lurched to his feet and half ran out of the room, leaving to Iris the task of righting the weeping fig. So silly and annoying of Tom Summerbee to get it all wrong, to interpret a mild flirtation as a declaration of love. It was a game, as she had said to Ash, and in grabbing at her like that, and in weeping like that, he had broken the rules.

★　★　★

It rained throughout the night; the following morning fat drops of water slid sullenly from gutter and rooftop. In the aftermath of the party a heaviness hung over Summerleigh. Lilian took to her bed once more, Joshua retreated to his study and the sisters sought the sanctuary of their accustomed bolt holes: a window seat, a summerhouse and the conservatory, where, it seemed to Marianne, an energy sparked by the events of the previous evening shimmered among the leaves and flowers.

After church Great-aunt Hannah asked Joshua if she could speak to him. Hannah Maclise had lived in Joshua's household since the death of his father, Hannah's brother, fifteen years earlier. Her bedroom and tiny sitting room were on the ground floor because she found stairs difficult. Her rooms were crammed with the accumulated belongings of several generations of Maclises. A watercolour which had once belonged to Joshua's father was squeezed between a daguerrotype of his grandfather (Dundreary whiskers and a judgemental Presbyterian glare) and a sketch Eva had drawn of Winnie as a puppy. A doll that had once belonged to a long-dead great-aunt nestled between a brass candlestick and a pouting china goatherd.

Hannah offered Joshua sherry in a glass the size of a thimble. Then she said without further preamble, 'I wanted to speak to you about Eva, Joshua.'

Joshua made a sound of incoherent rage. Hannah said firmly, 'My dear, Eva is very unhappy.'

'*Unhappy?* I should hope she is unhappy after the way she carried on last night!'

'Eva's behaviour was most reprehensible, it's true. But I think we must consider the cause of it.'

'The cause of it's plain,' he said slowly. 'It's Lilian. She's neglected the girls — aye, Aunt Hannah, *neglected* them. She's spent most of the last eleven years in her bed or travelling the Continent in search of a cure. A girl needs a mother, and my girls haven't had a mother. That's why they're turning out so bad.'

'They're not *bad* girls, Joshua,' said Hannah gently.

'Oh, Marianne and Clemmie are sweet enough, I daresay. They don't cause me much trouble. But Eva and Iris — '

'Eva's just headstrong, Joshua. And as for Iris — '

'Iris is a flirt,' he said bluntly. 'I saw her last night, keeping half a dozen of 'em on a string. There's talk about her, you know, Hannah — some old biddy took care to let slip the gossip to me last night. And she's been out for four years now, costing me a fortune in frocks and so on, and she still hasn't managed to find herself a husband! If she's not careful, she'll find herself on the shelf. Or worse.'

'Iris is a spirited girl,' said Hannah tactfully.

'Spirited!' said Joshua, with a snort. 'That's one word for it. As for Eva, she's spoilt. Ungrateful.'

'Eva likes to get her own way. Like you, Joshua.'

Joshua sighed. 'I don't want to make her unhappy. It's troubled me, seeing the lass so peaky. She's hardly spoken to me these past few weeks. I didn't know she could be so, so . . . *unforgiving.*' He drained the sherry glass in a single gulp, then added, 'All I've ever wanted was for them to have the best.'

'I know, my dear.'

'You've done what you can with the girls, Hannah, and Mrs Catherwood's been so kind, but I'm afraid they're running wild. Heaven only knows what will become of them.' Joshua ran a hand through his thick grey hair and glowered. 'And then there's James. The lad's a spendthrift — he has no self-control. All men like a drink and a pretty girl, but James doesn't know when to stop. He needs to learn the value of money. The trouble is he didn't have to fight for it, as I did.'

Hannah patted his hand. 'You must give him time. All young men can be wild — *you* could, Joshua, when you had a mind for it.'

His sons must eventually take over the business that Joshua had worked so hard and so long to build up. Maclise tools — files, saws, scythes, and parts and fittings for agricultural equipment — were shipped all over the world. He needed his sons to have good heads for business and his daughters to marry well. To Sheffield families, preferably, to build up alliances with other manufacturers. Sometimes he fretted that the world was changing and leaving him behind. Both America and Germany now produced good steel at a lower cost than Britain. Joshua's politics, a mildly paternalistic brand of conservatism, was falling out of fashion, threatened by the revolutionary impulses of firebrands and anarchists. The rise in trade unionism rankled with him: he didn't see the point of it. He knew every one of his employees by name, didn't make unreasonable demands of them, hadn't, like many others, cut wages because of the decline in demand. Yet he was aware of a growing mood of discontent. Even the women no longer seemed to be happy, but had become harridans who disrupted political meetings and chained themselves to railings. Old enmities seethed both in Ireland and on the Continent. Workers thought nothing of coming out on strike to force their employers to accede to their demands. There was no deference any more, thought Joshua fretfully, and little sense of responsibility. The tension in the air unsettled him; his beliefs, his morality, seemed increasingly at odds with this altered world.

Hannah interrupted his broodings. 'I have a suggestion to make, Joshua. I would like to pay for Eva to go to art school. No — hear me out, please. I have a little money of my own and I can think of nothing I would prefer to spend it on.'

'It's not the money I've a quarrel with. It's this whole nonsense. Why can't she just marry and settle down like a sensible girl?'

'Because she can't, Joshua,' said Hannah crisply. 'And if you force Eva to live her life in a way that is against her nature, then you will destroy her.'

There was a silence. Then Joshua muttered, 'That's not what I want. You know that.'

'Then you must swallow your pride and tell her that you were mistaken.'

He grumbled, 'Why must it all be so difficult? A man's home is supposed to be his sanctuary. These days I breathe a sigh of relief when I reach the works.'

'Of course, you do, Joshua,' said Hannah. 'You love your work.'

There was a pointedness to her tone that made him pause and think. Though he complained about the long hours his work demanded of him, he knew that he loved it, loved the acrid smell of the coke and the flare of the furnaces, the sense of industry and achievement. At the end of each day he had something to show for his labours. He loved to see the steel bars cooling in the furnace room and the boxes of files and saws and machine parts in the warehouse, each one individually wrapped in brown paper. He needed to make things, to hold in his hands the fruits of his labour.

Was that, Joshua found himself wondering, what Eva, too, needed? A girl couldn't follow in his footsteps at J. Maclise & Sons, of course, but did her painting give her the same sense of satisfaction and achievement?

'Humph,' he said, and wriggled uncomfortably on Hannah's slippery maroon sofa. The room was too hot, too small, too cluttered. And he'd sell his soul for a decent drink. His gaze met Hannah's. 'But — *London*, Hannah!' he protested. 'And on her own! Anything could happen to her.'

'Nonsense,' said Hannah briskly. 'Eva will be perfectly safe. I've another suggestion to make. She could stay with Sarah Wilde. You remember Sarah, Joshua.'

Joshua recalled a long-ago visit to a friend of Hannah's who lived in Bloomsbury. The house had been full of caged birds and chairs too small and spindly for a man to sit on.

'Sarah has agreed that Eva may board with her. Sarah would enjoy the company and she would keep an eye on Eva.' Hannah fixed him with a faded blue eye. 'Well, Joshua, do you agree?'

Reluctantly he gave his assent. Shortly afterwards, giving Eva his permission to go to art school in London, it took him aback that she didn't fling her arms around him and hug him, as he had expected, but instead confined her thanks to a few polite sentences and a dutiful peck on the cheek.

When she had gone, sitting alone in his study, Joshua poured himself a Scotch and drained it in one. Then he put down the glass, put his head in his hands and groaned aloud. He knew that he had been distracted recently, that he struggled to keep his mind on day-to-day affairs. The reason, which he could confide to no one, was Katharine Carver.

Mrs Carver was a widow. Joshua had known Stanley Carver, her late husband, for many years. Stanley had been the owner of a works in Attercliffe that made twist drills and cog-wheels. Just over a year ago Stanley Carver had died of heart failure, leaving Katharine with two young daughters and, Joshua suspected, not a great deal of money. As a friend of the family, Joshua had made tactful offers of assistance which Mrs Carver had brushed aside. At first his occasional visits to the Carvers had been prompted by duty, but as time passed he had become driven by something more. Though he had always thought Katharine Carver a fine-looking woman, it was only since Stanley's passing that he had found himself drawn by the rich tawny-red of her hair, by her height and upright carriage. Vitality informed her every breath — a sharp contrast with Lilian's pale languor.

He had found himself calling on Mrs Carver once a fortnight or so. Katharine had neither encouraged him to call again nor told him not to visit. Often, during the day, her features came into his mind. He hadn't felt like this for years, not since he had courted Lilian. He seemed to be sloughing off the cares and regrets of his adult life. He mentioned his visits to no one. It was nobody's business but his own, he told himself. There was no harm in keeping a kindly eye on the widow of an old friend. Because that was all they were: friends.

Until three months ago, that was. He had called one evening and found Mrs Carver in the scullery. The floor was under an inch of water. A pipe had burst, she explained. She had sent the maid out for a plumber; the cook had slipped on the wet tiles and had sprained her back and was lying down upstairs.

Amid a clutter of washing soda and Lysol, Joshua stooped under the sink and turned off the stopcock. When he stood up, she said, 'Joshua, your *coat*,' and tried to brush away the dust. He found himself taking her in his arms and kissing her. It was strange and wonderful to kiss a woman after so long, and she did not, as he had half-expected, push him away, but returned his kisses, her lips soft and hungry.

He had made love to her there and then, in the kitchen. Insanity: with the cook upstairs and the maid and the plumber expected any minute. Not that he had taken long about it — he had been starved of love for too many years to show much finesse. After the plumber had been dealt with and the servants dispatched, they had gone upstairs. In the wide oak bed that Katharine had formerly shared with her husband, Joshua had made love to her again, had taken his time, and had taken pride in giving her pleasure.

The events of that afternoon had transformed him. He felt young again, young and strong. Yet his elation was always tinged with guilt. He still loved Lilian, had never stopped loving her. Though she was now in her late forties, and though she had given birth to seven children, to Joshua she was still the fair, slender girl he had first fallen in love with. Yet Lilian had not shared a bed with him since before Philip was born and Philip was now eleven. Joshua could not remember when he had realized that he would never make love to his wife again. There had been no single moment of realization, only a gradual and soul-destroying awareness of loss. More than anything else, more than the grey hairs on his head or his thickened girth, the ending of that part of his life had made him feel old. At fifty-three, he was appalled to think that he might live another ten or twenty years without ever touching a woman again.

He could, of course, have paid for sex. There were back streets in Sheffield where it would be easy enough to make that sort of transaction. Sometimes, walking home at night, he had thought of catching the eye of one of the gaudy, painted creatures who stood in the shop doorways. He had not done so, though. The young girls made him think of his daughters, and there was a tired, deadened look in the eyes of the older women. He

74

had imagination enough to guess the self-loathing he would feel after such an encounter. And besides it was not only sex he wanted. He needed affection as well as physical release — or if not affection, at least the sense that he was in some way *chosen*.

That Katharine had chosen him seemed miraculous. When he closed his eyes he saw her, saw the folds and crevices of her pale skin, saw her soft, rounded shoulders, the curve of her belly. Sometimes, in the street or in a railway carriage, he would find himself thinking that he had smelt her perfume, and he would turn, searching through the crowds for her. Alone in the rattling gloom of a cab, he would run his thumb over the tips of his fingers, as if in doing so he could recall to himself the voluptuousness of her flesh.

Yet he knew that what he was doing was wrong, that he was wronging Lilian, and in breaking his marriage vows he was wronging God himself. Over and over again, he resolved to end the affair. Yet his resolve always faltered. Was it Katharine's proximity that wore away at his good intentions? Or was it Lilian's distance, Lilian's untouchableness, which daily reminded him of the loneliness he felt in his own house?

Before he could pour himself another drink, there was a knock at the door. The maid said, 'Mr Leighton would like to speak to you, sir,' and Joshua gave himself a shake, as if to clear thoughts of Katharine Carver from his head. Then he asked the maid to show Arthur Leighton in.

★　★　★

After Father had told the family that he had given Arthur Leighton his permission to marry Marianne, after a lengthy and excited discussion of wedding dates and bridesmaids and trousseaux, and after she had judged that no one would notice her absence, Iris

75

slipped out of the house into the garden.

The rain had stopped, but the ground was still wet underfoot. Iris sat down on the swing. Her head ached, had ached all day, and she felt wretched and fearful. Marianne was to be married; Eva was to go to art school. Sitting on the swing, drops of rain falling from the branches above to make crimson spots on her rose-pink dress, she recognized the desperate nature of her plight. She had left it too late. Her looks had begun to fade. She would end up the unmarried daughter, trapped at home, playing nursemaid to Mother.

Never, she thought fiercely. She would marry and marry soon. She had been too choosy for too long.

She heard a gate open and footsteps on the grass. Looking up, she saw Ash. Memories of the previous evening lingered like bruises beneath the skin, but she put up her chin and called out to him, 'Have you come to say sorry?'

He crossed the grass to her. 'I've come to say goodbye.'

'Goodbye?'

'I've decided to go back to Cambridge.'

Once, when they were children, they had been sea-bathing at Scarborough, and she had waded too far from the shore and a wave had struck her, knocking her feet from under her. She felt like that now, breathless, shocked, all at sea.

'I'm catching the train first thing tomorrow,' he said. 'I couldn't leave without saying goodbye.'

She cried, 'But you can't go away!'

'I have to.'

There was a steeliness about him that she recalled from the previous night. She blurted out, 'But you *can't* go, Ash! How shall I manage?'

'Oh, you'll manage, Iris. You're the sort of person who always manages.'

'What do you mean?'

He shrugged. 'Nothing.'

'You think I'm selfish, don't you? You think I don't care about anyone but myself.' As she slid off the swing, her silk shawl slipped from her lap. And in the time it took her to stoop and pick it up from the wet grass, she saw what she must do. This time she must not let her opportunity slip away. This was her chance. Perhaps her last chance.

'Well, it's not true. I do care about other people. For instance, I care about you, Ash.'

'It's kind of you to say so.'

'I mean it. You think I'm heartless. Well, I can change. I know that we don't always agree — '

'Perhaps that's what I'll miss.' He looked back at the house; his gaze lingered. 'The time I've spent with you all — it's been . . . different. Not like anything I've done before.'

'A nice sort of difference?'

'Most of the time.'

'Even though we argue?'

'Well, we're not the same, are we? You've said so yourself. You'd rather avoid the unpleasant things in life. Whereas I — ' He broke off, took a deep breath. 'Anyway, as I said, I'll be gone tomorrow.'

She said robustly, 'I think you're wrong. We've plenty of things in common. The same things make us laugh. The same pretensions bore us.' In the fading light she noticed for the first time the bluish marks beneath his eyes. 'You look tired, Ash.'

'A bad night,' he said, with a half-smile.

'Poor Ash,' she said softly. And then she drew him to her, cradling his head against her shoulder. He seemed to relax into her. Her fingers ran through his thick, fair hair. There was that patch of skin between collar and hair; she kissed it, and felt him still. He raised his head; his lips brushed against hers. Then, suddenly, he straightened, stepping back from her.

'Iris — '

She said quickly, 'It doesn't matter.'

'Of course it does.' He shook his head vehemently. 'I behaved badly enough last night. I didn't come here to behave even more abominably.'

'I mean . . . ' Her mouth was dry, she felt a sudden apprehension, but she had never been one to flinch from what must be done, so she said quickly, 'I mean, if we were engaged, it wouldn't matter.'

'Engaged?' He looked blankly at her.

'Would that be so terrible a prospect?'

'Iris, I hadn't thought — '

'What — ' she stared at him — 'never? Come now, Ash.'

'Never.' There was finality in his voice.

She began to feel cold inside. She whispered, 'But you must have. You called so often — you always stayed so long — and last night, we danced.'

'*You* asked me to dance.'

'Yes, I did.' Her voice faltered. Inside her, something seemed to plummet, to commence a long, dark fall. She heard herself say, disbelieving, 'But you must have cared for me!'

'I do — I do care for you.'

'But not in that way?'

He flung out his hands. 'Oh, Iris, what would we talk about, you and I? I want to make things better! I want to read books, to discuss great matters, to understand the world!'

'And I don't?' Her voice was small.

'It's not what you were made for, is it?' He gave his head a quick shake and said more gently, 'There's nothing wrong in wanting to be admired. You deserve to be admired, Iris, you're a beautiful girl. And plenty of men would be perfectly happy with a girl who's only interested in — oh, what colour her new gown is to be.'

She whispered, 'But you're not?'

He looked away. 'I'm sorry.'

Her head was pounding like a drum, but she drew herself up, and said proudly, 'You don't have to be sorry. I don't need to be pitied.'

He started to speak, but she interrupted him. 'I think that I'd like you to go, Ash.'

'Iris — '

'Go. Please go.'

She did not watch him as he walked away from her, but turned aside, her eyes fixed on the darkening garden, her nails pressed into her palms to stop herself crying out at her humiliation. When she was sure that he had gone, she opened her hands and looked down at them. Small red crescents marked her palms and she saw that where, just two months earlier, she had torn her hands after falling off Clemency's bicycle, her skin was still patched with white, as though it had failed to knit properly together.

Now her panic was so intense that for a moment she felt quite breathless. What was she to do? Where was she to go? Ash did not want her, no one wanted her. Marianne and Eva would leave home and she would be the only adult daughter left at Summerleigh. She would waste away the remainder of her youth keeping house and running errands for Mother.

And then she remembered what Charlotte had said to her. *You should think about nursing too, Iris . . .*

★   ★   ★

One morning Clemency was collecting her mother's letters for the post, when Lilian said, 'Of course, everything will be so different for me with three of my girls leaving home.'

Clemency said timidly, 'But you'll still have me, Mother.'

'Will I, darling?' Lilian smiled up at Clemency.

79

'You're such a good girl, Clemmie. Such a particular help to me.'

Clemency went pink. 'Me?'

'Of course! You're so . . . so *restful.*'

Clemency, who had always suspected that Lilian thought her second best to Marianne, was both flattered and moved. She said impulsively, 'I'd do anything for you, Mother!'

'Truly, darling? You won't leave me, then?'

'Never.'

'I wouldn't blame you at all if you did.' Lilian sighed. 'I'm such a tiresome old thing.'

Clemency protested, 'You're not tiresome at all, Mother!'

'Sweet of you to say so, darling, but no young girl wants to be stuck in a sickroom when she could be out having fun.' Lilian fiddled with the pots and jars on her dressing table. Then she said, 'And besides, I know how much you enjoy school.'

Clemency was confused. 'School?'

Lilian's small hand gripped Clemency's wrist. 'It's a terrible thing to ask of you. I haven't been brave enough to speak to you before. But what would I do, all alone every day, with none of my daughters to keep me company?' The grip on Clemency's wrist tightened, showing surprising strength. 'I don't want to force you into anything, darling. I'd understand perfectly if you don't want to leave school to keep your sick old mother company.'

'Leave school,' whispered Clemency.

Lilian continued as if she had not spoken, 'I'm sure I could manage somehow. The last thing I want is to be a nuisance to anyone. And perhaps Hannah . . . ' Lilian's brow crumpled. 'No. It would be too much to ask of poor Hannah at her time of life. Oh dear, I feel quite ashamed. That I should be reduced to asking my daughter to leave school to look after me. I sometimes

80

think — ' Lilian broke off, her eyes darkened.

Clemency was alarmed. 'What is it, Mother?'

'I sometimes think,' said Lilian quietly, 'that it would be better for everyone if I were dead.'

Just then, Clemency hated herself for the shock she had felt when she had realized that her mother wanted her to leave school. She cried, 'You mustn't say that, Mother!' and flung herself at Lilian's feet, clasping her hand. Between her own large, strong palms it felt so tiny and fragile, the pulse fluttering in the wrist. 'Of course I'll stay at home!' she cried. 'I'll do whatever I can to make you feel better, I promise! I'd love to stay with you!'

Lilian stroked her face. 'We'll have such a lovely time, won't we, darling? Such a lovely, special time.'

Sitting in the garden that evening, Clemency still felt ashamed of her momentary hesitation. With all her sisters gone, she quite saw that Mother had had no alternative but to ask her to step into the breach.

It wouldn't be so bad, she comforted herself. Her friends would call in on her in the afternoons on their way home. And perhaps, on Wednesday afternoons, she could walk up to school to watch a hockey match.

A voice called out her name. James was striding across the lawn towards her. He looked excited. 'I say, Clemmie, have you heard the news? Some chap's flown an aeroplane across the Channel. Some Frenchman. Can you imagine? Just think, being up there all on your own, with no one to bother you, heading off to wherever you wanted to go.'

Clemency lay back in the long grass, looking up at the sky. She thought of James's aviator flying across the English Channel. She had never seen the Channel, had never been to France. *Just think, being up there, all on your own.*

All on your own. With renewed force, she was struck by the implications to herself of the changes that had in the last few weeks swept through the Maclise household like a hurricane. By the end of the year Marianne would be married, Eva would be studying in London, and Iris would be training to be a nurse. In term time, Aidan and Phil would be at school; during the day, when James went to work, she, Clemency, would be alone. Now she felt a tightening of the heart, a sense of walls closing in and horizons lowering, trapping her. And she had an impulse to rise to her feet and to run, to run and keep on running, out of the garden, out of the street, out of the city, to run until she was too far away for anyone to call her back.

3

Love was Arthur's hand scooping back her curtain of hair because he could not bear to lose sight of her for a moment. Desire was waking in the night and turning to each other, silent because there was no need for words. The silk sheets were slippery against her limbs and her skin felt fevered, burning at his touch. Marianne could feel the pounding of Arthur's heart, the exhalation of his breath.

On honeymoon, in their room in the Gritti Palace in Venice, the remains of the wintry afternoon sun lingered, trapped in the engraved mirrors and Murano glass chandeliers.

'Annie,' he said, 'I think I shall call you Annie. It shall be my name for you. No one else shall use it.'

Marianne — whined, cross, commanding, a complaining heaviness on the final syllable — seemed to be becoming a creature of the past. *I am Mrs Leighton now,* she reminded herself. *I have been Mrs Leighton for three whole weeks.* Her married name was still unaccustomed, a thing of delight.

After Venice they went to Paris, where Arthur bought her clothes from Paul Poiret: long, loose tubular dresses and narrow coats trimmed with fur that swept the floor, a kimono with embroidered sleeves, and an evening gown of midnight blue and silver, a blue tinged with violet to match her eyes.

Released from the imprisonment of her whalebone corsets, her body became lithe and slender, her height enabling her to carry off the flowing, elongated lines. Examining her reflection in the mirror, Marianne noticed disparagingly, out of habit, her small breasts, her boy's hips. Yet curves would have spoilt the Poiret dress. And then there was her angular face, with its sharp cheekbones and long, thin Maclise nose — yet, miraculously, marriage seemed to have softened her features, rubbing out the marks of discontent and anxiety.

She and Arthur talked endlessly, late into the nights, as though time might run out before they had said everything they wanted to say to each other. Social engagements seemed an interruption to their voyage of mutual discovery. Some things she knew already, of course. She knew his birthplace (Surrey), his school and university (Winchester and Oxford), his family history (the Leightons had made their money first through sugar, then shipping). He was a partner in a shipping consortium; one afternoon he took Marianne to the London docks and showed her one of his ships, the *Louise*, sitting proudly on the Thames.

She discovered that he loved music, art and the theatre, and that he collected modern paintings; they hung in his Norfolk Square house, an Augustus John in the hallway, a Sickert over the study mantelpiece, and a Whistler, a dark, atmospheric blur of black and navy and grey, in the drawing room. She discovered that he had a soft heart, that he never left the house without pennies in his pocket for beggars. He loved animals, especially dogs and horses — the only time she ever saw him lose his temper was when he came across a carrier whipping his pitifully thin, mangy horse.

Arthur told her about his travels. Following his broken engagement, he had taken ship to the East. He described to Marianne the month he had spent in Egypt, en route to India via the Suez Canal, and the city of Bombay. He had remained in the East for two years, travelling round India and Ceylon. After the death of his father, he had returned to England, where he had invested much of his inheritance in a shipping consortium.

They travelled back to London in the middle of February. Grey slush clogged the gutters and ice made the pavements treacherous. The telephone rang and Arthur's friends called, leaving their cards. In their absence on the Continent invitations had arrived, piled on the silver tray in the hall: summonses to dinners and dances, receptions and recitals. Marianne felt dazed, the world too suddenly crowding in on her, reminding her that in becoming Arthur Leighton's wife she had obligations other than sharing his company, his bed.

He had a way of knowing what she felt before she spoke — because, of course, he felt as she did. He ran his thumb along the stack of cards. 'It's too soon, isn't it?' he said. 'Where shall we go? Not another hotel . . . I need to have you to myself.' He frowned. 'There's my Surrey house. It's been shut up for years — I hardly ever use it. My darling Annie, would you mind roughing it a bit?'

Of course she didn't mind. They drove to Surrey that evening. It was midnight when they arrived. Frozen in spite of her furs, Marianne first saw the house in the moonlight, iced with frost, white and strange and unearthly, its name picked out on the wrought-iron gates: Leighton Hall.

The housekeeper welcomed them. Marianne opened doors and peered into rooms. Much of the furniture was under dust sheets. Pale, sculptured shapes loomed out of the darkness, bulky and disconcerting in their lack of easy identification. Gaslight hissed in the mantels. A garland of plaster ivy leaves wound around a high ceiling, and long casement windows looked out over a garden made mysterious by moonlight.

They were looked after by the housekeeper and an odd-job man, who lived in the nearby village. At night they were alone. The weather remained cold, frost greying the lawns and a crystal covering of ice encasing the bare black branches of the trees. In the morning

Arthur rode while Marianne explored.

She didn't care about the threadbare carpets or peeling wallpaper, didn't even mind the cold. Instead, smiling to herself, she imagined children running through the corridors, their laughter echoing against the high ceilings.

After a month they returned to London. Arthur's town house was in Bayswater. He liked to rise in the early morning and ride along Rotten Row; often Marianne walked to Hyde Park to greet him at the end of his ride. Picking him out of the crowd, she saw how concentrated his expression was as he guided his horse along the busy thoroughfare, saw also that he was the handsomest man there.

The Norfolk Square house was spacious, light and elegant. There were electric lights, a modern gas range in the kitchen and a telephone. The telephone unnerved Marianne to begin with, lurking in the hallway like a menacing black toad that might at any moment erupt into shrieking clamour. But soon she began to see how useful it was: so easy to call Harrods or Fortnum's when one had run out of something.

The Norfolk Square servants seemed to be twice as efficient as the servants at Summerleigh. Marianne did not have to lift a duster or cut a slice of bread. After she had discussed the menus with the cook in the morning and had overseen the ordering of provisions and the paying of bills, there didn't seem a great deal more for her to do. Her clothes appeared in her wardrobe, cleaned and ironed, their missing buttons or torn lace replaced as if by magic.

Arthur introduced her to his friends. Older than Marianne, and with that indefinable glossy urban sheen, she encountered them at the theatre and the ballet, or they invited her to receptions and dinners. Though at first she thought of them en masse, these London friends — indivisible, similar in their social competence, self-assurance and sleek good looks — she soon saw that they divided into two camps. *Arthur's theatre friends*, she privately christened one group, *Arthur's business friends* the other.

Patricia Letherby, one of the theatre friends, took Marianne under her wing. Mrs Letherby was outspoken, cheerful, tactless and warm-hearted. Discovering that Marianne played the piano, she insisted that Marianne attend the music society, which met once a fortnight in her drawing room. There were also literary afternoons, when they drank tea and ate sandwiches cut so fine you could almost see through them, while a novelist read from his latest work. Some of the readings were quite racy, on the sorts of topic that would never have been mentioned at Summerleigh.

The Merediths were business friends. Edwin Meredith was a member of the shipping consortium. Laura Meredith was much younger than her husband. A succession of men, alike only in their adoration of her, accompanied Laura Meredith to the theatre and to dances. Mrs Meredith's eyes were grey, her hair was auburn, and her brows and lashes were delicate brush strokes of gold. She favoured rose pink and apricot, which complimented her unusual colouring, and she had a proprietorial manner with her escorts, a way of placing a white-gloved hand on a man's arm as if laying claim to him, a knack of keeping him in her immediate vicinity, recalling him with a sudden glance or flick of her fan if he threatened to stray too far. Patricia Letherby murmured to Marianne, 'Of course, it's a *mariage blanc*.' Marianne must have looked confused because Patricia then explained. 'Laura and Edwin don't share a bedroom. Laura needed Edwin's money and Edwin needed her social cachet. But he's a dry old stick so Laura finds her amusements elsewhere. There, don't look so shocked, my dear, it's how we go on, I'm afraid.' Patricia sighed. 'Sometimes I envy Laura. She only seems to have to *look* at them.'

It was as though Marianne had come to live in a foreign land, where there were different rules and customs. Behaviour that would have caused a scandal among the prosperous manufacturers of Sheffield was considered perfectly acceptable in London. It registered with Marianne that Patricia Letherby hadn't seemed to consider Mrs Meredith wrong in taking a lover. Amusing and interesting and rather fast, perhaps, but not *wrong*, not *immoral*.

That spring Marianne gave a dinner party. When Arthur came home in the evening his arms were full of violets, her favourite flowers. She was wearing the midnight blue and silver gown he had bought her in Paris. When he pinned a posy of violets to the bodice of her gown, the pin pricked his thumb. Closing her eyes, Marianne kissed the tiny bead of blood that had formed, like a crimson pearl, on his skin.

The dinner went smoothly; guests complimented Marianne on her table and on her appearance. Yet it occurred to her — a sudden thought, somewhere between the main course and the savoury — that she would rather not be here, among all these people she hardly knew. She would rather have been alone with Arthur in the Surrey house, that place of streams and shadows, would rather have been in bed with him. When she imagined his touch, she felt an ache of desire. She had to give herself a little shake to force herself back to the dinner table. Her thoughts disturbed her: they seemed inappropriate and unsuitable, and fleetingly her old fear that she was odd, different, returned. She could not know, could only guess, whether other women had the same desires, the same intrusive, ill-timed thoughts.

Looking round the table, she found herself wondering whether the polite conversation and carefully honed manners were only a veneer for something earthier and far more raw. She wondered whether the layers of silk and velvet concealed bodies that felt as hers did, that yearned as hers did. Her thoughts seemed to hint at something disruptive, something that could not be controlled. Searching for reassurance, she looked up to the far end of the table, to where Arthur sat. Their eyes met and, beneath the table, she stretched out her fingers towards him, as if by doing so she could reach him, touch him.

★　★　★

The Mandeville Hospital was in the East End of London. The Mandeville was a voluntary hospital which took in acute patients, the victims of accidents or sudden illness, many of whom paid a contribution towards their care. Various wings, paid for by charities and endowments, had been added to the hospital over the centuries, so that the original red-brick building, constructed in the eighteenth century, now sprouted tentacles that snaked into the cramped terraces and alleyways of the East End.

The first day Iris arrived at the hospital, the sight of her name, written in careful italic script on the label outside her room in the nurses' home, had brought home the finality of what she had done. Her heart had sunk and she was overcome by a wave of misery so intense that, once inside the room, she had to rush across to the window and pretend to look out at the view so that her father, who had escorted her to London, could not see her expression. It was a moment or two before she was able to look round and see that although the room was small, it was neat and well arranged, with a bed, wardrobe, washstand, desk and chair. And at least it was her own. At least she didn't have to share it with Marianne.

In the nurses' home, there was a dining room, a

sitting room and a lecture hall. The home was separated from the hospital by a garden, where the nurses sat when the weather was fine. Inside the hospital, the atrium and outpatients' waiting rooms echoed with different languages and dialects, from the birdsong twitter of a pretty little Cockney corset-maker to the low growl of a Polish stevedore. On the wards a dying Scotsman called out for water, and a grizzled Italian, the proprietor of an establishment that sold eel pies, serenaded Iris, singing of his love for her, falling silent only when Sister Grant scolded him.

Iris felt as though she had moved to a different country, a different world. All her old expectations and assumptions had been knocked away. Her former life, which had consisted of leisurely choices between a cycle ride or a game of tennis, now seemed unreal, as though it had happened to someone else. From the moment she dragged herself out of bed at six in the morning till she fell back into bed at ten o'clock at night, she had hardly a minute to call her own. She was always busy and always tired.

Her life was governed by the hands of the clock, by the commands of staff nurses and sisters and, of course, by matron. Matron was Miss Caroline Stanley. Miss Stanley wore black silk gowns with leg-of-mutton sleeves and pie-crust collars. Unlike her nurses, who were not allowed to wear jewellery, Miss Stanley wore a large cameo brooch at her throat and rings on her fingers. The probationers were expected to take tea with Miss Stanley once a month. Iris endured the quarter of an hour of polite small talk, making sure she did not fidget or glance at the clock, but some of the less poised probationers left Miss Stanley's room in tears, with stories of spilled tea or similar faux pas.

The first six weeks of the two-year training course consisted of lectures on basic anatomy, hygiene, physiology and practical nursing. It wasn't as difficult as

Iris had feared — her spelling and her arithmetic were a great deal better than some of the other girls', and she was neat-fingered at rolling bandages and making splints. Then, at the end of the six weeks, she was sent to work as a probationer on a men's general ward. Any of her remaining illusions about the job were quickly scotched. By the end of the first morning Iris had discovered that Sister Grant, who oversaw the ward, was a tyrant, and that nursing was every bit as dreadful as she had feared.

As the eldest daughter of a prosperous Sheffield manufacturer, Iris had been protected from many things. Once men's bodies had been a mystery to her; now, working on a men's ward, nothing was hidden. She was obliged to bathe every part of a man's body and to perform the most intimate tasks. Many of the men were as embarrassed as she, but others ribbed her. At Summerleigh all the unpleasant or dirty household tasks had been assigned to the maids. Now Iris was expected to empty bedpans, to clear up soiled dressings and fouled sheets. Though she had always secretly prided herself on her lack of feminine weaknesses, she now had to fight her queasiness at the sight of a terrible wound or disfiguring disease.

Yet much harder, in some ways, was to discover that she, Iris Maclise, was incompetent. Though she knew herself to be lazy, she had never before thought herself inept. Whatever she had chosen to do she had done well. It was just that she hadn't chosen to do all that much. Playing tennis, dancing and flirting with boys — at all of these she had excelled. She had left the dull household duties to Marianne. And now Marianne lived in luxury while she mopped floors and scrubbed iron bedsteads. Marianne dressed in silks and diamonds while she wore a blue calico dress with a white apron, cap and cuffs, and was forbidden to wear even her smallest pearl earrings.

Often she felt as though she had been picked up and turned about like a kaleidoscope, that all her complacent assumptions had been shaken up and reassembled in a different order. Preparing food, laundering linen and keeping a room clean and tidy were all a great deal more demanding than she had realized. Whatever she did, Sister Grant found fault. 'Cleanliness,' she said, pointing out Iris's streaky window sills to the other probationers 'is next to godliness, nurse. And dirt spreads infection. Didn't they teach you that at your lah-di-dah school?' Iris missed edges when she mopped and left smears on window panes. She didn't know how to make a bed; her corners refused to fit smoothly beneath the mattress. Sister Grant, click-clacking down the ward, spied Iris's corners with her eagle eye and harangued her, voice dripping with scorn.

Iris had to be on the ward at seven o'clock in the morning, to help the night nurse wash the patients. She always seemed to be short of time — five to seven would come and she'd still be pinning on her cap. If a nurse was late on the ward more than half a dozen times, she forfeited her day off. At eight o'clock Iris attended prayers, and then she returned to the ward, where she cleaned and dusted, washed glasses and jugs, and wiped the locker tops over with chlorinated soda. At a quarter past nine, she helped prepare and serve bread and milk to the patients. Then she cleaned the bathrooms and tidied the laundry before leaving the ward for a cup of tea in the nurses' home. Sometimes there was a lecture or a demonstration for the probationers; sometimes there was time to rush to the shops or to meet Eva or Charlotte for coffee. Then they had dinner and then, at half-past one, Iris returned to the ward for more cleaning and tidying before Dr Hennessy's round. Dr Hennessy was the moustachioed and dapper ward physician. While he and his junior doctors examined the patients, the nurses clustered behind Sister Grant, arranged in order of seniority, the staff nurses at the front, and Iris, the lowest of the probationers, at the back.

After the doctors had gone, the unconscious and fevered patients had to be washed and the steam kettles boiled. The patients had more bread and butter and tea in the late afternoon, then Iris left the ward for half an hour to have her own tea, and then there was a final rush to wash glasses and bottles, give the patients their supper and make the beds before the night staff came on at eight o'clock. At a quarter to nine, the day nurses went to evening prayers, and only then was there supper, followed by bed.

The one thing you could say for it, Iris often thought, was that all the rushing about didn't leave you much time to think. These days there were a great many things she didn't want to think about. For instance, she didn't want to think about Marianne's wedding, or to remember the fierceness of the envy she had felt as she had watched Marianne walk down the aisle on Father's arm. And she certainly didn't want to think about Ash. She had neither seen nor heard from Ash since that terrible evening. None of the Maclises had. With luck, she prayed, none of them would ever see him again. But something in his rejection of her seemed to have eaten into her soul and, since that night, she had not been able to see herself in quite the same way. It wasn't only that she now doubted the measure and power of her beauty, she also found herself questioning her worth.

Much of the time it seemed to her that she had slipped into the wrong life by mistake. Although she saw how a series of events — Marianne's engagement, Charlotte's decision to become a nurse, Ash's rejection of her — had led to her taking such a drastic step, she couldn't help thinking that some fundamental element of choice had been missing, and that she had stumbled, driven by fear and impulse and pride, each further step enmeshing her more deeply in a net of her own making. There had been moments, of course, when she might have changed her mind and admitted that she had made a mistake. At her interview Miss Stanley had grilled her about her vocation. Father, too, had tried to dissuade her. His parting words, just before he left Iris with her trunk and hatboxes at the nurses' home, had been an exasperated, 'I don't know what you're trying to prove by this, but you must come home when you've had enough, my dear. This won't suit you.' Then he had insisted on pressing money into her hand for the train fare back to Sheffield, before leaving her in the unfamiliar room, tears smarting in her eyes, fighting the need to call him back.

Iris's friends and acquaintances had expressed a mixture of shock and disbelief at her decision to become a nurse. She had scarcely bothered to argue with them: after all, shock and disbelief had been her own overriding emotions for some time. Shock and disbelief that it had been Marianne who had made the splendid marriage and not she. Shock and disbelief, and a terrible, enduring humiliation, that Ash had not wanted her. It wasn't that she had *loved* Ash, but she had liked him and she had believed him to be her friend. It had been a novel experience to discover the pain of rejection, and it hadn't made it one jot easier to know that such pain was commonplace and that she herself had inflicted it many times.

She hadn't expected to miss home, but she did. She missed the easy, unassuming comfort of Summerleigh, she missed the company of her family and friends. Most of all, she missed the feeling that she belonged somewhere, that she *mattered*. On the ward her value was measured by her ability to make a bed or take a temperature or prepare a tray of dressings. She knew that she wasn't particularly good at any of these things, that she was probably the least competent probationer on Sister Grant's ward. The Mandeville Hospital would not have suffered one jot had Iris Maclise decided to leave. Sister Grant, perhaps, would be relieved. Which was one reason, perhaps rather perversely, that made Iris stay.

She kept her unhappiness from her sisters. Convincing Marianne of her contentment was easy enough because Marianne, newly returned from her honeymoon and made beautiful by love, could think of nothing but Arthur.

Iris wrote to Clemency twice a week. Her conscience pricked her when she thought of Clemency: if she herself had stayed at home, Clemency would have been able to remain at school. And then Iris would have been Mother's companion. And even nursing was preferable to that.

She decided that she would endure it for a year. Anything less would be humiliating. Anything less and the friends and members of her family who, along with her father, had assumed that she would give up nursing within a week, would crow. In a year Charlotte, who had been so ridiculously pleased when Iris had told her of her decision to join her at the Mandeville, would have made other friends and wouldn't miss her. And in a year she might have thought of something else to do.

It was just that a year sometimes seemed an impossibly long time. Ash had also said to her: *You'd rather avoid the unpleasant things in life.* When she was washing out bedpans in the sluice, or bathing bodies that had been crippled by years of manual labour, she sometimes smiled grimly to herself and thought: *If only you could see me now, Ash. If only you could see me now.*

★   ★   ★

Aidan and Philip came home to Summerleigh for the Easter holidays. Then Eva, Marianne and Arthur arrived, and Clemency seemed to heave a sigh of relief. Summerleigh was almost like it used to be, with all the family together.

But Marianne and Arthur returned to London the day after Easter Monday, taking Eva with them. And afterwards Mother took to her bed, and Great-aunt Hannah, who had a chill, retired to her rooms, leaving just the three boys, Father and Clemency.

Eva and Marianne's departure seemed to make Father miserable and cross. As always, Father's moods and Mother's illness affected the tenor of the household, and tension settled over Summerleigh. Though Clemency tried to smooth things over, it was as if the balance of the family had gone wrong, that without her elder sisters to leaven them the rest of the family failed to mix together properly.

Things came to a head towards the end of the week. Mother had a bad night and Clemency had to call in Dr Hazeldene. The following morning, just as Mother was finally dozing off, Philip tripped, running down the stairs. He was carrying a tin tray of his model soldiers and the tray clanged onto the tiles, startling Mother awake and making her heart hammer alarmingly. Everyone was furious with Philip except Clemency, who suspected that Philip had stumbled because he couldn't see properly where he was going. She gave Mother a glass of wine with some drops of laudanum, then she sat beside Mother's bed till she slept.

By the time he came home from work Father's mood had worsened. At dinner Clemency read the warning signs — the gloomy downturn of his mouth, the sharpness in his voice, and the roaming, discontented gaze. To Clemency, Father's moods were as transparent as a child's, his lurches from infectious happiness to morose despair clearly signalled. It always surprised her

96

that James didn't seem to notice Father's changeable temper, and that he had the knack of lighting on subjects expressly designed to ignite Father's short fuse. Although, to be fair, Father had an equal knack of misinterpreting James, looking for slights.

Joshua surveyed the dining table. 'Hardly worth laying up this big table with so few of us here,' he grumbled. 'And at church — two pews, the Maclises used to fill and then we had to squeeze up. We'll be hard put to fill the one this Sunday.'

'I won't be here on Sunday,' said James. 'I'm going to London.'

Joshua's brows lowered. '*London?*'

Clemency felt herself tense. London, in her father's view, was crowded, noisy and populated by criminals, and not a patch, of course, on Sheffield.

'I can't think why all of you have to keep going off to London. Three of my girls have left me, and now you tell me you're off as well!'

'It's only for a day or two, Father.'

'Isn't your home good enough for you? What can you possibly want to do in London that you can't do here?'

'There's the restaurants — '

'*Restaurants!*' Joshua snorted scathingly. 'Why do people choose to eat in restaurants when they can get better food at home?'

'And the theatres — and the cinemas — '

'Theatres?' Joshua looked outraged. 'If your sister wasn't here then we'd have a little talk, you and I, about the sort of people who frequent such places. Rogues and scoundrels the lot of them.'

James flushed. Clemency said quickly, 'More potatoes, Father?'

Joshua wagged his finger at his eldest son. 'When I was your age, James, I was working six days a week, seven in the morning till seven at night. I didn't have time for all this gadding about.'

He fell silent, attacking his dinner with gloomy gusto. Clemency began to breathe again. Then Aidan said innocently, 'Theatres and restaurants cost a lot of money, don't they, Father? One of the fellows at school told me it cost five shillings a head when his people treated him to a spread in London.'

'Five shillings a head!' cried Joshua. 'You shouldn't be wasting your money on such frippery, James!'

James scowled and mumbled something under his breath.

Joshua's eyes narrowed. 'What did you say?'

Clemency threw James a warning glance. James muttered, 'Nothing, Father.'

Joshua, thwarted, threw his napkin onto the table with a vicious swipe. 'If you've something to say, then you can say it to all of us!'

James's head jerked up. 'Very well, Father. I said that you don't give me much money to waste.'

'Aye. For your own good! God only knows what trouble you'd get yourself into if you had money to spare. But you manage to make a good enough job of throwing away what you have, don't you?'

'It's my money to spend as I wish!'

Joshua's fist struck the table. 'It's *my* money! If it wasn't for me you'd all be starving in the gutter, every one of you! Every last penny comes from me!'

James stumbled to his feet, his napkin falling to the floor. As he left the room, he slammed the door behind him.

There was a long silence, eventually broken by Philip saying, 'I can't eat my cabbage. It tastes funny.'

Clemency froze, waiting for the inevitable explosion. Joshua roared, 'You'll clear your plate, young man! Every mouthful! I'll not have another son of mine grow up a spoiled brat!' And then, without warning, he rounded on Aidan, hissing, 'And you can take that smug expression off your face, my

98

lad! You're no better than the rest of them!' Aidan whitened. Philip began to cry.

After dinner, when Philip, teary and snuffling, had finally eaten the last of his cabbage, Clemency plucked up her courage and tapped on the door of her father's study.

'I wondered whether you wanted anything, Father. A cup of tea, perhaps.'

Joshua was sitting at his desk, smoking. 'Nothing, lass.'

She made to close the door, but he said suddenly, 'You're a good girl, Clemency. I expect you miss your sisters too.'

'Yes, Father.'

She went upstairs and knocked on the door of the bedroom that Aidan shared with Philip. Aidan was lying on his stomach on the floor. A row of coins, in neat towers, was arranged in front of him.

Clemency asked, 'What are you doing?'

'Counting out my funds, that's all.'

'Dear me, Aidan, you must have been saving up! All that money!'

'People waste money,' he said, 'on sweets and toys and silly things like that. I *never* waste money.'

She said ruefully, 'I don't know where my allowance goes.'

'You should keep accounts,' he said. '*I* do.' Rising to his feet, he took a notebook from a drawer, and showed her the columns. *Nib for pen*, she read, *2d. Paper gum, 6d.*

'Goodness,' she said. Glancing at him, she added, 'Father didn't mean it, you know.'

'Didn't he?' In the darkness Aidan's eyes, paler than all the other Maclises', were as hard as granite. He muttered, 'I always try to please him. I never cross him, as James does.'

Clemency found James in the summerhouse. Seeing

her, he made an angry stab through the air with his cigarette.

'Why does he have to take it out on us?'

'That's just Father's way.' She went to sit beside him. It was cold in the summerhouse and she shivered, so he gave her his jacket. It smelt pleasantly of James, of tobacco and Pears' soap and smoke from the works, and she hugged it around herself, comforted by it. She said, 'It's not the same, is it, now Marianne and Iris and Eva are gone. The family seems to be getting smaller and smaller. What if everyone goes away? What if, one day, there's only me left?'

James hugged her. 'That won't happen, you idiot. You'll have a family of your own one day, won't you?'

She remembered the day Philip had been born, how miraculous it had felt to fit her fingertip into his tiny palm. 'It would be nice to have babies,' she said slowly, 'but I can't imagine getting married.'

'A bit tricky to have one without the other.'

'I didn't mean — ' She blushed. 'I can't see why anyone should prefer *me*.'

'Some chap will some day. A couple of years and they'll be queuing up.'

She thought how nice James was, how strong and kind and reliably cheerful, and she asked, 'Who are you visiting in London?'

'Just some old friends,' he said vaguely. 'How about you, Clem? Do you see anything of those school chums of yours?'

Clemency fiddled with her shoelace. 'Not much. And when I do see them, I never seem to have anything interesting to say. They've done so much and I haven't really done anything at all. I'm afraid I'm rather dull company.'

'Nonsense. You're a sport, Clemmie. We couldn't manage without you.'

'James.'
'It's true,' he said.

★ ★ ★

Eva loved London. She loved the busyness and the jumble of language and culture and class. She pictured the city's beating heart, strong and forceful, its pulse resounding through the churches and factories and palaces. She wanted to see *everything*. She walked along the Thames from the Embankment to the docks, and saw the cargo ships and ferry boats moored on the olivine water. The dark, cramped little pubs and warehouses that lined the river kept their secrets, their windows curtained with cobwebs and dust. She visited the National Gallery and the department stores and parks of the West End; at night she watched men and women going into the theatres in Leicester Square, and saw the sheen of the women's satin capes, and the tiaras catching fire in the light from the street lamps.

Though the city entranced her, it was hard to admit even to herself that, in the middle of her second term at the Slade she was still struggling to find her feet there. Previously Miss Garnett's prize private pupil, for the first time she was surrounded by students as talented as her. Some were more talented: the accomplishment of a few made her own work appear in comparison lifeless and clumsy. Increasingly she felt as though a mainstay of her life had been kicked out from beneath her. Eva was good at art, it had always been so. In a family with no particular talents, she had been proud of her own. But now her work was mercilessly pulled apart, its faults revealed to an unsympathetic light, no weakness too insignificant for critical comment.

The life class, too, jolted her. She had said it so easily all those months ago: 'But I need to learn to draw from *life*, Father!', and yet, attending her first class, she was thrown into confusion. She had never before seen a grown woman naked. The women of her acquaintance hid their bodies beneath skirts and petticoats, never removing one layer until another was safely in place. The only nudes Eva had seen were in paintings and the women who modelled for the Slade did not bear much resemblance to the pale, perfect nudes of classical art. They were working class and middle-aged, and the robes they cast off before they sat on the podium were patched and darned and, like the women themselves, faded with age. Flesh rolled unrestrained around breasts and bellies, skin sagged beneath upper arms and hair sprouted from crevices. Was *this* what the female body was, or what it came to? Eva wondered. She found it curiously troubling to draw those women, as if by committing their imperfections to paper she was diminishing them.

She lodged with Sarah Wilde, who had once, a very long time ago, been to school with Great-aunt Hannah. Where Great-aunt Hannah was vast, Mrs Wilde was tiny and fragile, her wrists the circumference of a child's, her spine bent with age. She kept a parrot called Perdita, who had a habit of getting lost. As she herself was now too infirm to chase after Perdita, it was one of Eva's duties to extract the snarling bird from whichever dusty laurel bush or railings she had taken refuge in. Eva supposed it was because Mrs Wilde had no daughters of her own that her chaperonage was eccentric. She accepted without question Eva's explanations about visiting friends or having to attend evening classes. Knowing that she took advantage of Mrs Wilde's innocence, Eva sometimes felt a pang of guilt.

She went to meetings of the Women's Social and Political Union, the National Union of Women's Suffrage Societies, the Women's Freedom League, and the Women's Labour League, and, because she couldn't decide which to join, joined them all. She went on marches and stood on windy street corners, wrapped up in coat and hat and gloves, begging passers-by to sign her petition or buy a copy of *Votes for Women*. She cheered speeches given by other suffragettes and wrote letters to Members of Parliament.

Before Eva left Sheffield, Miss Garnett had given her Lydia Bowen's address. At Lydia's flat, Eva met artists, actors, writers and the oddities whom Lydia could never resist: a psychic, a Russian princess, who claimed to have been a confidante of the tsarina, and a woman who had walked ('*Walked*, my dear!') to Nice, sleeping in haystacks and supporting herself by singing for her supper in cafés and bars.

One evening Lydia invited Eva to a private view at her gallery in Charlotte Street. The rooms were crowded by the time Eva arrived. Covertly she studied the guests. The women were *soignée* and elegant in their long, narrow gowns, and all the men wore evening dress. Eva was wearing a green and red checked woollen dress that she had made herself. It had been raining and her stockings were spattered with mud, and her hair, quite neat when she had left Mrs Wilde's Bloomsbury house, had been cork-screwed into wild curls by the damp weather.

The exhibits were a mixture of landscapes and portraits. Eva was studying a painting of a child and a puppy when she heard someone say, 'Don't you feel that the artist's loathing for both dogs and children shows in his treatment of the subject?'

She looked up. The man standing at her shoulder was wearing a long black overcoat over a navy-blue workman's shirt. An emerald green scarf was looped several times around his neck.

Eva studied the picture again. 'The little girl's face is rather yellow.'

'Positively jaundiced. And as for the dog, it has a

rabid look in its eye. May I show you my favourite painting?'

He led her to a large canvas in the far corner of the room. The caption beside the painting said, '*Fields at Avebury* by Gabriel Bellamy'.

He asked, 'Do you like it?'

The landscape was banded with ochre, green, yellow and white stripes. 'I think so,' she said slowly. 'It's so . . . *undisturbed*.'

'Undisturbed . . . That's an interesting word for it. Do you know Wiltshire?'

'Not at all, I'm afraid.'

'It's one of my favourite places. You can feel the history. And I love the way the chalk shows through the grass, like bones.' He turned aside from the canvas. 'What about you? Where do you come from?'

'Sheffield,' she said.

'Satanic mills?'

'Steelworks, actually.'

'How long have you been living in London?'

'Six months. I'm studying at the Slade School of Art,' she added proudly.

His eyes raked over her. 'I would have taken you for a gypsy. Or a dancer, perhaps. Your colouring . . . and the way that you move.'

She felt herself blush. She heard him ask, 'How do you know Lydia?'

'My art teacher in Sheffield, Miss Garnett, introduced me to Miss Bowen. She and Miss Garnett are friends.'

'And comrades in arms?' he said, and his fingertip lightly brushed the purple, white and green ribbon Eva wore on her lapel. She blushed again: his proximity, she supposed. He was enormously tall, more than a foot taller than her, and broad-shouldered. He seemed to tower above her, almost enveloping her; she felt like a rather small moon that has been swept into the orbit of a large planet.

She explained, 'Miss Bowen and I go to meetings of the WSPU. I think it's absolutely appalling that here we are, at the beginning of the twentieth century and women still can't vote. It's disgusting that laws can be made that decide our fate, and yet we have no say in them. I think — '

'Of course,' he said. 'It's completely ridiculous.'

The wind knocked out of her sails, she followed him round the room as he glanced briefly at painting after painting.

'You do?'

'Naturally. Women are far more sensible than men. Men are too much victims of their own desires. Women govern themselves better, so I don't doubt they would make a much better job of governing the country as well.'

He had paused in his perambulations and was staring at a portrait. The woman in the portrait was dark-haired, full-lipped and sensual. Her dress, cut close around the upper part of her body, was of a dark-red, shimmering fabric. 'Of course,' he said slowly 'men don't want women to have the vote because they are afraid of the consequences. They say that they're afraid that involvement in politics will make women lose their unique charm, when what they *really* fear is that women will no longer be submissive, and that women may impose on them standards of morality that they deem unacceptably high.' He gave Eva a piratical grin. 'In other words, men are afraid that the standards they demand of women will be required of them also.' He threw a glance over his shoulder. 'Here's Lydia. Dearest Lydia, have you come to scold me?'

Lydia kissed his cheek. 'You should be *mingling*, my darling.'

'Lydia, please. You expect too much of me.'

'Don't be ridiculous.' Lydia took his arm. 'Please excuse us, Eva.'

Eva was putting on her coat in the lobby, about to leave, when Lydia reappeared. She said, 'I've introduced Gabriel to the Stockburys. If he's nice to them, he might sell a painting or two.'

'Painting?' Eva was confused. She remembered the caption on the landscape. '*Gabriel . . .* ' she repeated slowly. '*He* was Gabriel Bellamy?'

'Of course.' Lydia frowned. 'Didn't you realize?'

Eva shook her head. She felt mortified.

'The landscapes are his. He doesn't do many landscapes, mostly portraits, but they are rather lovely, aren't they? So I snapped them up.' Lydia lit a cigarette. 'Gabriel's very up and coming. I'm not sure my little gallery will be grand enough for him for much longer.' She exhaled a thin stream of blue smoke as she studied Eva. 'I thought I'd better rescue you. What did you think of him?'

'I thought he was very nice.'

'Of course he is. He's perfectly sweet. And terribly interesting and attractive. And he has had a string of mistresses and, the rumour is, an illegitimate child or two besides. He doesn't behave himself at all, I'm afraid.' Lydia patted Eva's shoulder. 'Gabriel's a darling, really. But he's not to be trusted, Eva. He is absolutely not to be trusted.'

A few days later, Eva caught sight of Gabriel Bellamy as she left the Slade one afternoon. He was standing beneath a lamp post, wearing the same black coat and emerald scarf; the scarf flapped in the breeze. Remembering their conversation, she wanted to turn and run. But she was wheeling her bicycle, rolls of paper cradled against her chest, and in her haste they spilled to the ground. As she stooped to gather them up, she saw him coming towards her.

'What a lucky chance,' he said, as he plucked one of

her sketches out of a puddle. 'I've been catching up with a few old friends. How nice to meet you again.' He beamed at her. 'I never found out your name.'

'Lydia Bowen told me yours, Mr Bellamy,' said Eva pointedly.

'You're not annoyed with me, are you?'

'You might have told me who you were!'

'But that — ' he smiled mischievously — 'wouldn't have been so much fun. You would have felt obliged to pay me bland compliments about my paintings. Or you might even have refused to speak to me. Some people do. My reputation, you know.'

To her horror, he was unrolling her sketch. 'Please don't,' she said.

But he was already looking at the drawing. '*Antiquities*,' he said, and sighed. 'All those hours we used to spend drawing those wretched statues and bas-reliefs.' He handed it back to her. 'Won't you let me look at the others?'

'No.'

'Why not?'

'Because they're not very good.' She shoved the papers into the bicycle basket.

'Where are you headed?'

She told him and he said, 'I'll walk with you. I'm going to Russell Square. Let me.'

He took the bicycle from her and began to push it along the pavement. She opened her mouth in protest, but he was already yards away from her, walking fast.

'You really should introduce yourself,' he said, as she caught up with him. 'Such bad manners not to do so.'

She was about to make a furious response when she caught the laughter in his eyes. She said stiffly, 'My name's Eva Maclise.'

'*Eva Maclise*,' he repeated. 'Eva Maclise from . . . where was it? I remember. Sheffield.' He held out his hand to her. 'I'm very pleased to make your acquaintance, Miss Maclise.'

His hand was large and brown and warm and enveloped hers completely. 'And what made you come to London, Eva Maclise? You could have studied art in Sheffield, I presume.'

'But London's so exciting!'

'Do you think so?'

'Of course! I adore it. Don't you?'

'Sometimes I love it and sometimes I hate it. I came back to London a couple of months ago and just now I'm longing to escape. So I'll go back to my place in the country, I expect, and when I'm there I'll feel perfectly happy at first and vow to stay forever. But then, as the weeks pass, I'll begin to feel restless, and after a while — six weeks, or maybe a couple of months — I'll find myself longing for London. And then the whole process will start all over again.' He gave a rueful smile. 'I often think the two places answer different parts of my character, the good side and the wicked side. In the country, I grow my own vegetables and tend my animals, whereas in the city — ' He broke off, looking at her. 'What is it?'

'Do you *really* grow vegetables?' She found it hard to imagine the scandalous Gabriel Bellamy digging and weeding.

'I certainly do. I grew a splendid crop of peas last year. I sowed sweet peas among the garden peas so that it pleased the eye as well as the palate. Have you never grown vegetables, Miss Maclise?'

She shook her head. 'But I sew. I make all my own clothes.'

'You have an eye for colour.' His gaze travelled down her, from head to toe, and she had to look away, suddenly disconcerted.

'Sadie, my wife, makes all her own clothes. And the children's too. And she spins yarn and weaves cloth with the wool from our sheep.'

Sadie, my wife. Eva had to adjust her image of Gabriel Bellamy again, from rake to family man.

'Sadie and I wanted to bring our children up in the countryside. I don't believe in children being penned up, made to sit still and only speak when they're spoken to, that sort of nonsense. Children should be allowed to run free.'

'How many children do you have, Mr Bellamy?'

'Four and another one on the way.' *Four*, she thought, and made yet another mental readjustment. He told her, 'Orlando is eight, Lysander is six and Ptolemy's five. And my little Hero's just three.'

'All boys?'

'Hero's a girl. The name's from *Much Ado About Nothing*, of course. We're hoping for another girl. Even things up a bit.' His hand swept through the air. 'It makes me angry to think what some people put their children through. They claim to love the poor beggars, but then they torment them. When I was a boy, I was sent to bed each evening at seven on the dot. I used to lie awake for hours. If anything made me the insomniac that I am it was that. So my tribe go to sleep when they want and get up when they want.'

'But — school? What about school?'

He snorted. 'I've no intention of sending them away to be beaten and bullied. I lost count of the times I was beaten at my school. We tolerate violence too easily in this country. We encourage our children to grow up accustomed to it. I don't want that for my four. Sadie teaches the children now and some of my friends help out. I don't believe in making them learn times tables and lists of kings and queens — such rubbish. Far more useful to them that they should know how to milk a cow or sail a boat.' He peered at her. 'Or do you think I'm talking nonsense, Eva Maclise?'

'Not at all. Though some people like school and other people hate it. My brother Philip cries all night before he has to go back to his boarding school. But my sister Clemency loved school.' She explained, 'I have hordes of brothers and sisters, I'm afraid. I sometimes used to think that my mother would have hardly noticed if one of us had got mislaid. Especially me, in the middle.'

'Oh, I shouldn't think so. I shouldn't think *that* at all.' He looked at her again, that same look which made her shiver. 'You've got something about you. I saw it the moment I set eyes on you. You look to me like a girl who knows her own mind. Schools — and all the paraphernalia of bourgeois bureaucracy — are there to crush the spirit out of people like us. They're there to make us toe the line, keep our mouths shut, put up with all the cant and hypocrisy that goes on.' He stopped suddenly and, turning to her, said fiercely, 'People mouth their disapproval of me, but I only do what they long to do — what some of them actually do, if truth be known. In their book, anything goes as long as you keep up appearances. Cover up God knows what sins with a conventional, pious exterior and no one cares. Speak your mind, be honest about your imperfections and you're painted as the Devil incarnate. I despise all that.'

Eva thought of her father climbing into a hansom cab, stooping to kiss Mrs Carver; her father at home, the upright family man, the respectable manufacturer, pillar of the Sheffield business community. She bit her lip and heard Gabriel Bellamy say gently, 'I'm sorry, I didn't mean to frighten you. Sadie tells me I'm too loud. She says I scare the children.'

'I'm not frightened. And I think you're right. I hate that sort of hypocrisy too.'

It was six o'clock. Office workers were hurrying home, their umbrellas furled and their starched collars wilting at the end of a long day. Gabriel slapped the palm of his hand on the bicycle handlebars. 'I used to do what I was told, the same as everyone else, just like these poor drones who have to eke out their lives sitting at a desk. Then one day I thought — why not live my life as I choose to live it? Be damned to other people's opinions. After all, you only have one life, don't you?' He threw her a glance. 'There, I've shocked you now. Was it my language, or my lack of belief in the afterlife?'

'Neither.'

'You should come to Greenstones, my home in Wiltshire. There, I've shocked you again, haven't I? Inviting you to meet my family and after only half an hour's acquaintance.'

4

On 6 May 1910 King Edward VII died. Theatres closed and stock exchanges ceased trading; crowds gathered on the pavements before dawn on the day of the funeral, waiting for a glimpse of the coffin on its way to Windsor for burial. At the Mandeville Hospital Iris's thoughts dwelt momentarily on the king's death (all those years of waiting, and then to reign for only nine years!) and then turned back to her usual preoccupations: her sore feet, her wrinkled hands.

At Summerleigh Clemency read the newspaper aloud to Lilian. *President Taft has sent Queen Alexandra a cable of condolence. The House of Rep — Rep —* Clemency stumbled over the word — *Representatives,* supplied Lilian impatiently. *The House of Representatives, of course, Clemency.*

A letter arrived from Gabriel Bellamy inviting Eva to stay at his Wiltshire home. As Mrs Wilde talked about her distress at the king's death, Eva thought, with a ripple of excitement: *He remembered. I thought he would forget, that he was just being polite, but he remembered.*

Newly introduced to London society, Marianne heard whispers and a murmur of apprehension. *The upper echelons of society take their tone from the king,* one of Arthur's friends explained to her, *and Edward was the embodiment of bonhomie and good living. George is a different kettle of fish altogether; times are on the turn.*

★ ★ ★

Iris had blisters on her feet from the miles she walked on the ward each day, and her hands were puffy and red

112

from washing soda and Lysol. She no longer curled her hair, which she had always been so proud of, in rags at night. It was as much as she could do to pin it up neatly beneath her cap each morning. Her tiredness had accumulated to a point where she could hardly think straight. Without the patients, her allies, she would have been in trouble even more often than she was. When Sister Grant wasn't looking, the men would beckon Iris over and remind her that it was time to boil the kettles for their Bovril, or point out to her the tray of soiled dressings she had left on a window sill. There never seemed to be enough time to get through all the work that had to be done. She would have run from one task to the next had running not been forbidden. Sister Grant's caustic words sometimes made tears burn behind her eyes; only her pride, her wretched pride, which had made her take this dreadful job in the first place, enabled her to hold her head high.

Had it not been for Charlotte, banging on her bedroom door to wake her in the mornings, she would have been late on the ward each day. She lost count of the number of times she decided to give up nursing and would have done so — gone to matron and handed in her resignation, perhaps, or just walked out of Sister Grant's ward and never come back — if she could only have found either the time or the will. She longed for her days off. Once, she went to the West End and wandered around the shops; sometimes she visited Marianne, in her cool, light London house. Even her envy of Marianne had lessened these last few months. She no longer had the energy for envy. And, besides, it was nice to spend a day in a place that was civilized and didn't have that hospital smell.

Yet, as time passed, almost without her noticing it, nursing became easier. As she became more competent, she was also less tired — because, she supposed, she did not have to do everything twice over. Because she was less tired, she learned new skills more quickly. Tasks with which she had at first struggled she now did without thinking. Now it embarrassed her to remember her early fumbled attempts to make a bed or cook a simple supper.

At the Mandeville there were isolation wards for cases of scarlet fever, diphtheria, smallpox and venereal disease, as well as special wards to treat osteomyelitis and puerperal fever. There were the children's wards and a mental ward, and a ward for patients with diseases of the eye. Sister Grant's ward took in men suffering from a wide variety of complaints. Septic infections, respiratory infections and acute abdominal conditions were the most common. Workmen in the prime of their lives died in a day of lobar pneumonia; young men entering adulthood faded away from valvular diseases of the heart, the consequence of rheumatic fever in childhood.

On Saturday nights and at Bank Holidays there was an influx of injuries from street fights. Iris nursed men who had had their throats slit in Whitechapel's back alleys, and victims of pub brawls who lay white and still, their fractured skulls wrapped in bandages. And then there were the industrial injuries, labourers admitted to the hospital with their limbs broken by falling girders, or their spines snapped in half after a ladder had slipped or a rope had given way.

Alfred Turner's legs had been crushed in an accident at the docks. Twenty years old, he had a mop of brown curls and an open, snub-nosed countenance. He called out to Iris as she passed his bed.

'Oy, Blondie!'

'Yes, Mr Turner?'

'Alfie, Blondie. Call me Alfie.' He flashed her a smile. 'I need a drink. Beer would be nice. Or a tot of rum.'

'I'll get you some water.' She fetched a cup and a straw.

He gulped down a few mouthfuls and then fell back on the pillow and grinned at Iris. 'What yer doing on yer night off, Blondie?'

'Darning my stockings and writing letters, I should think.'

'Ain't you got a sweetheart?' He called out to the other men, 'Blondie 'ere ain't got a sweetheart!'

There was a chorus from the surrounding beds. 'Shame — '

'Got more sense, 'aven't you, ducks — '

'I'll be your sweetheart, love — '

In the probationers' common room, they were one fewer that night. Elsie Steele had been taken to the nurses' sick room with a septic throat. Charlotte worked on the same ward as Elsie. 'Elsie's very unwell,' Charlotte told them. 'Sister Matthews said she has a high fever.'

Back on the ward the next day, Alfie Turner seemed to have taken a shine to Iris. As she worked, his voice followed her with requests for a drink or a smoke.

'Mr Turner,' she hissed one afternoon, 'you are being a nuisance!'

'Just need my pillows done. Feels like someone put stones in 'em.'

'This is the last time — ' Iris pulled out his pillow — 'then you must let me get on.'

'I just wanted — '

'What?'

'To see your face.'

'Mr *Turner* — '

'Don't be snappy with me, Blondie. You've got a pretty face. Can't think why you're in this place. You could be on the stage. You're as pretty as any of the girls down the Gaiety Theatre.'

Iris gave the pillow a thump. 'The only thing is I can't sing for toffee.'

'Go on, bet you can. Give us a song, love.'

'If I did, you'd definitely have a relapse.' Smiling, she slipped the pillow under his head.

'Bet you can dance, though. I'm a nifty dancer. When I'm out of 'ere, I'll take you to the Palais.'

In another life she had worn white silk and had waltzed round a ballroom. Now that other life seemed insubstantial: if she looked at it too hard it might fade away, as though it had never happened.

That evening Iris sat in Charlotte's room, eating the biscuits that Charlotte's mother had sent from home. Elsie Steele was still very unwell, Charlotte told Iris; the fever wasn't falling as quickly as the doctors had hoped.

The following afternoon Dr Hennessy lanced the wound on Alfie Turner's leg. From the ward kitchen, where she was boiling up the kettles, Iris heard him cry out.

He had recovered by teatime, though, to plague her again.

'Tell us yer name, Blondie.'

'You know my name. It's Nurse Maclise.'

'I meant yer *Christian* name.' He grinned. 'Me and the boys are 'aving a bet. Whether you're a Florrie or an Ethel. Go on, tell us, Blondie. I think you're called Gertie. Or maybe Marie.'

She couldn't help smiling. 'None of those.'

'How can we go dancing if I don't know your name?' His voice followed her as she pushed the trolley along the ward. 'Liz, then, or Sal — '

Elsie Steele's condition deteriorated during the day. The doctors were afraid that the infection had spread to her lungs; matron had sent for Elsie's parents. In the probationers' common room that night, they were quieter, the laughter subdued. The following morning, in chapel, prayers were offered up for Elsie Steele's recovery. Iris was aware of a sense of disbelief. Patients died every day, felled by accident or disease. But surely not slight, perky, slapdash Elsie, twenty-two years old,

116

four foot eleven in her stockinged soles, with her stringy blonde hair and Midlands accent.

There was a curtain around Alfie's bed when Iris went on the ward that morning. His temperature had gone up and he was running a fever, the staff nurse told her. He was awake, wide-eyed and restless, when she wheeled the trolley behind the curtain. 'Hope you 'aven't forgotten,' he said hoarsely.

'Forgotten what?'

'Our night out, 'course. You and me, Poppy. Dancing.'

'Poppy?'

'Night nurse told me you was called after a flower.' His gaze darted nervously to the trolley. 'What's that?'

'It's a poultice. The heat will draw the poison out of your wound and stop it swelling up.'

He whispered, 'Fed up with doctors carving me up like a piece of meat.' He flinched as she folded back the bedclothes. 'We'll go for supper after we've been to the dance 'all,' he said. His voice was taut with pain. 'I'll buy you fish and chips.'

Iris saw that the unbandaged parts of his legs were black with bruises. 'Hawser on the crane broke,' he muttered. 'All them sacks of wheat fell on me. Wouldn't think a few bits of wheat could make such a mess, would you?'

On her day off, Iris went shopping. At five o'clock, laden with bags and parcels, she met James, who was in Town for the weekend, at the Lyons Corner House in Coventry Street.

He kissed her. 'My treat,' he said as the waitress showed them to a table. 'I had a little win on the horses.'

James ordered supper and told Iris all the family news. She found her attention wandering as he spoke. There it was again, that curious sense of being separate from what had once been her entire life, the dances and picnics and the daily round of home.

He said after a while, 'I say, cheer up. You look a bit down in the dumps.'

'I'm fine,' she said. 'Just rather tired. But then I'm always tired.' She told James about Elsie, adding, 'Charlotte told me that Elsie was careless on the ward. That she skimped on her cleaning and didn't always wash her hands after dressing a wound.' Sister Grant's voice rang in Iris's head: *Cleanliness is the only defence we have against infection*. She said slowly, 'Elsie might die. It seems a high price to pay for carelessness, doesn't it?'

'Is she a particular friend of yours?'

'Not really.'

'Shame though. Poor kid.'

Iris felt suddenly angry. 'There, and I hadn't meant to talk about that horrible hospital at all! I'd meant to have an entire day without thinking about it once.' She stared down at her Welsh rarebit. 'What on earth possessed me to think I could ever endure nursing . . .'

'I envy you sometimes,' he said.

'Don't be ridiculous, James. If you only knew — '

'Coming here meant that you could leave home, didn't it? Perhaps you were the lucky one. *You're* free now.'

Iris wanted to laugh. She thought of the awfulness of dragging herself out of bed in the mornings, and of her sore hands and blistered feet. It was perfectly ridiculous to say that she was free when every moment of her day was taken up by some task or other.

'How's everyone at home?' she asked. 'How's Mother? Is she bad again?'

'Mother's just the same.'

'And Father? Have you and Father been quarrelling?'

'No more than usual.' He shrugged. 'I don't mean to make him cross. It just *happens*.'

'If you tried not to do the things that annoy him

— you know what he's like about money — '

'He's so tight-fisted — '

'I meant gambling, James!' she cried, exasperated. 'If Father *knew*!'

His eyes brightened. 'But I won!'

'And how often have you lost?'

'Once or twice,' he admitted. Then he said slowly, 'It's fun, Iris. It's exciting. That's why I do it. Everything else is so ordinary. Sometimes I'm afraid that everything's going to go on the same way forever. Fifty years from now I'll still be living in Sheffield and working at Maclise's.'

'Would that be so bad?'

'I'd like to do something glorious. Something heroic.' His eyes shone. 'Something people will remember. I'd like to hike to the South Pole. Or fly across the Atlantic Ocean. But I haven't even been out of England!'

'I've never understood why men are so bothered about glory,' said Iris scornfully. 'Or heroism. I suspect both are thoroughly uncomfortable. Much like nursing.'

James smiled. 'I could get married, I suppose. That would let me escape from the parental home, wouldn't it? Only that's another thing Father and I don't seem to see eye to eye about. He wants me to tie the knot with any old bag of bones who has a bit of money and comes from a respectable family. But I like a girl who's soft and sweet,' he said wistfully. 'With a complexion like a peach and a nice little figure.'

'*James*,' she said.

The next day the surgeons operated on Alfie Turner's leg, cutting out the dead bone and packing the wound with gauze. When Iris looked in on Alfie, he was white-faced and weak.

'Feel like they've been 'itting me with 'ammers.' He glanced out of the window to where grey clouds scudded across a restless sky. 'Might be a week or two before I can take you dancing, Poppy.'

There was better news about Elsie Steele when Iris went back to the nurses' home that night. Elsie was on the mend, Charlotte told them. Charlotte had been allowed to see her for a few minutes. Because of the fever, they had cut off Elsie's hair. 'She looks like a boy, a funny, skinny, little boy,' said Charlotte. Then she said, 'Elsie told me that when she's well enough she's going home. She's decided that she doesn't want to be a nurse after all. So that'll be one less of us.'

The first thing Iris saw when she went on the ward the next morning was that the screens around Alfie Turner's bed had been cleared away. A split second later and she realized that the bed was empty, the sheets and blankets stripped off.

The night nurse was stooped beside the locker. 'Passed away in the night, poor kid,' she muttered as she bundled Alfie's few belongings into a sheet of brown paper. 'Best thing, really — I can't stand it when they linger. You'd better make up the bed for the next patient, nurse.'

But he can't be dead, Iris found herself wanting to protest. *I spoke to him only last night.* But she went instead to the laundry room, where she found herself staring blankly at the stacks of linen. So ridiculous, she told herself, to feel so suddenly upset. Men died on the ward every day, strong young men like Alfie. She should be used to it by now.

Yet the sheets and pillowcases blurred, and she had to press her fingertips against her forehead to stem the tears. Then she took a deep breath and, arms full of bedlinen, went back onto the ward.

★   ★   ★

At the railway station on the branch line from Salisbury, there was a pony and trap waiting to take Eva to the Bellamys' house. 'Gabriel's gone out,' the young man driving the trap told Eva as he took her overnight bag from her and helped her onto the seat beside him. 'And Sadie's, you know, *enceinte*, and God knows where Nerissa is, and Max and Bobbin are probably still asleep, damn them. So you've got me.' He held out his hand to her. 'My name's Val Crozier. Some people assume Val's short for Valentine, but I'll tell you the truth because you've got a nice face. My parents christened me Percival, God rot 'em.'

'Eva Maclise,' she said and shook his hand.

He clicked to the pony and they headed away from the station. 'Maclise? You're not Scots, are you?'

'No. My great-grandfather — '

'Good. Dreary place, Scotland. Even drearier than bloody Wiltshire.'

They were trotting down narrow roads walled with high verges, where honeysuckle spilled from the hedgerows and the hawthorns were heavy with pink and cream blossom. Eva said, 'I think it's very pretty.'

'I've been staying with Gabriel and Sadie for three months now and, believe me, it's dreary. I hate the countryside.' He sneezed. 'And I've always got a cold.'

She asked, 'How do you know Mr Bellamy?'

'Met him in a pub. Some den in Paddington.'

'Are you an artist?'

'God, no. To tell the truth, I haven't really been doing anything for a while. I took the exam for the Indian Civil Service and failed it dismally, and then I met Gabriel and he asked me down here. I help out, fetching water and feeding the animals, that sort of thing.'

'Animals?'

'Gabriel's beastly pigs.' A farmer driving a horse and cart was coming down the lane towards them; Val edged the pony and trap into the opening to a field to let them pass. 'I hate the pigs almost as much as I hate the children. I'm supposed to be teaching the little beasts ancient Greek,' he explained gloomily. 'The children, not the pigs. Gabriel has a notion that children can learn anything if you start them off young enough. They'll just absorb it somehow.'

'And have they?'

'Not at all. I don't think I'm cut out to be a teacher. Yet another profession closed to Val Crozier.' He waved towards the hills. 'There's Greenstones.'

Eva followed the direction of his hand and saw a distant group of buildings. There was a grandeur and isolation about the setting of rolling hills, streams and woodland.

They left the road, taking a track that branched off across fields golden with buttercups. As they drew nearer to the farmhouse, Eva saw that it was made of a patchwork of stone, flint and brick, and that a number of barns and other outbuildings clustered round it.

Val steered the pony and trap into the courtyard. A small child with tangled black hair, dressed, it seemed to Eva, in a selection of colourful rags, darted out of a nearby barn.

'Guess what I've got,' he said to Eva.

'I've no idea.'

'Look.' The child thrust his cupped palms towards her.

'I shouldn't if I were you,' advised Val. 'Buzz off, won't you, Lysander. Where's Sadie, by the way?'

Lysander opened his hands to reveal a large black beetle.

'He's lovely,' said Eva politely.

A sly glance towards Val. 'I'm going to call him Percival. Percival the beetle.'

Val picked up Eva's bag and headed towards the house. 'Horrid little creature,' he muttered under his breath.

Inside Greenstones clutter spilled from every shelf and covered every surface. A collection of flints, some in the process of being knapped into axe heads, were strewn across a grate. Children's toys, wooden blocks and miniature engines, were sprayed across rugs, as though blown by a gust of wind. The rooms were unevenly shaped and low ceilinged, the furniture worn but comfortable looking, and there were pictures everywhere — sketches in red and white chalk, pencil drawings, prints and, over a fireplace, a large oil painting of a woman, her calm, arresting face framed by a cloud of dark hair.

Val led Eva into a kitchen where there was the smell of coffee and newly baked bread. Another black-haired little boy was perched on the draining board eating a bun, and a cat lapped milk from a saucer on the floor. A large cast-iron pot bubbled on top of the stove. The sink was crammed with unwashed baking tins and saucepans.

Eva recognized the woman standing at the large pine table as the woman in the painting. She was making pastry. Her apron curved over her pregnant belly. A little girl — Hero, Eva guessed — was coiled round one of her legs. Black-haired and dark-eyed like her brothers, Hero was wearing a smock made out of something that looked like red and green striped sacking.

'Hello, Sadie,' said Val.

The woman glanced up. 'Val, thank goodness. Is Orlando with you?'

'Sorry, no.'

Sadie looked worried. 'I thought he must be with you. I haven't seen him all morning.'

'Perhaps he went with Gabriel.'

'Would you mind having a look for him? You know what he's like.'

'Of course. This is Eva, by the way.' Val headed back down a corridor.

Sadie wiped a floury hand on her apron and offered it to Eva. 'I'm pleased to meet you, Eva. I'm sorry everything is rather — ' The words trailed away as her gaze swept round the kitchen.

'It was so kind of you to invite me, Mrs Bellamy.'

'Call me Sadie, please. And any friend of Gabriel's . . . But you must be tired and hungry after your journey. Coffee?'

'Please.'

'Sit down, if you can find a space.'

Sadie poured coffee into a mug from an enamel jug and handed it to Eva. 'I can never drink coffee when I'm expecting,' she said ruefully. 'Dreadful how children rob you of so many of the pleasures of life. Though I am hungry. I always seem to be hungry.' She sawed a couple of slices from a loaf of bread. 'Here, help yourself, Eva. And there's some of Gabriel's honey . . . ' She took a jar from a shelf. Eva noticed that when Sadie walked, Hero clung to her leg, so that she was doubly burdened, by her small daughter and by the unborn baby.

Eva spread honey on her bread. 'Does Mr Bellamy keep bees?'

'I'm afraid so. They swarmed last year. They came down the chimneys into the house. They were all black from the soot, buzzing around the children's bedrooms like furious lumps of coal. Have some more.'

'Such lovely bread,' said Eva.

'It's kind of you to say so. Now I really must get on, I'm afraid.' Sadie stood up.

She had sat down, Eva estimated, for less than five minutes. There was a difference between the Sadie of the painting and the woman rolling out pastry. This Sadie was paler and she had a tired, strained look around her eyes.

Eva said, 'Can I help? I'm not very good at cooking, but I could wash up.'

'Would you? Nerissa said she would, but she has a headache and is lying down. And all our other guests are men.' Sadie added waspishly, 'And men think washing up is beneath them, don't they?'

Eva hauled some of the dishes out onto the draining board. The small boy perched nearby stuck his tongue out at her. 'Ptolemy,' said Sadie sharply.

'Mama.' Ptolemy held out his arms to his mother.

'Mama can't pick you up. You're too heavy.'

'But mama — '

'Finish your bun, Tolly. The hot water's on the stove, Eva. You'd better refill the kettles and boil them up straight away or you'll run out. If you run out of cold, I'll have to find one of the men to fetch some more from the well. And while you wash up, talk to me, if you would. Did you come from London? You must tell me about London. I miss it so much. You must tell me what's in all the shops — *everything*. Especially the clothes — what are women wearing nowadays?'

Eva told Sadie about the dress materials in Selfridge's and Marianne's trousseau. Then she described the play she had been to at the Haymarket and the ballet she had seen at the Empire.

Sadie looked wistful. 'I adore ballet. When I was a girl I wanted to be a ballerina.' She opened the door of the stove. 'Hero, *please*! Don't cling so.' She prised the little girl off her knee. Hero began to cry. Disregarding her, Sadie stooped with difficulty and slid the pie dishes into the oven. 'Now tell me about yourself, Eva. What do you do?'

'I'm studying at the Slade School of Art.'

'I went to the Slade too,' said Sadie. She straightened, rubbing her back one-handedly as her great dark almond-shaped eyes slid from the heaps of washing-up to the crying child. 'Years ago,' she said softly, 'in another life, I went to the Slade, too.'

★ ★ ★

125

Eva didn't meet the others until dinnertime. After she had washed up, Sadie showed her to her room. Eva unpacked, bathed and changed into an evening frock. At six o'clock she went downstairs. The sound of voices led her back to the kitchen, where the table was laid for dinner. A young woman was sitting at the table. She wore a deep-red, close-fitting dress, and her shining dark hair was coiled around her ears, framing her long, oval face. A very handsome young man — light brown curls, tweed jacket patched at the elbows — lounged decoratively against the sink. In a corner of the room Lysander and Ptolemy squabbled over a game of jacks.

Sadie was standing at the stove, stirring the stew. She introduced Eva to the other guests. The young man in the tweed jacket was called Max Potter, and the woman in the red dress was Nerissa Jellicoe. Max poured Eva a glass of red wine. Nerissa said, 'Gabriel used to make wine from peapods and nettles, but he has given up, thank goodness. Now he buys it in France. *So much* nicer.' She had a rich, drawling voice.

More people drifted into the kitchen. Val was carrying Hero on his shoulders, and there was a short, round-faced man, whom Max introduced to Eva as Bobbin. Then a lanky boy of nine or ten, who, with his black hair and almond-shaped eyes was unmistakably another child of Sadie's.

'Orlando,' said Sadie 'you should go upstairs and have a wash. And where's Gabriel?' She looked fretful. 'The vegetables will get cold.'

'You look as though you've rolled in a haystack,' said Max to Orlando. He had straw in his hair and streaks of mud over his face.

'I was trying to kill rats.' Orlando brandished a catapult.

'Did you get any?' asked Lysander.

'No, but I caught a frog in my fishing net. He's a really good jumper. He's in a box in the bedroom.'

Sadie repeated, 'You should wash your hands, Orlando.'

Just then, the back door was flung open wide. Gabriel Bellamy was standing in the yard, a shotgun broken over his arm and half a dozen rabbits slung over his shoulder.

'Brought you a present, Sadie.' He strode into the kitchen and put the rabbits on the draining board.

'Gabriel, not so near the *pies* — '

'I've had a marvellous day.' He put his arm around Sadie and pulled her to him, kissing her.

'The dinner's ready. And you must put those rabbits in the larder.'

'Don't you want to hear about my day?'

'The vegetables — '

'Up at the crack of dawn, dew still on the fields.'

'*Gabriel.*' Sadie's voice shook slightly. Then, in a tightly controlled tone, she said, 'You need to put the rabbits in the larder and sit down at the table. And, Orlando, go *now* and wash your hands.'

Gabriel swept up the rabbits and Orlando shuffled out of the room. Nerissa said, 'Can I do anything, darling Sadie?'

'If you would just reach down the plates for me. I can't — ' Her palm rested on the curve of her belly.

'I'll get them,' said Val and reached up to the shelf.

'And I'll look after darling little Hero,' said Nerissa. She swept the resisting child onto her lap.

Sadie served the stew. Gabriel, returning from the pantry, caught sight of Eva, gave a roar of pleasure, flung his arm around her neck and kissed her cheek.

'Leave the poor girl be, Gabriel,' drawled Nerissa. 'You're ruffling her hair.'

Eva explained, 'My hair's always ruffled, I'm afraid. It's that sort of hair.'

'You should brush it a hundred times a day,' said Nerissa. 'That's what I do.' She patted her smooth coils.

Hero dipped her finger into Nerissa's glass of wine and sucked it.

'Don't do that, darling,' said Nerissa sharply. 'Naughty girl.'

Hero's face crumpled; she began to cry. Gabriel swept his daughter up into his arms and spun her into the air; the tears vanished and she laughed with delight.

There seemed, thought Eva as the meal went on, to be a great deal of to-ing and fro-ing at the dinner table. If the Bellamys wanted more potatoes and couldn't reach the dish, they simply slid out of their seats, circled the table and grabbed it. Sadie's quiet pleas: *Do ask for things to be passed, don't talk with your mouth full,* went unheeded. Halfway through the first course, Gabriel left the table to search for the flowers he had picked that morning, and then Bobbin disappeared, returning with an enormous tome to identify the poor bedraggled things. Then Orlando dashed off to fetch the frog, which escaped from its box and leapt all over the floor to great shrieks from the Bellamys and their guests. When the frog gained its freedom by jumping out of the back door, Hero, upset by the loss, burst into tears and had to be comforted, until she fell asleep on Sadie's lap. Val carried her up to bed, still sleeping. And between all these incidents, Gabriel and Max planned a sailing trip to Bilbao, and Nerissa told them about her plan to purchase a gypsy caravan and travel round the country. 'I shall wear a green dress, I think, and the darlingest straw hat with ribbons under the chin, like a shepherdess.'

Sadie was serving the apple pie when Gabriel fixed his gaze on Eva and said, 'Well, Eva Maclise! And are you enjoying yourself? Has anyone showed you round my farm? No? Then I'll do the honours myself tomorrow.' Sadie passed him a piece of pie. 'I'll introduce you to the pigs. Splendid pigs, aren't they, Val? Do you like pigs, Eva? Lovely animals. And I'm thinking of damming the stream so that we can make a pond. We could keep carp in it.' He smiled at Eva. 'You can help me dig the pond, if you like, Eva. Stay a couple of weeks — a month — as long as you like.'

'Gabriel, Eva has to go back to London. To art school.'

'Of course.' Gabriel looked suddenly downcast. 'Shame. I like to have company.'

'You've plenty of company, Gabriel.'

'The more the merrier, though.'

'Cream or custard?' Sadie passed Gabriel two jugs.

Gabriel brightened. 'So what do you think of us all, Eva? I hope we're not too loud for you. Some of our guests have run shrieking for the railway station after a couple of hours with the Bellamys.'

'Gabriel, really, there was only *one* — '

'And she was mad.'

'Quite, quite dotty.'

'Eva's made of sterner stuff, aren't you, Eva?' Gabriel poured cream and custard liberally over his apple pie. 'You come from a big family, don't you? *Hordes*, you said.'

'I've six brothers and sisters.'

'There,' said Nerissa, with a little smile, 'something for you to aspire to, Sadie. Only two more to go after the new little one.'

Sadie muttered under her breath, 'Dear God, I hope not. I think I'd kill myself.'

'*Sadie*,' said Gabriel.

Sadie was standing at the sink, the empty pie dish in her hands. 'It's just that I'm so tired.' Her face was a pale, papery white. 'And we've run out of clean spoons.'

'Oh, for heaven's sake, sit *down*, Sadie.' Gabriel guided his wife to a chair. 'You always make such a performance of things. We can use teaspoons, can't we?' He fetched half a dozen from a drawer. 'Tell you what, you needn't do a thing tomorrow. You must have a rest

129

— you can stay in bed all day. I'll make the dinner. I'll cook the rabbits over a fire in the field and we'll dine like gypsies, under the stars.' Gabriel sat down beside Sadie and, taking her hand, kissed it, and she smiled at him.

★　★　★

The following morning Gabriel took Eva round the farm and showed her the vegetable garden and the hay meadow, the beehives and the pigsties. 'I bought the pigs only last year,' Gabriel explained, 'so they're a bit of an experiment. They eat all the potato peelings and they should make marvellous bacon in the autumn. And I'm thinking of getting a couple of cows.'

They crossed the courtyard. 'Doesn't it all take rather a lot of time?' asked Eva. 'Time that you could spend painting?'

'I escape to London if I need a bit of time to myself. I've a studio in Paddington. And besides — '

He broke off; she looked up at him. He grimaced. 'Having a bit of a fallow period, you might say, at present. I haven't done anything much since the landscapes.' He glanced at her. 'Not something that's happened to you yet, I daresay.'

'Not really.'

'How old are you, Eva?'

'Nineteen,' she said.

'*Nineteen.*' They were walking towards the grassy hollow where Gabriel intended to make the fish pond. He said, 'When I was nineteen I didn't have time to paint all the pictures I wanted to paint. I thought it would always be like that. Now that I'm thirty . . . well, I find that it's not so.'

Picking up a fallen branch, he began to slice a swathe through the long grass and nettles. When they reached the edge of the hollow, he paused. 'You know that feeling you get when you're going to start a painting, Eva. When you're certain that it's going to be the best thing you've ever done. It's a sort of a . . . a mental *itch*. A feeling of excitement, bubbling away, that you have to seize and act on. It was like that when I bought this place — I painted half a dozen landscapes that first winter. And when I first met Sadie — I've never done anything as good as those portraits of Sadie. And Nerissa, too. The *Girl in a Red Dress* paintings. I seem to need something . . . or someone . . . to spark me off.' He tapped his forehead. '*Then* it all comes out of here.' He smiled. 'Let me show you why I bought this place. Let me show you why I love it so.'

They walked away from the farm, heading up the hillside. Larks soared up from the meadows to either side of them, bubbling with song as they spilled into the blue sky. Below them the tiled roofs of the farm and outbuildings glittered in the sunlight.

At the top of the hill the oval hummock of a long barrow swelled out of the grass, crowned with gnarled hawthorns. 'No bones of ancient kings or buried treasure inside it, I'm afraid,' said Gabriel. 'Grave robbers must have got to it long ago.' He climbed on top of the barrow. 'Yet I always feel as though I'm trespassing here. Odd, isn't it? As though this is someone else's domain. Look. What do you think?'

The landscape spread out around Eva, hill, wood and meadow, threaded silver with streams. A breeze blew her hair around her face and made the leaves of the hawthorns sway.

'It's beautiful,' she said. 'So beautiful.'

He ran down the side of the barrow to stand on the meadow below, frowning as he looked up at her. She wondered whether she had said the wrong thing. It's beautiful, so beautiful. *For goodness sake, Eva,* she thought, cross with herself, *so unoriginal.*

131

But he said, 'Come on, it must be time for lunch,' and gave her his hand to help her down the slope.

★   ★   ★

In the afternoon Hero fell asleep in an armchair, the men disappeared to make the bonfire, and Eva and Sadie had tea in the room with the flints and the children's toys.

Sadie said, 'This is supposed to be my sitting room, but it always seems to be invaded.' She moved a jigsaw puzzle and a child's paintbox so that Eva could put down the tray. 'Still, how civilized to have afternoon tea with a friend.'

A *friend*, thought Eva, with a flicker of delight. Perhaps the Bellamys were going to be her friends. Perhaps there would be other weekends like this, other Fridays when her classmates at the Slade would ask her what her plans were, and she'd say: *I'm spending the weekend with the Bellamys — you know, Gabriel Bellamy, the artist, and his wife.* Perhaps she would become one of the Bellamys' circle of interesting, unconventional friends; perhaps one day she would know fascinating Greenstones as well as she knew dull old Summerleigh.

Sadie lowered herself into a chair. 'Tell me about yourself, Eva. You're at the Slade, you said? Are you enjoying it? Is Henry Tonks still there? And those bedraggled women who modelled for the life class — where on earth do they find them? A brothel, Gabriel once told me, but I think he was trying to shock.'

Eva told Sadie about the female students who had fled Henry Tonks's classes in tears, and about the long afternoons spent drawing Greek statues and Etruscan bas-reliefs.

'Oh, you have reminded me how much I miss female company,' said Sadie with a sigh. 'There always seem to

132

be so many men at Greenstones. I suppose Hero will be company one day, but just now she's too young for sensible conversation.'

'There's Nerissa,' suggested Eva.

'Nerissa's only topic of conversation is herself, which becomes a little limiting. I end up talking to myself sometimes. If I could only find even a kitchen maid who could talk about — well, all the things that women like to talk about. But, of course, no one good will come all the way out here. So we have to make do with the halfwits and the ninnies. There's a girl who comes up from the village during the week, but she can hardly string two words together — it's just 'Yes, mum,' and 'No, mum,' and a dumb look if I try to talk to her about anything other than washing soda and starch. I've lost count of the number of girls we've had. Some of them leave because they're frightened of Gabriel — he can be rather loud, I suppose, and he does have a piratical look. And some of them go because they're shocked by Nerissa.' Sadie handed Eva a cup of tea, adding by way of explanation, 'Nerissa believes in being in touch with nature. She doesn't always wear a great many clothes. One girl fled screaming when she came across Gabriel painting Nerissa in the orchard.'

Eva giggled.

'I know,' said Sadie with a smile. 'It was funny, in a way. And some of Gabriel's other friends are rather, well, unconventional.' Sadie stirred her tea. 'And then, of course, there are the children.'

'They're lovely children.'

'Are they?' Sadie looked doubtful. 'I suppose they are. Or they would be, if they ever brushed their hair or washed their faces. If I were a better mother then I'd make them do so.' She attempted a smile. 'I'm sorry, I'm being miserable again. You mustn't take any notice,

I don't mean it. It's just this.' She patted her swollen belly. 'I always seem to get a bit down in late pregnancy.'

'It must be very tiring.'

'More tiring when they're born, believe me. When it's your fifth, you know what you're in for. There's having it, of course, all that frightful business — and then, when it's born, all the sleepless nights. It makes me miserable to know that I'll be exhausted for the next six months at least. That I'll be lucky if I have as much as half an hour to myself for months and months.' She frowned and bit her lip. 'You must forgive me, Eva. I'll put you off marriage and motherhood for good if I'm not careful.'

There was a wail from another room. 'Hero,' muttered Sadie. She stood up. As she reached the door, she turned back to Eva and said more calmly, 'You mustn't think I don't like it here. I do. Sometimes I love it. And Gabriel loves it. Gabriel's happy here and that's all that matters to me.'

★ ★ ★

They made a bonfire in the meadow behind the house. At dusk they stood in a circle around it, watching the fire consume the dead leaves and dry branches. Their faces were black and gold in the reflected light, like Aztec masks. A breeze stirred the flames, making them leap higher, and orange sparks scattered like powder in a lavender-grey sky. On the hill that Eva and Gabriel had climbed that morning, the tumulus was a dark inky lump backed by scudding clouds.

When the flames died down, Gabriel placed the rabbits that he had shot the previous day to cook in the embers. Eva thought of the stiff little picnics of her girlhood, the sedate venturings into the hills in charabancs and motor cars, with servants and hampers

134

and folding chairs. Here they sat on the grass and were warmed by the heat of the bonfire; here, instead of cucumber sandwiches and finger rolls, they ate rabbit and baby carrots and spring greens from the vegetable garden.

Max poured wine; after they had eaten, Bobbin produced a guitar and began to play. Nerissa danced, circling around the fire, swaying in her red dress to the music. She carried a white paper fan with which she drew patterns in the air.

Max whispered in Eva's ear, 'She's such a bitch, but you can understand what Gabriel sees in her.'

Nerissa's movements were fluid, hypnotic. Eva said, 'Nerissa models for Gabriel, doesn't she?'

He threw her a glance. 'Yes, that's right. She models for him.' He melted back into the darkness.

The dance ended and there was a ripple of applause. Eva heard a snuffle behind her. Looking round, she saw Ptolemy.

'What is it, Tolly?'

'I want a fan.' His face was tear-stained; he held out a crumpled piece of paper. 'I want a fan like Nissa.'

Eva took the piece of paper from him and pleated it into a fan shape. Ptolemy slid into her lap, the fan clutched in his plump hands. It occurred to Eva that he was a middle child, like herself. Not the oldest, nor the youngest, not important at all, in fact. She put her arms around him and he leaned his warm little body against her.

Bobbin was singing. It was dark now, and there was only his voice, haunting in the darkness, singing of love and loss.

'Now I'll go off to some far-off country
Where I'll know no one and no one knows me.'

135

Eva thought: *Even if I never come here again, even if I never see the Bellamys again, I shall remember that this was a perfect weekend. I shall remember the night and the fire and the song and the warmth and weight of the child on my lap.*

A shape in the darkness: Gabriel. He sat down beside her. For a big man, his movements were fluid, graceful. He said, 'Dear old Bobbin collects songs. He has the face of a tax collector and the soul of a poet. What is it with music? How is it that a song so simple, so commonplace, can affect one so?' He touched Eva's arm. 'Even church music . . . especially church music . . . How can I be an atheist, find the whole God business quite repulsive, in fact, and yet some church music — Christmas carols, for pity's sake — can move me to tears?'

'Are you an atheist?'

'In my mind.' He thumped his fist against his chest. 'Not, perhaps, in my heart. Are you?'

'I don't know. Everyone in my family goes to church. There would be a terrible fuss if one of us refused to go. But we don't all do the things they tell us to do in church.' She knew that she sounded bitter. 'We just mouth the words.'

He threw her a glance. 'Always a big gap between what one means to do and what one actually does.'

'But not *you*!' she exclaimed, smiling as she looked up at him. 'This wonderful place — you manage to live according to your principles, don't you? If you and Sadie can do it, then why can't others?'

'Dear Eva,' he said softly. 'Never change, will you?' His tone changed. 'I should put this boy of mine to bed or he'll be grouchy as hell in the morning.' He scooped Tolly out of her lap and strode off.

Sometime after midnight they began to trail, yawning, back to the house. In her room, Eva took off her coat and pulled a brush through her hair. Then she sat for a while at the window, looking out.

There was a knock at the door. She opened it. Gabriel was standing in the corridor. 'Couldn't sleep,' he muttered.

He had mentioned that he was an insomniac. She felt flattered that, wakeful, he should come to her for help.

'Shall we go for a walk?' she suggested.

His eyes widened slightly. 'If you like.'

They went outside. In the meadow a crimson glow marked the remains of the bonfire. The night was clear, the sky sprinkled with stars. Eva shivered.

'Poor thing, you're cold.' He put his arms around her in a way that she at first thought was friendly and then, with a shock, realized was not. He was pressing her to him, burying his fingers in her hair.

'Mr Bellamy — '

'Oh, for God's sake, *Gabriel*.'

He lifted her face and kissed her forehead. Then her lips. Ludicrously, through her alarm came the only piece of advice she could remember Lilian ever having given her daughters on the subject of men: *If a man tries to impose himself upon you, then you must stamp down hard on his foot with the heel of your boot.*

Which with Gabriel would be much like an ant treading on the foot of an elephant. Instead, she put her palms against his chest, gave him as hard a shove as she could, and said clearly and coldly, 'Mr Bellamy, you seem to have forgotten yourself.'

His hands fell to his sides. 'Eva — '

'I don't know what you're thinking of. I'm going back to my room.'

He said, bewildered, 'But you must have known — '

She looked back at him. 'Known what?'

'How I feel about you.'

137

She hissed furiously, 'If I'd thought — if I'd thought for a moment that you were going to do that, then I would never have come here!' Then she ran back into the house.

In her bedroom she turned the key in her lock and wedged a chair against the door. Then she threw her belongings into her bag and sat, fully dressed, her heart pounding, on the bed, staring at the door.

He did not come to her room again, though. At five in the morning, she rose and crept out of the house, leaving a note on the kitchen table for Sadie, explaining that she had remembered that she had an early morning class at the Slade. Then she walked across the fields, following the route that Val had driven her only two days before.

On the train, heading back to London, she was almost overwhelmed by the great muddle of her feelings. Mortification, disillusionment and shock seemed to be uppermost. Yet, when she closed her eyes, her head falling against the window pane as she dozed, she remembered his kiss: the strength and warmth of his arms around her, and his kiss.

★ ★ ★

The following week, coming out of college, Eva saw Gabriel Bellamy on the far side of the street, leaning against a lamp post, smoking. Any faint hope that he might be waiting for someone else, or that she might be able to cycle away before he caught sight of her quickly evaporated as he threw his cigarette end to the ground and crossed the road.

'Eva,' he said. 'I have to speak to you.'

'I don't think we've anything to say to each other, Mr Bellamy.'

'That night at Greenstones — '

'I don't want to talk about it.'

'Eva — '

'Really, Mr Bellamy, we've nothing to say to each other.'

'Oh, for God's sake! I was drunk! I came here to apologize!'

'Then I accept your apology.' She climbed onto the saddle and began to cycle down the road.

To her annoyance, he jogged along beside her, his long legs keeping pace with the bicycle. 'So when will we see you again?'

'I don't think that would be a good idea.'

'*Eva.*' He seized the handlebars, bringing the cycle to a halt. 'I *told* you — I'd had too much to drink. I didn't know what I was doing.' He asked fiercely, 'How long are you going to punish me?'

'I'm not trying to punish you, Mr Bellamy.'

'Then come to Greenstones.' His voice softened, cajoled, and Eva was aware of a sudden longing for chalk hills and for freedom.

Then he said, 'And all for a kiss! Just one foolish kiss that didn't mean anything at all!'

Yet she had not forgotten that kiss — her first kiss, her only kiss. It disturbed her to realize that, however wrong it had been, it had meant something to her.

'Come to Greenstones on Saturday,' he coaxed. 'We've almost finished the carp pond.'

'I'm afraid I can't,' she said stiffly. 'I'm rather busy just now. And I have an appointment, so if you would please let go of my bicycle — '

Gabriel's hands fell to his sides. He looked suddenly forlorn. As she cycled off, he cried out, 'For pity's sake. I only wanted to paint you!'

Surprised, she glanced back over her shoulder at him. '*Paint* me?'

'Yes! I'm sorry, I went about it the wrong way. That first time I saw you at Lydia's gallery — you looked so wild, somehow! Eva, it was the first time I've really

139

wanted to paint anything in months!' He pulled out his trump card. 'And Sadie misses you! Sadie keeps asking me why you don't visit.'

She said icily, 'I don't think you'd better tell her that, had you, Mr Bellamy? And besides, I have to go home to my family. It's the end of term.'

His voice grew fainter as she drew away from him. 'I only wanted to paint you! That's all! *Eva!*'

★   ★   ★

That summer seemed to Marianne to be a rainbow of colours, bright or muted or gaudy. There were the jarring shades of the costumes of the Ballets Russes as they danced *The Firebird* and *Schéhérazade* to the music of Stravinsky and Rimsky-Kovsakov in a theatre in Paris. There were the sombre hues of Black Ascot, where they wore mourning in deference to the late king. There were the whites and greys and faded pinks of Arthur's Surrey house, and the slow infiltration of colour as they began to redecorate the rooms.

In August they were invited to the Merediths' country home, Rawdon Hall. Marianne made lists. She must take day dresses, tea gowns and evening gowns; she must take outfits for walking, riding and tennis. And she must take a maid: it would be thought odd, Arthur told her, if she did not take her maid.

Rawdon Hall was in Yorkshire. The grey stone façade looked out over a circular lake; beyond the lake was a great sweep of lawn dotted with oaks and horse chestnuts. Parkland spread on every side of the house as far as the eye could see. A chauffeur parked Arthur's motor car and a butler greeted them. In the hall their voices were swallowed up by the marble floor and the great upward sweep of the stairs. Vast, multi-coloured arrangements of flowers burst from the giant vases on the side tables, and suits of armour leered emptily from

alcoves. The house seemed designed, thought Marianne, to intimidate, to belittle.

For breakfast, there were hot-house peaches and
pineapples, and raspberries and out-of-season
strawberries. Curls of butter nestled in circlets of ice,
while dishes of porridge and cream, poached eggs,
haddock and bacon kept warm on a sideboard.
Plump devilled kidneys and sausages glistened and
quivered, as if about to burst their skins. Cold meats
and game, galantines and pheasant, tongue and
ptarmigan, made dizzying concentric cartwheels on
vast silver plates.

At half-past one they sat down in the park beneath
canvas awnings to an eight-course lunch. At four they
assembled in the drawing room for an afternoon tea of
sandwiches and brioches, scones and fruit cake. Laura
Meredith presided, making a theatre of the tiny spirit
lamps and kettles and silver tea service. Between meals,
every moment of the day was planned, fixed,
pre-ordained. Marianne must walk in the park, must
play tennis, must take part in a rubber of bridge. She
must change her gown three or four times, and her
maid must dress her hair ever more elaborately as the
day went on, and must heap on earrings and necklaces
and bracelets. She must not remain silent but must join
in the bright, empty conversation, must talk much but
say nothing.

Yet she, who liked to observe, noticed how some
married couples moved apart and then paired up
differently. She saw which man's wife favoured another
woman's husband, and which married woman flirted
with a bachelor. She noticed which couples no longer
spoke to each other and which, preserving appearances,
uttered polite phrases with a sort of cold loathing.
Fingers linked together in shadowed corners of the
room, heads bent and whispered in jewelled ears.
Returning to her room to fetch a forgotten pair of

gloves, Marianne heard a woman's laughter from behind a closed door.

She was separated from Arthur for much of the day. In a green tunnel of pleached hornbeams, she sat down on a bench; a man paused in front of her.

'Mrs Leighton, isn't it?' He smiled. 'My name's Fiske, Edward Fiske. Can I help you?'

Leaves cast their dappled shadows on his handsome face. Marianne had taken off one of her shoes. She saw that he was looking down at her stockinged foot.

'Thank you, Mr Fiske,' she said, 'but I'm quite all right. There was a stone in my shoe.'

'Teddy. You should call me Teddy.'

She put the shoe back on. He offered her his hand to help her up, his fingers lingering a little too long. As she hurried to catch up with the others, she heard him call after her. 'Newly married, aren't you? Lucky old Leighton. Shame for me, though. Still, I can wait.'

As the day wore on a sense of purposelessness seemed to settle over the company. Yawns were stifled behind gloved hands; at tea fingers crumbled pieces of cake into pyramids of crumbs. They played games they did not care to play, thought Marianne, and they ate food they did not want to eat. Outside it had begun to rain; in the fields, rain soaked the mountain of game, falling on dulled eyes and bloodstained feathers.

In the evening, after a ten-course dinner, the men remained in the dining room for cigars and port while the women were served coffee in the drawing room. When the men joined the women, Marianne searched through the company for Arthur. She could not find him and felt a sudden pang of loneliness.

A voice said, 'My dear Mrs Leighton, on your own again?' Turning, she saw Teddy Fiske. He smiled. 'Your husband really should take better care of you.'

Murmuring excuses, Marianne went upstairs. In the bedroom she pulled back the curtains, but did not yet put on the light. Strands of moonlight illuminated the bands of silver on the bodice of her violet dress. Looking out of the window, it seemed to her that parkland, lake and trees had acquired a hard, black, deadened appearance, like the lacquered illustrations on a Chinese box. The optimism and happiness she had enjoyed since her wedding day seemed for the first time to falter. Might she and Arthur grow apart as these couples had grown apart? Might she never have the child she longed for? Might the disappointment she endured each month continue relentlessly, month upon month, year upon year?

The door opened; turning, she saw Arthur. She gave a small cry of relief. 'I'm so sorry,' he said. 'Such an interminable evening.' He crossed the room to her. 'My poor darling. You look exhausted.'

'Such a long day.' She took his hand, pressing it against her shoulder, closing her eyes. 'I missed you.'

'And I you, my darling Annie.'

'I never knew enjoying oneself could be such hard work.'

'They make rather a career of it, don't they?' Arthur pulled off his tie. 'Except Edwin, who will insist on discussing business at the most impossible times. Two in the morning, everyone has indigestion after that frightful dinner, and he wants to talk about *shipping*.' He stroked her face with the tips of his fingers. 'You look sad. Don't be sad, darling.'

'It's this place, I think. There's too much . . . *everything*. That breakfast — '

'It was rather overwhelming, wasn't it?'

'I didn't know what I was going to find next.'

'You mean, lift another lid and find suckling pig, perhaps — or songbirds — four and twenty blackbirds baked in a pie?' When she smiled, he kissed her. 'That's better.'

'How dreadful if you and I were to end up like these people!'

'Hideously rich and eating blackbirds for breakfast?'

'*Darling.*' She stroked his face. 'I meant . . . so separate from each other.'

'We won't. Not a chance of it.'

'But they must have been like us at one time, musn't they? When they first married they must have liked one another.' Marianne took off her earrings, fitting them into their velvet-lined box. 'Such emptiness, these loveless marriages. And half the husbands seem to keep a mistress!'

He raised an eyebrow. She said, 'I've *seen* them, Arthur! I know what they are.'

'It's the way of the world, I'm afraid, darling.'

'Not of my world,' she said fiercely. 'What kind of world is it where a man can make love to another man's wife and no one seems to mind?'

'I don't think it's a question of not minding. More of turning a blind eye. Or perhaps not even that. Laura is always very tactful in her arrangement of rooms. Some of the known roués would be most put out, for instance, if they were to find their bedroom surrounded by the rooms of happily married couples. And Laura always puts those who are known to be established lovers within easy reach of each other. Doesn't do to have too many guests wandering around in the middle of the night, knocking on bedroom doors.'

He unclasped Marianne's pearls and passed them to her; they slid into her palm, cool, almost liquid. 'Do you mind, darling?' he asked. 'Does it upset you?'

She thought of Teddy Fiske: moustachioed, hard-eyed, professionally charming. 'I don't think I'd mind so much if only they cared about each other,' she said slowly. 'If only they loved each other.'

'Love conquers all?' Arthur began to unhook the fastenings at the back of her dress. 'Or love excuses all?

Even marital infidelity?'

She considered. 'It makes it more forgivable, perhaps.'

'Some of the cuckolded husbands or neglected wives might not agree with you. A great passion might be more of a threat to a marriage than a mere entertainment, which is what most of these affairs are.'

'They make it . . . trivial,' she said angrily. 'Love isn't trivial.'

'Of course not.' He stroked her neck. 'And perhaps we should feel sorry for them. After all, we're the fortunate ones, to have found each other. And you're wrong about one thing, darling — they were never like you and me, these people. I doubt if many of our fellow guests married for love. Some will have married for dynastic reasons, and others — like Laura herself, of course — married for money.'

He beckoned to her; she sat on his knee. 'It probably isn't thought fashionable to be in love with your husband,' she said.

'I expect we're considered to be in extremely poor taste.' He caressed the hollows of her collarbones.

Something nagged at her. 'So they don't love each other, these men and their mistresses. Yet they share a bed.'

'Dear Annie, one can enjoy sex without love.'

'*I* couldn't.'

'Of course not.' He unlaced her camisole. 'Now — talking of bed — '

She lay on linen sheets and watched the moonlight, filtered through the ivy that half-covered the window pane, playing on the ceiling. All those long years, she mused, between Arthur's first engagement and their marriage. How had he occupied himself? How had he passed the time?

In the darkness she asked, 'Could *you* share a bed with someone you didn't love?'

145

'There's only one woman I want to share my bed.'

'But before you met me — '

He ran the flat of his palm along her belly. 'I was thirty-eight when I married you. I'm not a monk, Annie.'

She felt a stab of jealousy, black and poisonous. '*Who?*' she whispered. Images flickered through her head, the faces of his friends, his friends' wives.

'No one that mattered.'

'Patricia Letherby? Laura Meredith?'

In the darkness, she heard him laugh. 'Certainly not. Patricia is very happily married. And Laura is possessive. You must have noticed that. Of all things, I dislike possessiveness.'

She rolled onto her side to face him, sliding her hand beneath the stiff folds of his dress shirt, and touching the warm flesh beneath. She thought, but if not Laura Meredith, then there were others.

He said, 'I do not love easily, Annie. Some would say that was a fault. That's one of the things I adore about you — you seem to love so many people. All those brothers and sisters.'

When he took her in his arms, she felt safe, safe and warm. But she said, 'And if I told you that I had known other men before I married you?'

'Did you?'

'No. But if I had, then would you mind?'

In the silence she heard the rise and fall of his breathing. 'Yes,' he said. 'Yes, I would. Of course I would. It's different for women, isn't it? We expect more of you. Men are too easily subject to their animal instincts. We look to women to set an example.'

She thought once more of Teddy Fiske, prowling, searching out his prey. What of the women who succumbed to him — were they beyond the pale? Were their sins to be judged greater than his?

Arthur's fingertips traced the curve of her hip and

146

waist, and Marianne's weariness vanished, replaced by a dark stir of excitement. Yet, as he drew her to him, it occurred to her that if she had not, more than a year ago, gone to the Hutchinsons' ball — if she had had a cold, for instance, like Eva, and had been unable to attend — then she and Arthur might never have met. What then? Would she have lived the rest of her life without knowing passion or love? Or would she have known that she was missing something, and, if so, might she have searched endlessly for it as the people in this house, perhaps, did?

5

A few days after the start of the autumn term, Mrs Wilde's parrot, Perdita, disappeared. Hurrying from street to street, Eva eventually caught sight of a flash of emerald green high in a lilac tree. Scrambling up the iron railings round a front garden, she leaned precariously over and made a grab. With a snarl and a vicious peck, the parrot shuffled higher up the branch.

Someone said, 'Let me,' and Eva stilled, recognizing Gabriel Bellamy's voice.

'You'll impale yourself,' he said. Then he put his hands round her waist and lifted her down. Too surprised to protest, she watched as he reached up and slid his fingers beneath Perdita's belly. The parrot stepped obligingly onto his hand.

'She bites,' warned Eva.

'You're not going to bite me, are you?' Gabriel ruffled Perdita's neck feathers; to Eva's annoyance, the parrot's eyes glazed over and she bowed her head submissively.

'What a pleasant surprise, running into you,' he said to Eva as he sheltered the bird beneath the folds of his coat. 'Is she yours?'

'My landlady's.'

They began to walk back to Eva's lodgings. 'How was your summer?' he asked. 'Were your family well?'

She had spent only two weeks at Summerleigh, two tedious weeks which had confirmed what she knew already to be true, that she did not belong there any more. She had felt marooned, cut off from the new world she had discovered, and had quickly returned to London.

'Yes, thank you,' she said. 'I didn't stay long.'

'That bad? Arguments or just grim silences? That was

my family's speciality, silences. We went to Spain, Max and I. Took the boat. Marvellous.'

'Lucky you,' she said enviously.

'You should have come with us. Are you a good sailor?'

Eva imagined blue-green seas and waves topped with white foam. 'I don't know. I've never really sailed anywhere.'

He talked about Spain for a while. It seemed to Eva that he had forgotten their kiss — he had, after all, been drunk that night, and he had since made it plain to her that the incident had meant nothing to him. How ridiculous, she had found herself thinking during the long weeks of summer, how unsophisticated and provincial, to make such a fuss about something so unimportant.

'How's Sadie?' she asked.

'Sadie's in splendid form. And so's the baby.'

She stared at him. 'Baby — '

'Another boy, I'm afraid. We're calling him Rowan. He weighed ten pounds — he looks like a prize fighter. You must come and see him. Sadie's been asking for you. You will come, won't you?'

'Well, I — '

'Good, that's settled then.'

They had reached Mrs Wilde's house; Gabriel handed Eva the parrot. As she fitted her key in the lock, he called from the far side of the road, 'And you have to let me paint you! I'll make you immortal!'

'I've no wish to be immortal.' But she smiled as she let herself into the house.

★   ★   ★

The baby was a funny, crumpled little thing with black eyes like raisins and fine black hair that grew out of his scalp at all angles. Since the birth Sadie's features seemed to have blurred, to have become less defined. The sharpness of tongue that Eva had previously noticed had gone; she spoke less, smiled rarely and gave scant attention to the older children.

Eva slotted back easily into life at Greenstones. She fitted here, she thought, in a way that she no longer fitted into Summerleigh. She ploughed through mountains of washing-up for Sadie; she pushed the baby round the garden in his pram when he cried too long. Tolly took to following her around like a small, grubby dog, and Max took her out for a ride on his motor bike. In the evenings, when they all sat together round the big pine kitchen table, she thought: *This is how I want to live, this is how I shall live one day.*

You have to let me paint you, Gabriel had said. At first Eva resisted, baulking at the thought of placing herself on a dais like the models at the Slade, subjecting herself to the judgement of the male eye. He misinterpreted her reluctance. 'Must you be so damnably bourgeois?' he cried one day. 'Fussing about impropriety!' So she gave in: because she did not want him to think her a prude and because she was curious.

Gabriel's studio was at the back of Greenstones. The brick walls were whitewashed and the floor was made of stone flags. Eva sat on a high stool. Sunlight poured through the window panes and fell onto the red and green dress Gabriel had asked her to wear, the dress she had been wearing the first time he had seen her at Lydia Bowen's gallery.

To sit in his studio seemed to Eva like treading on enchanted ground. She came to know the room by heart, could have closed her eyes and listed its contents: the old coat and hat hanging on the peg on the back of the door, the confusion of easels and canvases and lay figures and half-finished sketches and the colours of Gabriel's palette, a great slur of scarlet and emerald.

He, too, seemed printed on her retina, like the

aftermath of the sun. His concentration was absolute; he disregarded all the sounds of the house — the barking of the dogs, the shouts of the children and the cries of the new baby. She wondered whether that was the key to his accomplishment: his single-mindedness. For hours at a time there were only herself and Gabriel and the soft sweep of his brush as it moved across the canvas. Much later it occurred to her that, if she had not been a middle child, then she might not have fallen in love with him. No one had ever looked at her for so long or with so much attention. There was an intimacy about his gaze that stirred her, wakening her. When he let her glimpse the finished canvas, and she saw herself through his eyes, she was shaken, as though he had taken a part of her she had not known to exist, had revealed it to her and, in doing so, had changed her forever.

★ ★ ★

Clemency's friend, Vera, dropped in one day after school. She said, 'I must tell you my news. I've met the most adorable man. He's called Ivor Godwin and I've been longing to tell you all about him.' She went rather pink. 'Oh, it's not like that at all. We're just terribly good friends. Ivor's married. His wife's called Rosalie and she's an invalid, poor Ivor.'

Clemency noticed that Vera said 'poor Ivor', not 'poor Rosalie'. 'Where did you meet him, Vee?'

'At a musical recital. He plays the harpsichord. He's so terribly clever and talented. He used to live in London, but they had to move up here because of Rosalie's health. For the air, you see — they live out in the Peaks. He misses London dreadfully.' She beamed. 'He's so sweet — he let me put out the programmes at his last concert! You must meet him.'

Vera invited Clemency to Ivor's next recital. When Clemency told her mother about the recital, Lilian looked at her vaguely and said, 'Of course you must enjoy yourself, dear. I shall be perfectly all right by myself.' Clemency felt a wash of guilt at the thought of poor Mother confined all alone to her rooms.

The day of the recital arrived. After lunch Clemency put on her best dress and went to say goodbye to Mother. Lilian was sitting at her dressing table. 'Dear me, Clemency, you look very smart,' she said. 'All dressed up to the nines. I'm sure Dr Roberts will be very flattered.'

'Dr Roberts?'

'The specialist from London. You haven't forgotten that Dr Roberts is coming to see me, surely?'

'I don't think you mentioned it, Mother.'

'I'm quite certain that I did.' Studying her reflection in the mirror, Lilian patted her hair. 'If you had forgotten about Dr Roberts then why are you wearing your silk tussore dress?'

'Vera and I are going to a concert.'

'I'm afraid that's quite impossible.' Lilian unstoppered a scent bottle. 'How can I receive Dr Roberts on my own?'

'Surely Edith — '

'You know that Edith won't do at all. She's far too slapdash.' Lilian dabbed eau de cologne on her neck. 'If you had managed to find a reliable parlourmaid . . . '

Clemency said desperately, 'But I *told* you about the concert, Mother.'

Lilian looked wounded. 'Please don't be cross with me, Clemency. You know how sad it makes me feel when you're cross with me. And I really don't think you did tell me.'

'But Vera's expecting me.'

'I'm sure Vera will understand that you're needed here. You can go out with your friends another time, can't you, dear?'

Just then Clemency felt such sudden and overwhelming rage that she had to dig her nails into her palms to stop herself screaming out loud, or with a sweep of her arm throwing her mother's perfume and medicine bottles to the floor.

Yet Lilian seemed oblivious to her anger. 'Oh dear,' she murmured, 'I feel quite nervous.' Her small, slim hand ruffled her lace collar. 'I mustn't get myself into a state, must I? That would never do. Perhaps you'd better read to me, Clemency. Tennyson, I think.'

Clemency's rage left her as suddenly as it had come and she felt tired and ashamed of herself. She sat down, her legs shaking. Out the corner of her eye she could see the clock on the mantelpiece. As the hands moved inexorably round the dial, she felt a sense of panic so sharp she had to grip the book hard to steady herself. 'Man for the field and woman for the hearth,' Clemency read, rather unsteadily. 'Man for the sword and for the needle she. Man with the head and woman with the heart: man to command and woman to obey.' Lilian made a little snorting sound.

★　★　★

Eva caught sight of Gabriel across the street and her heart gave an odd little bounce.

He was gloomy, downcast. 'I had to get away,' he said. 'Couldn't get any work done. Too many children, and they always seem to be howling or fighting. Sadie's in a foul mood, hardly speaking to me, and the place is so bloody *boring*.' He dug his hands into the pockets of his greatcoat as they walked. 'And we've had no visitors in months. I tell you, Eva — rural idylls are all very well in June, but, come the winter, well, I almost slit my throat. I needed to be somewhere civilized for a couple of months. So you can model for me again.'

She said, 'Gabriel — ' and he interrupted with a

153

snarl. 'What? Still worried about your virtue?'

She felt herself redden. 'Of course not.'

'You shouldn't be. I know where that sort of thing gets me. Six mouths to feed, which is why I have to do some decent work to pay the bloody rent.' He was walking fast along the leaf-swept pavements; she had to half-run to keep up with him. 'Or are you too busy to see an old friend? Is the Slade so marvellous that you can't spare me an hour or two?'

'Certainly not. It's not marvellous at all.'

He threw her a glance. 'The first time we met, you told me how much you loved London. Has it begun to pall?'

'It's not *London* — '

'What, then?'

Her boots kicked up clouds of fallen leaves. 'It's college,' she muttered. 'I didn't think it would be like this. I didn't think it would be so hard. I used to think I was good at art. Now I seem to be so . . . so mediocre!'

He said more kindly, 'Bring your portfolio to my studio tomorrow evening. Let me have a look. It may not be as bad as you think.' Then he glared at her. 'Unless, of course, you're more concerned about propriety than you are about painting.'

Gabriel's studio was in Paddington, squeezed between a watchmaker's and a manufacturer of cardboard boxes. Opening her portfolio seemed to Eva as great a self-exposure as modelling for him. He studied her sketches and paintings one by one. After what seemed a very long time, he said, 'This is better,' and Eva, who had not until then realized that she was holding her breath, let out a gasp of air.

'The colours are good,' he said. 'I told you before, you have an eye for colour. And this — ' he held up a drawing — 'this shows promise.'

From memory she had drawn the children dancing in the street to the music of the barrel organ. She had caught their rapt and serious expressions, the swirl and flick of their ragged skirts and pinafores.

He said, 'You paint better when you are painting something you care about. It's the same with all of us, I believe.'

He drew her that evening standing at the window, her hands resting on the sill. She could see the railway station and the great cloud of steam and smoke that hung over it, and hear, from behind her, the rasp of the charcoal as it moved across the paper. While he worked, he talked to her. He told her about his family. He was the son of a Baptist minister; he had been brought up in Christchurch on the south coast of England. From his upbringing he had retained a love of the sea and a loathing for religion. 'My parents always tried to take all the colour out of life,' he said. 'Adventure, travel, parties — they disapproved of them all. Afraid of them, I suppose. Even the rooms of our house were papered in dreary shades — browns and buffs and eau de Nil.' His gaze swung to Eva, then back to the easel. 'One day, when I was sixteen, I threw a few things into a knapsack and walked out the door. I've never been back.'

'But how did you eat?' she asked. 'Where did you live?'

'Oh, I did this and that. I've always had the knack of drawing likenesses — I used to set up my easel in a marketplace and charge people sixpence a sketch. And I worked on building sites or helped at harvest time on a farm. And when I didn't have anywhere to live, then I'd sleep in a barn or in a ditch. Cold doesn't bother me.'

She had noticed this in him, that he wore much the same clothes — corduroy trousers, a rough blue workman's shirt and his greatcoat — whatever the weather. While she shivered in the unheated studio, he flung off his coat and rolled up his sleeves before he set to work.

'I haven't taken a penny from my family since I left

home,' he told her. 'If you don't think much of the way people live, then you shouldn't take their money. That's my belief, anyway.'

She told him, 'My married sister, Marianne, has asked me to decorate some fire surrounds and bedheads for her. And I'm trying to persuade her to let me paint her a mural.' Eva smiled. 'I wish you could see Marianne and Arthur's country house, Gabriel. It's beautiful. There's a magic about it. When you're there, you feel as though you might turn a corner and see — oh, I don't know. Something unexpected. Something marvellous.'

He said, '*That's* it. Don't move. That's the expression I want. That look in your eyes. Such *passion*.'

★   ★   ★

Sometimes Clemency felt as though her life had become stuck, frozen solid, as if she had leapt into a puddle and ice had clamped itself around her. She could feel her friends growing away from her. Their lives moved on while hers stayed the same.

Mrs Catherwood called one afternoon. After she had sat with Mother for an hour, Clemency saw her out. At the front door, Mrs Catherwood said, 'I thought Lilian seemed a little brighter today, Clemency dear. Perhaps the new treatment is proving beneficial.' Mrs Catherwood peered at Clemency. 'But you look a bit peaky. Such a miserable time of year, autumn. Ronnie and Gerald both have dreadful colds. I hope you're not coming down with a cold, Clemency.'

Clemency muttered, 'I'm fine. I've a headache, that's all.'

'A brisk walk,' Mrs Catherwood suggested. 'I always find a brisk walk a good cure for a headache. Though in this rain . . . ' She was struggling to open her umbrella. She said sympathetically, 'It must be hard for you,

Clemency, now that your sisters have left home. I'm having a little tea party on Thursday afternoon. Just a few friends. Won't you come, dear?'

'I don't think I can. Mother may need me.'

Mrs Catherwood paused in her fight with the umbrella. 'Surely Lilian could spare you for an afternoon?'

Clemency did not reply. Mrs Catherwood looked concerned. 'You really don't look quite the thing. And you've always been such a bonny girl. Do you get many headaches, dear?'

'Quite a lot,' she mumbled.

'Are you worried about something, perhaps? Your mother, for instance?'

When she spoke Clemency's voice was quick and rough, as though she had to get the words out before she had second thoughts. 'I think I'm ill! I'm afraid I've caught Mother's illness!'

Mrs Catherwood did not laugh as Clemency was half-afraid that she might, but said, 'Why not put on your coat, dear, and walk with me part of the way? I would appreciate the company. And if you could help me with this wretched umbrella . . . '

Clemency fetched her coat, put up Mrs Catherwood's umbrella for her and they left the house. Mrs Catherwood said, 'Tell me what makes you think you are unwell, Clemency.'

'My heart beats too fast. And then, there's the headaches. I never used to get headaches.'

They walked in silence for a while. A storm the previous week had blown the leaves from the trees and they lay, dirty and bruised, in the gutters. Then Mrs Catherwood said, 'Do you manage to get out much nowadays?'

Clemency shook her head. 'Not really. Vera invited me to a concert a few weeks ago, but I couldn't go.'

'Because of your mother?'

157

'Yes.'

'I don't believe that Lilian's illness is infectious,' said Mrs Catherwood. 'Not in the way that scarlet fever and influenza are infectious. And I've always been a great believer in fresh air and exercise. I'm convinced that they do far more good than any medicine. As for bed rest — well, doctors are forever telling us to rest, aren't they, but I can't help thinking that one can have *too much* rest.' Mrs Catherwood patted Clemency's arm. 'I haven't seen enough of Lilian lately. How would it be if I came and sat with her two afternoons a week? Wednesday and Friday, perhaps, if that suits you. And then you could see your friends and Lilian would have company. Would you like that, Clemency?'

Mrs Catherwood sat with Lilian while Clemency met Vera and Erica one Wednesday afternoon at the beginning of November. Ivor Godwin was giving a recital in the drawing room of a house in Oakholme Road. Chairs were placed in a circle round an instrument that looked to Clemency like a very small piano. The sound it made was like raindrops falling into a pool. The music was quiet and intricate, and all the ladies in the audience — there were only ladies, Clemency noticed, most of them a good deal older than herself — kept very silent and still. There was a collective exhalation of breath whenever he came to the end of a piece.

Ivor Godwin was dark and slight and he crouched over the keyboard, his shoulders hunched and his head at a tilt. He had an expressive, mobile face. Clemency noticed how, sometimes, while he was playing, he closed his eyes and how, often at the end of a piece, he gave a flicker of a smile.

When the recital finished, there was a ripple of applause. Vera whispered to Clemency, 'Wasn't he *marvellous?*'

The music had taken Clemency to another place.

158

While Ivor Godwin had played she had imagined hills and streams and woodland. It jolted her to return to the drawing room, with its over-stuffed chairs and heavy, dark green curtains.

'Marvellous,' she agreed.

Ivor Godwin was borne away by a bevy of ladies, who plied him with tea and cake, and fussed over him when he murmured about his aching hands. 'And, of course,' said Erica slyly, 'he's very handsome, isn't he?'

'Shh, Erica!' Vera had gone crimson. 'He'll hear you!'

After tea, as the other ladies began to drift out into the drizzle, they went back into the drawing room, where Mr Godwin was tidying up his music. Vera introduced Erica and Clemency and they all shook hands. Then Ivor Godwin said, 'So exhausting. And one is compelled to eat when one really doesn't feel the least bit hungry.'

'Poor Ivor,' said Vera. 'Mrs Hurstborne can be so smothering.'

'Our hostess?' Ivor threw a glance at the adjacent room. 'You did rather leave me at the mercy, Vee.'

Vera giggled. Ivor took out a cigarette case. 'I always feel so strung up after a concert. You don't mind if I smoke, do you, ladies?' He offered round the case.

Vera offered to tidy up Ivor's music for him. As Vera scuttled about, picking up sheet music, Ivor Godwin, who was leaning against the mantelpiece, smoking, asked, 'Are you musical, Miss Maclise?'

'Not in the least, I'm afraid.'

'You shouldn't apologize. Talent can be a curse.'

'It must be marvellous to be good at something!'

'Sometimes it's a burden. One has one's duty to one's talent as well as all one's other obligations.'

'Vera mentioned that your wife was unwell, Mr Godwin.'

'Rosalie has been ill for many years. Which is why I'm forced to live out in the wilds.' He was smoking in little

159

short, jerky puffs. 'Hills and crags and woodland — I know poets are terribly keen, but they don't suit *me*.'

He looked, she thought, rather like a poet, with his Roman nose and tousled brown hair. 'I prefer London,' he said. 'I had such a marvellous circle of friends there. And the music — the concerts and recitals — so exhilarating.'

'It must have been very hard for you having to give all that up.'

He said bitterly, 'Talent sometimes has to take second place to duty.'

'Do you give many concerts?'

'Once a month or so. Just little recitals. Rosalie doesn't like me to be away from home, so I have to restrict myself. And I teach — piano, mostly. Ambitious mothers drag their poor little children out to my home in Hathersage in the hope that one day they'll become concert pianists. And not one of them has an ounce of talent, I'm afraid. But I haven't the heart to tell them. You can't kill hope, can you? The trouble with teaching is that it's so draining. My pupils are like leeches, taking from me every ounce of inspiration. When I should be practising or composing, I'm listening to the poor things plod through their scales and arpeggios.'

'How awful for you!'

He smiled at her. His eyes, she noticed, were a very dark brown, warm and understanding. 'It's so marvellous to talk to someone who has a sympathetic ear,' he said. 'Rosalie is never the least bit sympathetic. She simply doesn't understand how hard it can be. But *you* understand, don't you?'

It seemed to Clemency that invalids never noticed anything much about anyone except themselves. When Ivor added, 'I could be half-dead with exhaustion and Rosalie wouldn't give me the least attention. It's because she's ill, I suppose,' it struck her how closely he had voiced her thoughts.

And then Vera was standing between them, the music bundled in her arms, and she was saying brightly, 'There, Ivor, all done! And I've folded up your scarf and your gloves as well.'

'Dear Vee,' he murmured, and beamed at her. 'Such a help. How could I manage without you?'

★   ★   ★

Most evenings, after Eva had finished at the Slade, she went to Gabriel Bellamy's studio and sat for him. Sometimes they talked, on other days he was silent, intent on his work. Since that first, that only kiss, he had given her no indication that he wanted any more from her than friendship. *I only wanted to paint you*, he had told her and, as the weeks passed, she wondered whether he had spoken the literal truth. He touched her now only to adjust the angle of a limb or the tilt of a head.

She told herself that she didn't mind. She distrusted love: it made people behave in ways they wouldn't otherwise. Yet when, every now and then, it seemed to her that Gabriel thought of her as a piece of dough rather than a woman, to be pushed and pulled this way and that for artistic effect, she was surprised to find that she felt disappointed. She was nineteen years old and in her entire life only one man had kissed her. She was too short, too plump, too dark, perhaps. She, who had never cared about the way she looked, began to peer at her reflection in the mirror, worrying at her unruly hair, pulling and pinching at the folds of her dresses.

Gabriel told her about the day he had first met Sadie. 'I'd left the Slade,' he said. 'Sadie had just started to study there — I'd gone back to visit Tonks or Wilson Steer or someone, and I passed her in the corridor. She was with her friends and she was laughing. She was always with her friends in those days, and she was always laughing. There were four girls — two dark, one fair, one redhead. You couldn't prise them apart.' His eyes narrowed. 'I knew the moment I saw her that I had to have her.'

Eva wondered what it would be like, to love someone like that without thought or compunction. She wondered whether she was capable of such love.

'She made me chase her for a year,' said Gabriel. 'She didn't make it easy. Once, she went to Edinburgh. It took me a while to find her. She and her friends were staying in lodgings near the castle.' He grinned. 'So I bought myself a mandolin from a flea market and stood on the pavement one night and serenaded her. Then she had to come out and speak to me.' His mood changed abruptly, his brows lowering. 'We were married three months after that. I don't believe in marriage, never have. But Sadie's mother insisted. She's a terrifying old trout, lives in St John's Wood in one of those lumpen, hideous houses that look a bit like a mausoleum, with red and black tiles in the hallway and pointless bits of stained glass in the windows.'

'Summerleigh is like that.'

'Then I quite understand why you had to escape.' He scowled. 'The first time I met Sadie's mother, I had to endure an appalling half-hour drinking tea with her. And she hated it as much as I did — I know she did — but neither of us said anything, we just went through the ritual. When I got up to leave I could see the relief in her eyes. I knew that as soon as I was out of the house, she'd be plumping up her cushions and smoothing out the little lace things on the back of the sofa, trying to erase any trace of me. People like that, they pay so much attention to possessions. Even Sadie,' he said angrily, 'even Sadie fusses about servants and housekeeping, that sort of nonsense. It's marriage, you know, Eva, that's what does it. Sadie was never like that before we married.' He squeezed paint from a tube onto his palette. 'Marriage changes women,' he said morosely. 'For the worse, I'm afraid.'

★　★　★

Marianne and Arthur were bringing the Surrey house back to life. An army of decorators had begun to strip off the faded wallpaper and repair the damaged plaster. In her mind's eye, Marianne saw how the house would look when it was finished. The drawing room would be cream and gold, the music room a pale sea-green. They would cover the hall and stairs with a crimson carpet, and would paint the banisters, with their barley-sugar twists, white. For their bedroom, she had chosen a plum-coloured paper and wall lights of coloured glass that reminded her of the chandeliers in the Gritti Palace in Venice.

'And this one?' Arthur asked Marianne.

They were in a light, airy room on the second floor. Tall windows looked down onto the overgrown garden. Dust motes floated, suspended in the weak autumn sun, over a floor of waxed wood.

'The nursery, I thought,' she said.

He put his arms around her. 'Are you . . . ?' She could hear the hope in his voice.

She shook her head. 'I thought I might be expecting a child, but I'm not. But it'll happen soon, won't it, Arthur? Surely it'll happen soon.'

He hugged her again. 'There's plenty of time. Are you feeling unwell?'

'Pretty bad.' She had always had painful monthly cramps. The doctor had told her that they would be better after she had her first baby.

'Poor thing.' He caught the look on her face and said again, 'There's plenty of time, Annie. And it means that I have you to myself for a while longer.'

'Two boys and a girl would be nice, I thought.'

'Or two of each. Boys can be so uncivilized. They need sisters to tame them.'

She kissed him. 'You didn't have any sisters.'

'I have only a thin veneer of civility. I'm a caveman at heart.' He scooped her up in his arms and made ape sounds. Laughing, she protested only weakly as he carried her out of the nursery and to their room, where he laid her carefully on their bed.

'This house needs children,' she said. 'I can imagine them here. I can *see* them.' She placed the flats of her hands on her belly. *Next month*, she promised herself silently. *Next month*.

She slept badly that night. She went down to the scullery in the early hours of the morning to make herself a hot-water bottle and a cup of tea. When she fell asleep properly at last, she dreamed tangled, overly vivid dreams and did not wake when Arthur rose for his early morning ride.

The sound of his voice and his hand, gently shaking her shoulder, woke her at last. 'Annie, wake up. I'm afraid you must wake up. There's been a fire at the shipyard where they're building the *Caroline*. Edwin Meredith sent me a cable,' Arthur was holding a crumpled piece of paper. 'I must go to London, I'm afraid. I need to find out how much damage has been done.'

She sat up. 'I'd better get dressed.'

'Annie, it may be nothing. A few scorch marks, a few days' work lost. You could stay here, if you prefer. And someone should keep an eye on the decorators.'

She must ask Mrs Sheldon, the housekeeper, to stay at the house overnight, he told her. He would be back in a day or two. He went to the wardrobe. Staring at the rows of shirts and jackets, he punched his fist angrily into his palm. 'We've had no luck with this ship. The work schedule's already weeks behind.'

She said, 'Arthur, your *foot*.'

He was barefooted; scarlet marks now imprinted the white rug from bed to wardrobe. He looked down. 'I stood on a nail in the boot room when I was changing after my ride. That floor's full of nails.'

'Let me clean and dress it.'

'It's nothing, Annie. Just a pin prick.'

'Darling — '

'Really, it's nothing. And I must hurry.'

After Arthur had left the house, Marianne went to the boot room. She saw the nail jutting out of the floorboard, a sharp, thick old thing that was red with rust. She had the handyman go over the floorboards and fix all the protruding nails. As she sat in the drawing room writing letters, the sound of the hammer echoed through the house.

★ ★ ★

On Friday, 18 November, three hundred women marched from Caxton Hall to the House of Commons in protest at the government's abandonment of the Conciliation Bill, which would have legislated for a limited measure of women's suffrage. As the women neared the House of Commons the police attacked. Standing back from the mêlée, Eva drew policemen punching women's faces, policemen kicking women as they lay curled on the ground, and a policeman yanking a handful of hair from a woman's bloodied head. She drew until her sketchbook was pulled from her hands and hurled aside, and she herself was thrown to the ground. Then she gathered up her things and made for Paddington.

As she let herself into Gabriel's studio, she heard him say, 'You're late.'

He was at the easel; he sounded annoyed. She stood in the doorway, her belongings clutched to her chest, wondering whether to leave. She could not have borne just then for him to be angry with her.

'You know it's hopeless when the light's gone,' he said irritably. He looked out at her from behind the easel. His tone altered. 'Dear God, what's happened to you?' He crossed the room to her. 'Eva, you're shivering . . . and you're hurt.'

Wrapping his coat around her shoulders, he helped her sit down. Then he lit a fire, scrunching up odd bits of paper, running down to the coal merchant's along the street for a sack of coal that he hauled on his back up the three flights of stairs. Then he sloshed an inch of brandy into a cup and placed it in her hands. 'Eva. What happened? Who hurt you? Tell me who it was and I'll kill them.' He looked ferocious.

'It was the police.' The brandy scorched her throat, but steadied her.

'The police?'

'We were marching to the House of Commons. I was with Lydia — ' She gripped his sleeve. '*Lydia*. I don't know what's happened to Lydia!'

'Lydia will take care of herself,' he said soothingly. 'She's been taking care of herself for years.'

'They were hitting everyone. Old women. Young girls.' She put up her grazed hands to her face, covering her eyes. 'They didn't give us a chance, Gabriel. We were only marching!' She took a deep breath to steady herself and said more quietly, 'I thought I was going to faint, so I ran away. And then I remembered that I had my sketchbook, and I thought that even if I wasn't brave enough to stand and fight then at least I could draw what was happening, and people would know what brutes they were. But then a policeman saw me. So I haven't even got the drawings.'

He put his arms around her and she buried her head into his chest. She heard him mutter, '*Bastards*. Such bastards.'

She drew her sleeve across her wet face. 'They

166

wanted to humiliate us,' she said. 'And they did. They were stronger than us. They might be ignorant brutes, but they could make us do what they wanted just because they were stronger than us.' She looked down at her hands, watching them tremble. 'I heard someone say that those policemen had come from the East End and that was why they were so rough. They were treating us the same as they always treat the women of the East End. Which no one minds about and no one is shocked about.'

When she looked out of the window she saw that the sky was now black. It was late, she should go home — Mrs Wilde would be worried.

There was a looking glass on the mantelpiece. In its cracked, dusty surface she saw that her face was dirty and bruised and that her hair had come down round her shoulders. She cleaned herself up as best as she could, but her fingers shook too much to pin up her hair. Gabriel took the pins from her; she felt him twist her hair into a knot. She was glad of the poor light, glad that he could not see her closed eyes as he pinned and tucked.

They went down to the street. In Praed Street he stood on the pavement, his hand raised to hail a taxi. She watched him covertly, learning him, imprinting his features on her memory, and remembering the treacherous, glorious touch of his fingertips as they brushed against the back of her neck.

★   ★   ★

Arthur had left Leighton Hall on Thursday morning. On Monday afternoon Marianne heard his motor car coming down the drive. She watched him park and climb out of the car. Rain darkened the sleeves of his mackintosh. She noticed that he was limping slightly.

'That wretched nail,' he said, after he had embraced

167

her. 'You wouldn't think a little pin prick could be so bothersome.'

Over lunch he told her that the fire had been fierce, that it had started in an adjacent timber yard and had quickly spread out of control. 'And the ship?' she asked. 'The *Caroline*?'

'Badly damaged, I'm afraid.' He pressed his fingertips against his forehead. 'It's so good to be back. Always so good to see you, Annie.'

'You should rest. Such a long drive.'

'Yes. Yes, I think I will.'

'And soak that foot. I'll fetch you iodine.'

They drove back to London the following day. That afternoon and throughout Wednesday Arthur remained at the shipyard. When Marianne woke on Thursday morning, he was lying beside her. She stroked his face, and his lids fluttered open.

'You didn't go for your ride.'

'Felt a bit tired.' Rain hammered against the window. 'And the weather's vile.' He took her in his arms. 'I don't want to move. We could stay in bed all day.'

'We could pretend to be unwell.'

He grinned. 'What would the servants say?'

She rested her head on his chest. 'The only thing is,' she said, 'I promised Patricia I'd sell flags for her.'

'Flags?'

'For one of her charities. The Snowdrop Society. It's for poor widows, I think.'

'What of poor husbands?'

'Oh, husbands are always mollycoddled. They're thoroughly spoiled.' She kissed him. 'It's the sort of thing I loathe, but Pat's been so good to me and I really shouldn't let her down. And I won't be long.' She laid the back of her hand against his face. 'You feel rather warm, darling. Are you sure you're quite well?'

'I may have caught a chill. All that standing around in rainy dockyards.'

'I'll telephone Patricia and put her off.'

'Nonsense. All I need is a few hours' rest. Off you go now.' He gave her a pat on the bottom to speed her on her way as she climbed out of bed. 'And sell dozens of flags,' he called after her.

Marianne stood in a shop doorway in Oxford Street, sheltering from the rain, carrying a basket of paper flowers and a card of pins. Because she couldn't bear to approach strangers, she only sold a flag when passers-by noticed her and took pity on her. By midday she had sold only two dozen. So she emptied the contents of her purse into the money box and threw the remaining flags furtively into a litter bin. Then she had lunch with Patricia in Fortnum's.

When she went home, Arthur was in the library, sitting by the fire. She put her hand on his forehead again; his skin was hot to touch. For the first time she felt a stab of unease.

'Darling, you have a fever.'

'So infuriating,' he said fretfully. 'And when there's so much to do.'

In spite of the fire, he was shivering. She said, 'I'll call Dr Fleming.'

He caught her hand, drawing her back. 'There's no need, Annie. You know I hate fuss. I don't want the wretched old sawbones hovering over me. And I'll be fine by tomorrow morning.'

She had noticed this about him: that he loathed doctors, hospitals, anything to do with the medical profession. When Iris called, he left the room if she talked about her work. He, who was so physically confident and afraid of so little, had his fears, his antipathies.

She said doubtfully, 'If you're not well tomorrow — '

He held up his hands. 'I promise. You can call in the leeches.'

She slept fitfully that night, waking every now and

169

then and turning to him. Yet, when he woke the next morning, his fever seemed to have fallen.

Marianne had a fitting at her dressmaker's at ten o'clock. As she left the house, she saw that a fog was settling over the city, blurring the outlines of the buildings, beading the railings and the leaves on the trees with tiny pearls of moisture. At the dressmaker's the seamstress pinned and tacked. As the evening gown was fitted to her, Marianne looked down at the crimson cloth. She no longer liked the colour: it was too rich, too dark, too heavy. There was something nauseating about it. It was the colour of blood; she wished she had not chosen it. Her unease remained, needling her, so that she could hardly bear to stand still. She thought of Arthur, turning in his sleep at night, and the hot paperiness of his skin beneath her palm. Every time the seamstress pushed a pin into the cloth, she had to bite her lip to stop herself wincing. *It's just a chill*, she told herself. *When I go home he'll be well again*. But when the fitting was done she did not visit the shops, as she had intended, but hurried back to Norfolk Square.

As the day had progressed, the fog had thickened, so that now Marianne could hardly see to the other side of the road. Outside, sound was muffled, negated by the fog; inside the house, her footsteps tapped emptily in the corridors.

Arthur was not in the library, nor in the drawing room. Marianne went upstairs to the bedroom. He was lying in bed, his head turned away. 'Arthur?' she said. 'Darling?'

At the sound of her voice, he turned to her. His eyes glittered, and she saw that something — something she could not quite put her finger on — had altered since she had left him that morning.

'Arthur?' When she touched his face, he recoiled from her fingers. 'Arthur, my love?'

'Annie. Where were you? You were gone so long.'

'I was at my dressmaker's. I told you, darling.'

'I was waiting for you. For hours and hours.' He winced. 'My head aches.'

There was a flannel and a basin of cold water beside the bed. She soaked the flannel in the water, squeezed it out and placed it on his forehead. 'Is that better?'

He closed his eyes. 'Thirsty,' he muttered. 'So thirsty.'

He could not drink from the glass unaided. Marianne's fear turned to alarm. Arthur, who rode like a prince in Hyde Park, and who had dealt so easily with gondoliers in Venice and cab drivers in Paris, could not drink without her help.

'I'm going to telephone the doctor,' she said. 'I think you're quite unwell.'

As she turned to go, he grabbed her hand. 'Don't leave me, Annie. You mustn't leave me.'

She said gently, 'I'll come back as soon as I've telephoned Dr Fleming. I'll only be gone a minute or two, I promise. Of course I won't leave you. Always and forever, remember, my darling. Always and forever.'

She ran downstairs. She saw that the parlourmaid was in the hallway, arranging the midday post on a side table. She had always been a little afraid of Arthur's servants. *Arthur's servants*, as she had thought of them, not *her* servants.

But now she hissed at the girl, 'Why didn't you call me? Why did no one call me? Why did no one send for the doctor?' And when the maid stared at her blankly, she screamed, 'Mr Leighton is ill! Didn't you notice? Mr Leighton is very ill!'

Her hands shook as she lifted the mouthpiece of the telephone. She heard the operator asking for the number, and the doctor's maid, distant and disembodied. Then her own voice, listing Arthur's symptoms. And Dr Fleming himself, saying soothingly, 'I'm sure it's nothing to worry about, Mrs Leighton. Most likely a winter chill. This weather, you know.'

Some of the tension drained out of her. Dr Fleming would know what to do. He would make Arthur better. She went back to the bedroom and drew up a chair to sit beside the bed. Arthur whispered something to her; she could not catch the words and leaned towards him.

'It hurts. It hurts so much.'

Fear rose again in her throat. She could taste it. '*Where* does it hurt?'

'Everywhere.' He looked frightened. 'What's happening to me, Annie?'

'You're unwell, darling. You'll be better soon. It's just a fever.'

'My foot,' he said. 'It hurts so. My damned *foot*.'

Marianne remembered the rusty nail, and those small, bloody footprints on the rug. She tore off the blankets. What she saw made her clamp her hands over her mouth to stop herself crying out in terror. The skin around the puncture wound on the sole of Arthur's foot was blackened and swollen. A dark discoloration blotched his ankle and leg, making livid, angry bruises beneath the skin where the blood vessels had fractured and bled.

She did what she could, knowing all the time that it would not be enough. She washed his foot with carbolic soap and painted it with iodine and propped it up on pillows to relieve the pain. She knew that she must lower his temperature, so she sponged him down and gave him sips of water. She could not think why the doctor was taking so long. It seemed hours since she had telephoned. And all the time her fear was unbearable, nauseating, like something solid and alive, trapped in her throat.

When she looked out of the window again she saw that the fog had closed in. The movement of the traffic on the road below was almost indecipherable, picked out only fleetingly by headlamps and lanterns. There were two voices in her head. One angry and impatient:

172

Hurry up, why can't you? that voice said. *What can be keeping you? This wretched fog, of course. Don't leave me alone. Hurry up.*

The other voice was pleading, terrified. *Don't let anything dreadful happen. Please God, don't let anything dreadful happen to Arthur. Please. Please.*

★   ★   ★

Dr Fleming was a square, pink-faced man, with a patronizing air. *Blood poisoning*, he told Marianne. *Mr Leighton is suffering from blood poisoning. Septicaemia*, he added, with a little cough, *but you need not trouble yourself with long scientific names, Mrs Leighton*. Though the wound from the rusty nail was small, it had dug deep into Arthur's flesh, carrying a cargo of germs into his bloodstream. Dr Fleming proposed to lance the wound. Arthur was young and strong and they must hope and pray that he was able to fight off the infection. Marianne noted the word *pray*: a lack of certainty there. She grabbed the doctor's arm, her fingertips digging into the cloth of his coat sleeve. *You must make him better*, she hissed. *You must.*

She stood at Arthur's bedside, holding his hand, as Dr Fleming lanced the wound. Arthur had asked her not to leave him, so she wouldn't, even though the doctor tried to make her go. As the incision was made, she imagined the poison draining away, running out of all the little veins and vessels. When the knife dug deeper and Arthur cried out, she bit her lip so hard she tasted blood. She did not turn aside as Dr Fleming washed out the wound with peroxide, nor when he packed it with gauze and bandaged it. Then she sat beside the bed, waiting. In her head, there were still the voices, one imploring, the other chattering. *Surely he'll be better soon. The fever should be falling — why isn't it falling? Why doesn't he open his eyes and speak to*

173

me? Please, God, make him better, and I'll do anything, anything you like. I'll even bear it if there isn't a baby, if there's never a baby.

Outside, the fog thickened, so that it seemed to press against the window panes. The greying of the ochre air was the only indication of nightfall. Dr Fleming drew Marianne aside.

'I've sent for a nurse to relieve you, Mrs Leighton.'

She said stubbornly, 'I shall stay with my husband.'

'We can manage perfectly well, my dear. You should rest.'

'I won't leave him!' In spite of herself, she heard her voice rise. 'I'm not going to leave him!'

'There, there, my dear.' He put his hand on her shoulder. 'If that's what you'd prefer.'

More than a year ago, in the conservatory at Summerleigh, Arthur had promised her that he would never leave her. When she closed her eyes now she could remember the rain on the glass, and the heavy, earthy scent of the palms and ferns. Arthur was the sort of man who kept his promises. She must keep hers too.

She whispered in Arthur's ear, 'I'm here. I'll always be here. You have to get well for me, darling.'

But he turned on the pillow, and said, 'The cannon. Don't you hear the cannon?'

Her heart gave a twist of fear. 'There's nothing, Arthur. No cannon. Just the motor-car horns in the fog. Or one of the maids dropped something, perhaps.' His eyes were like a sleepwalker's, distant and unsteady, and she was not sure whether he saw or heard her. She stroked his face. 'Hush now. You mustn't worry. I'm here.'

His lids closed. The nurse arrived. Her starched apron crackled; she took Arthur's pulse with a brisk, efficient flick of the watch at her breast. There it was again, that momentary relief, the fleeting confidence that Nurse Saunders, with her doughy face and plump,

174

red fingers, would know how to make Arthur better.

In the early hours of the morning, Marianne found herself drifting off to sleep as she sat beside the bed. When she jolted awake she did not know whether she had slept for a minute or for an hour. Once she dreamed of the Surrey house. Arthur was standing in a corridor and she was walking towards him. It was summer and sunlight was streaming through the tall windows. Her movements were slow, as if she were impeded by an invisible barrier. He seemed to shrink away rather than come nearer. When she woke there was the shock of the unfamiliarity that the bedroom had acquired during the last twelve hours: the nurse sitting in a chair beneath the standard lamp, the tray of bottles and bandages, the smell of disinfectant and, beneath it, another smell, of staleness and decay. There was a moment of choking panic, and for the first time it occurred to her to send for Iris or Eva. So that she would not feel so alone.

Yet she did not do so. She still had a lingering conviction that if she just blinked, or gave herself a hard enough shake, all this horror would dissolve, there would be a whirring and creaking of machinery, and everything would be put to rights. To send for her sisters would be to admit to herself that something terrible was happening. To admit that there was a possibility that Arthur might —

She broke off the thought. She sat watching him, concentrating, willing him her own strength. He must get better. He had to get better soon because she didn't see how she could bear another such night. Clergymen always said, didn't they, that God only required you to endure what you were capable of enduring. And this was unendurable.

Towards dawn, he woke with a gasp. 'I saw — ' He was sitting up, his gaze darting round the room.

'What is it, darling?'

'There. Over there.' He was staring into the shadows. She could see the horror in his eyes. 'So many of them!' he whispered.

'So many of what, Arthur?'

'The Indian gods. Multitudes of them. Hundreds. *Thousands*.'

'Hush, darling, it's just a dream.'

'The elephant god. What was his name . . . ? I saw a procession. All the people. So many people. And the noise. The music. Such strange music. I can't remember . . . *Ganesh*. That's it. And the blue-skinned god, Krishna.' He was talking very fast. When he seized her arm, his fingers clawed into her flesh and he hissed, 'What if they're right and we're wrong?'

The nurse had risen from her chair. Arthur stared at Marianne, wild-eyed. 'We always think we're right, don't we? Our way of doing things must be the only one, the right one. Our God, not theirs. But what if they're right, not us? What if *their* gods reign in heaven, not ours?' He rubbed his forehead. 'Or hell,' he muttered.

His voice faded away. He was retreating from her, travelling somewhere she could not follow. She wanted to shout at him, to shake him, to force him back.

The nurse counted drops onto a spoon. After he had taken them, Arthur fell back onto the pillow. Then the nurse lifted the bedclothes to look at his foot. Marianne took his hand again. His lids fluttered, and the skin around his eyes and cheekbones was sunken and drawn.

As Nurse Saunders unpeeled the bandages, Arthur groaned. Marianne prayed: *Tell me it's better. Tell me the swelling has gone down and the bruising has lessened.*

But the nurse said, 'I think I should call Dr Fleming, Mrs Leighton.' She left the room.

Time passed. Dr Fleming came back to the house. After he had examined Arthur, he beckoned Marianne into the adjacent room. The fever showed no signs of abating, he told her. Arthur's heart was showing evidence of exhaustion and would not hold up for much longer. 'His *heart*,' she repeated, stunned, dazed, her own heart squeezing painfully.

Dr Fleming frowned. The lancing of the wound had not succeeded in stemming the infection, he said, and there were indications that gangrene had set in. A little cough; his eyes evaded Marianne's. He was sorry to have to tell her that he had decided he must take more radical measures.

She said furiously, 'I don't know why you're waiting — if you know of some medicine that will make him better — '

'There is no medicine,' he said bluntly. 'Unless the infection is stemmed, Mr Leighton's circulation will be impaired and the vital organs — the heart and brain, you understand, Mrs Leighton — will be starved of oxygen.'

Then he told her of the operation he proposed to perform. She fell silent and did not speak again as he patted her hand and returned to the bedroom.

When she was alone, she went to the window. Outside, there was nothing, only the swirling, yellow-grey wall of fog blanking out everything familiar. She pressed her hand against the pane and saw the drops of water gather together and slide down the glass. But beyond there was still the fog. If the sun had risen, then she could not see it. There was only her own reflection in the window pane. Her pale face, her bedraggled frock, her untidy hair. She began to pin her hair back into place, but then her hands fell away. Why pin up her hair when *he* could not see it? Why change her frock or wash her face when they were doing *that* to him?

★ ★ ★

177

A staff nurse stopped Iris as she came out of the ward kitchen.

'Matron's sent for you, Maclise. Wants to see you straight away. In her office.' The staff nurse smirked. 'You must have been a very naughty girl, Maclise.'

As she left the ward, Iris ran through a list of recent errors in her mind. There weren't a great many — far less than there would have been a few months ago. Iris racked her brain — yesterday she had dropped a tray of soiled dressings on the floor. Surely they wouldn't dismiss her for that. It would be just like Sister Grant to send her packing for such a trivial offence. Well, she wouldn't put up with it. When she left the hospital it would be at a time of her own choosing. She wouldn't be thrown out, ignominiously dismissed.

Outside matron's office, she paused, patted her hair into place, straightened her cap, gave her shoes a quick shine on the backs of her stockings. Then she knocked on the door.

Miss Stanley called out for her to come in. 'Nurse Maclise. Please sit down.'

Which threw her rather. Surely one was usually scolded standing up.

Then Miss Stanley said, 'I'm afraid I have some bad news for you, nurse. I've received a telephone call from your sister.'

Sister, thought Iris. A quick, jolting rearrangement of thought. And then: *Clemency. Mother.*

But then Miss Stanley said, 'Mrs Leighton has asked me to tell you that her husband is dangerously ill. She requests that you may go to her, nurse. Though I dislike my nurses taking time off in working hours, you have my permission, in such circumstances, to go to your sister. You can make up the lost hours on your day off.'

Crossing London, it seemed to Iris that matron must have made a mistake. Arthur couldn't be ill. Arthur was in the prime of his life, handsome and strong and virile.

And yet she knew, of course, that men in the prime of their lives died every day at the hospital. She had watched them, had held their hands as the breath ebbed from their bodies.

At Paddington Station she ran up flights of steps and fought her way through the crowds. Steam from the engines mingled with the fog. Shapes loomed out of the grey-brown air. A girl with a basket of holly sprigs, workmen crowding round a blur of red coals in a brazier. All sound was muffled: the click of horses' hooves, the flower girl's calls. So easy to lose her bearings. Where the fog was thickest, she had to trail her hand along the iron railings outside the houses to guide herself, feeling them beat against her palm.

There was the fear of losing herself in the fog, and then, as she neared Marianne's house, a much worse fear. She had always, with elder sisterly contempt, thought Marianne rather idiotic, with her timidity and her romantic novels and her ineptitude at anything that required physical prowess. And then there had been that huge turning of the tables, Marianne's wedding, when contempt had turned to envy. Now, perhaps for the first time in her life, she thought about Marianne objectively. She thought, soberly, that she herself was incapable of loving as deeply as Marianne loved. Marianne loved, perhaps, too recklessly. And if Arthur should die . . . Iris found that she was afraid to think what might happen to Marianne if Arthur were to die.

A servant answered her ring of the doorbell. Inside, she was shown to an upstairs room. Marianne was standing at the window, her back to the door. When the maid announced Iris, Marianne turned.

Her face was like stone. Her dress was crumpled and stained. Locks of hair hung limply from the coil at the back of her head, and it occurred to Iris that Marianne, who had looked beautiful since the day she had met Arthur Leighton, had become plain again.

It was only a short distance from the Leightons' Norfolk Square house to Gabriel Bellamy's Paddington studio. A few twists and turns and crossings of the streets, a narrowing of a wide road into something meaner. Then Eva was running down an alleyway, past the coal merchant, past the watchmaker and the manufacturer of cardboard boxes. And then she saw him.

It hadn't occurred to her that he might not be alone. But, of course, it was late — nine o'clock — much later than she usually visited him. And there he was, just a few yards ahead of her, spilling out of the tenement block in which he rented his studio, surrounded by half a dozen friends.

'Eva,' he said, catching sight of her. 'My lovely little Eva.'

Seeing him — his flushed face, and the knowing grins of his friends — she wondered whether she had made a mistake in coming to him. Perhaps there was no solace to be found here. Perhaps there was none to be found anywhere.

But he took a few steps towards her and, studying her face, called over his shoulder to his friends, 'You push off, why don't you?'

'*Gabriel*,' they complained as they moved up the street.

'Something's happened,' he said. 'Tell me, Eva.'

But she could not speak, could not yet bear to put it into words. He frowned and said, 'Come up to the studio. You'll feel better there,' and she shook her head violently.

'No. I want to go somewhere different. I want to *see* something different.'

He hailed a cab and took her to the Café Royal. There was a large room filled with tables. Men — and a scattering of women — sat at the tables. Ornate pillars sprouted from the floor, soaring up to a panelled and gilded ceiling. Eva found herself staring at the pillars. Some were encircled with wreaths of gilded vine tendrils, heavy with grapes; others were surmounted by carved figures. She registered that all the figures were of women, pale and naked and full-breasted.

Gabriel ordered drinks. Then he lit two cigarettes and put one of them between Eva's fingers. The drinks arrived: a glass of wine for Eva, and something clear and yellowish-green for Gabriel.

She said, 'What's that?'

'Absinthe.'

'I'd like to try it.'

'You probably won't like it.'

She hissed fiercely, 'I want to try *everything*!'

'Eva — ' He broke off. 'Dear God, I'm beginning to sound like my father. Anyone's father.' He pushed the glass towards her.

She took a mouthful. It tasted bitter; she screwed up her face. He smiled and said, 'Vile, isn't it? It's the drink of poets and neurotics.'

'Which are you, Gabriel?'

'I like to think I'm one, but sometimes I fear I'm the other.' He looked around the room. 'And what do you think of the Domino Room?' he asked. 'Everyone comes here. Orpen and William Nicholson and Augustus John.'

'It's like a cave.' Her eyes travelled over the painted ceiling. 'You could hide away.'

He said gently, 'Eva, my darling, why don't you tell me what it is that you want to hide away *from*?'

Her head ached and her eyes were gritty with the tears she had shed. She drank half of her wine, then put down her glass and pressed her hands against her face. Then she whispered, 'My brother-in-law, Arthur, is dead.'

'Your elder sister's husband?'

She nodded. 'Marianne's husband. They'd only been married a year, Gabriel! Not as much as a year — eleven months!'

'Dear God,' he said. 'Poor souls.'

'I've been with Marianne . . . ' She screwed up her eyes, trying to remember. 'For just a day, I suppose, but it feels like *months*. In that house — and with Arthur so ill, so pitiful.' She drank the remainder of her wine in one gulp. Gabriel signalled to the waiter to refill their glasses. 'Poor Marianne, I don't know how she'll bear it. She loved him so much, Gabriel. But I had to get away. It felt as though everything was dying there. And my father's there, and so are James and Iris, so Marianne has someone . . . So I told them I was going back to Mrs Wilde's house. And they were very kind and sympathetic because they knew I was tired and upset, but . . . ' She paused. 'But it wasn't just wanting to get away. I had to be somewhere that made me feel alive. I had to be *with* someone who makes me feel alive!'

He put his hand over hers; when his thumb rubbed against her palm, she shivered. He said, 'And I make you feel alive?'

'Yes.' The word was like a sigh. She made herself meet his gaze. 'Even though it's wrong.'

'It isn't wrong. Love is never wrong.'

The word love made her shiver again. But she said defiantly, 'Isn't it? Then what of Sadie? What of your children?'

'I love Sadie. I shall always love Sadie. Nothing could stop me loving Sadie. And the same, of course, goes for the children. I would give my life for each and every one of them.'

She thought of her father stepping into a hansom cab. 'I hate deceit!' she cried. 'I hate dishonesty!'

'Isn't it dishonest to pretend that you don't love?' He frowned, gathering his thoughts. 'The way I see it, Eva, my darling, is that I don't pretend to be anything other than I am. I have a bad reputation and, in the eyes of the world, of course, I *am* bad. I don't keep to the rules, but then I don't make a pretence of keeping to the rules. I have my own rules. I believe that love is good. And I don't believe that love is exclusive. I don't pretend to have loved only one woman in my life. I'm honest in admitting that I have already loved two, three — more.' He raised her hand to his lips and kissed the inside of her wrist. Then he said, 'I told you before that I don't believe in marriage. I only married Sadie because she — and her mother — wouldn't have it any other way. If it's marriage you're looking for, Eva, then you should walk away from me. And this time, I promise you, I won't come after you.'

'I don't want marriage. Marriage cages women!'

'Then we see eye to eye about that.'

She said softly, 'I should walk out of here and never see you again. Only — '

'Only what?'

'Arthur,' she whispered. 'Poor Arthur. What if Marianne had waited? They'd met only a handful of times before they became engaged and they had only a short engagement. What if she'd insisted on a longer one? They would have had *nothing*. They thought they had years ahead of them, but they hadn't, had they? And who knows what will happen to me — or to you — tomorrow, or in a week — or in a year or two?'

'*Carpe diem*, you mean?'

'Days have to be seized, don't they? Not wasted.'

'That's always been my philosophy. You said you wanted to try everything. What do you want to try, Eva?'

'I want to paint. I want to paint pictures that will make people gasp. Or make them cry. Or laugh. And then . . . ' She stopped and, looking him in the eye, said defiantly, 'And then there's love, isn't there?'

'Yes, I suppose there is.'

Some of the wine had spilled onto the table top. She drew shapes in it with her fingertip as she said, 'The doctor amputated Arthur's foot. They thought the operation might save his life. But the shock was too much for him and he died.' The worst memory: a memory she knew would remain with her all her life. 'Marianne wouldn't leave him. After he died, I mean. She sat with him for *hours*. In the end, Father and Iris and I almost had to drag her away.' Eva stared at the crimson marks on the table. 'I know now that you can't wait for love. It isn't safe.'

He said, 'I can't stop thinking about you. I dream about you,' and her fingertip paused, stained with red.

She thought of Sadie rolling pastry on the kitchen table at Greenstones. She thought of Marianne, whose eyes had been like dark thumbprints in a face from which all colour had gone.

And a wave of exhaustion washed over her, draining away the last of her scruples, so that when he raised her hand to his mouth and sucked the drops of wine from her finger, she did not resist.

6

In the weeks and months that followed Arthur's death Marianne went over the events of the last days of his life time and time again. Sometimes out loud to her friends and sisters; more often silently, in her head. Arthur's accident, his illness, the operation, his death. *If,* she thought. *If* she had insisted on dressing his cut foot before he drove to London. *If* she had not mistaken blood poisoning for a chill. *If* she had called Dr Fleming sooner. *If* she had cancelled her dress fitting. *If* there had not been the fog. Her listeners reassured her, but there remained that persistent nugget of guilt, hard and black, embedded in her heart.

At night she dreamed of the protruding nail in the floor of the Surrey house. In her dream it grew, piercing through the wooden boards like a dagger. When she brushed her hand against it, blood spilled from the cut.

Sometimes she dreamed of small, bloody footprints on a white rug. Once, she dreamed that she was in an unfamiliar house following that trail of crimson footprints along a long corridor. From the many doors that lined the corridor, she chose one at random. Looking into the room, she saw that it was empty but for the bed on which Arthur lay, sick and bloody and bandaged. She realized that they had all made a terrible mistake, that he was not dead at all, that he had survived and was suffering in some forgotten place, his torment unabated, alone and neglected. When she woke, gasping for breath, her skin was iced with terror and her hands clawed at the darkness.

She had her clothes dyed black. In her mind's eye she pictured the stain creeping over the blues, cerises and purples like a dark mist. She seemed to be living in that dark mist, as if the fog that had enveloped the house during the last days of Arthur's life had never lifted.

At the funeral she scattered violets into his grave. The violets were dried and papery, the ghosts of the flowers he had given her before their first party, pressed by her, kept between the pages of her diary. As they crumbled between her fingers, she breathed in their scent. Then she watched the sharp wind catch them and toss them about before they were swallowed up by the earth.

★ ★ ★

Arthur's solicitor, Mr Marshall, called. Father sat beside Marianne in Arthur's study while Mr Marshall read the will. Though she tried to concentrate on what Mr Marshall was saying, she couldn't. These days she couldn't seem to hold a thought for more than a moment or two, couldn't seem to allow any new thoughts into her head. In her mind the continuous loop of Arthur's illness and death turned and turned. As Mr Marshall spoke, Marianne thought of the furnaces at Father's factory consuming the great heaps of coal, turning them to fire and ashes. It seemed to her that all her memories, all her thoughts, had been turned to horror and guilt, fire and ashes. Her first meeting with Arthur, their courtship, their wedding, all that they had shared had led only to this.

Mr Marshall told her that because the Surrey house was entailed, and because Arthur and Marianne's marriage had had no issue, the house would pass to Arthur's nearest male heir, a distant cousin she had never met. The Norfolk Square house, however, was now hers. At the loss of the Surrey house she felt a flicker of relief. Though she had once loved it, she felt it to have been complicit in Arthur's death.

Mr Marshall spoke of trust funds and stocks and shares. He named a sum of money. After he had gone,

186

Father hugged her and said, 'You are very well provided for, my dear, and that's a comfort, isn't it?' Marianne made some suitable reply. Since Arthur's death, she had become adept at making suitable replies. She knew that if her family were to realize how the inside of her had been hollowed out, left scourged and empty, then they would not leave her alone. And that was all she longed for now.

★ ★ ★

One morning she sorted through his things. Pressing his coats and shirts against her face, she breathed in the scent of him, which was still trapped in the scratchy tweed and white cambric. Sliding her hands into his gloves, she tried to believe that his fingers were folded over hers. She hugged his jacket round her shoulders, wrapping it tightly as she closed her eyes, enveloped in the memory of him.

Among his handkerchieves and neckties she found a white hair ribbon that she recognized as her own, which she had believed lost at the Hutchinsons' dance. He must have kept it, treasured it. She found the letters that she had written to him during their engagement; she could not bear to read them and the paper had already begun to yellow. She found a receipt from the Venice hotel, a programme from the Paris Opera and an old, screwed-up boat ticket from a trip they had once made on the Thames. Carefully, she unfolded the ticket, ironing out the creases with her thumb and placing it on top of the pile of his possessions that she intended to keep.

Other discoveries unsettled her. A heavy gold repeater watch that she had not seen before: was it his father's, perhaps, or his grandfather's? She found a grey cashmere scarf: when she let the back of her hand drift against it, it felt as soft as a cloud. She wondered why he had never worn it and who had given it to him.

At the back of his bureau's bottom drawer she unearthed a handful of postcards. The postcards were French, and all the pictures were of women. The women were undressed, their simpering faces framed by ringlets and their bodies plump and shapely. Their breasts, shoulders and haunches looked to Marianne like so many smooth, white cushions.

Sitting on the edge of the bed that she and Arthur had once shared, studying the women on the postcards, Marianne felt a flicker of envy. They looked so — so *content*. Their eyes were vacant and untroubled. If only her brain was as empty as theirs, she thought savagely; if only she could learn from them the knack of not thinking.

★   ★   ★

She was thankful that the conventions of mourning allowed her to remain indoors behind drawn curtains. In bed she hugged Arthur's old tweed jacket to herself. Her nights were short and broken and, waking each morning before dawn, she would find that she was still clutching the jacket and that her lashes were wet with tears. The doctor offered her laudanum to help her sleep; thinking of her mother, afraid that it would only thicken the fog, she did not take it.

Some of the servants left; she heard them whispering that it was an unlucky house. When they were gone, she was relieved. She preferred the emptiness and the silence. She did not replace them, and those who remained, knowing themselves to be unsupervised, became lazy. Days passed and the Norfolk Square house acquired a slovenliness it had never had in Arthur's lifetime. Dust gathered in the corners and the floors went unpolished.

Her life seemed to be emptying out; soon, she

thought, there would be nothing left in it. She no longer bothered to put up her hair and she forgot to change her dress. Some friends fell away, discomfited or repelled by her silence, her coldness. Her sisters persisted; she found it harder to put on a front for them. She thought, idly, but more and more often, of killing herself. She wondered how she would do it: a slash of a knife across the wrist, perhaps, or a fall from a high balcony. She was tired of getting through the days.

Iris called. Iris ran a fingertip along a window sill, wrinkling her nose as it came away grey with dust. Then she harangued the servants so that they ran round the house, dustpans and brooms in hand, a mixture of shame and resentment in their eyes. Iris brushed Marianne's hair for her; she winced as the bristles stung her scalp. Iris made her bathe and change into a clean and pressed dress, and then announced that they were going for a walk in Hyde Park, making it clear that if Marianne refused she would cable Father. And then Father would make her go back with him to Summerleigh. Away from this house, with all its reminders of Arthur, the inexorable process of losing him that had begun with his illness would have been completed.

★   ★   ★

Marianne made another list.

All the things she lost when Arthur died.

She lost her belief in the rightness of the world. She knew now that good people can die terrible deaths. That there is no justice, only luck or ill luck.

The loss of company, of friendship, of growing old together. The loss of her old pleasure in music because music, of all things, rubbed away at the thin scab that barely covered her wound. The loss of possibility: the places they would have seen together, the family they

189

would have made. She yearned for the baby she had never had.

She had lost the person she once was. If she must go on living, then she supposed that some day she must remake herself. But with what a paucity of ingredients! No hope, little belief. No desire to please, no wish to fit in. Only fire and ashes and what would she make of that?

She had lost love. Six months after Arthur's death her dreams altered. He was whole again and he took her in his arms. She felt his body mould itself to hers, the warmth of her skin melt into his. When she woke, she was on fire. Closing her eyes, she touched herself, imagining her hand to be his.

★　★　★

Eva had worked on Saturday at Lydia Bowen's gallery since the beginning of the year. She helped Lydia plan exhibitions, sent out invitations for private viewings and manned the desk when Lydia was busy. Lydia also insisted she learn to type and to keep the books. 'Because you never know when such skills might come in useful,' Lydia pointed out. 'It isn't easy to make a living as an artist, especially for a woman.'

Eva liked working at the gallery. When, every now and then, someone bought a picture, she felt flushed with pride, almost as if she had sold one of her own paintings. And besides, working at the gallery and studying at the Slade during the week seemed to keep her feet on the ground. Sometimes she thought that if it hadn't been for these things, then she might have just floated away, buoyed up by excitement and elation.

In the six months since she and Gabriel had first become lovers she had discovered the sheer force of physical desire. Until then all her pleasures had been intellectual or creative. She had never enjoyed sport like

190

Clemency, or dancing like Iris. She was short, untidy Eva, whose clumsiness only deserted her when she held a pencil in her hand. It was a surprise to discover that her body could instinctively know what to do, a surprise that the joining of bodies could make her feel so transformed.

She had her rules, though. She never allowed Gabriel to touch her when they were at Greenstones. In an entirely different way Eva knew that she loved Sadie as much as she loved Gabriel. No matter how often Gabriel reassured her that his marriage was different, and that Sadie knew and understood that he needed a life of his own and that he would not be shackled, a part of her struggled to be convinced. Now her friendship with Sadie could never be uncomplicated, but must always be tainted by guilt and secrecy. She told herself that as long as what they did did not affect Gabriel's marriage to Sadie, then it was not wrong. Ruthlessly, she divided her life into compartments. In London she was Gabriel's lover, but at Greenstones they were friends, nothing more. At Greenstones she made a special fuss of Tolly, and pushed the new little baby with the blackcurrant eyes around the fields in his pram. Loving Greenstones seemed to her part of loving Gabriel. She loved it in all seasons: in winter, when a raw wind blistered the chalk hills, and now, in summer, when the blossom bubbled over the hedgerows.

In a whirl of creativity, Gabriel had completed three large oil paintings of her. In the first, painted at Greenstones, Eva wore the green and red checked dress in which Gabriel had first seen her at Lydia's gallery. In the second she had on her coat and hat, and her hands were resting on the sill as she looked out of the studio window. In the third she wore a ragged skirt trimmed with rickrack, and a wide picture hat that shaded her face. The three paintings sometimes seemed to Eva to be of three different women: the prim student, the

191

young woman curious to see the world that lay beyond the window, and the ragamuffin.

When Gabriel worked he was quiet and intense. All his energy and thought were focused on painting. He rarely spoke or moved except to readjust a fold of her dress, a lock of her hair. If she tried surreptitiously to stretch out a cramped limb, he was angry. 'How can I work when you won't sit still?' he cried. 'It's impossible!' Much later, looking back, she often thought that she first learned patience and endurance in those long, quiet hours in Gabriel's studio. These were not qualities she had previously possessed. She, who had always rushed from one thing to another, must now sit still for hours at a stretch, her only distractions the swirl of the brush on the canvas, the rumble of the traffic in the street.

She did not mind because Gabriel was with her. Only in those still hours in the studio could she be sure of him. With Gabriel, there was always excitement and surprise and impulse. She fed off it; it made her feel more alive than she had ever felt before, and it was the antithesis of the routine and conformity of her upbringing. On the spur of the moment Gabriel travelled to Holland with Max, to sketch flat lands and vast skies. He was away for a month, reappearing without warning one morning, begging Eva to drop everything, forget college, spend the day with him. And she did: he bought her champagne and steak in Simpson's-in-the-Strand, and afterwards, in his studio, with sunlight pouring like honey into the bare, whitewashed room, they made love, her body folded into his, his strong arms round her, the beat of her heart against his.

One warm June afternoon she fell asleep in his studio. The hot air had gathered in the room, making her drowsy. When she woke, she saw that he was perched on the window sill, sketching her. She quickly pulled on her clothes.

'*Eva*. Why won't you let me paint you properly?' He threw down the chalk. 'Still so prudish. You have a beautiful body. You shouldn't be ashamed of it. There's nothing more beautiful in this room — nothing more beautiful, damn it, in the whole of London. So why won't you let me draw you?'

'I do let you draw me. Just not like *that*.'

He came to sit beside her. 'Funny little thing,' he said indulgently, his irritation vanished. 'How would you feel if I wouldn't let you paint all your hideous old women and tramps?'

'They're not hideous,' she said indignantly. '*I* think they're beautiful. What would you prefer me to paint, Gabriel? Society beauties?'

'Certainly not. You're quite right, Eva. You stick to your old crones and don't end up selling your soul.'

She had drawn a series of studies of ordinary people at work or having a night out. She had shown them to Gabriel and he had been encouraging. Her notebooks contained sketches of seamstresses and dockers and artificial-flower makers. The great beauties of classical art often bored her, their passivity bored her. In so many portraits the female subjects seemed to live out their lives waiting, waiting, waiting.

She had in common with Gabriel that she loved the London night. She loved the flicker of gaslight in the darkness, the shimmer of a reflection on damp cobbles. One night she was sketching the crowds going into the Empire Theatre in Hackney when she caught sight of a familiar face in the crowds. She had to look twice to check that it really was James. She was about to call out to him when she saw that he was with a girl. James's arm was around the girl, protecting her from the buffeting of the crowd. She was slight and young; she wore a navy jacket over her narrow cream-coloured

193

dress, and fair ringlets peeked out from beneath the brim of her black straw hat. As she put up her face for James to kiss, Eva saw that she was delicately pretty. *Well*, thought Eva, *I don't expect you've introduced her to Father, have you, James?*

She, too, had her secrets. There was the secret of Father's love affair with Mrs Carver and there was Gabriel, of course. She had told no one about Gabriel, though she sometimes had the uncomfortable feeling that Iris guessed something. She knew that James would never tell her about his midinette in a black straw hat, just as she would never tell him about Gabriel. *Secrets*, she thought as she cycled away, *secrets*. As they grew older, they seemed to gather to themselves more and more secrets.

★ ★ ★

Joshua Maclise had bought a motor car; James learned to drive it. He took Clemency out for a spin around town. The motor car was huge and heavy and cumbersome. The maroon paintwork had the sheen of satin and James had polished the brass till Clemency could see her face in it. She watched him intently, noting every press of a lever, each turn of the wheel, asking questions.

'What does that one do?'

'It changes the gears.'

'Gears?'

James explained what gears were for and how they worked. Then he said, 'Would you like a go?'

'Could I?'

'Why not? You'd be good at it, Clem, I know you would.'

They were in a quiet side street. Clemency took the driver's seat and James cranked the starter motor. Then he showed her how to depress the clutch and put the car into gear. When the vehicle began to move slowly forward, she felt a thrill of excitement.

They stuttered along the road. James was patient and encouraging. 'You're a natural,' he said after Clemency had slowly but successfully negotiated a corner. 'Another lesson or two and you'll be charging around Sheffield like nobody's business.'

Clemency told Ivor Godwin about the motor car. 'It was marvellous,' she said. 'It reminded me of when I used to play hockey, that feeling you get when you know you're going to score a really good goal. As though everything's going to happen just the way you want it to.'

They were in the Botanical Gardens. That afternoon Ivor had given a concert at a house in Rutland Park. Over the last six months Clemency had been to several of his concerts. When the weather was fine he liked to take a walk afterwards — it made him feel less strung up, he said. Vera and Clemency often accompanied him.

Today, for the first time, there was only Clemency, as Vera had to help in her mother's shop. They were sitting on a bench, smoking Ivor's dark, pungent cigarettes. Ivor said, 'If only I could afford a motor car. It's such a slog, battling out here from the wilds.' His brow darkened. 'Sometimes I wonder whether it's worth the trouble. Whether anyone would notice if I didn't bother.'

'I would.'

'Sweet of you, Clemency.' When he looked at her like that — so appreciative, so affectionate — she blushed.

He said, 'It's people like you who give me the strength to keep going.'

'How is your wife?'

'Oh, Rosalie's just the same. Your mother's an invalid too, isn't she? Vera told me.'

'That was why I left school. To help look after Mother.'

'We have so much in common, don't we? That's why you understand. Rosalie always seems to be not quite ill and not quite well. We moved up here for her health, but it doesn't seem to have made the slightest difference.' He threw his cigarette stub onto the gravel path. 'The worst thing is that she doesn't like me having any life of my own. She gets upset if I come home half an hour late. I suppose she's lonely, but it's such a burden. Sometimes I find myself longing for a week off.' His dark brown eyes, the colour, Clemency thought, of molasses sugar, focused on her again. 'Do you think that's wicked of me?'

'Not at all. I often feel just the same. That's why I love coming to your concerts, Ivor. It's like a little holiday.'

'Dear Clemency,' he said, and she was suffused by a warm happiness.

'Don't you have any relations who could help you out?'

Ivor shook his head. 'I've a brother living in Winchester, but I hardly ever see him. I've invited him to stay but he always has some excuse — his family, or his business. And Rosalie has only her uncle and a cousin. She doesn't get on with the cousin and her uncle is old and rather infirm. He lives in Hertfordshire and we go to see him once a year. Such an ordeal — Rosalie always seems to feel faint at the most inconvenient moments. And there never seem to be any porters at the railway stations. Last time we visited, I had to haul the bags out of the carriage and I strained my hand. I couldn't play for a fortnight.'

'Poor Ivor.'

'Between you and me, Clemency, we make sure to keep in Rosalie's uncle's good books because he's rather wealthy and he has promised to leave everything to Rosalie. And though I know that it's bad form to talk about money, I'm afraid that when one hasn't got enough, one does tend to think about it rather a lot.' His dark eyes brooded. 'It would make such a difference to me if I wasn't always scrimping and saving. I could give up teaching.' He sighed. 'What a pleasure that would be.'

'Wouldn't you miss it?'

'Oh, not at all!' he cried. 'So utterly dreary, most of them — and the mothers are even worse than the pupils!'

'What would you do instead?'

'I would write a concerto. I've always wanted to, but sometimes I wonder if I'll ever have the time.' He sighed.

★   ★   ★

The summer of 1911 was hot and dry. In London the streets were acrid with exhaust fumes and soot. At lunchtime office boys and shopgirls sat on the scorched grass in the parks, loosening their collars and cuffs and rolling up their sleeves.

As the hot weather continued, tempers flared. Scuffles broke out in pubs as labourers quenched their thirst on the way home from building site or factory. In parliament, the speaker was forced to adjourn proceedings in the House of Commons when the prime minister was howled down by opposition MPs during a debate on the reform of the House of Lords. At the docks workers went on strike to secure better pay and conditions, and the government sent troops in to the Port of London to keep essential supplies moving. In Liverpool and South Wales strikers were shot dead when the troops opened fire on them.

In Gabriel's tenement studio the air was hot and still. Gabriel posed Eva sitting at the table, arms folded in front of her, wearing a blue silk blouse, her hair loose and falling in heavy curls over her shoulders. On the table in front of her was a bowl of cherries.

Gabriel worked from first thing in the morning until the light faded. He must complete the portrait, he told Eva, before he took Sadie and the children to Brittany for their summer holidays. He could never bear to be interrupted in the middle of a painting. If he was forced to stop halfway through, he was frustrated and bad-tempered, knowing that he would never quite be able to recapture his original inspiration, knowing that something would have been lost. He forgot to eat and seemed surprised when Eva, ravenous with hunger, begged for a sandwich or an apple. He did not answer Sadie's daily letters, but glanced at them cursorily, throwing them quickly into a drawer before he picked up his paintbrush again.

He finished the painting the morning before he was due to travel down to Sadie at Greenstones. As always after completing a major piece of work, he was both elated and exhausted. He took Eva to the Café Royal, where he ordered oysters and champagne. She found herself looking up at the pillars in the Domino Room once more, with their entwined vine leaves and carved caryatids, and remembering the day Gabriel had first brought her here. So much had changed since then. *She* had changed since then. Change seemed to drift in the air like a heat haze, distorting everything she had once taken for granted.

For the first time they spent an entire night together. Eva had told Mrs Wilde that she was leaving for Sheffield the previous day. When, in the morning, she opened her eyes, Gabriel was already up and dressed and throwing his clothes into a bag. He escorted Eva to the railway station, where he saw her into a carriage, gave her a quick kiss, said, 'I can't bear long-drawn-out goodbyes, can you?' and disappeared into the smoke and crowds.

As the train pulled out of London, Eva sat in the

corner seat, looking out of the window. She had wondered whether she might cry at the thought of not seeing Gabriel for a month, but instead there was, to her surprise, a small flicker of relief. It was the sun, she decided, and the way the hard blue sky seemed to press down on London, that gave her the uneasy feeling that everything that was normal, everything that was everyday and expected, was starting to dissolve, cracking and splintering in the heat.

One Friday at the beginning of August Eva went with her father to the works. There she drew the girls who worked in the packing shed, wrapping the knives and scythes in waxed paper. Later, sitting in her father's office, she peered out of the window to draw the carters loading crates and boxes to be taken to the docks. When her father was called out of the office, she slipped outside and, darting across the courtyard, went into the furnace room. Sheltering in a corner, she drew the furnacemen as they worked, picking up the crucibles containing the molten steel with iron tongs, their muscles contorted with the weight, their bodies black silhouettes against the harsh oranges and reds of the furnaces. A trickle of sweat ran down Eva's spine and the pencil slipped in her damp fingers. Light-headed, she ducked outside.

Her eyes were narrowed because of the sun; she caught sight of Mr Foley, crossing the courtyard towards her.

'You mustn't tell my father I was in the furnace room, Mr Foley.'

'Only if you promise not to go in there again. It's dangerous and, besides, you'll get heatstroke in there today.'

'I don't know how they can breathe.'

'They're used to it. Some of them have worked in there since they were twelve years old.' He glanced at her. 'Can I get you a drink of water, Miss Eva?'

They went to his office. He gestured to the sketchbook. 'May I look?'

'On one condition.'

'What?'

'That you let me draw you.'

'I can't see why you'd want to do that. Now, the steelworkers — I understand why you might want to draw them, though you shouldn't have gone in there.'

'Don't you ever break the rules, Mr Foley?'

'No,' he said shortly. 'No, I don't.'

'How very law-abiding of you.' But she saw that she had disconcerted him, so she said, 'I'm sorry, I didn't mean to cause any trouble. And I'd like to draw you because you have an interesting face.'

★ ★ ★

During the week, Rob Foley lodged in Sheffield, but on Fridays he took the train home to spend the weekend with his mother and older sisters in Buxton. Travelling, he was aware of the familiar stirrings of dread.

His father had died ten years earlier, when he was fifteen, leaving extensive debts. A week after his father's death Rob had left school and started work at J. Maclise & Sons. He knew that he had been lucky to get the job — Joshua Maclise was a fair-minded employer and Rob had learned early on to see through the moodiness and uncertain temper to the good heart that lay beneath. During his time at Maclise's, he had worked his way up from clerk to become Mr Maclise's assistant. He had paid off most of his father's debts, though the mortgage on the Buxton house remained and took a large bite out of his monthly salary. He had also supported his mother and his older sister, Susan. His other sister, Theresa, taught in the National School in Buxton, much to Susan's disapproval. When Theresa had told her family that she intended to take the job, Susan had expressed the fear that Theresa would bring unmentionable diseases into their home. Rob suspected that Susan's real dread was of a more insidious disease, that of a further loss of the status that she and Mrs Foley had clung to so desperately since his father's death.

Rob often thought that his mother's and Susan's lives were made almost unbearably difficult by their determination to keep their poverty a secret from their neighbours. During the week they restricted their diet so that they might offer their visitors — their neighbours, a retired doctor and his wife, and the vicar, Mr Andrews — a lavish spread for Sunday tea. Rob had remonstrated with them, pointing out that they risked their health, but when his mother had said, 'Susan and I are perfectly happy with a slice of bread for our tea,' and had then burst into tears, he had given up the unequal struggle. He knew that his mother had never come to terms with the disgrace of his father's death. He sometimes suspected that the complicated business of keeping up appearances was all that stood between her and breaking down entirely.

Yet the household often seemed to weigh on him like an iron chain around his neck. Downstairs, where visitors might see, all was gentility with a respectable, if meagre, degree of comfort, but as you climbed the stairs you felt the first shiver of the Arctic regions to come. Winifred Foley never lit a bedroom fire in the winter, not even on the coldest night. Once, during a particularly foul January, when a snowstorm had blanketed the town in white, Rob had arrived home late, the train having been delayed by the snow, to find his mother and Susan huddled together in bed for warmth, and Theresa wearing her coat over her nightdress, curled up beneath heaps of blankets on the rug near the dying embers of the sitting-room fire.

He knew that his mother economized partly for his sake. Though at the weekends the food was often plain and dull, there was always plenty for him to eat. He was given the choicest cuts of meat, the largest piece of cake. He did not protest because he knew that to do so would make his mother unhappy. He loved his mother and sisters utterly, even Susan, whose passionate nature, allowed no satisfactory outlet, led her to ever more outlandish diversions. Yet the mixture of his mother's constant gratitude to him and his own fear that he might never be able to lift his family out of the genteel poverty they had endured since his father's death, oppressed him: thus the apprehension that always settled on him as he travelled home on a Friday.

Years ago he had suggested to his mother that they sell the Buxton house and buy somewhere smaller in another part of the country. Then they might drop the pretence that they were something they no longer were. His mother had been horrified by the suggestion. She had come to Buxton on her marriage. How could she possibly start again somewhere new? Rob had felt the chains become longer, heavier.

Arriving at the house, he saw the curtains twitch as he started down the path and knew that his mother was looking out for him. Inside, he was greeted with hugs and kisses.

His mother said, 'You look tired, Rob. Susan, don't you think Rob looks tired?'

Rob thought it was his mother who looked tired and strained. Winifred Foley was barely five foot in height. Grey, wispy curls framed a face that, though still pretty, was drawn and lined.

'I'm fine,' he said firmly. 'And I'm looking forward to my holiday.' J. Maclise & Sons had closed down that afternoon for a fortnight for the annual summer break.

'Such a treat for us all, to have you home for two weeks!' exclaimed Winifred. 'But you look thinner, Rob. Are you sure your landlady is looking after you properly?'

'She's looking after me well enough, Mother.' The door opened. 'And here's Hetty, so dinner must be ready.'

The Foleys had only one servant, a slow-witted girl called Hetty, who was given to having fits when required to think about more than one thing at a time. Rob ate his dinner of boiled cod, boiled potatoes and carrots, followed by sago pudding, with the best appearance of enthusiasm he could muster. Afterwards they went back to the sitting room. Theresa read a book, while Susan and Winifred told Rob the events of the week. Eventually Winifred said, with an air of someone who is imparting exciting news, 'And Mrs Clements has invited us to a picnic!'

'I detest picnics,' said Susan. 'Last time I went on a picnic, I was stung by a wasp. It swelled up terribly and I was very unwell.'

'Rob will keep away the wasps, won't you, dear?'

'I can never think why people choose to go on picnics,' said Susan sourly. 'I dislike eating outside. I think it's coarse.'

'The Clements would never be coarse.' Winifred had begun to look flustered. 'They're one of the best families in Buxton, aren't they, Theresa?'

Theresa glanced up from her book. 'Yes, Mother.'

'I'm afraid I shall have one of my headaches in this heat,' continued Susan relentlessly.

Winifred wailed, 'But I *told* Mrs Clements we would all come!'

Theresa snapped her book shut. 'And we will, won't we?' she said briskly. 'If you wear a sunhat, Susie, then you should escape a headache. And you can take a bottle of vinegar, in case of wasp stings. Now — ' she glanced at the clock — 'isn't it time for your seance?'

'Seance?' asked Rob.

Susan clasped her hands together. 'Last week Mrs Healey's cousin tried to contact us. At least, I'm almost sure it was Mrs Healey's cousin. You'll join us, won't you, Rob?'

'I should unpack,' he said hastily. 'Next time, perhaps.'

He left the room. Theresa followed him. 'A wise decision,' she whispered, when they were alone.

'*Seances*,' said Rob. 'Good grief.'

They went into the kitchen. Hetty had retreated to her attic; Theresa folded tea towels and put saucepans away. 'Mother isn't sure,' she said, 'that seances are entirely respectable, so they have to be kept secret from Mr Andrews. Susan believes that she has a spirit guide, you know.'

'A spirit guide?'

'He's a Red Indian warrior called Running Deer.' Theresa opened a tin. 'Cocoa, Rob? Running Deer guides Susan's hand on the ouija board. He spells out the letters of the names of the dead who are trying to contact her. I have noticed that Running Deer spells almost as badly as Susan herself.'

They both smiled. Then Theresa sighed and said, 'Poor Susie. If only she could find a sensible occupation. She fusses so about little things because she has only little things to think about.'

'If only she'd married.' Many years ago Susan had been engaged to a curate, who had broken off the engagement shortly after Mr Foley's death. Rob said grimly, 'Father chose his time well, didn't he?'

'Susan has no hope of marriage now.' Theresa boiled milk on the stove. 'She's thirty-three, Rob, and she has no money, of course. Neither of us will ever marry.'

There was no bitterness in Theresa's voice, only resignation. Rob put his hand on her shoulder. 'Theresa — '

'I'm not being miserable, only realistic. There's no point in hoping when one is in a hopeless situation.

And, anyway, I enjoy my work, I truly do. I would miss it if I were to marry.'

Theresa poured boiling milk into the cups and stirred. As she put a cup of cocoa in front of her brother, she said, 'It's different for you, though, Rob. You have a good job, and your prospects will surely improve.'

'You know I can't think of marriage, Tess. I couldn't possibly support two families.'

'Then you must find a way,' she said firmly. 'I can bear that Susan and I remain spinsters. What I can't bear is that none of us should marry. It seems so . . . so arid. So desiccated.'

Her vivid features, dark like his own and in a woman too strong for beauty, looked troubled. He squeezed her hand and said lightly, 'Let's not worry about that now. This is my summer holiday.'

'One of us has to escape,' she said fiercely. 'You must meet girls in Sheffield, Rob. Don't any of them take your fancy?'

They had always been close, he and Theresa. There was only eighteen months between them, and, in the cataclysm that had enveloped the family after his father's death, they had been allies, understanding, as Susan and Winifred did not, both the gravity and reality of their situation.

So he could not quite lie to her. He said, 'There is someone.' Her eyes brightened and he added quickly, 'It's hopeless, Tess. Utter folly on my part. There's no possibility of anything ever coming of it.'

'Circumstances may change.'

He shook his head. 'I would need to earn ten times what I earn now were I to have any prospect — ' He broke off. Then he looked Theresa in the eye. 'And even if it weren't for money and position, then there's the other thing.'

'Doctors are not agreed — '

'Enough of them are,' he said harshly. 'So how could I possibly take the risk?'

Later, alone in his bedroom, he found himself recalling yet again his meeting with Eva Maclise earlier that day. He had looked up through his office window and had seen her coming out of the furnace room. She had been wearing a narrow skirt of blue flowery stuff and a white blouse. Her jacket, which she must have taken off because of the heat of the furnace room, had been slung over one arm. Tendrils of dark hair had clung to her flushed face. He had watched her for a moment, drinking in the sight of her, and then he had gone outside to meet her.

It was the recollection of their conversation that made him clench his fist and strike it angrily against the wall. *Don't you ever break the rules, Mr Foley?* she had asked him, and he had replied, *No. No, I don't.* Which was the truth. His father had been a rule breaker, and the four of them were still paying the price for that, would probably pay it for the rest of their lives.

Yet he had seen in Eva Maclise's eyes that she thought him stuffy, conventional, dull. His fists relaxed and he sat down on the edge of the bed. Not so stuffy, he thought grimly. Falling in love with the boss's daughter — that wasn't stuffy. Merely ridiculous.

★ ★ ★

Philip left his prep school at the end of the summer term and in the autumn started at public school. It was four weeks into the spring term that they received the telegram from Philip's headmaster telling them that he had gone missing. Joshua gave a roar of displeasure and leapt on a train to the boys' school in York. When he came home the following evening Clemency hoped that Philip would be with him. But Joshua was alone: in the hallway, as he took off his hat and scarf and handed them to Edith, Clemency saw deep lines of tiredness in his face.

When Joshua was seated by the fire, a glass of whisky in one hand and a cigarette in the other, she said, 'Have they found him, Father?'

Joshua shook his head. 'No, lass.' He took her hand. 'Don't look so worried, Clemmie. He'll turn up safe and sound, I promise you.'

She voiced her worst fear, the one that had come to her in the middle of the previous night, lying awake, wondering where Philip was. 'But Father . . . he might have been *kidnapped*!'

He gave a strained smile. 'No, love, he hasn't been kidnapped. We know that much, if not a great deal else.' He patted the arm of his chair; Clemency perched beside him. 'I doubt if kidnappers would have taken his outdoor clothes, his pocket money and penknife, and his food from his tuckbox along with him. No, the silly little blighter's run away.'

'*Run away* — '

'Yes. Cut and run.' Joshua drew on his cigarette. 'The school told me that in the evenings the boys are allowed to do their hobbies — make model ships, practise the piano, that sort of thing. And when Philip didn't turn up, his teachers assumed he was somewhere else — well, as you can imagine, I told them what I thought of that! Damned shoddy — pardon my language, Clemmie, but it was damned shoddy. They searched the school first, of course, so by the time they realized he'd gone he must have been miles away.' Joshua stared broodingly at his glass of Scotch. 'Fool of a doctor tells me I ought to drink less!' he muttered irritably. 'Small hope of that, with a family like mine. Not you, Clemency, you're a good girl. Anyway, that chap, the headmaster, Dr Gibson, cold devil, likes to look down his nose at you, said Phil was *difficult* — ' Joshua stubbed his half-smoked cigarette furiously into the ashtray, scattering tobacco on the carpet. 'Phil, *difficult*! Ridiculous! That boy wouldn't say boo to a goose!'

Joshua fell silent, glowering into the fireplace. Clemency asked, 'Will he come home, do you think, Father?'

'Hard to think where else he could go. The headmaster said he was a bit of a loner. Didn't fit in. But I thought that was the point of the place! To make him fit in!'

'But surely Aidan — '

'*Aidan!*' Joshua snorted. 'Aidan lent Phil money! For his train fare presumably, though he claimed not to know. Charged him interest, the avaricious little wretch! And now — ' Joshua rose heavily from the chair — 'I should go and speak to your mother. I only hope this doesn't set her back all over again.'

In the middle of the night Clemency woke, uncertain what had disturbed her. She rose and went to the window to look out. At first everything seemed as it always was: the orchard, the trees' bare branches glistening with frost, and the flower beds with their shrivelled remains of chrysanthemums and Michaelmas daisies.

Then her attention was caught by a light at the summerhouse window. She blinked, staring at it. Pulling on a jersey over her nightdress, she wrapped her dressing gown around herself, stuffed her bare feet into her shoes and went outside, drawing in a sharp breath as the cold air struck her. Approaching the summer-house, she wondered whether she should have taken the poker. What if a tramp, or even a burglar, was hiding in there?

Pushing open the door, she gave a muffled shriek as she caught sight of the huddled figure in the far corner of the room. Then, '*Phil!*' she cried.

He grinned. 'Hello, Clemmie.'

'Phil, thank goodness you're safe!' She flung her arms

round him. 'But what are you doing here? Why didn't you come inside? You must be so cold!'

'I don't mind. It's not bad, really.'

Philip was wearing his overcoat over his school uniform, and his scarf was wrapped several times around his neck. His hair stuck out in unruly tufts and he had a grimy, unwashed look. He had made a small fire of twigs and dried leaves on an old tin tray. On an upturned tea chest beside the fire was a candle, a handful to toffee wrappings and the remains of a currant cake.

'Phil,' she said gently, 'please come indoors.'

He shook his head. After a moment or two Clemency sat down on the floor beside him. 'The dorms at school are as cold as this, Clemmie.'

'Phil, everyone's been so worried!'

'I didn't mean to worry you. Is Father cross?'

'He's always cross when he's worried. You know that.'

'It's just that I couldn't bear it any longer.'

'Did you hate it so much? Was it the lessons? Couldn't you keep up with the lesson?'

'Oh, the lessons were all right. Anyway, they don't like you if you're good at lessons. They call you a swot.'

' "They . . . ?" '

'The other boys. The top boys.'

Clemency recalled Philip's innate clumsiness, his inability to catch a ball. 'Is it sport? Aren't you any good at it?'

He shrugged. 'It's pretty awful. Especially boxing.'

'Boxing?'

'So stupid, hitting people.'

'And . . . and did the other boys make fun of you?'

'Oh yes.' He was fiddling with grimy fingers at the tangled laces of his boot. 'They said I was unpatriotic.'

'Unpatriotic?' Clemency repeated blankly.

'Because I said fighting was stupid. Fighting wars, I mean.' He added, with sudden passion, 'Well, I think it

209

is, Clemmie. They're as stupid as boxing, but more people get killed. If no one fought, there wouldn't be any wars, would there?' He looked down at the floor and muttered, 'They said I was a coward. The thing is, I am, I am a coward. I even hate watching the others fight. Everyone else likes fighting. So I must be a coward, mustn't I?'

'So you ran away?'

'I only had enough money for a train ticket to Doncaster. So I sang some songs and got some more money.'

'You *sang*?'

'Mostly hymns. People put money in my cap. But then a policeman came so I thought I'd better scarper. I took a bus to Rotherham and then I walked for ages and ages. I've masses and masses of blisters,' he said proudly, pulling down his sock to show them to Clemency. 'Then a man gave me a lift on his cart, and then I walked for miles more, and then I came here.'

'But Phil . . . where did you sleep?'

'The first night, in a waiting room at a railway station.' He looked suddenly guilty. 'I told them my aunt had died and I had to go home for the funeral. So they let me sleep there. I suppose it was a pretty bad lie.'

'Phil,' she said, 'how can you possibly think you're a coward after a journey like that, all by yourself?'

'I was running away, wasn't I? They'll say that's cowardly, I know they will.'

The fire had died down to a heap of pink embers. Beneath her nightgown, Clemency's bare legs were goose-pimpled. 'How about coming inside and I'll make you some cocoa, Phil?' she coaxed. 'Better than sitting out here freezing.'

He looked anxious. 'Father will be angry with me, won't he?'

'I'll talk to him. I promise you it'll be all right.'

'Father will make me go back, won't he?'

'I don't know, Phil,' she said sadly. 'But probably, yes.'

After a while he stood up and followed her indoors. In the morning she got up early so that she could tell her father about Philip before he left for work. There was the predictable eruption of fury and relief, then Clemency said firmly, 'I think he should be allowed to stay at home for a few days. He's very tired and he might be coming down with a cold. And, besides, there's something I have to do.'

The next day Clemency took Philip to an optician's in the centre of the city. The optician fitted him with a pair of glasses, which Clemency paid for from her dress allowance. On the way home Philip sat with his face squashed against the window of the tram. 'Look at that ripping motor car — and that one . . . '

She told Ivor about Philip. Ivor's chocolate-brown eyes widened. 'The poor boy! How frightful! I *hated* school. My mother let me leave after a year because I was too sensitive. She taught me at home, and I had my music lessons, of course.'

Then Clemency asked after Rosalie. The corners of Ivor's mouth turned down. 'Poor old Ro hates the winter. She's convinced that she won't survive another English winter. She wants us to go to the south of France again next year. We went before and it was so dreary, Clemency, away from all my friends and only a frightful old upright piano in the *pension* to practise on. And I don't see how we could possibly afford it. I told Rosalie that, but she didn't seem to listen.'

Though Clemency had never met Rosalie, she imagined her to be a pampered, self-centred woman, who took advantage of Ivor's kind heart. In doing so, Rosalie had deprived Ivor of the career and recognition he would otherwise have had. Secretly, Clemency loathed Rosalie.

At first, Lilian had made clear her dislike of

211

Clemency's concert going. 'It's not as though you've ever been musical, Clemency,' she had pointed out. 'Marianne was always the musical one.' Yet Clemency continued to attend Ivor's concerts. She would not give up Ivor as easily as she had given up school, her friends, and any chance of a life outside the home. Something stopped her weakening when Lilian, changing tactics, whispered pathetically, 'Leaving your poor mother alone again, dear? I'm afraid I'm more often by myself than in company, these days.' Clemency plumped up the pillows, made sure the drops and pills were to hand, and reminded her mother that Mrs Catherwood was coming to sit with her. Lilian's sighs followed her as she left the house. 'But Lucy is so dull, darling, compared to you!'

But it was not until she quarrelled with Vera that she thought of Ivor as anything other than a friend. Throughout the winter she had seen Vera only occasionally and, on the rare occasions they met, Vera had been noticeably stand-offish.

Clemency decided to talk to her to try to find out what was wrong. One afternoon at the end of March, she called on Vera at her mother's shop in Bridge Street. The shop had the gloomy, dusty look, Clemency thought, of a white elephant stall. Three-legged stools decorated with painted flowers jostled against faux-marble fire surrounds and needlepoint table covers. There never seemed to be any customers.

Vera was sitting in a corner of the room, gilding a plant stand. Clemency said brightly, 'Hello, Vee.'

Vera looked up, said, 'Oh, it's you,' and returned to the plant stand.

'I missed you at Ivor's last concert.'

'Did you?'

Vera's cool tone disconcerted Clemency. 'Ivor wondered where you were,' she said.

'I expect you managed to stop him worrying too much about *that*!' Vera gave a trill of laughter.

'Vee — '

Vera's expression altered. 'I don't know how you have the nerve to come here!' She set the paintbrush down on the table with a thump; gold paint sprayed over the floor. 'Sweet little Clemmie!' she hissed. 'Miss Butter-wouldn't-melt-in-her-mouth! Well, *I* can see through you!'

'Vera, I don't know what you're talking about — '

'I'm talking about *you* stealing Ivor from me!'

Clemency gasped. '*Stealing* him?'

''Oh Ivor,'' mimicked Vera in a high-pitched tone, ''let me put out the programmes! Oh, Ivor, let me write your letters for you!' When you knew how much I wanted to!'

'I thought you couldn't because of the shop.'

'Yes, very convenient for you, isn't it, Mummy needing me here.' Vera scrubbed the gold paint from the floorboards with a rag. Then, looking up, she said pointedly, 'You should remember that Ivor's a married man, Clemency.'

It took a second or two for the implications of Vera's words to sink in. Then she could hardly speak for shock. 'There's nothing like that — there really isn't — ' The words stumbled over each other.

'You're madly in love with him. Anyone can see that.'

'I'm not.' Clemency struggled against tears. 'How can you say such an awful thing?'

'Mrs Braybrooke remarked on it. I heard her say to Mrs Carter that you followed Ivor Godwin around like a puppy dog.' Vera went back to the plant stand. She added spitefully, 'You always were a bit of a doormat, Clemency.'

'Ivor's my *friend*.'

'Oh, Clemmie, you really are fooling yourself, aren't you? You can't take your eyes off him. You'd do anything for him!' Vera studied Clemency disparagingly. 'Well, I won't get in your way. I hope to become engaged soon and I don't suppose my fiancé will want me running around after a married man.'

Walking home, upset and shaken, Clemency struggled to dismiss Vera's accusations. *You're madly in love with him.* Was it possible? Did she love Ivor — and not only as a friend? Was there something underhand — distasteful, even — about their friendship?

She hadn't told her mother about Ivor. Why not? Because she needed to keep a part of life separate from her mother — or because she knew that her mother would, quite properly, disapprove? She didn't really, she reflected wearily, know what love was. She loved her family, and it seemed to her that the feelings she had for Ivor were as strong as her feelings for her brothers and sisters.

But did she love him as a sweetheart? Would she, had it not been for Rosalie, have wanted to marry him? Fleetingly she allowed herself to imagine living with Ivor in a dear little cottage, looking after him, giving him the love and understanding that he deserved and that she had concluded long ago he failed to get from Rosalie. If, as was perfectly possible, Ivor and Rosalie went away to the south of France, then how would she feel? Desolate, she thought. Without Ivor, her life would become empty once more.

Could she be in love with him? Did she want to touch him, to kiss him? She had only ever kissed her family and her closest friends. Now, remembering how Vera had once let her brush out her long nut-brown hair and plant a kiss on the top of her head, Clemency felt the tears rush to her eyes again and she had to bite her lip to stem them.

7

After Marianne's first year of mourning was over, friends began to invite her to little suppers and away for weekends in the country. There was sometimes a single man, a bachelor or a widower, at the little suppers. She knew that they meant well, these people who sought to pair her off, that they believed a new love to be the only cure for the loss of the old, but inside she raged at their obtuseness. Why could they not see that she would never love again? What man could possibly compare to Arthur? And if, in all the wide world, there was one, then how could she lay herself open to such pain again?

She could see in their faces that they thought she should be getting better, that she should be starting not to mind so much. She suspected that they were growing impatient with her; it made her angry to wonder whether they were thinking: *After all, they were only married for a year.* They were waiting for her to go back to normal, she supposed, to revert to the person she had been before Arthur had died.

She had bad days and better days. On the bad days the fog of loss and depression weighed on her, and inside her a layer of darkness persisted, like a black striation in rock. She did not go out; on the very worst days she did not leave her bedroom. Yet, slowly, the bad days became less frequent. She supervised the running of the house, she ate and talked and was sociable enough to stop her sisters fussing too much. But she found something in common only with the bereaved, in whose eyes she glimpsed kinship. Those people who had not been touched by grief seemed to her naive, lacking an essential understanding.

In the April of 1912 the Merediths invited her to stay

at Rawdon Hall. 'Just a quiet little get-together,' Laura Meredith told her, but, arriving at the house, Marianne was dismayed to find it filled with fashionable, glittering couples.

Dressing for dinner and looking out of the window to the gardens and parkland, she remembered her previous visit to this house, the touch of Arthur's lips on the curve of her neck, and felt a surge of anger that memory could still be so vivid, so hurtful. Hadn't she endured enough? Hadn't she earned that small mercy, the power to forget?

Something made her ask her maid to help her change her dull grey dress for a gown of silvery silk and thread her chain of moonstones into the dark coils of her hair. At dinner a handsome, moustachioed man with slicked-back hair caught her eye, and smiled and raised his glass to her. *Teddy Fiske*, she thought, recalling the practised roué she had met in the garden on her earlier visit, and the way his hand had lingered too long as he had helped her up from her seat.

She let her gaze move on. A different face: she paused again. Much later she struggled to remember that moment. Had she known? Had she some inkling, perhaps, of how he would shape, mould, *distort* her life?

She had not. She noticed him because, in the constricted world in which she moved, he was unfamiliar. She noticed him also because there was something arresting about him — something angelic, perhaps, in the lightness of his hair and eyes against his tanned skin. And an impression of strength and power in his broad shoulders, and in the way he sat back in his seat, self-contained, quiet, watching.

After dinner the party seemed to fragment, two or three to the glasshouses to search, shrieking with amusement, for pineapples; others to play cards for high stakes; and the lovers, of course, pairing off to shadowy corners, or to lie on velvet sofas in little-used rooms.

Alone, Marianne wandered through the house. Turning a corner, her eye was caught by a gleam of white through an open door. Entering the room, she looked at the sculpture standing on a side table. Moonlight fell on four dancing marble figures. Flares of fabric and locks of hair had, in a moment of joy and abandonment, been turned to stone, as if by a basilisk's stare.

Hearing footsteps, she looked and saw Teddy Fiske.

'Mrs Leighton,' he said. His head cocked to one side as he studied her. 'All on your own?'

'As you see.'

He closed the door behind him. 'Such a pleasure to find you here.'

'Is it?'

He came to stand beside her. 'Cigarette?' He offered her his case, lit their cigarettes, and leaned against the edge of the table, looking out of the window. Smoke drifted along the shafts of moonlight; she had not put on the electric light.

He said, 'These weekends can be dull affairs, can't they? The same people, the same conversation.'

'Then why do you come?'

'I always hope for distraction.'

Distraction, she thought. *That's what I need.* Something new to cover over the memories, as one papers a wall. Something to make the layers of skin form into a scar, puckered and ugly, sealing off the heart.

She said coolly, 'What sort of distraction?'

'Oh, you know.' He stubbed out his cigarette. 'The usual sort.'

'Is there a usual sort?'

'Well, it's a matter of taste, I suppose. But one suits me more than others.' He glanced at her. 'You are not gambling, Mrs Leighton, and you are not dancing. So I assume that, like me, you find those things unsatisfactory.'

When she did not reply, he said softly, 'Might I suggest something different?'

He let his fingers trail over the back of her hand. She did not push him away, but stood motionless, passive, waiting. The palm of his hand ran up her arm; a fingertip sketched the curve of neck and shoulder. She wondered whether she felt anything at all. She wondered whether flesh would be able to stir flesh, as it had once done.

The door opened; the sudden light shocked her and she pulled away. The pale-eyed man she had noticed at dinner drawled, 'So sorry. I thought the room was empty.'

'*Melrose*,' muttered Teddy Fiske. 'You have damnably bad timing.'

Muttering a quick excuse, Marianne ran out of the room. Upstairs she locked her bedroom door behind her. She did not call for her maid, but tore off her dress and pulled the pins from her hair herself. Moonstones spilled to the rug, and she sat hunched on the bed, staring at them. If they had not been interrupted, what would she have done? Would she have stood there, as hard-hearted and unmoving as those stone girls, and let Teddy Fiske seduce her?

She heard a tap at the door, a voice murmured her name. She stared at the door handle as it moved up and down, suddenly afraid of herself, afraid of the grief and fury that bubbled and boiled inside her, that had made her, Marianne Leighton, the good wife and obedient daughter, burn to break rules, to shock, to provoke. Tonight, she had almost given herself to a man she did not care for. Whom she actually disliked. Such desperation, she thought, and knelt to gather the moonstones from the floor as she heard footsteps fading away from her door.

★ ★ ★

218

Her punishment was a tiresome game of hide-and-seek with Teddy Fiske. By the afternoon her head ached and her nerves were ragged, and she felt tired and out of sorts.

The weather was fine enough for tennis, so Laura Meredith decreed they make pairs. Marianne slipped away, darting between bushes and flower beds, heading for the sanctuary of the avenue of hornbeams. By the time she saw Mr Melrose standing at the entrance to the avenue, it was too late to avoid him.

He called out to her, 'Don't you play?'

'I detest tennis.' She glanced quickly back at the courts.

'Don't worry, I don't think your admirer saw you go.' His gaze rested on her. 'Unless you'd like him to come after you.'

'Certainly not.' She said hesitantly, 'Last night — '

'I apologize if I interrupted something.'

'You didn't. He's a loathsome man.'

'And the sort of fellow who fancies himself irresistible in tennis whites. His vanity won't allow him to pursue you.'

The bones of his face were finely drawn, and his mouth was curved and sensual. She noticed that his eyes were not blue, as she had supposed, but a pale, cloudy grey, the colour of moonstones. She said suddenly, passionately, 'This place — this house — I hate it!'

'Then why do you stay?'

'It passes the time.' She frowned. 'There. I sound like Mr Fiske. How abominable!'

'His ennui is practised — a pose. Yours is heartfelt.'

'I shall go home tomorrow. I should never have come. Please excuse me.'

The pleached hornbeams towered above her, their new leaves making yellow-green walls. Tears welled in her eyes; she forced them back as she hurried along the avenue.

She had meant to escape him, but she saw that he was keeping pace with her. 'I'm so sorry,' he said. 'How impolite of me. I can't recall whether I've been introduced to you. I'm Lucas Melrose.'

She told him her name. He said, 'You're widowed, aren't you?' and glanced at her quickly.

She said sharply, 'It's all right, Mr Melrose, you may be direct. I prefer it. So many hedge around the subject. Perhaps they're afraid of upsetting me. Perhaps they think that I might have forgotten my husband's death if they hadn't tactlessly reminded me.' She paused, gripping her parasol with both hands, once more afraid that she was splintering, fragmenting, no longer capable of abiding by the rules of polite society. 'I shouldn't have said that,' she muttered. 'I know people mean well. I should be grateful to them for their concern.'

'Should you?'

She was unnerved by his question and the directness of his gaze. 'Of course I should. It's not their fault that something terrible happened to me, so why should I be angry with them? The fault is in me that I am no longer content. That I find company . . . unsatisfactory.'

'This company in particular or all company?'

She began to walk faster, desperate for the solitude of her room. Then something in his expression shifted and he said, 'You must forgive me. I've annoyed you.'

She shook her head. 'It's not you, Mr Melrose. My husband, Arthur, died almost eighteen months ago. And people are forever telling me to pick up the pieces. As though my life could be glued together like a broken vase. I accepted the Merediths' invitation because I thought I should begin to make an effort. But I've realized that I'm not fit to be in company yet.'

'Perhaps you're trying to pick up the wrong pieces.'

'What do you mean?'

'Perhaps you're trying to remake your old life, which is impossible. Perhaps you should look for something different, something new.'

She considered. They were crossing the lawn, heading for the steps at the front of the house. She heard him say, 'But how impertinent of me to offer you advice. I assure you that I'm not usually so tedious, Mrs Leighton. I'm afraid I'm not quite myself at present.'

She said politely, 'I'm sorry to hear you're unwell, Mr Melrose.'

'Oh, I'm in perfect health. But horribly homesick.'

'Homesick for where?'

'For Ceylon.'

When she looked at him, surprised, he laughed and said, 'What were you expecting me to say? For Hampshire? Or Surrey?'

'*Ceylon.*' She thought that might explain his difference, and her instinct that he was, like herself, an outsider.

'I own a tea estate in the highlands,' he explained. 'And all this — ' his gaze swept over the lawns, the flower beds, oaks and beeches — 'all this seems pallid in comparison.'

'Have you always lived in Ceylon, Mr Melrose?'

'I was born there. I'm here for a few months, partly for business reasons, partly for personal ones.'

'Have you relations in England?'

'Scotland,' he corrected her. 'My family comes from Scotland, from near Aberdeen. Where do you come from, Mrs Leighton?'

They had reached the terrace. 'I was born in Sheffield,' said Marianne. 'Not as romantic as Ceylon, I'm afraid.'

At the front door of the house, they parted. He offered her his hand. She took it briefly: it felt cool and dry, as though the warmth of the day had not touched him.

★ ★ ★

A few days later, returning to London, Marianne heard the first news of the loss of the *Titanic*. Over the next few days the enormity of the tragedy unfolded. When the great ship, holed by an iceberg, had sunk, one thousand five hundred people had drowned. For the first time since Arthur's death, news from the outside world truly touched her. She found herself imagining the horror of that moment when those remaining on the ship must have realized that death was imminent and unavoidable. That final choice: when and how to die — clinging to the rail of the sinking ship as it began its long fall to the sea bed, or jumping from the prow into the waves. The last long flight through the empty air. Then the shock of ice-cold water in eyes, nose, mouth. Then nothing.

★   ★   ★

Earlier in the year Gabriel had left for the Continent. He had not asked Eva to go with him; instead, she had found herself saying: *Just for a few days — I could come with you as far as Dieppe.* She had hated the pleading tone in her voice. *Another time, poppet,* Gabriel had answered vaguely. *I promised old Max, you know?*

Val Crozier, Gabriel and Sadie's friend from Greenstones, sent Eva a note asking her to dine with him. She met him in a small café in Frith Street. From the glitter of his eyes and the slight clumsiness of his speech and gestures, she guessed that he had had several drinks before she arrived.

'Eva.' He gave her a noisy kiss on the cheek. 'How are you?'

'Very well.' They ordered steak and potatoes and a bottle of red wine. 'And you, Val?' she asked. 'What are you doing in London?'

'Nothing much. Just mooching around. I couldn't stand Greenstones any more.'

'How's Sadie?'

He shrugged. 'She's just the same.'

'I suppose she misses Gabriel.'

'I suppose so. And Max, perhaps.' He glanced at Eva. 'Not Nerissa, though, I shouldn't think.'

'Nerissa? Has she gone away as well?'

A widening of the eyes. 'Didn't you know?'

'Know what?'

'That Nerissa went to Spain with Gabriel and Max.'

Eva froze in the act of raising her glass. 'No. No, you're wrong, Val. It was just Gabriel and Max.'

He shook his head. 'Nerissa too. Quite a relief, really — we were all sick of the sight of her at Greenstones. You didn't know?'

Mutely, she shook her head. It was not possible that Gabriel had taken Nerissa with him. Val must have made a mistake. Gabriel could not have refused to take her and then taken Nerissa instead. Eva drank some wine and felt a little calmer. Even if Val was right, and Nerissa had gone with Max and Gabriel to Spain, there must be a perfectly reasonable explanation. Nerissa must have persuaded Gabriel to take her. She imagined Nerissa coaxing him in the little-girl voice she liked to affect: *Take me with you, Gabriel darling. I will be good, I pwomise.*

'I expect Nerissa nagged poor Gabriel,' she said. She was pleased that her voice was steady, that she had not betrayed her shock. 'And she does like to travel.'

'So Gabriel will be happy. Not Max, though.' Val sniggered. Eva noticed that his gaze continually flicked in her direction. He added, 'Wouldn't like to be a gooseberry with those three.'

'I don't understand — '

'Rather a tricky little *ménage à trois*.' Now she saw the naked contempt in his eyes. 'You do know that Max is in love with Nerissa, don't you?'

'But he's always so — so *unpleasant* to her!'

223

'Hides a broken heart. The poor sap has been besotted with her for years,' said Val nastily. He poured more wine into their glasses, spilling some so that it left a dark crimson smear on the tablecloth. 'So you see what I'm saying.'

'No, not really.' Yet there was the sudden certainty that she was going to hear something terrible. She would have liked to clap her hands over her ears or run out of the café.

Val gave a little smile. 'Gabriel always sleeps with his models, of course. And his ex-models. Everyone knows that.'

She stared at him. Then she shook her head violently. '*No.*'

He blinked. 'You mean I've got it wrong? That you and Gabriel aren't sleeping together?'

She felt herself flush. But she said coldly, 'That's my business.'

'Is it? Sadie's business too, I'd have thought.'

She looked away, clenching her hands under the table. 'I'd never want to hurt Sadie,' she whispered. 'You know that. Gabriel and I — we've never — '

But she broke off, unable to complete the sentence. *Gabriel always sleeps with his models.* Could it be true? Even if Gabriel had loved Nerissa in the past — and now, recalling the seductive beauty of the *Girl in a Red Dress* paintings, she saw how foolish she had been not to have guessed — it did not mean that they were lovers now. Trust was a part of love and she must trust Gabriel.

Yet Gabriel had admitted to her that he had loved several women. Faithfulness was unimportant to him; more than that — he despised it. Having already betrayed his wife, why not betray his mistress as well?

But she managed to say, 'Not *Nerissa.* Not *now.* That's what I meant.'

'Oh, Eva.' An expression of feigned sympathy. 'Oh

dear. I thought you knew. How careless of me to let it slip.' Then his voice hardened. 'And how stupid of you not to realize.'

'It's not true — '

'Ask Max — ask Bobbin — if you don't believe me. Of course they're still lovers.'

There was the possibility that nothing was as she had believed it to be, that Gabriel had betrayed her and that they had both betrayed Sadie. She felt a deep wave of shame wash over her. She whispered, 'Why are you telling me this?'

'Because I thought you'd like to know.' Val lit a cigarette. 'You could always ask Sadie. If you have the gall, that is.' He shrugged. 'Sadie was clever. She was the only one of Gabriel's women to realize that he'd never marry her if she went to bed with him first. So she held out until she had a ring on her finger.'

The bitterness in his voice made her look up at him, and suddenly she understood. '*You* are in love with her. You are in love with Sadie.'

He gave a twisted grin. 'Of course I am. Why did you think I hang around? You didn't think I was another of Gabriel's acolytes, did you?' His expression soured. 'Much good may it do me. Funny, isn't it? You are in love with Gabriel and Max is in love with Nerissa and I'm in love with Sadie. It's like one of those bloody awful country dances Bobbin is so keen on. The rotten thing is that Nerissa lets Max into her bed often enough to keep him on a string, whereas Sadie won't have anything to do with me. Good old Val, who feeds the pigs and keeps the children quiet. That's all *I* am.'

She whispered, 'And Sadie?'

'Oh, Sadie has only ever loved Gabriel.' His lip curled. 'I'm not sure she even cares that much about the brats. She adores Gabriel, always has done. She'll do anything to keep him. Have a litter of his kids, live out in the middle of nowhere. Even put up with his mistresses staying in her house.' His lids shuttered, half-masking the coldness and cruelty of his expression. 'Sometimes I'm glad he hurts her,' he muttered. 'Sometimes I'm glad he humiliates her. It means she knows what it's like, doesn't it? To love someone who doesn't care tuppence about your happiness.'

★   ★   ★

Marianne had spent the morning with Patricia Letherby when, returning home, she saw Lucas Melrose standing at the corner of the street. Catching sight of her, his eyes widened and he crossed the road to her. 'Mrs Leighton. What a remarkable — and pleasant — coincidence.'

'Mr Melrose.' She felt ruffled. Because one slotted a person into a particular place, she thought, and so Mr Melrose belonged to Rawdon Hall and not to Norfolk Square. She asked, 'Do you have business in London?'

'I've just escaped from a very long morning with my agents in Mincing Lane. I needed some fresh air, so I thought I'd explore. But I'm afraid I'm a wretchedly ignorant colonial because I seem to have got myself hopelessly lost.'

'Can I help you? Which street were you looking for?'

'Not a street, a park. I wanted to see Hyde Park. Perhaps you'd be kind enough to tell me the way.'

'It's not far at all. At the end of this road you must turn right — no, left — ' her hands darted first to one side, then to the other — 'no, it's right, I'm sure of it . . .'

'Mrs Leighton.' His smile widened. 'Being an incorrigible bachelor, I claim no great acquaintance with women, but I have noticed that the fairer sex often struggles with directions.'

'My husband used to laugh at me,' she admitted. 'I never could manage to read the map for him when he

226

was driving. We used to get horribly lost.'

'Then I have a suggestion. If you'd do me the honour of walking with me to the park, then there'd be no need to bother with lefts and rights.'

When she hesitated, he made a quick, deprecatory gesture. 'There, I'm being presumptuous, aren't I? I hope you'll forgive me, Mrs Leighton. I'm just a rough old planter who must mend his manners.'

'Not at all.' She was ashamed of her lack of generosity. Making an effort, she smiled at him. 'In fact, I could do with some fresh air too. I've spent the last three hours at a meeting of the Snowdrop Society. That's what we widows do — we sit on committees and endure interminable meetings planning flag days or arranging little concerts. I write the minutes. My friend, Mrs Letherby, persuaded me to act as secretary to the committee. I think she thought that I'd benefit from an occupation. That it would take my mind off things.'

'And does it?'

'Not at all.' They were walking along Sussex Gardens. 'My mind wanders dreadfully and afterwards I discover that my notes are almost illegible. Have you ever tried inventing the minutes to a meeting?'

He laughed. 'I haven't, I'm afraid. I spend most of my time outdoors — there aren't many meetings or committees on a tea estate.'

'Then you're fortunate.'

'If you don't care for charity work, what do you prefer to do?'

'Oh, I call on my friends and relatives and I run my house and I go to church every Sunday.' Catching his glance, she muttered, 'I ought to be content with my life. I know that it's a great deal easier than most people's.'

'But you're not content, are you?'

'No, Mr Melrose, I am not content,' she said and regretted the confidence immediately. She felt the need

227

to pull back, to distance herself from him. To admit her misery to a man she hardly knew seemed inappropriate, overly intimate.

But he said only, 'Perhaps you need a change.'

'It may be different in Ceylon, Mr Melrose, but in England a woman such as myself hasn't a great deal of choice in how she may spend her time. It's not as if I had any talent. I used to play the piano, but I haven't touched it for more than a year. And, as I've said, charitable work bores me. I suppose that's very selfish of me, but it's true.'

'I didn't mean pastimes. I meant, what would you do if you could do anything?'

If I could do anything, she thought, with a stab of longing, *then I would wipe away the past and have Arthur here, at my side.* But she said, 'None of us really does as we wish, do we? Other things — duties and obligations and misfortunes — prevent us.'

'I do as I wish.'

'Then, as I said before, you're lucky.'

'I've never believed in luck.' A curl of the mouth and something feral in the narrowed grey eyes, as he said, 'You must decide what you want and then take it.'

'That sounds . . . ruthless.'

'Does it?' Once before at Rawdon Hall she had noticed his sudden change of mood. Now his expression seemed to lighten, and his smile became gently encouraging. 'I don't mean to be fierce. Merely to point out that life is short and one should please oneself if possible. So, if you could do anything, anything at all, Mrs Leighton, then what would it be?'

The opaque grey gaze settled on her, demanding an answer. She plucked one out of the air to satisfy him, to stave off questions, to hide from him the void that had remained in her since Arthur's death.

'I suppose I should like to travel.'

'Trips to the Lake District . . . or something further afield?'

'I hadn't thought.'

'Then perhaps you should. Perhaps you should see the world, Mrs Leighton.'

'I couldn't possibly — '

'Why not? One only needs the fare for the ship. Unless — '

'Yes, Mr Melrose?'

'You'll say that I'm being impertinent again.'

'I promise I won't be offended.'

'I was going to say, unless your husband didn't leave you well provided for.'

'Arthur left me very well provided for.'

'Then you're fortunate, Mrs Leighton.'

'Am I?' She felt a surge of anger. 'I would happily exchange every penny I have for just one more day with Arthur!'

'I'm sorry. I've annoyed you again.'

'No.' She sighed. 'Not at all. It's only that a great many people seem to find money so interesting and spend so much of their time amassing it, yet it seems to me . . . unimportant.'

When he did not reply, she said, 'You think I'm spoiled — indulged — to disdain wealth when so many are in want.'

'I think that you forget what money can do. Or — ' once more, he flashed a smile at her; she saw white, even teeth — 'or perhaps you haven't had the opportunity to find out. Money gives you a choice. It allows you to do things you wouldn't otherwise be able to do. That's its importance. And I don't mean to labour the point, but I should have thought that seeing the world might be more interesting than sitting on committees.'

They were strolling along the gravel paths she had so often walked with Arthur. Marianne said slowly, 'I'm not sure I have the courage.'

'To travel alone?'

She had meant: *I'm not sure I have the courage to start again, to leave my home, to challenge myself. All that takes a spirit, an energy, which I seem to have lost, and that I'm not sure I ever had in great measure.*

'You told me you had many relatives,' he said. 'Couldn't one of them travel with you?'

'All my brothers and sisters have busy lives of their own.'

'Mrs Meredith travels a great deal, I believe.' He glanced at her. 'You don't consider her a close friend, I suppose? No, there's a superficiality about Laura Meredith that I suspect wouldn't appeal to you.'

'Laura's a generous hostess. And she was very kind to me after my husband's death. It's just that she's not — *I'm* not . . . ' Marianne broke off. 'As I told you before, Mr Melrose, the fault's in myself. I do not seek out closeness.'

'Well then,' he said, 'you'd like to travel. Is there anything else you'd like, Mrs Leighton?'

Two little girls were bowling hoops near the Round Pond. Toy yachts bobbed on the water and small boys in sailor suits crouched at the edge of the pond, clapping their hands in excitement. Watching them, Marianne felt a wave of longing so intense that she closed her eyes momentarily, almost giddy.

She gave a light laugh. 'I really have no idea,' she said, as she put up her parasol to shade her face. 'And I seem to have talked about myself at great length when I would far rather hear about you. And Ceylon. Tell me about Ceylon, Mr Melrose.'

★　★　★

In the December of 1911 Iris had completed her probationary period and become a fully qualified nurse.

Several of the other girls in her set had left the hospital soon after qualifying. Charlotte took a job as a private nurse in Belgium. Seeing her friend onto the boat train at Victoria, Iris hugged her hard, knowing how much she would miss her. Charlotte's plain face, beneath a sadly unflattering hat, was stained with tears. She gripped Iris's hand. 'You will write to me, won't you? You must promise that you'll write to me!'

Iris herself had remained at the Mandeville. The newly qualified nurses were given four weeks' holiday. In January Iris had gone home to Summerleigh, where she caught up with old friends, went to dances and dinners and to a succession of parties. It was a delight to be at no one's beck and call and an unaccustomed, almost sinful, pleasure to sleep for as long as she wanted in the mornings.

Yet after a fortnight something began to grate. Mornings spent trimming hats and helping Clemency in the house seemed painfully long. She felt herself slipping back, chained once more by the benevolent surveillance that was the lot of every middleclass daughter. She realized that she was missing the Mandeville, and wondered whether she was turning into that dreary creature, the hospital nurse, with her bunions and her red, raw hands and her brisk, sensible smile.

She could not pinpoint the moment at which she had begun to enjoy nursing. It seemed to have crept up on her gradually, in odd moments at first, and then with a realization that an hour, a morning, and eventually a whole day had flown by almost without her noticing. And then Arthur had died. The importance of cleanliness and asepsis, hammered into every probationer's head by every ward sister at the Mandeville, had been made hideously real by the tragedy and futility of Arthur's death. And though nursing might still sometimes be loathsome, it was rarely boring. She had discovered that she hated to be bored. When she recalled her life before nursing, it seemed so constrained, so lacking in incident. Away from the hospital, she missed the banter with the patients and the variety and bustle of life on the ward. She missed the camaraderie of the other nurses. She missed being useful, and being needed.

Towards the end of April Eva came to see her. The grey, rainy weather mirrored the gloomy cast of Eva's expression. Eva had forgotten her umbrella and locks of her dark hair clung to her face in soaked rat's tails. She sat on Iris's bed in the nurses' home, half-heartedly drying her hair as a soupy light seeped through the window and rain lashed against the glass.

The contents of Iris's sewing box trailed across the bed: lengths of ribbon and lace, pearl-headed pins, and a silver thimble. Choosing a reel of thread, Iris said, 'Tell me what's wrong.'

'Nothing's wrong.'

'Eva.' Iris took a hat out of a box.

'It's my painting. I've worked till midnight these past few nights, but everything I do is hopeless.'

Iris didn't believe Eva for a minute. Eva wasn't the sort to look that miserable because of work. But she said, 'Perhaps you should take a break.'

'How can I possibly do that?' cried Eva angrily. 'That's the last thing I can do!'

Eva looked awful, Iris thought, white-faced and pink-lidded, as if she had been crying for days. 'Why don't you go home for a while?'

'Home?'

'Yes, why not? It may be dull, but at least you get your meals cooked for you and your bed made for you. And you always like seeing Clemmie and James.'

'Yes, but Father — '

'I don't see why you're always so hard on Father.'

'Because I know — ' Eva pressed her lips together.

'You know?' Iris threaded her needle. 'What do you know, Eva?'

Muffled by the towel, Eva said coldly, 'He's a liar and a cheat. That's why I'm hard on him.'

'*Eva*.'

'He is. It's true.' The towel was lowered; Iris saw that Eva was on the verge of tears again. Then she whispered, 'I *saw* him.'

'Saw him what?'

There was a long silence. Eva twisted a lock of hair into a tight, hard knot. She said dully, 'I saw Father with Mrs Carver.'

'Mrs Carver?' It took Iris a moment or two to place the name. 'The widow with the lovely hair? And the two plain daughters who have freckles?'

'I saw them kiss. Twice, actually.'

'Oh.' Iris delved into her bag of trimmings.

'Is that all you can say? *Oh*?' Eva sounded furious. 'So you thought they were having a love affair?'

'Of course they were! I expect they still are!'

'A kiss isn't necessarily an affair.'

Eva snorted. Iris took two ribbons out of the bag. 'I've kissed plenty of men, but I haven't had an affair with any of them. It was just — kisses. Just a bit of fun. It never meant anything.'

Eva bit her lip. 'It was the *way* they kissed.'

'When did this happen?'

'The summer we met Ash.'

Ash. The garden at Summerleigh, after the rain. She had kissed Ash. And then he had said: *Oh, Iris, what would we talk about, you and I?*

'Aren't you shocked, Iris?' cried Eva. 'Don't you think it's awful?'

She considered, found she wasn't, not really — perhaps she should have been, but there it was — and said tactfully, 'Awful for you, of course.'

'And awful for Mother! What if she found out? It would kill her!'

'Do you think so?' Iris thought of Lilian, pale and fragile and untouchable. 'I don't suppose Father and Mother have had a proper marriage for years. Not since Philip was born.'

'I don't see that that justifies — '

'No. But it makes it more understandable, perhaps.' Iris held the two ribbons against the navy blue hat. 'The pale pink or the fuchsia? Which do you think?'

Eva looked enraged. 'Honestly, Iris! You're so — so unreasonable sometimes!'

'I daresay. But still. Now you must help me. You're better at colours than me. And I spent a fortune on this hat and navy blue can be so difficult.'

'The fuchsia,' Eva muttered.

Iris cut a length of dark pink ribbon. 'Father likes to have people around him, doesn't he? He hates to be by himself. And Mother hasn't been much company for years.'

'That's hardly her fault! She's ill!'

There was a measurable pause before Iris said, 'Of course.'

Eva stared at her. 'Sometimes I think you disagree with me on purpose.'

'Eva, *think*. What are Mother's symptoms? A rash? Vomiting? Fever?' She shook her head. 'None of those.'

'You think she's *pretending* — '

'No, not at all. Mother believes she's ill and so she is, in a way.'

'No one would choose to be like Mother!'

'Wouldn't they? It's not so bad a life. Mother's illness means that everyone's at her beck and call. We go out of our way not to trouble her. And she's free from all domestic duties. Well, I can perfectly understand that writing the grocery order for a family of ten might begin to pall after a while. Mother's an intelligent woman, but what outlet has she ever had for her cleverness? She could neither go to college like you nor take up a profession like me.' Iris folded the ribbon into a rosette.

'You surely can't think that Mother's taken to her bed for the last twelve years because — because she's fed up — or bored?'

'It is rather extreme, isn't it? But then perhaps we're a rather extreme family.' Iris glanced at Eva — Eva, in her ragbag of brightly coloured wools and velvets, Eva, whom for some time Iris had suspected of being in love with some perfectly unsuitable man. 'Perhaps we only pretend to be conventional,' she said coolly. 'Perhaps each of us has our secrets.'

Eva flushed and looked away. Iris began to stitch the rosette onto the hat. 'I should have thought you of all people, Eva, might understand the lengths a woman might have to go to to have control over her own life. You're forever pointing out to me how powerless we are because we don't have the vote.'

'Well, so we are!'

'Mother's illness has given her power over the family. Not one of us — not even Father — dares disobey her openly. We all go on tiptoe and if any of us crosses her she has a bad turn and we feel full of guilt. And then there's Clemency. She loved school, yet she gave it up without a fuss because Mother needed her.'

'That's hardly unreasonable. Why should poor Mother be left alone?'

'And if Clemency had not agreed — or if we had been only three sisters — what then? Would you have given up art college and all chance of a career for Mother?'

Eva reddened. 'You think I'm selfish — '

Iris put down the hat. She said gently, 'You're no more selfish than I am. Goodness me, I took up *nursing* to escape Mother. Out of the frying pan, one might say.' After a silence she went on, 'When I was last at home I spoke to Mother. She's been having the same treatment for more than a decade — bed rest, isolation, only one visitor at a time — and none of it seems to have done her any good. I put it to her that she might consider a change of treatment. I was very gentle, very tactful. The room was like an oven, so I suggested she might feel better if she had some fresh air and exercise. Nothing too strenuous to start with — just a stroll in the garden at first, and then a little more each day to build up her strength.'

'What did Mother say?'

'She told me I was heartless. Well, she's not the first person to accuse me of that.' Iris recalled the hot gloom of Lilian's room and the clutter of medicine bottles on the dressing table. 'Mother takes laudanum and port wine every day. They're very old-fashioned treatments and the patient tends to have to take more and more to have an effect. If she could stop taking them, she might not feel in such a fug all the time. She might think more clearly and feel stronger. But when I explained that, Mother told me she had palpitations and felt faint. She wouldn't let me take her pulse and poor Clemency had to spend the rest of the morning calming her down. And after that — ' Iris picked up the hat again and squinted at it — 'I gave up.'

Eva said obstinately, 'I still don't think that excuses Father.'

'I wouldn't dream of suggesting that it does. But illness suits Mother. For one thing, it's meant that she doesn't have to have any more babies.'

'Babies?' Eva looked confused.

'Poor Mother. Seven of us in . . . how many years? Fourteen? That's a baby every other year. And I dare say she had a few miscarriages, besides. I see women like that in the hospital. They have one baby after another, and they never know good health because they're always either expecting a baby or have just given birth or are nursing one. Not long ago I nursed a woman who was in hospital to have her tenth. It was a difficult birth and after the infant was born she didn't even want to look at it.' Iris sighed. 'Oh, Eva, Father isn't perfect — I've yet to meet the man who is. You thought he was perfect when you were a little girl, and then you learned, in a rather horrible way, that he isn't. But he's not a bad man. Just flawed, like the rest of us.' She gave the hat a tweak and, standing in front of the mirror, tried it on. 'Have you told any of the others about Father and Mrs Carver?'

Eva shook her head violently. 'Of course not. I didn't mean to tell you.'

'Good. You mustn't.' Iris studied her reflection. 'What do you think? Rather chic, or does it look like a coal scuttle?'

★   ★   ★

Lucas Melrose's tea estate in Ceylon was called Blackwater. 'Blackwater was the name of the Scottish hamlet my grandfather originated from,' he explained to Marianne. Archibald Melrose, Lucas's grandfather, had been one of five brothers. The Aberdeenshire farm on which he had been born was too small to support such a large family, so Archibald had decided to seek his fortune elsewhere. He had arrived in Ceylon in the 1830s. 'I think he fell in love with the island,' Lucas said. 'He'd meant to stay a few years, make his fortune and then return to Scotland. In the end, he never went back. Ceylon has a magic, an enchantment. The Muslim traders who came to it centuries ago called it Serendib, the island of jewels.'

Archibald had spent six months working in a sawmill in Colombo before going on to work in a coffee-pulping house in Kandy. Eventually he amassed enough money to buy land in the hill country. He had planted his estate with coffee, prospering, like so many other Europeans, in the coffee boom of the 1850s. Archibald married, and had a son, George. Through careful husbandry and investment Blackwater had increased in size until, at Archibald's death, the Melroses had owned over three hundred acres of land.

After coffee blight struck the island in the 1870s, many of the estates went bankrupt. Not Blackwater, though. George Melrose hung on by the skin of his teeth, through tenacity and sheer hard work, and because he had the foresight to switch quickly enough from coffee to tea. 'I was twenty when my father died,' Lucas Melrose told Marianne. 'He was just fifty. He'd worked from dawn to dusk for decades — he'd worked himself to death. He'd felled trees and hacked away undergrowth with his bare hands, he'd shot rogue elephants when they trampled the tea plants and he'd built the bungalow that I now live in. There was nothing my father wouldn't do. It's because of him that I still own my estate, when so many others were bought up by tea companies after the blight. Because my father refused to let anyone take what was his.'

He took from his jacket pocket a leather billfold. 'Would you like to see my home, Mrs Leighton?'

He handed her a photograph of a whitewashed one-storeyed building set among gardens. At the front of the bungalow was a hexagonal porch; through the open doors Marianne had a glimpse of a cool, dark interior with palms, cane furniture and white-robed servants.

'You'd like my garden,' he said. 'My mother planted the roses. They're sadly neglected now, I'm afraid. I know what to do with tea, but not with roses. When my mother was alive, the roses were glorious.'

'Did your mother pass away recently?'

'I lost her a long time ago.'

'I'm sorry.'

238

His eyes narrowed into slits of crystalline grey. 'Blackwater's five miles from the nearest town,' he said. 'In truth, I don't suppose you'd think it merited the name of town. There's a railway station and a bazaar with a post office and a few shops. Apart from my own, the only other houses on the estate are my managers' bungalows and the coolies' lines. Sometimes, in the middle of the day, all you can hear is birdsong and the whisper of the leaves in the trees.'

His voice held her. 'It sounds,' she murmured, 'like paradise.'

'Oh it is.' There was a look of longing in his eyes. 'I have over five hundred acres planted with tea. I own another fifty or so acres which have been left barren because the hillside's too steep or rocky to be planted, or the forest's too dense. And yes, it's paradise. I've always thought of Blackwater as my paradise.'

★ ★ ★

The housemaid's, Edith's, hands were now so badly swollen with rheumatism that Clemency had taken over helping Great-aunt Hannah dress in the mornings. The old lady was invariably in her petticoat and stays by the time Clemency tapped on her door at half-past seven; Clemency sometimes found herself wondering whether Great-aunt Hannah ever took her stays off, or whether perhaps she slept in them. Clemency buttoned Hannah into her gown, which was made of a rusty greenish-black material so old it had begun to crack and fray at the seams, and helped her put on her stockings and shoes. While she was dressing, Great-aunt Hannah talked about this and that. Because she was often hazy about who exactly Clemency was, muddling her up with Marianne and Eva or with her own long-dead sisters, and because she spoke of events that might have happened yesterday but might equally well have

239

happened eighty years ago, Clemency had to concentrate hard to follow the conversation. After Hannah was dressed, after Clemency had found the old lady her handkerchief and her cachous and her lace gloves, and had sat her in her chair by the window, they were both exhausted, and Hannah often took a little nap while Clemency dashed to the kitchen to check that Mother's breakfast tray was ready.

It was Hannah's birthday in May. No one knew how old Hannah was — even Hannah herself was unsure — and Clemency couldn't think what present to give a person of such immeasurable age.

She confided her problem to Ivor, who had just returned from a month with his wife in Switzerland. They were in the teashop that they had come to think of as their own. 'We usually give Great-aunt Hannah handkerchieves or soap,' Clemency explained, 'but she has a drawerful of handkerchieves and plenty of soap. And Eva always buys her writing paper, and I bought a new lead for Winnie last year — and it's not as though Winnie goes out much any more because she's so fat.'

Ivor said, 'Perhaps a treat rather than a present. I always adore treats.'

'Me too.' She smiled at him. It was a source of delight to her that they had so much in common.

'Such a treat,' he said, 'to be here with you.' He slid his hand across the table and their fingers interlinked. He had beautifully shaped, long, thin fingers — musician's fingers, Clemency thought.

'I missed you,' she said.

'And I missed you *terribly*. Switzerland — I detest it. So unutterably dreary.'

'I've always thought it sounded rather nice. I've never really seen a mountain. Derbyshire doesn't count, does it?'

The waitress was approaching their table; Ivor withdrew his hand. He said vaguely, 'I suppose the mountains are rather splendid. But such a grim hotel and no one to talk to.'

'You had Rosalie.'

'Rosalie and I don't talk. Not really. Not like us.'

Clemency loved it when Ivor said *us*. It made her feel that she was important to him. Ivor was so clever and talented, he had so many friends, from the coterie of women who regularly attended his concerts to the London friends he visited on the rare occasions when Rosalie could do without him for a day or two. Although, since her quarrel with Vera, Clemency had known that she loved Ivor, she had at first been unsure of his feelings for her. Then, one day, they had been walking in the Botanical Gardens and he had raised her hand to his mouth and kissed it. 'Do you mind?' he had asked and she had shaken her head. Ivor looked relieved. 'I've been wanting to kiss you for ages, but I wasn't sure whether you'd mind.'

Since then he had kissed her several times on the mouth, a fleeting brush of the lips, like a feather's touch. Though, because of their responsibilities, they were never able to spend much time together — half an hour, perhaps, once or twice a month — those half hours seemed to Clemency quite perfect. If it was fine, they walked in the Botanical Gardens; if it was raining, they went to the little teashop on Ecclesall Road. The teashop was dingy, with brown oilcloth covering the tables and chipped cream-coloured crockery. No one they knew ever went there. Clemency supposed she should have felt guilty, sitting with a married man in a teashop and holding his hand beneath the table, but she did not.

Sometimes Ivor looked at Clemency in an intense sort of way and said, 'If it wasn't for Rosalie . . . ' He never finished the sentence, but she supposed that if he had, then it would have been to say that if it wasn't for Rosalie, then they could have married. Gradually

241

Clemency's dislike of Rosalie had turned to loathing. Previously she wouldn't have thought it possible to loathe someone you had never met. Every now and then Ivor made a vague suggestion that she come to tea at his house and meet Rosalie, suggestions that were never followed up by an invitation. In place of meeting the real person, Clemency conjured up her own picture of Rosalie, imagining her pretty in a blonde, fragile way, a woman who spent a great deal of her time reclining on a sofa or chaise longue, surrounded by medicine bottles.

When Clemency thought of how Rosalie constantly demanded Ivor's time and attention, and how she leached from him his time and energy, time that he could have spent nurturing his talent, she felt a surge of rage. She imagined telling Rosalie what she really thought of her, berating her for her selfishness. The words would flow from her with a fluency that she did not possess in real life, and Rosalie would weep and apologize and promise to be less self-centred in future.

More and more often, though, this fantasy was being replaced by a different one, in which the tiresome Rosalie suffered a particularly bad coughing fit or a sudden fever. Clemency pictured herself comforting Ivor, who, poor love, would be distraught if Rosalie died. She would put her arms round him and would stroke his hair and then, of course, they would kiss. And then (the exact progress of events was hazy) they would marry and live in Ivor's cottage in Hathersage, and she would look after him and he would be able to write his concerto at last. In time, they would have a baby or two. Perhaps, if Ivor preferred, they would move to London, where they would live in a lovely little mews house. She would keep house and he would give concerts. It would be perfect.

Though her fantasies were pleasurable and satisfying, after letting herself indulge in them, Clemency always felt guilty and ashamed. She knew that it was wrong to imagine someone's death, and a wicked thing to *wish* for someone's death. Yet on the days that Ivor looked particularly tired and despondent, her dislike of Rosalie was so fervent that she could almost have throttled her herself. Sometimes it frightened her, the depth of her loathing for Rosalie. It was as though, in the years since she had left school, she had lived a half-life, rarely feeling anything at all very deeply. She seemed to be waking up, coming alive again. Before she had met Ivor her strongest emotions had been for her closest friends, for Vera especially. Yet she had not seen Vera for months; Vera had not invited her to her wedding later in the year. That Vera's neglect did not hurt as much as it once might have was, Clemency knew, because of Ivor.

Taking Ivor's advice, she decided to give Great-aunt Hannah an outing in the motor car for a birthday treat. Father and James had to heave the old lady into the motor car, and Clemency drove very slowly and carefully. They were halfway down the hill, when Hannah said, 'Such a splendid machine! It reminds me of the first time I travelled on a train. So extraordinary, to see the trees and houses fly by so fast.' Through the mesh of her veil Clemency could see the gleam of delight in Hannah's eyes.

★ ★ ★

Marianne found herself looking forward to Lucas Melrose's visits. She hadn't realized how routine her days had become, and how much she had needed distraction. She was never quite sure why he visited her. Because he was lonely, she concluded, because he was far from home and had no family and few friends in England. It crossed her mind, of course, that he might be attracted to her. If he was, he gave little indication of it. He was always formal, never flirtatious, always addressed her as Mrs Leighton and never asked if he might call her Marianne. He never touched her except to take her hand on meeting and leaving, or to help her into a cab. His visits were short and not so frequent as to become tiresome.

Mostly he talked to her about Ceylon. 'The moment your ship docks at Colombo,' he told her, 'the difference assaults you. Even the air you breathe is different. It's warm, naturally, because Ceylon's a tropical island only a few degrees north of the equator, but it's not the warmth of an English summer's day. It's a balmier, headier warmth. The air is perfumed with the smell of the sea and it seems to be soaked in spices. And then there are all the strange sounds, the chatter of the mynah birds and monkeys, the hawkers calling out their wares, and the beggars imploring you to find them a cent or two. In the city there's a crush of motor cars and bicycles and bullock carts. And, if you're lucky, maybe you'll see an elephant.'

'An *elephant*!' she exclaimed.

'I use them on the estate for pulling heavy loads. Have you ever seen an elephant, Mrs Leighton?'

'Yes, at the zoo.'

'Have you ridden on one?'

'Never. Have you?'

'Many times. I wouldn't recommend it after a substantial meal. It's choppier than a small boat.'

She laughed.

He said, 'And the colours — '

'I remember you told me that England seemed pallid.'

'England has a beauty of its own, of course.'

'I sense that you're being polite, Mr Melrose. That your heart's in Ceylon.'

'You've found me out. Well, there are the colours of the fruitsellers' stalls at the roadside — huge green jackfruit, and yellow bananas and golden king coconuts. And the streets always seem to be decked with flags

— the statues outside the Hindu temples are so gorgeously painted that they make your English churches look drab by comparison.' He smiled. 'The hill country is different to the lowlands, though. The first planters settled there because it reminded them of Scotland. There are conifer forests and thickets of azaleas and rhododendrons. There's always a mist over the treetops and, in the distance, the hills are blue. The air becomes cooler as the railway line climbs into the mountains through the cloud forest. The track curves so sharply and rises so steeply that to look out of the window would make you dizzy. Yet the native boys delight in hanging from the open doors of the carriages as they go over the chasms. *They* are not frightened. Or they like to test their fear, perhaps, to hone it. It's only the interlopers, the Europeans, who are afraid the train might lose its grip and fall.'

'And you, Mr Melrose? Are you afraid to look out of the window?'

'Not at all. I like to see the edges of the world.'

One afternoon they visited the Tate Gallery. Marianne had had a raw, dreadful night (crimson footprints on a white rug, and the terrible emptiness of the bed when she woke) and, walking through the gallery, she felt exhausted and despairing. The paintings seemed to her the stuff of nightmare, the portraits distorted and garishly coloured, and the landscapes arid and ugly.

After leaving the gallery, they strolled along the Embankment. She could never afterwards remember how the conversation had begun, or how it had shifted, in small stages, to the offering of confidences. She had been miserable and tired, she supposed, and her defences had been down. Perhaps, noticing her pallor, he had made some enquiry, had murmured something well meaning to comfort her. But a door had opened, a

245

floodgate had burst, and the words had poured out of her.

She told him about Arthur. Their courtship and marriage, his death. 'I'm not sure whether what I feel is grief,' she said. 'If it is, then it's not what I thought grief was. Mostly, I feel angry.'

'Angry? With whom?'

'With everyone.'

'I can't believe that. Not you.'

'Arthur's death was meaningless, the consequence of a stupid accident. If he had died for some great cause — if he had died for his country or for the people he loved — then perhaps there would have been some comfort in that. But he died for nothing. Quite often I'm angry with God, or at least I would be if I still thought he existed. Friends try to comfort me by telling me that Arthur is with God now, and all I can think is that if that's so, then God must be cruel and very selfish.' She looked at him. 'Have I shocked you, Mr Melrose?'

'I'm not easily shocked. Nor as much given to platitudes as, it seems, some of your friends are.'

'And sometimes,' she went on slowly, 'I'm even angry with Arthur. I'm angry with him for leaving me when he promised me he wouldn't. He made me love him and then he left me. And I'm angry with him for not letting me call the doctor sooner. He didn't want to admit there was anything wrong with him. I think he felt that asking for help was a sign of weakness.'

'That's a fault of our sex. And of our nationality, perhaps.'

'The stiff upper lip,' she said bitterly. 'Oh yes, Arthur was a true English gentleman. And it killed him, Mr Melrose, it killed him.' She paused, then she said more quietly, 'But most of all, I'm angry with myself. For my weakness, my lack of any useful skills. Nothing in all my ridiculous upbringing prepared me for Arthur's death. I was made to be decorative, not to be useful. Others might have saved him, but not *me*.'

'You think too harshly of yourself, Mrs Leighton. You have many admirable qualities. The first time we spoke, at Rawdon Hall, I noticed your gentleness, your sweetness.'

Later, alone in the Norfolk Square house, Marianne felt embarrassed by her loquaciousness. She wondered whether Lucas Melrose would visit her again. Perhaps, shocked and repulsed by her atheism and her self-pity, he would return to his island paradise, brushing the English dust from the soles of his shoes with relief.

The fine weather vanished overnight. The following morning Marianne woke to the sound of rain hammering against the window. She noticed a difference in Lucas Melrose when he called on her in the afternoon. He seemed edgy, nervous. The cup and saucer trembled as he accepted them from her, and a little tea spilled into the saucer.

They spoke of the weather, of their mutual acquaintances, and of his visit to the theatre the previous night. Then he said abruptly, 'I came here today to ask you . . .' Breaking off, he rose from his seat and went to the window.

'What would you like to ask me, Mr Melrose?'

The clouds seemed to press down from the sky, trapping the streets in a grey pocket of smoke and rain. His knuckles were white where he gripped the sill.

'I came here to ask you, Mrs Leighton,' he said, 'whether you would consider marrying me.'

8

Eva longed for Gabriel to come home. If she could only see him, speak to him, find out the truth. Yet he remained absent, his sole communication a hastily scribbled postcard. *Ask Max, ask Bobbin*, Val had said to her. But Max was with Gabriel, and she did not know where Bobbin lived.

Ask Sadie, Val had then said, *if you have the gall*. She could never have asked Sadie about Nerissa, of course. It was hard, waking in the night, to work out which was worse — that Gabriel might be Nerissa's lover, or that Sadie might know that she herself was Gabriel's lover. One filled her with rage and despair, the other with an overwhelming shame.

At college her concentration drifted as she weighed up her affair with Gabriel. In her drawings folds of fabric bulged, unnaturally stiff, and hands drooped, the fingers boneless and misshapen. Sometimes she rubbed away at the paper so hard that it became a lace-work of holes and ribbons. Gabriel had told her that he could not stop thinking about her. He had told her that he loved her, adored her. When she remembered that she was certain of him. But then her certainty evaporated as she saw, quite clearly, that Gabriel loved everyone. He loved Sadie and his children and the friends who visited Greenstones. He loved the louche, disreputable artists who drank with him at the Café Royal and the Tour Eiffel. He loved the flower girl on the corner of the street and the stray dog who ran up to him in the park.

Sadie wrote to her. Threaded into anecdotes about the children and enquiries after Eva and the Slade and London, were the lines: *Gabriel came back from Spain a fortnight ago. He is as brown as a gypsy and has taken to wearing a gold earring. He seems restless again and plans to return to London shortly.*

A few days later Eva went to Gabriel's studio. The door was ajar; pushing it open, she saw him, a great, dark shape silhouetted by the window.

'Eva!' he cried, and held out his arms to her. His embrace enveloped her.

'I didn't know you'd come home.'

'I've only just got here.' Letting her go, he began to unpack his knapsack. 'I was going to send you a note.'

'How was Spain?'

'Spain was wonderful. Such an extraordinary country.'

'Did Nerissa enjoy it?'

He was shaking out a shirt. 'I think so. She's been before. She complained of the cold when we were in the mountains.'

There it was again, that feeling in the pit of her stomach, the sensation you had when your foot slipped on a step and you found yourself falling. She said, 'I didn't know Nerissa was going with you.'

'It was all rather last minute. You know Nerissa. She's a creature of impulse.'

Eva sat down on the arm of the chair. From the heap of crumpled clothes beside the knapsack, Gabriel drew out a necklace of tiny cowrie shells and fastened it round her neck. 'Do you like it?' The shells were cream and gold and blush rose. Eva nodded. 'I bought it from a boy in Almería,' he said. 'If you gave him a peseta, he'd dive into the sea for shells. There were dozens of boys throwing themselves into the water like pebbles.' He beamed at her. 'Let's go out for a drink. I haven't seen the crowd in the Café Royal for months.'

'*Nerissa.*' The name jerked out of her mouth as if she was spitting poison. 'Val told me that you and Nerissa — '

'What of Nerissa?'

249

She said flatly, 'Val told me that you and Nerissa were lovers.'

He was knotting a scarlet muffler round his neck. 'Nerissa and I go back years. You know that, Eva.'

She might have left it at that — better not to know — but some need to end the uncertainty made her ask, 'And are you still lovers, Gabriel?'

'Sometimes. Yes.'

She couldn't speak, but took a swift, indrawn breath as if she was drowning, struggling for air.

He threw her a quick glance. 'It doesn't make any difference to us.'

'But you didn't tell me!'

'You didn't ask.'

She whispered, 'I thought you loved me!'

'And I do.' His fingertip traced her cheekbone and jaw. 'I do love you, Eva. So put on your hat and we'll go out on the town.'

'You can't expect me not to mind!'

His smile cooled. 'Why can't I?'

'Because it makes me feel — '

'What? How does it make you feel?'

'Betrayed,' she whispered.

'That's nonsense.' He put on his coat.

Tears gathered at the corners of her eyes. 'It's not nonsense. It's true.'

'I cannot — I will not — believe that love is about having exclusive rights. You know that won't do for me, Eva.'

She looked up at him. 'And me?'

His expression softened. He took her hands in his. 'I've been honest with you from the start, darling girl. You can't say that I've deceived you. I won't ration love.'

Yet she shook him away, saying coldly, 'So you expect me to share you?'

A sudden exhalation of breath. 'If that's how you wish to put it.'

'How else might I put it?'

'It sounds to me as though you're behaving as everyone else does, dividing people into little slices, doling them out like pieces of property. I didn't think you were like that.'

'But I didn't know!' she wailed. 'How do you think I felt, hearing something like that from *Val*? And he enjoyed it, Gabriel — he enjoyed telling me!'

'I'm sorry if he hurt you. He has his cruel side. Val isn't clever enough to have any real aptitude for anything, but he is clever enough to know that he has no real aptitude — and human enough to care. That's his tragedy.' Gabriel surveyed her dispassionately. 'But, come now, Eva. You've always known that you must share me.'

'With *Sadie* — '

'So what are you saying? That it suits you to share me with Sadie, but it doesn't suit you to share me with Nerissa?'

She looked away, suddenly ashamed. She heard Gabriel say quietly, 'Eva, dearest Eva, I've never wanted to hurt you. But I won't limit who I love. Because I love Sadie — and because I love Nerissa — doesn't mean I love you any less.'

The desire to cry, to rage, suddenly faded. It was hard to ask the question but she knew that she must. 'And Sadie? Does she know about Nerissa? Does she know about *me*?'

'Sadie has always understood.'

'*Oh*.' She thought of Sadie in the kitchen at Greenstones, baking bread and chopping up vegetables to feed her husband's mistresses. She wondered what price Sadie paid for understanding. As she stood up, she heard Gabriel say, 'Come, Eva, I've missed you. Come and have a drink with me,' but she shook her head.

She gathered up her bag and hat. As she opened the door, he said, 'I should never have married at all if Sadie hadn't made it clear that she wouldn't accept anything less. I know myself, and I know I'm not the kind of man who should marry.' His voice hardened. 'So the last thing I want is another wife. I thought you understood that.'

'So did I.' Glancing back at him, she made herself smile. 'So did I, Gabriel.'

'Eva — ' As she ran down the stairs, his voice followed her, hurt and exasperated. 'Eva! You're being ridiculous! For heaven's sake, Eva!'

★ ★ ★

She thought he would write to her, that he would explain, apologize, and somehow make everything better again. She thought that, leaving the Slade at the end of the afternoon, she would find him waiting for her as he had done when they had first met. His persistence then had both frightened and enchanted her. So she dashed downstairs every morning to grab the letters when the postman knocked at the door. Yet none of them were from Gabriel, and later, scouring the street outside the Slade and failing to find him, her heart seemed to shrink into a small, hard lump.

Her three years at the Slade had almost come to an end. Looking through her portfolio, she felt a flicker of panic. It seemed sparse, too many of the paintings unfinished, too many others showing promise rather than fulfilling it. A poor showing for three years' work. She found herself adding up all the long hours she had spent posing for Gabriel. She wondered how much improved her own work might have been if she had given it those same hours. She remembered the mornings Gabriel had waylaid her, cycling to the Slade, pleading with her to forget college and spend the day with him. She had never refused him. She had fudged excuses and invented colds and sick relatives to be with Gabriel. Might she have been a better artist if she had not fallen in love with Gabriel Bellamy? Might she have better justified the faith shown in her by Miss Garnett and Great-aunt Hannah?

Eventually, belatedly, she took Iris's advice and caught the train to Sheffield. It was annoying to discover that Iris had been right, that she hadn't realized how much she wanted to go home. Even more annoying to find herself, as she lugged her bag from the tram stop to Summerleigh, breaking every now and then into a run.

At home there were banged doors and raised voices. Her arrival was scarcely noticed in the heat of the quarrel, and the unexpectedness of her visit hardly remarked on. Joshua was redfaced and furious; Clemency was trying to patch up a peace.

That evening James fled the city to catch the train to London, and Great-aunt Hannah retreated from the fray to doze in her chair in the drawing room, Winnie and a heavy black Bible on her lap. Only Mother remained indifferent to the storms and tempests around her, serene and untouched in her hot, dark eyrie. Eva remembered Iris saying: *You, of all people, should understand the lengths a woman might have to go to to have control over her own life.*

In the sanctuary of the conservatory, with the remains of the evening sunlight flickering through the glass roof, Aidan explained the events of the past few days to Eva. He had refused to go back to school after half-term. Philip had taken the train back to York the previous morning; Aidan had not gone with him. Father insisted that he return, but Aidan was unmoving — thus Father's anger. There was no point in him staying at school, Aidan told Eva calmly. He had always intended to leave as soon as he was sixteen. He was going to work

253

for the family business, which was all he cared about. He had no interest in anything else. Father would accept it; Father would, as soon as his temper had cooled, be pleased.

His certainty jarred her. She had always thought of Aidan as the quiet one, never as a provoker of dissent. For the first time she recognized that Aidan was his mother's son, both in appearance — his slightness, and the fragile colouring of his fair skin and light, strawberry-blond hair — and in his obduracy.

She was beginning to think that she had misread everything: her family, Greenstones, Gabriel. She had not known about Nerissa because she had closed her eyes to the truth, refusing to read the signs. She had not known that Sadie knew that she and Gabriel were lovers because she had not wanted to know. Gabriel had hidden nothing from her. She had only to ask, to see. If the truth hurt her, then she had only herself to blame.

As for her family: three years ago, leaving Summerleigh for London, she had dismissed them as old-fashioned and hypocritical. Yet what right had she to judge? There was little to choose between herself and her father; they both transgressed, they both risked hurting the people they loved. The self-deceptions she had practised to justify her affair with Gabriel now seemed to her contemptible. Of course she was doing wrong. You could not keep the compartments of your life separate; they bled together, the colours mingling, inescapably interlinked.

She avoided her father, seeing her own failings in his impulsiveness and in the transparency of his emotions, fending off his questions about her life in London with brusque monosyllables, afraid that her unhappiness must show. She was irritable with Clemency and Aidan, and the hours she spent in her mother's overheated rooms made her head ache.

One morning she was coming downstairs after

reading to her mother when the doorbell rang. There was no sign of Edith, so Eva answered the door herself. Mr Foley was standing on the doorstep. He raised his hat to her.

'Miss Eva. I didn't realize you were at home. I've a telegram for your father.'

She let him into the house. Sunlight poured through the stained glass in the door. He said, 'Are you all right, Miss Eva?'

He had a way, she thought, of coming across her when she was at her worst — hot and perspiring after leaving the furnace room, or soaked and tearful, having lost herself in the slums of Sheffield.

'I'm fine, Mr Foley.'

'You look . . . upset.'

She said coldly, 'I assure you, Mr Foley, I'm perfectly well. You said you'd come to my house on an errand to my father?'

He flushed and took a step back. Then Edith arrived to escort him to Joshua's study, and Eva escaped into the drawing room, closing the door behind her.

Alone, her anger drained away, leaving her miserable and exhausted. In the mirror over the mantelpiece, she caught sight of her reflection. A white face with dark circles around the eyes. Red, swollen lids because the poem she had been reading to her mother had made her cry (*Come to me in the silence of the night; Come in the speaking silence of a dream* . . .)

She heard the front door close and footsteps on the gravel as Mr Foley left the house. Her own voice echoed in her ears, her haughty dismissal of him making clear the difference in their station. That she was the boss's daughter, that he was her father's employee. No amount of unhappiness made her behaviour excusable. She knew that Mr Foley had been born a gentleman and that his family had, in some way her father had never properly explained, come down in the world. She had always been taught to be kind to those less fortunate than her. Yet she, who was scornful of rank, had used her position to humiliate Mr Foley. And all because he had noticed that she had been crying and had had the temerity to be concerned about her.

The following morning, she cycled to J. Maclise & Sons. There was the smell of hot metal and the clank and roar of the furnaces. Mr Foley answered her knock at his office door. Seeing her, his mouth tightened and his gaze flicked away.

'Your father's in the packing room, Miss Maclise.'

'I didn't come to see Father. I came to see you.'

He was gathering together papers, putting them in a leather case. 'I'm afraid I have to go to the other site.'

'Then may I walk with you?'

For a moment she thought he was going to refuse, but then he said curtly, 'If you wish.'

She waited until they were out of the factory gates before saying, 'I came here to apologize to you, Mr Foley.'

'That isn't necessary.'

'I think it is.'

He looked at her properly at last. In his dark eyes she read a mixture of emotions: pride and anger and hurt. He said, 'I spoke out of turn yesterday. You had every right to express your displeasure.'

She shook her head. 'No. I was horrible to you because I was upset. It had nothing to do with you. You just caught me at a bad moment.' She saw him weighing her words and she added quickly, 'None of which excuses my unpleasantness. I'm asking you to forgive me, Mr Foley.'

'There's nothing to forgive.'

They were crossing the river. The water's oily surface was sheened with iridescence; flotsam and jetsam from the docks bobbed in the slick.

Eva said, 'I didn't know about the new site.'

'Your father bought it six months ago. The firm that owned it before had gone bankrupt. Mr James manages it now.'

'What do you make there?'

'Clutch plates. For motor cars.'

'Clemency, my sister, drives my father's motor car.'

'I know. I've seen her waiting for him outside the factory.'

'Everything's changing.' She glanced around wildly. 'Everything's different.'

'I suppose it is. That's progress.'

'I wish everything would stay the same!'

'That's not possible, I'm afraid.'

'But my *family* . . . ' There it was again, that treacherous tremor to her voice. 'I thought *they'd* always stay the same.'

'Families? We all think we know our families.' He sounded bitter. 'But often we don't know them at all.'

'Clemency's driving a motor car and Aidan's going to leave school. And I've hardly seen James for ages — he always seems to be dashing about London. And Great-aunt Hannah keeps calling me Frances — that's her sister who died decades ago. And even Father — Father looks so *old*!'

'It only seems so because you've been away. People often seem changed when you haven't seen them for a while. And setting up the new plant has been very tiring for your father. We've had teething problems and labour disputes, days lost through strikes over pay, and because of that we've lost orders. It's been a difficult year.'

Yet another adjustment to be made. That the family business, which she had always assumed unassailable, smoothly jogging along of its own volition, might encounter problems jarred her.

'But everything's all right now?'

'There's nothing we won't ride out. But it's all placed a burden on your father.'

257

It occurred to her that although Mr Foley had been familiar to her since she was quite a little girl, she knew almost nothing about him.

'Do you have any family, Mr Foley?'

A flicker of impatience. 'What did you think? That I was put together in a factory somewhere? Standard-issue limbs, features, brain — '

She felt herself flush. 'I didn't mean that.'

'I have a mother and two sisters. They live in Buxton.'

'Your father?'

'He's dead. He died eleven years ago.'

'I'm sorry.'

He stopped suddenly and the crowds divided, flowing round them. 'Are you? I'm not. He was a drunk and a gambler, and he ruined my mother's life and blighted my sisters' and my own.'

In the middle of the clamour of the road and the steelworks there seemed to Eva to be a silence. As they began to walk again, Mr Foley said, 'Forgive me.'

'What is there to forgive?'

'My sordid family history. It's hardly something to be proud of.'

'You're not responsible for your father's behaviour, Mr Foley.' She went on, trying to lighten his mood, 'I should hate to be held responsible for *my* family's behaviour. There are far too many of us, for one thing.'

They had reached a red-brick building. Mr Foley stopped. Eva offered him her hand. 'I've enjoyed talking to you, Mr Foley. Are we friends now?'

When he smiled, his dark face lightened and became suddenly handsome. 'Of course we are,' he said, and shook her hand.

★   ★   ★

Marianne had refused Lucas Melrose, of course; had managed, in the midst of her shock, to stutter out the formula: *I am conscious of the honour you do me but I'm afraid I cannot accept your proposal.*

Yet he continued to call on her, did not, as she had half expected, go away and leave her alone. *It isn't possible,* she said to him, *it can never be. Why?* he asked her. *Why isn't it possible? Think what I can offer you. You told me that you wanted to travel. Under my protection you can see the world. I can show you sights you never dreamed of, beauty that would take your breath away. I can show you cloud forests and moonstone mines and flame trees. You could dip your fingers in the Indian Ocean and you could breathe the tropical air. You would know what it is to live on a mountain top, to walk to the end of your garden and look out to miles and miles of hills and valleys sweeping down to the sea. What have you to lose in marrying me except loneliness and tedium and an existence that you admit only wearies you? What have you to lose by starting afresh?*

She found herself putting up objections, as though marriage was a logical business, a weighing of gain and loss. One by one he dismissed them. She knew nothing of the life of a planter's wife, she told him. 'You could learn,' he said. 'It's easy enough. Your only duty would be to oversee the running of the house. You wouldn't have to trouble yourself with the estate or the factory. They're my responsibility. You'd have many more servants than you have here; you'd hardly have to lift a finger. I live well enough; you'd want for nothing.'

'The climate,' she said. 'The fevers and the snakes and the tigers . . . '

He took paper from the writing bureau and his pen from his pocket. With strong, confident strokes he sketched the tear-drop shape of the island. 'This is Blackwater.' His blunt fingertip stabbed the middle of the wider end of the tear drop. 'And these are the malaria swamps, many miles away, in the flat plain near

259

the coast. The climate in the hill country is known to be health-giving. Oh, there are fevers, of course, but there are fevers in London, too, surely? And as for snakes, my men know how to deal with them. And you'd not be troubled by tigers — they keep to the forest, by and large, and if one did venture out, then I'm a good shot.'

'My family,' she said. 'I'd miss them so much. Ceylon seems so far away.'

'A modern passenger steamer can take you from Colombo to London in a matter of weeks,' he told her. 'Some of the wives visit England every other year. And if you're homesick — well, there are letters, of course. You needn't be lonely — we're a sociable lot and most weekends we see each other at the club.'

One day he sat down beside her and took her hand in his. When he looked at her, when that pale, lucent gaze fell on her, she found herself unable to turn away.

'You say that you'll miss your family, Mrs Leighton. Yet you told me that your sisters are often busy. They'll only become busier as the years pass. They'll marry and have children and have establishments of their own to look after. Is that what you want? Do you want to watch other people's lives become fuller while yours remains empty? Do you want to be an aunt but never a mother?'

Another day it was raining, and a gusty wind tugged the pink blossom from the cherry trees.

'This weather,' he said, with a shiver. 'The cold. I don't know how you tolerate it, year after year. I'd sail home tomorrow, but it's only . . . sometimes the *loneliness*. My empty house. I'd never thought all that much about it before. Just took it for granted, being alone. I suppose I've been too often in your company. It's made me realize what I've been missing.' He was pacing around the room. He said suddenly, 'I quite understand why you won't have me, Mrs Leighton. I can boast of the comfort of my home and tell you of my small social circle till I'm blue in the face, but I do quite see that it can't compare to this. To this house. To London society.'

'It isn't that,' she said. 'I've never cared for society. I wouldn't miss *that* one bit.'

'Kind of you to say so, Mrs Leighton. You have a generous heart, putting up with me all these weeks.' A quick, sad smile. 'I should never have come here. I should never have met you. It's made me . . . dissatisfied. Perhaps I'll end up going native. Or taking to the bottle. I've known several fellows who have, you know.'

The flicker of fear in his eyes took her by surprise. Fear was not an emotion she had come to associate with Lucas Melrose. His voice lowered so that she had to strain to hear what he said next. 'It's been twelve years since my father died. But every now and then, I think he's there, in the next room. I wake up in the night and I think I can hear his footsteps.'

Then he seemed to give himself a little shake and there it was again, that sudden shift in aspect that she had noticed once or twice before, a darkness deliberately obliterated. 'I'm sorry, I'm being morbid, aren't I?'

'We all have dark thoughts, Mr Melrose, after losing a loved one.'

He paused at the window, looking down to where people hurried along the pavement, umbrellas jostling like so many black stars. He said slowly, 'I've been in England long enough to know that my ways aren't London ways. In Ceylon I don't spend much of my time in the company of women. I suppose you must find me rather brutish. And then there's my birth. Two generations back the Melroses were common farming stock.'

'And three generations back mine were blacksmiths. There's little difference.'

He swung round to her. 'If it isn't my birth, my manners or my way of life that stops you marrying me, then perhaps it's my person? I had hoped I was not entirely repulsive to you, but — '

'It's not that. You are not repulsive at all . . . ' She broke off, suddenly confused.

'Then . . . ?'

She tried to make it as plain as she could. 'Can't you see, Mr Melrose, that I'm not fit to marry you or anyone else? I lost the better part of me when Arthur died. If you'd known me longer, then you might not much like what's left.'

'Oh, I think I know you well enough.' Suddenly he smiled. 'I think I know you well enough by now.' He crossed the room to her. 'I'm not asking you to love me as you loved your husband,' he said softly. 'I know you can't do that. But perhaps my respect and love for you might do for both of us. Or perhaps I'd settle for friendship and liking. And there's something else you might consider. Wouldn't your husband have wanted you to be happy? If he loved you as much as you believe he did, then would he have wanted you to spend the rest of your life mourning him?'

★   ★   ★

The outpatients' department of the Mandeville was always busy on a Saturday night.

The nature of the patients' ailments changed as the hours lengthened. In the early evening a young woman dashed into the clinic weeping, her scalp scorched from too-hot curling irons, and handfuls of burnt hair clutched in her fists. Then there were cut fingers and fevers and broken bones from falls. As the evening wore on, an entire family, from infant to grandmother, appeared, vomiting after eating sandwiches made with tainted potted meat. A twelve-year-old girl, badly burned after standing too near a fire in her best dress, died shortly after her father had carried her into the hospital.

And then there were the drunks. Some of them came in supported by their friends, blood pouring from cuts to their heads, mumbling the words to 'Rose of Tralee'. Some of them were found by the police in the gutter, covered with bruises, their pockets ransacked. They were belligerent or affectionate, comatose or cheerful. Iris cut the clothes off unconscious men and women, bandaged cuts and made slings for sprains. She fended off beer-laden advances from men who begged for just one kiss and combed lice from the hair of an old woman who screamed curses at her.

There was a lull at around eight o'clock and they all escaped into the kitchen. One of the staff nurses had a birthday and had brought in a cake with pink icing. Iris gave a sigh of pleasure as she slid her feet out of the stout lace-ups she wore in the hospital and stretched out her toes. It was her day off tomorrow, and she and another nurse, Rose Dennison, were to go on a picnic with Lionel and Tommy, Rose's brothers. Iris closed her eyes, and thought what bliss it would be to wear a nice dress and hat instead of her uniform and cap. She checked her watch: fifteen minutes to go. Just fifteen minutes and then she would be free.

There was a roar of 'Rule Britannia' from the outpatients' hall and they all gave a sigh, twitched their aprons into place and went back to work. In the hall half a dozen young lads were bawling out a chorus — 'Britannia rules the waves! Britons never never *never* shall be slaves!' — while supporting their friend, who was bleeding profusely from a gash on the leg. Other patients crowded in — an elderly woman, clutching a towel round her scalded hand, and a pregnant girl with her young, pale husband.

And two men. The younger man was supporting the older one. The older man wore a patched jacket and a cloth cap, and was crouched over, coughing into the handkerchief that he held over his face. Iris saw bloodstains on the handkerchief.

The younger man was scanning the hall, looking for help. He was fair-haired, hatless. When he turned towards her, Iris, recognizing him, froze. She looked wildly round, searching for escape and then, realizing that all the other nurses were busy and that she had no alternative, crossed the hall to him.

'Ash,' she said.

He turned to her. 'Good God.' His eyes widened. '*Iris.*'

There was a moment of stillness and silence, while all the rush and clamour of the outpatients' hall seemed to retreat. Then Ash's companion coughed again. Iris said briskly, 'If you'd take a seat, Ash, I'll find a doctor to look at your friend.'

When she was sure he could not see her, she pressed her palms against her face, trying to cool her cheeks. *Ash, here*, she thought. The one man in England she never wanted to see again, here. It was so unfair.

As she checked with sister when the doctor would be free, and as she escorted Ash's friend to a curtained cubicle and took his name and address and made a note of his next of kin, she seemed to hear in the back of her head, as if played over and over again on a gramophone, the entire length of her last conversation with Ash in the garden at Summerleigh. *If we were engaged*, she had said, after she had kissed him. And then Ash's voice, as crushing as a physical blow: *Oh, Iris, what would we talk about, you and I?*

As she went back to where Ash was sitting, he rose to meet her. 'Mr Reynolds,' she said crisply. 'Is he a close friend of yours?'

'Not close, exactly, but I've known the family for about six months. How is he?'

'We're keeping him in for the night.' Iris frowned. 'Mr Reynolds told me that he has a family.'

'Eric has a wife and four children.'

She motioned Ash to a quieter corner of the hall. 'I'm sure you realize that Mr Reynolds has tuberculosis. The disease is in its final stages. All we can do is to try to keep him comfortable. I'm sorry.'

As she turned to go, he said, 'Iris,' and she paused, biting her lip.

'I have to go.' She hated that her voice shook slightly. 'I have other patients. You must speak to the family. You must prepare them. Mr Reynolds won't live out the week, I'm afraid.'

★ ★ ★

Marianne visited Patricia Letherby. After lunch they sat in the garden watching Patricia's children play.

'Molly will insist on trying to walk,' said Patricia. The little girl, just thirteen months old, was examining stones, grass and flowers with great interest, her progress impeded by her nappy and by the unsteadiness of her chubby legs. 'Nanny disapproves terribly. She doesn't think babies should walk until they're at least eighteen months old. I feel dreadfully guilty — she'll probably grow up bow-legged, the poor little thing. But she looks so sweet, doesn't she, and she'd rather be mooching around the garden than sitting in her pram.' Molly tottered a few steps towards her mother. 'Is that for me? Thank you, darling girl.' Patricia held out her hand to receive Molly's gift of a leaf. 'Yesterday,' she confided to Marianne, 'she gave me a worm.'

'I hope you were grateful.'

'Immensely.' There was a howl. 'Oh, *John*,' cried Patricia, and dashed across the garden to rescue her son from the fish pond.

While Patricia took John into the house to change him into dry clothes, Molly advanced on Marianne, smiling widely, her hand outstretched. Marianne lined up her gifts on the grass: a pebble, a snail shell and the mangled remains of a flower.

After a while Molly seemed to flag, so Marianne scooped her up in her arms. The little girl had fallen asleep, her head a sudden weight on Marianne's shoulder, by the time Patricia returned.

'Oh, the poor darling!' Patricia cried. 'Is she too heavy for you? She's such a pudding.'

'She's not heavy at all. She's adorable.'

As Patricia took the little girl from her, she said, 'Such a pity that you and Arthur never — ' She broke off. 'Forgive me.' She patted Marianne's arm. 'I'm a tactless fool. I open my mouth and a great deal of nonsense flows out.'

Walking home, Marianne noticed the branches heavy with green leaves that trailed over the railings outside the houses, and the bees that burrowed in the lilies to emerge powdered with orange pollen. Whenever there was a lull in the traffic, she seemed to hear the rhythms of summer, a mixture of birdsong and insect hum, a beating in the air that celebrated the return of warmth and life.

Sitting on a bench in the park, watching the children play, her anger and despair returned. That she could not be a part of this greedy, hungry life. That she must remain an onlooker.

How many times had she come here to greet Arthur as he rode down Rotten Row? She remembered how he had looked, the handsomest man in the park, and tears stung her eyes. Even now, a year and a half after his death, she still found herself searching through the crowds for his beloved face. Each time, she endured the unutterable pain of his absence. Could she choose to leave all these reminders of him?

She must, she thought, because the alternative was a lifetime of waiting for a man she would never see again. She remembered the day he had died. After Dr Fleming had operated, she had sat at his bedside. His breaths had come further and further apart and, in that terrible space between one breath and the next, she had pleaded with him, begged him to live. After he had taken his final breath, she had remained with him. It was not that she had been, as her sisters had believed, unable to accept that he had gone, more that she could not think what to do next. That absence of breath had robbed her life of meaning. All the small acts that make up everyday life — eating, sleeping, dressing, speaking — had since then been questionable to her.

Arthur had died in agony because of a small carelessness, a little neglect. To accept that had been a cruelty almost beyond endurance. And yet she had endured. A year ago she had considered killing herself. In not doing so, she had made a choice, she supposed. She must make other choices. She must settle for *something*. She must amuse herself, or she must be useful, or she must find the courage to seek out love again.

It seemed to her that the only thing she had ever been good at had been marriage. Marriage had suited her, it had brought out the best in her. Unmarried, she would always be prey to men like Teddy Fiske. Lacking certainty herself, she needed to draw her strength from someone more vigorous and resilient. Strength and conviction attracted her because they were qualities she herself lacked.

She walked back through the park. Every now and then she paused to look at the roses. Once she broke off a flower and pinned it to her lapel. All the way home she breathed in the rose's heady scent and, reaching up her fingers, stroked its crimson velvet petals.

★ ★ ★

Seeing Ash had brought back to Iris all the humiliation of their last meeting. She wondered whether he might have forgotten what had passed between them, but dismissed the possibility immediately. No one, however unworldly, forgot that sort of thing. Such encounters seared themselves onto your memory, sticking like glue.

For the next few days, she was edgy and ill at ease. She could not quite convince herself that he would not come back. Any other man, she thought, would have the tact to keep away. But tact had never been one of Ash's qualities.

She was on her Saturday morning break, dashing out to the shops, when she heard him call out to her. As she turned towards him, she put up her chin defiantly. This time, she promised herself, she would make sure not to appear shocked or upset. *She* would keep the upper hand.

She said coolly, 'What, more patients for the Mandeville, Ash?'

'Not this time. I wanted to speak to you. Have you a moment?'

'I'm on duty. I have to go back on the ward in a few minutes. I have to match some thread.'

To her annoyance, he followed her into the shop. Ignoring him, she searched through reels of cotton for the ashes of roses colour that would match the length of material she had bought to make a blouse. She heard him say, 'Seeing you the other week . . . it was so unexpected.'

'Unexpected?' She glanced at him, her brows raised. 'In what way, Ash?'

'I didn't know you were in London.'

'Oh, Ash, you disappoint me!' she cried. 'Finding me in London was the least of the surprise, I should think!' She glanced back at the reels once more, running a fingertip across the different colours. 'What you meant,' she said, 'was how unexpected to find Iris Maclise doing hospital nursing. How unexpected to find Iris Maclise getting her hands dirty.'

He flushed. 'That wasn't what I meant at all.'

'Of course it was.' She turned to face him. Somewhere in the back of her mind it registered that he, too, had changed. That he looked older, more sure of himself. Not tidier, though: his hair needed a cut and he was wearing a jacket of dusty, greenish-black stuff that looked, she thought disparagingly, as if it was made of dead moles.

She said coldly, 'You made it perfectly clear what you thought of me three years ago. Don't pretend that this is just a polite passing of the time of day between old friends. You were curious, weren't you? Curious to see why silly, frivolous Iris Maclise was doing something useful at last.'

'I never thought you were *silly* — '

'Don't lie to me, Ash!' she hissed furiously. 'I may not live up to your high standards, but I'm not a fool!' Grabbing a reel, handing a few coins to the assistant, she stalked out of the shop.

Yet he ran after her, calling out, 'Iris. *Please!*'

She was halfway up the hospital steps. In the shadow of the entranceway to the Mandeville, she took a deep breath to steady herself. 'People change, Ash. I've changed. The greatest insult would be for you to think me just the same. You can't work in a place like this without seeing some dreadful things. I don't go to political meetings, like Eva, or anything like that, because I have little enough spare time as it is. When I have time off, I enjoy myself and I'm not ashamed of that. But please don't assume that I'm as foolish and ignorant as I was before. Because I'm not.'

There was a silence. Then he said, 'I missed you.'

Again her chin jutted out. 'Missed me? Or missed my family?'

'All of you. But you most of all.' He gave a wry grin.

'No one quarrels with me like you used to, Iris. I miss that. It's true.'

There was a glint in his eye; reluctantly, she found herself beginning to remember why years ago she had liked him, and why, in spite of their differences, she had enjoyed his company.

'I have to get back,' she muttered.

'Of course. But you'll let me see you again, won't you?'

'Ash — '

'That's settled then.' And he was gone, disappearing into the market-day crowds.

Iris looked down at the reel of thread in her hand. It wasn't ashes of roses at all, but a nasty salmon pink. With a hiss of exasperation she stuffed it into her pocket and went back into the hospital.

When she came off the ward at eight o'clock, there was a note in her pigeonhole at the nurses' home. It was from Eva. *Iris,* she had scrawled in wild black ink, *you have to do something. Marianne is going to marry an awful man and live in Ceylon. You have to stop her.*

★   ★   ★

Marianne was in the scullery of the Norfolk Square house when Iris arrived. She was wearing an old blue dress which Iris remembered from their Summerleigh days, and her thick, dark hair was pinned up in an untidy knot. Always pale, the blue of the dress and the poor light in the room made her complexion look colourless.

She looked up when Iris came in. 'I forgot to do the flowers.' Vases and bunches of pinks and roses stood on the draining board. 'I picked them this morning and left them in here and forgot all about them. The poor things will die of thirst.' She threw Iris a glance. 'Isn't it rather late to call?'

270

'Terribly.' Iris went to stand by the sink. 'And home sister will hang, draw and quarter me if I'm not back in my room by ten.'

Marianne was cutting the ends off the blooms with a knife. 'I suppose Eva's told you?'

'That you're engaged to be married? Is it true?'

'Yes. And if you've come here to try to make me change my mind, then you may as well go away because you're wasting your time.'

'If it's what you really want, Marianne, I wouldn't dream of trying to make you change your mind.'

'Well, that's a pleasant change. Eva shouted at me.'

'Eva was shocked, perhaps. We didn't realize there was anyone you particularly cared about.'

'There isn't.' Marianne's voice was grim. She looked over her shoulder at Iris. 'But Lucas has asked me to marry him and I've accepted.'

'Lucas?'

'Lucas Melrose.'

Iris watched the swift, ruthless motion of the knife. 'I don't remember hearing of him before. I don't remember you mentioning him.'

'He's perfectly respectable, if that's what you're concerned about. He's a tea planter in Ceylon.'

'And after you're married you mean to live in Ceylon?'

'We sail in a fortnight's time. We're going to marry by special licence.'

'Marianne . . . ' *You mustn't do this*, she was about to say, but just managed to stop herself. 'Have you told Father?'

'I wrote to him yesterday. And I daresay Eva will have cabled him.' Marianne gave a taut smile. 'No doubt Father is rushing down to London even as we speak. Maybe he'll have James in tow for moral support. I'd better ask the maids to air the guest rooms, hadn't I?' The sarcasm ebbed from her voice and she muttered stubbornly, 'It won't make any difference. I've thought and I've thought about it and I've decided that this is the only way.'

Iris felt as though she was floundering, fighting to see her way in the dark. 'Where did you meet Mr Melrose?'

'At Rawdon Hall. Laura Meredith introduced us.'

'And you found that you enjoyed each other's company . . . or that you had things in common?'

'We talked a little. And then we met, by chance, in London. And he's often called since.' Marianne paused. 'We were both on our own. I suppose that's what it was. At Rawdon Hall we were both . . . outsiders.'

Which didn't reassure Iris one bit. 'How long have you known him?'

Marianne filled a vase with water. 'Eight weeks.'

This time she couldn't help herself. '*Eight weeks!* Good God, Marianne, are you mad?'

'Well, yes.' A small smile. 'I often think I am, a bit. Since Arthur died there are things I think about all the time, terrible things. I have to bite my tongue to stop myself saying them out loud. And sometimes I can't stop myself and the dreadful things come out and everyone looks shocked, as if I've said something indecent. So, yes, perhaps I am a little mad.' She leant her back against the sink. The twilight emphasized the hollows and shadows of her face and the slightness of her figure. Always thin, Marianne had lost weight since Arthur had died. 'To tell the truth,' she said quietly, 'sometimes I don't even try to stop myself because I don't see why I should. After all, *I* see the world as it is, while they deceive themselves. I'm not the same person any more, you see. I pretend to be, but I'm not. But sometimes lately I've shocked even myself. I'm afraid I'll do something dreadful. Something rash.'

'This marriage sounds rash enough to me.'

Marianne put down the knife. 'I meant worse than

that. There are worse things than marrying a man you don't love.'

'Are there? Marriage is so final — for a lifetime — '

'Dear me, Iris, have you such a small imagination?' Marianne gave a brittle laugh. 'I could do much worse than marry Lucas Melrose. I could have a string of lovers. What would Father think of that?'

'Marianne — '

'I'm not so mad that I don't know what I'm doing.' She looked fierce. 'I'm choosing to marry again.'

'And no one would deny you that right. But to a man you've known for only eight weeks?'

'Time has nothing to do with it. I knew I loved Arthur the first time I met him.'

'So you feel for this man — for Lucas — something of what you felt for Arthur?'

'Of course not.' Marianne's voice was scornful. 'I told you, I feel nothing for him. But he's good enough. As good as anyone.'

'*Good enough?* That's no foundation for a marriage!'

'Isn't it?' It was Marianne's turn to sound angry. 'I don't know what right my sisters think they have to advise me on marriage. Eva doesn't approve of it and poor Clemency will probably remain a spinster all her life. And as for you, are you suggesting that I wait for something better? As you did, Iris?'

In the silence there was the drip of the tap and, from outside in the garden, the glorious peal of a song thrush. Iris remembered Summerleigh: warm nights and a man's arms around her as she danced. And the scent of roses and a stolen kiss or two in the moonlit garden.

'I suppose I deserved that.' She picked up a fallen petal and crushed it between finger and thumb. 'I let slip a good number of chances, didn't I?'

Marianne closed her eyes. 'I'm sorry. That was unkind. I didn't mean — '

'Yes, you did. And you're quite right, of course. I was too proud to accept any of the men who proposed to me. I always thought there'd be someone better just round the corner. And by the time I discovered there wasn't, it was too late. And who'd want to marry me now?' She gave a little laugh. 'Eau de carbolic soap isn't exactly seductive, and just look at my poor *hands*.'

'You must forgive me, Iris,' whispered Marianne. 'It was a mean thing to say.'

She looked white and drawn and desperately unhappy. Iris said gently, 'You look tired. Aren't you sleeping?'

'Not really.' Marianne tucked away a stray lock of hair.

'Marianne, it's been only eighteen months since Arthur died. That's not long at all. And to marry a man you hardly know — to go and live thousands of miles away from your family — can you wonder we're worried?'

Marianne had begun to arrange the flowers in a vase. 'I know you used to think me rather foolish and romantic. And I was, I suppose. When I was a girl, all I wanted was to fall in love. I didn't care whether he was rich or poor, handsome or homely. I thought that falling in love would change my life. Well, it did, it changed it forever. And I know that it's hard for other people to understand how I feel, but since Arthur died I've felt as though I were made of stone — ' she put her fist to her chest — 'here. I may not love Lucas, but he seems a good man and he says that he loves me. Is it so terrible to let him believe that I might be able to love him too? I can pretend, Iris — I've become good at pretending.' Her voice fell. 'You see, I don't think I'm capable of loving another man, and even if I were, I'm not sure I'd want to. You can lose love, can't you? *Better to have loved and lost*, people are forever saying to me, but I don't think it is, I don't think it is at all!'

Iris chose her words carefully. 'I know you still miss Arthur terribly. All I'm suggesting is that you wait.'

'But don't you see, Iris, that there's nothing to wait *for*? I spent most of my girlhood waiting. That was all I did — it was all any of us did. We waited. For something to happen — for love — for marriage. When I married Arthur I thought that was an end to waiting. But then he died and ever since I've felt that I'm in limbo. I've nothing to look forward to and I can't even take pleasure in thinking of the past because all my memories of Arthur are tainted by his death. And there's nothing to fill the gap. Nothing at all. I haven't a talent like Eva, and I'm not clever enough to have a career like you. I'm twenty-three years old, and I feel as though my life is over!'

There was a finality in Marianne's voice that made Iris feel cold inside, a growing suspicion that there was nothing she or anyone else could do to stop her marrying Lucas Melrose. But she still tried. 'In time — '

'No.' Marianne shook her head violently. 'Time will make no difference. Waiting will make no difference.' She put the vase on the side table. Iris saw that the flowers were arranged with great artistry and precision. 'This house — ' Marianne's gaze flicked around the room — 'is like a mausoleum. Every room has reminders of him. I used to cling on to those memories, but lately they've come to haunt me. Whenever I go into our bedroom, I see him lying there in agony. I have to get away from here. I have to go somewhere different and see different things. I have to have different thoughts. Or I shall die, Iris. I shall simply die.'

'Oh, *Marianne*.' Iris hugged her, but Marianne was stiff and unyielding. 'I just don't see why it has to be such a rush. Couldn't you settle for becoming engaged? Then the family would have time to get to know Lucas and you'd be absolutely certain in your own mind that you're doing the right thing. And then, if you still felt the same in six months or so, you could marry with our blessing.'

Marianne turned back to the flowers. 'Lucas must return to Ceylon in a fortnight.' Her voice was clipped and emotionless. 'He will not return to England in the foreseeable future. We marry now or we don't marry at all. He's made that quite clear.'

Something Marianne had said earlier made Iris say, 'You told me Mr Melrose noticed you at Rawdon Hall. Perhaps he noticed you because you were on your own. Arthur left you a wealthy woman, Marianne. I'm afraid that makes you a target for a certain type of man.'

'You mean that he might be a fortune hunter?' Marianne was placing white rosebuds in a glass vase. They gleamed, luminescent in the twilight. 'If he is, I don't particularly care.'

'You *must* care.'

'Well, I don't,' said Marianne sharply. 'It may be wicked of me, but I don't. After all, we'd both be using each other. He'd be marrying me for my money, and I'd be marrying him for a child.'

'A child?'

'I know I'll never love another man. But I might be able to love a child. I've made a bargain with myself, you see. I'll be a good wife to Lucas. His life sounds rather rough and ready and I think he wants a wife to run his home and make it more comfortable. I know I can do that and I know I can do it well. And in turn, he'll give me what I want — a child of my own.'

And at last Iris understood. 'So that's why you are marrying? So that you can have a baby?'

'Yes.' Marianne looked defiant. 'I'm tired of being alone. I'm tired of waking up in the morning and wondering how I'll get through another day. I want someone to love again.' She put the vase of flowers on the table. 'I've always done what other people wanted of me,' she said softly. 'I was a good daughter and a good

276

wife. Now I'm taking something for myself. I'm taking what *I* want. The only thing that I want.'

★ ★ ★

Standing at the altar, Marianne was gripped by a panic so fierce she wanted to run out of the church. She could not do it. She could not marry a man she hardly knew, a man she did not love. A man who every now and then showed a glimpse of something that frightened her.

Yet the vicar continued to speak, and she stood motionless at Lucas Melrose's side, her veiled face betrayed nothing of her inner turmoil. *Just think of the fuss*, she thought. The explanations she would have to find, the comments of family and friends she would have to endure, the curiosity and gossip she would expose herself to. The very thought of it wearied her.

And besides, if she did not marry, then what would she do? Nothing would have changed. She would have no choice but to return to a life that had become meaningless to her. She would have lost her last chance of happiness, a child of her own. Some spark inside her, already almost obliterated by Arthur's death, would finally fade and die.

She heard her own voice, firmer now, repeating the vicar's words. She felt the ring slide onto her finger.

★ ★ ★

Two days later they set sail for Colombo. As the ship drew away from the port, Marianne waved until she could no longer see her family standing on the quayside. But she remained on deck, watching as first the great cranes and cargo ships disappeared, then the city of Southampton, and then, at last, the coastline of England itself was lost in the curve of the earth.

9

Eva went back to Gabriel because she could not have done otherwise. She needed him, needed his energy, his love of life and his easy laughter.

Something had changed, though. Her loathing for Nerissa was black and jealous. It made her watch Gabriel, suspicious of where he might have been, who he might have been with. And Gabriel hadn't painted for months. 'A fallow period,' he said moodily. 'Whenever this happens to me, I'm afraid that's it, I'll never paint again.'

In July Eva helped Lydia Bowen move into a new flat. They painted walls, hung curtains and made chair covers. When the decorating was finished, Lydia gave an impromptu housewarming party. Jars and vases filled with long-stemmed daisies stood on tables and mantelpieces. Light streamed through high arched windows. Guests crowded into the rooms and the pop of champagne corks beat a rhythm to the music of the gramophone.

Though she had arrived at the party with Gabriel, Eva seemed to keep losing him in the crowd. He would be there, at her side, and then she would spend a few minutes talking to a friend and look round and find him gone. It seemed imperative to her to stay with Gabriel. Familiar faces flickered in the crowds: her fellow students and tutors from the Slade, Lydia's suffragette friends, artists and patrons Eva had met at Lydia's gallery.

Talking to Lydia and May Jackson, Eva lost track of Gabriel. Excusing herself, she wove round the huddles of guests in search of him. She caught sight of him at last, standing at the far end of the hallway. He was talking to a girl. The girl was dark and slender; she wore an ankle-length, emerald-green velvet skirt and a black knitted sweater. Her feet were bare and her wild, curling hair fell free of pins or ribbons down her back. When she laughed, she threw her head back, displaying the long, pale column of her throat.

At around midnight the guests began to drift away. Lydia's escort, a wiry, foreign-looking man, took his leave of them as Eva stood in the kitchen, washing glasses. 'Fabrice is a fearfully dull conversationalist, but the most divine dancer,' confided Lydia after she had seen him out of the front door.

'Have you ever been in love, Lydia?' asked Eva.

'Just the once. Cigarette, my dear?'

'Please.' Eva dried her hands on a tea towel. 'What was he like?'

'Laurence?' Lydia smiled sadly. 'He was tall and rather thin and he had eyes the colour of black coffee. I think that's why I fell in love with him, because of his eyes.'

'But you didn't marry him?'

'No.' Lydia flicked a lighter. 'Those lovely eyes had a habit of roaming, I'm afraid. Laurence collected beautiful things. Dutch interiors and pretty young women. He was married when I met him. To be fair, he never made a secret of it. So you could say that I knew what I was doing. Though one never does, of course. One never does.'

The silence seemed to hang rather heavily in the air. Eva thought of the portraits of herself hanging in Lydia's gallery. How many people knew, or suspected, that she was Gabriel Bellamy's mistress? Val had said: *Gabriel always sleeps with his models. Everyone knows that.*

'That girl . . . ' she began.

'Which girl?'

'She was wearing a green velvet skirt. And no shoes.'

'She's called Ruby Bailey.' Lydia stubbed out her cigarette. 'One of the others must have brought her. I've seen her once or twice but I don't really know her. She's a dancer, I believe. Rather striking.'

'Is she — '

'Is she what?'

'Nothing.'

Eva rinsed glasses and put them on the draining board to dry. *Is she married?* she had wanted to ask. *Is she attached to anyone? Is she the sort of woman Gabriel might fall in love with?* But, remembering dark, gypsy-like Ruby Bailey, she already knew the answer to that question.

★ ★ ★

Slowly, cautiously, Iris and Ash became friends again. Iris discovered that for the past two years Ash had been articled to a firm of solicitors in Leman Street, only half a mile from the Mandeville. He had met Adam Campbell, the senior partner of Campbell, Sparrow & Blunt, through the university settlement. Campbell was in his mid-forties, a quiet, principled man who considered it a part of his job to represent the interests of the poor and powerless. 'You must be in your element,' said Iris, when Ash showed her round his shabby, busy offices. 'All those Good Works to be done.'

They saw each other only occasionally. Iris worked long hours and, in the evenings and at weekends, Ash taught politics and economics at a technical college, gave lectures for the Workers' Educational Association, and attended political meetings. An assortment of waifs and strays drifted through his house in Aldgate. His kitchen often saw heated discussions that lasted into the early hours of the morning.

Through Ash, Iris discovered an East End previously unknown to her. Together they explored the warren of little streets and alleyways that branched off from the Whitechapel Road. Peering through the windows of the shops, Iris glimpsed parrot cages and ostrich feathers, mandolins and mantillas. She saw flat bread knotted into strange shapes, glass bottles of humbugs and boiled fruits, and trays of pink and yellow Turkish Delight. Ash showed her the anarchists' haunts in Jubilee Street, and the club where Prince Kropotkin and Enrico Malatesta had made speeches. He took her to tiny, dark cafés where photographs of foreign-looking gentlemen with flourishing moustaches were pinned to the walls and bought her thick, sweet Turkish coffee, which they drank sitting in a booth upholstered with threadbare purple plush. He himself was not an anarchist, Ash explained; anarchists were too fond of the bullet and the bomb for his taste.

They talked about everything — or almost everything. There was one subject they shied away from. They never spoke of their quarrel the day after the party at Summerleigh. They skirted round it, avoiding it. It occurred to Iris that Ash might think she was embarrassed by the memory. There was an even more unpleasant possibility: that he might think that she had really been in love with him. If so, it was a misapprehension that must be nipped firmly in the bud.

She went for a walk with Ash on her Saturday afternoon off. On the way home they stopped at the shops. Iris chose ribbons and braid, lace and thread, selecting colours and estimating lengths with practised efficiency. It had begun to rain; Ash carried her brown paper parcel and they fitted themselves beneath his umbrella. 'That's what I admire about you, Iris,' he said, as they left the shop. 'You always seem to know exactly what you want.'

'I don't believe in dithering.'

'Half a yard of this and three yards of that and a dozen pearl buttons . . . What on earth are you making?'

'A gentleman should never ask a lady that. What if it was something unmentionable?'

'Then I apologize unreservedly and withdraw the question.'

'I'm only teasing. I'm making a blouse for Clemmie's birthday and a skirt for myself and two nightdresses for a friend's new baby.'

The traffic along Commercial Road was heavy; crossing the street, Ash took Iris's hand as they darted between trams and brewer's drays. As they reached the pavement she said, 'And besides, you're wrong. I can be quite dreadfully slow at knowing what I want. I spent years convinced I wanted something which probably wouldn't have suited me at all.'

There was a crack of thunder, a heavy burst of rain and they darted into the shelter of a shop doorway. Ash collapsed the umbrella. 'What was that?'

'Marriage, of course. There, Ash, I'm admitting I was wrong, and you know how I hate to do that. But perhaps I didn't care about diamond rings and wedding dresses as much as I thought I did.'

'So you mean to be a nurse for the rest of your life?'

'Goodness, no. What a hideous thought.' Iris gave a little laugh. 'Do you remember that a very long time ago, for the teeniest of moments, I wanted to marry you?'

He drew her closer to him, out of the rain. 'I remember.'

'Yet you've never spoken of it. Were you being tactful, Ash?'

'It would make a change, wouldn't it? I don't recall being particularly tactful then.'

'Weren't you?' she said lightly. 'I don't remember.'

'I'm afraid I was an appallingly pompous ass.'

'Then it's just as well I've forgotten, isn't it?'

There was the noise of raindrops drumming on the pavement, and they did not speak for a while. When the downpour lessened, they walked on. Iris said, 'The dreadful truth is that I seem to like nursing. And I'm rather good at it — I wasn't at first, but I am now. I suppose that makes me terribly dreary and worthy. I shall probably end up a bossy old spinster with only my pet cats for company.'

'Oh, undoubtedly,' he said with a flicker of a smile.

Iris hooked her hand through his arm. 'What about you, Ash? Has there been anyone?'

'Nothing that came to anything. And you? Are you seriously expecting me to believe that not one man has so much as glanced in your direction?'

She dimpled. 'Well, my friend Rose's brothers are rather sweet on me . . . and several of the doctors at the hospital . . . '

'The same old Iris.'

'But I've never been in love with anyone at all, and one is supposed to be in love with the man one marries, isn't one?'

'I believe so.'

'I still have a heart of granite, you see. And I haven't yet met the man who's capable of chipping it.' She beamed at him. 'It's so nice to know that you'll never be anything more than a friend, Ash. So much less bothersome than being in love.'

★ ★ ★

At the end of the summer term Eva's friends from the Slade drifted away, some to return to their parents' houses, one or two to be married. Several went to study art in Paris and asked Eva to go with them, but she prevaricated. Maybe later in the summer, she said. Maybe when she had saved up more money.

Gabriel's private viewing was in September. His portraits of Eva were displayed on the walls of Lydia's gallery along with landscapes and sketches of his children. The evening after the reviews were published Eva found him in the Tour Eiffel in Percy Street, hunched over a glass of absinthe. 'That bastard in *The Times* had the nerve to call me old-fashioned,' he said savagely. 'Just because I don't stick bits of old newspaper or cigarette packets to my bloody paintings. If I made beautiful women look as if they were made of cardboard boxes, or if I wasted my time painting *machines*, then they'd be fawning after me.' He knocked back the remainder of his drink and ordered another. 'I want to paint beauty, not ugliness. What's wrong with that? Why should we prize ugliness? There's more than enough of it in the world, isn't there? So why should I add to it? Art should lift the heart, not lower it. Most of us have a hard enough time keeping out of the gutter as it is, without deliberately wallowing in it.'

He had lurched to his feet, a massive figure in his long black coat and fedora. The other customers in the café turned to stare at him. 'Beauty's the only thing that matters!' he shouted and thumped the table with his fist so that the glasses jumped. 'Can't you fools see that?' He swayed slightly, his gaze sweeping the room, his voice becoming low and contemptuous. 'But beauty's not the fashion now, is it? And we must be fashionable, mustn't we, at all costs? God help us if we should allow ourselves to become unfashionable!'

Eva dragged him out of the café. They went on to Soho, trailing from one pub to another. Friends and hangers-on gathered, clinging to Gabriel like burrs on a coat sleeve. Later in the evening Max whispered to Eva, 'I should go home if I were you. I'll keep an eye on him.'

She learned later that, very drunk, Gabriel had got into a fight in a pub, had spent the night in a police cell and had been bailed out by Max the next morning, before being escorted back to Greenstones and Sadie.

She hadn't posed for Gabriel since the beginning of

the year. Once, when they were alone in his studio, she began to unbutton her blouse and take off her stockings. 'What are you doing?' he asked her. 'I thought you might want to paint me,' she said. 'To paint me properly, like you always said you wanted to.' He did up her buttons himself. 'Dear little Eva, you don't have to do *that*.' There was pity in his eyes.

She knew that she received less and less, that she hoped for less and less from him. Once they had spent entire days together; once his studio had seemed to them a whole world. Now, after an hour or so, she would see the restlessness in his eyes, the wish to move on to another friend, another place. In six months, maybe a year, she thought, she would have become his *cinq à sept*, the mistress who, a remnant of an old passion now spent, must be fitted in between the more important parts of his life for old times' sake.

* * *

Though he had lived in the East End for some time now, Ash still found it impossible to reconcile himself to the deprivation he encountered daily. His affluence seemed obscene in a place where hunger constantly stalked the poorest familes. He hated to see the effects of poverty clearly visible in the children's sunken faces and listless eyes, hated even more to see the bruises on their legs and backs. Though he knew that there were many loving families in the East End, there were others where the parents beat their children because they were too exhausted and too uneducated to know how else to discipline them. And there was worse, he discovered: in some of the poorest houses there lived children who should never have been born. Adolescent brothers and sisters were crammed into one small bedroom; every now and then such close proximity would produce a baby whom no one spoke about. The family's shame was hidden and no one was ever prosecuted — and in any case, he thought angrily, who would you punish? The infant itself by taking it away from the only home it had ever known? Or the ignorant child who had given birth to it? Or the parents for not earning enough money to house their family decently?

Though he did what he could, it never seemed to be enough. His pockets were empty because he could never pass by the one-legged soldiers, forgotten casualties of the Boer War, who held out their caps to him, or the old women who chose to beg on the streets rather than go to the workhouse. He shared his food with families whose bellies were empty, gave up his sofa to men without a bed for the night. Taking Iris to his home for the first time, he saw her blue eyes widen with disapproval. 'I know it looks untidy,' he said quickly, 'but I know where everything is. And I like having friends to stay.'

He wrote articles for left-wing newspapers on the causes that stirred him: on child malnutrition, on the condition of the dockers, always only a step or two away from poverty because of their conditions of employment. He took photographs of East End streets and squares, photographs that were sometimes shown in shabby little Jubilee Street galleries which, Ash suspected, passers-by only ever went in to get out of the rain. He wrote pamphlets pointing out the need for change in simple language aimed at the working man, and had them printed on a noisy, clattering press in Inkhorn Court. He delivered the pamphlets himself, stuffing them through letter boxes with a gaggle of curious children and stray dogs following behind him like the train of a comet.

Proceedings were well under way by the time Ash arrived at a Labour Party meeting one evening. After the meeting was over, tea was served. They gathered in a corner of the room — Ash, Harry Hennessy, who was the branch secretary, Harry's brother, Fred, and a ginger-haired man of about Ash's age called Charlie Porter. A young woman Ash had not met before joined them. Harry introduced her to Ash. Her name was Thelma Voss. Slender and of medium height, she wore a threadbare mackintosh and a navy-blue beret. Her face was round, high-cheekboned and sallow-skinned, its most notable feature the straight, strong black brows that framed her lively greenish eyes.

They were discussing the difficult progress through parliament of the government's Home Rule for Ireland Bill.

'The Unionists won't give an inch,' said Fred. 'They don't care what Asquith wants and they don't care what the people of Ireland want.'

'It's the same old story.' Harry stirred sugar into his tea. 'The landowners mean to keep hold of power. They don't want ordinary working men to have a say in what goes on.'

'Or working women,' muttered Miss Voss. 'Women should have their say just as much as men.'

'We shouldn't let ourself be distracted by everyone with an axe to grind,' said Charlie.

'An axe to grind? Is that your opinion of the representation of women?' Thelma Voss's eyes sparked.

'You have to get your priorities right.'

'And women's rights are pretty low down on your list, aren't they, Charlie?' Thelma's voice was scornful. 'I'm surprised to find you here. Why don't you head off down the road to the Liberal Club? It sounds as though you're of much the same mind as Mr Asquith.'

Charlie lit a cigarette. 'Ireland's been ruled long enough by absentee landlords. Didn't think to find you sticking up for the aristocracy, Thelma.'

'I'm not! Of course I'm not!'

Charlie winked at Ash. 'Thelma doesn't care for the

ruling classes. You'd do away with the lot of 'em, wouldn't you, love?'

'Well, what good do they do? They're just parasites and spongers!'

'Thelma would send them all to the guillotine.'

'Of course I wouldn't, Charlie,' said Thelma stiffly. 'You know I don't approve of violence.'

Charlie laughed. 'Give you half a chance and you'd be sitting there, knitting away, as the heads rolled.'

'I told you, I'm a pacifist.'

'Click, click, click . . . '

Thelma hissed, 'Why must you always make fun of me?'

Charlie grinned. 'Just having a laugh. Where's your sense of humour, love?'

Thelma had gone pink. 'All I meant is there's one rule for the rich and another for the poor — '

'Miss Voss is quite right,' said Ash. 'Suffragettes endure the miseries of forcible feeding in gaol while Sir Edward Carson, who has openly advocated armed Unionist rebellion in Ulster, goes free.'

'Carson's a Member of Parliament, isn't he?' said Fred. 'He's one of their own.'

'And he's rich.' Thelma sounded bitter. 'That's what makes him different.'

Charlie gave her a sly glance. 'Some of those wildcats screaming for the vote have a bob or two, I believe.'

'Wildcats — '

'Throwing stones through shop windows . . . it's hardly ladylike behaviour.'

Thelma's colour deepened. 'Being ladylike hasn't got women anywhere!'

Charlie took out papers and a pouch of tobacco. 'I haven't seen you rushing to go to prison for your beliefs, Thelma.'

'You know that I can't — '

'Not that I'm suggesting you make a fool of yourself

like some of those women.'

'It isn't only women who make fools of themselves! Men make fools of themselves easily enough!' Thelma's eyes blazed. 'I see them every night in the pub down my road!'

Charlie smiled. Leaning forward, he said softly, 'And there's a fast piece or two at the Bull who'll do anything a man asks him for the price of a gin and orange, Thelma, love.'

Thelma went white. She grabbed her mackintosh. Harry Hennessy said, 'Thelma — '

'I have to go. My father will be worried.' Her voice shook slightly.

She left the hall. Harry began to follow after her, but Ash said, 'No, let me. I'll go.'

He caught up with Thelma as she headed down the Commercial Road. She was carrying two heavy bags of shopping. She looked at him sharply. 'What do you want?'

'I came to see if you were all right.'

A quick little jab of the shoulders. 'Why shouldn't I be?'

'I'm sure Charlie didn't mean any harm.'

'Are you?' This time, her fury was directed at Ash. 'And what makes you so certain of that?'

'Some people like to provoke. Charlie's one of them.'

'Charlie likes to provoke *me*.' She flung a glance at Ash. 'Charlie and I used to walk out together. But I put a stop to it.'

'I'm sorry.'

'I'm not.' Thelma put down the shopping bags. 'I saw him with another girl. He has a roving eye, Charlie does. When I told him I'd seen him, he said she wasn't important. So I said that he wasn't important to me. He didn't like that.' She drew her mackintosh more tightly across her chest in a defensive gesture. 'Thinks himself God's gift, that one. He enjoys needling me. He knows how to get under my skin.' She swung round to Ash. 'Did you notice how many women were at the meeting tonight?'

He thought back. 'About half a dozen, I'd say.'

'And how many men were there?'

'Twenty-five — maybe thirty — '

'It's not that girls don't care about politics. But they're at home looking after their babies or sitting with their old folks. That's why they don't come out. Men don't have to be troubled with things like that, do they?'

'I suppose not.'

Her chin jutted out. 'Did you notice who made the tea and biscuits? And who served them?'

'Two of the women — I don't know their names — '

'Of course you don't. Why should you? But it'll always be two of the women, never two of the men. Yet nine out of ten of the speeches are given by men. Oh, they're kind enough to let us have our say every now and then. A mill girl visited a few months ago and spoke to us. She was very interesting, I thought. Afterwards, I overheard some of the men mocking her. They said she was like a mouse, a little, squeaking mouse.' She broke off. 'I must go. My father . . . '

'I'll walk with you.'

She looked startled. 'That's not necessary.'

'It's dark, Miss Voss.'

Her brows lowered over her eyes. 'All right, then,' she said ungraciously.

'Let me carry your bags.'

She handed them to him and they set off. Eventually she stopped outside a greengrocer's shop. 'This is where I live,' she said. Ash saw a curtain twitch. Thelma rapped on the window pane with her knuckles and called out, 'It's all right, Dad, I'm back!' Turning to Ash, she said fiercely, 'That's why I'm not out marching with the other girls! That's why I can't take the risk!

Who'd mind the shop if I went to prison? Who'd look after my dad?'

Then the sullen, angry cast lifted from her features and she said brusquely, 'It was kind of you to help me with the shopping. And thank you for standing up for me back there with that lot at the meeting.' She opened the door. 'I've seen you around before, putting pamphlets through letter boxes. I don't mind giving you a hand, if you like. As long as I can fit it round Dad and the shop.'

⋆ ⋆ ⋆

In her heart of hearts Clemency understood that Great-aunt Hannah was dying. It wasn't that Great-aunt Hannah was ill, exactly, more that she seemed to be retreating from the world. Slowly her faculties were fading. Her sight had dimmed so that she could no longer read her bible, though she still liked to hold it in her hands when she sat in her chair in the drawing room. Clemency had to speak very loudly and clearly for Great-aunt Hannah to hear her, and for some weeks now the old lady's longest journey had been from her bedroom to the drawing room. Sometimes Clemency wondered what it was like inexorably to lose everything that made life worth living. Not to be able to hear the voices or see the faces of the people you loved. Not to be able to feel the sun on your skin or the wind in your hair.

It was unfortunate that just as Hannah seemed to be fading, Mother had taken a turn for the worse. Clemency seemed to spend a great deal of that summer and autumn dashing between Mother's room and Great-aunt Hannah's with trays of medicine and pots of tea and plates of invalid food. The doctor visited almost every day. Father, who had an irrational dislike of the perfectly pleasant Dr Hazeldene, said grumpily one

291

dinnertime, 'I think you should have a room made up for the wretched man, Clemmie. He seems to have taken up permanent residence.'

However busy she was, Clemency always made time to go to Ivor's concerts. Father had become an unexpected ally in that. Though he did not know — and must never, of course, know — how she felt for Ivor, he seemed to realize that the concerts were important to her, and took her part when Mother complained of Lucy Catherwood's dullness, or the servants wordlessly made clear their resentment of the extra work that Clemency's absence entailed. On recital afternoons Father would sometimes give her a lift in the motor car on his way back to work after lunch. As they left the house, he would look about in a conspiratorial fashion and say, 'The coast's clear. Enemy nowhere in sight. Better make a run for it, Clem.' Depositing her at whichever house the concert was to be held, he'd slip her a half-crown.

It was in September that Clemency finally met Rosalie. There was a concert at Mrs Braybrooke's house. Ever since Vera had made her spiteful remark about Mrs Braybrooke having said that Clemency followed Ivor around like a puppy dog, Clemency had made sure not to pay too much attention to Ivor when he played at Mrs Braybrooke's house. Because Mother had needed her to tidy up her letter case, Clemency was late leaving home, and Ivor had already reached the Braybrookes' by the time she arrived. Standing beside Ivor as he spoke to Mrs Braybrooke was a tall, dark-haired woman Clemency had not seen before. The woman was wearing a purple skirt and jacket and matching purple hat. When she first heard Mrs Braybrooke address the purple-hatted woman as Mrs Godwin, Clemency thought she must have made a mistake. This tall, well-made woman with the high-coloured complexion could not possibly be Rosalie

292

Godwin. Rosalie was fair, pallid, slight. It took Clemency a second to recall that the slight, pallid Rosalie existed only in her imagination.

During the concert Clemency hardly heard the music and her gaze constantly slid to Rosalie Godwin. Mrs Godwin gave Ivor an encouraging smile before he began each piece and applauded politely afterwards. Once, halfway through one of the longer sonatas, she gave a little yawn behind a purple-gloved hand. Clemency saw how, when the recital was over, Rosalie went to Ivor and gave him a little pat on the arm to congratulate him on his performance. And how she straightened the handkerchief in his breast pocket, and how she quickly and neatly put back the lock of dark hair that had fallen over his brow, something that Clemency had always wanted to do, but had never quite plucked up the courage. At tea Clemency noticed that Rosalie Godwin made sure that Ivor's tea was as he liked it: weak, with one sugar. Cakes were offered round; as Ivor reached for the plate, Rosalie said, 'Not the almond cake, Ivor. You know it always makes your dyspepsia worse.'

Before the afternoon ended, Clemency was introduced to Rosalie Godwin. 'This is my dear friend, Clemency Maclise,' Ivor said, and then she and Rosalie shook hands. There was, of course, no opportunity that afternoon to linger in the Botanical Gardens.

After that day she no longer fantasized about Rosalie dying. What had formerly been distasteful seemed, now that she had met Rosalie, contemptible. Though she tried to loathe Rosalie she could no longer do so with as much conviction. Though she reminded herself of that yawn halfway through Ivor's piece, she acknowledged that the sonata had been very long and mostly scales and arpeggios. She recalled Rosalie's officiousness in directing poor Ivor's choice of cake — yet Clemency herself knew that Ivor had a very delicate stomach. Once, at their café, he had eaten a currant bun and had been in *agony*.

A few weeks later Clemency knew the moment she went into the drawing room at Summerleigh that something had changed. An absence: something gone forever. Hannah was sitting in her chair. Her eyes were closed, as if she was sleeping, and the bible lay open on her lap. But when Clemency touched the old lady's hand it was already chilling.

That night they wrote letters and sent cables. 'I remember Aunt Hannah taking me to Ecclesall woods,' said Joshua, blowing his nose hard. 'I loved to play there — I loved to climb the trees and run through the paths and imagine I might get lost and never find my way out. Once Hannah climbed a tree. Did I ever tell you that, Clemency? I'd got myself stuck — I was only a little lad — and she clambered up and helped me down. Just imagine, climbing a tree in crinoline and petticoats and whatnot.' Joshua placed blotting paper over his letter and thumped it hard with his fist. 'Hannah was the only person left alive who knew me when I was a little boy,' he said sadly. 'With her gone, I've lost a part of myself, too.'

★   ★   ★

Eva had a letter from Sadie.

> The children have had chickenpox. They didn't have the decency to all catch it at once, and have had it one after the other, so we've been in quarantine for months. Dearest Eva, if you've had the wretched illness already, and can put up with a Sadie who's lately found herself talking to the pigs, please, please come and visit me.

There was no one to meet her at the station, so Eva walked across the fields to Greenstones. The yard and outbuildings had a neglected, shabby air. The fallen leaves had not yet been swept up from the cobbles, and a few scruffy hens wandered around pecking at the mud.

Sadie was unpegging washing from the line. She hugged Eva. 'I'm so glad you've come. Now I won't go entirely mad.'

The house, too, seemed bedraggled. Children's belongings were strewn around the floors. A heap of picture books was scattered across the kitchen, as though blown by a gust of wind; Eva tripped over a bow and arrows left in a dark corridor.

'I try to put the children's things away,' said Sadie, 'but they only take them out again, so it all seems pointless. And my daily woman has deserted me — not that I blame her, things being as they are, and not that she was a great deal of help anyway. I often thought the floors looked dirtier after she'd mopped them than before. But she was company, at least. At the moment there's only me and Val and the children, and you know how moody Val can be. I keep catching him scowling at me. So you can't imagine how pleased I am to see you, Eva. You simply can't imagine.'

Eva washed up and ironed the children's clothes and read stories to Tolly as he scratched his fading spots. Later, in the afternoon, Sadie came into the drawing room, looking worried. 'I can't find Hero. Have you seen her?'

Eva looked downstairs while Sadie went upstairs to the attics and Val searched the garden and farmyard. For a while there was only the echo of Hero's name as they all called out for her, and then there was a sudden shout and Eva and Sadie ran outside.

The shout came from the carp pond. By the time they reached it, Val was emerging from the water, ribboned with pond weed, the little girl limp in his arms.

Sadie went white. 'Oh God. Oh no. Please God.' She ran to the pond. Val put Hero face down on the grass and knelt beside her, pressing her ribcage. There was a long, awful moment when she lay quite still, and then she gave a cough and spat out water and weed. Then she sat up and cried, and Sadie scooped her up into her arms and carried her into the house.

As Sadie ran a hot bath and stripped off Hero's wet clothes, Eva saw that her hands were shaking. Her face was still very pale and there was a taut, frightened look in her eyes. But she said quite calmly, 'If you would be so kind as to keep an eye on the dinner, Eva, please. The stew will burn.'

Eva went downstairs to the kitchen. She, too, was shaking. After she had checked the stew, she sat down at the table. Val, still wearing his wet clothes, came in. 'Apparently it was some sort of a game. Orlando made a boat out of an old log. It was the *Titanic* or something.' He reached under the sink and drew out a bottle of brandy. 'Drink?' Eva shook her head. 'Suit yourself,' he said. Throwing his head back, putting the bottle to his mouth, Val took several large gulps. Then he wiped his mouth with the back of his hand and said, 'I'd better get changed. I smell like a bloody sewer.'

Dinner was a subdued affair, with even Orlando eating his meal in silence. Eva noticed that Sadie hardly ate a thing, every now and then poking at the meat and potatoes with her knife, her face white and set. After dinner Eva washed up while Sadie put the children to bed. Eva was drying the last of the cutlery when she heard Sadie come downstairs. 'Are they all settled?' she asked.

Sadie nodded.

'Where's Val?'

'He went to the pub. Had enough of family life, I expect.' Sadie sat down and covered her face with her hands. Eva only just caught the muttered words. 'If she had died — if Hero had died — it would have been my fault!'

Sitting down beside her, Eva patted Sadie's tense shoulder. 'Children always have accidents.'

'My children have more than most.' Sadie's hands slid away from her face; her dark eyes were wide and tearless. 'I'm not a good mother, Eva, and that's the truth of it. I don't care for them as I should, and I don't love them as I should. I never wanted five children. I'm not sure that I even wanted one. And since I had Rowan I seem to have given up.'

'You're just tired, Sadie.'

'Yes, I suppose I am. I've been tired — oh, since Orlando was born. I can't remember what it's like not to be tired. But that's no excuse, is it? Other mothers are tired and they manage to care for their children properly.' She gave a quick, frightened smile. 'I must have tea. Will you be a darling and make me some tea, Eva? I live on tea and cigarettes these days.'

Eva filled the kettle and put it on the hob. Sadie said quietly, 'I haven't felt right since Rowan was born. I haven't *loved* him, you see. When I look at him, I feel nothing. I keep thinking that it'll change — I've never much cared for little babies, I've always preferred them when they were older — but Rowan's two now, and I still feel nothing for him.' She frowned as she opened her cigarette case. 'I haven't told anyone. Not Gabriel — not even my mother. It's not the sort of thing one wants to talk about, is it? A mother should love her children.' She struck a match. 'But this afternoon, when I thought Hero was . . . ' She broke off, biting her lip. Then she gave a short laugh. 'Perhaps I should be thankful. Perhaps poor Hero nearly drowning was a blessing in disguise. At least it's proved to me that I do love my children a bit.'

Eva made the tea and put a cup in front of Sadie.

'Perhaps you've just had rather a lot of children in quite a short time,' she said. She remembered Iris saying: *Poor Mother. Seven children in fourteen years.*

'I neglect them, Eva, I know that I do. They're dressed in rags because I can't keep up with the washing and the mending, and they're lucky if I remember to bath them once a week. The village children won't play with them, did you know that? They call them names — pikey and gypsy — and throw stones at them. And even if I could manage to persuade Gabriel to let me send them to school, then how on earth would they manage? They don't know their times tables, and I don't think they've ever recited the Lord's Prayer in their entire lives.' She looked around the untidy kitchen. 'This is not what I want for them,' she said softly. 'This is not want I want for Hero. Men don't mind mess, do they? They don't care if a room doesn't look nice, but women do. And it's not that I don't want things to look nice, Eva, it's just that I can't — I can't — ' She broke off, pressing her palms together.

'It's a big house,' said Eva consolingly. 'There must be so much to do.'

'I managed at first. But I can't seem to find the spirit any more. I feel *defeated*.' Sadie gave a shaky smile. 'It's all very well for a man to be a Bohemian, but it doesn't do for women, does it? Gabriel's forever romancing about how, before we were married, he used to wander round the country, sleeping in hedges and ditches. And he loves café life, doesn't he, and all those noisy, rumbustious friends of his.' Her voice lowered. 'But that sort of life wouldn't work for a woman. You know how disparaging men are about women who frequent cafés and pubs. As for sleeping in hedges and ditches, they'd probably carry us off to an asylum.'

Eva poured out more tea. 'I can't say that hedges and ditches have ever appealed to me. Too cold, for one thing.'

'Quite.' Sadie sighed. 'There, I've been talking about myself for hours. How dull. Tell me about yourself, Eva. You must have finished at the Slade by now.'

'Yes. I finished in June.'

'You'll keep on painting, won't you?'

Eva turned away, busying herself with emptying tea leaves into the bin. 'You have to be so good to succeed. Even Gabriel, who's so brilliant, finds it hard sometimes.'

'He was in a foul mood for weeks after his last show,' said Sadie ruefully. 'Those wretched reviewers. I'd happily throttle them. And he's always in a foul mood when he isn't painting.' There were jigsaw pieces scattered across the table; Sadie drew them to her, one by one. 'An artistic life is harder for women than for men,' she said slowly. 'You have to give up so much. I don't think it mixes with husbands and children. When I first married Gabriel, I tried to keep up with my painting. But I couldn't, it was quite impossible. Domestic things kept getting in the way — tradesmen would ring the doorbell, or I would have to rush out to buy the supper things, or the washing would need doing. I used to have servants then because we were in London, but even so, you have to keep an eye on servants, don't you? And it was always my job, of course, to remember to buy the bread and pay the milkman and change the sheets on the bed, never Gabriel's.' Her eyes darkened. 'When I was trying to paint he often used to come into my room — just to ask me where something was, or to find out when we were next going to see this or that set of friends. But I have never interrupted him, Eva. And I've never let the children interrupt him either.' She stubbed out her cigarette in a saucer. 'And after a while I stopped trying to paint. It didn't seem worth the effort. And then Orlando came along and I've hardly touched a paintbrush since.'

'Perhaps when they're older . . . '

'Perhaps. Though I suspect any scrap of talent I once had will have vanished by then.'

There were more jigsaw pieces on the floor; Sadie knelt on the flagstones to gather them up. 'Of course,' she said, 'the ironic thing is that, though men depend on us to do the domestic work, they find domesticity so unattractive. Especially Gabriel. He loved me far more before I became so caught up with houses and babies. In fact, all that horrifies him — the grim meals with the children, and the nagging wife telling him that the drains need mending. That's why he dashes off to London, to escape from all that.' Standing up, Sadie put the jigsaw pieces on the table top. 'And that's why he falls so, poor dear, for his nymphs, his gypsies.'

Eva could not speak. Her throat felt constricted, her face hot.

Sadie was fitting jigsaw pieces together. 'Gabriel has a habit of falling in love with wild, unobtainable women,' she said lightly. 'Sandals and uncombed hair and ill-fitting clothes, you know the sort of thing. He pursues the poor things so fiercely they can't refuse him. He can be so terribly persistent when he chooses, the wretch. When he courted me, I kept saying no, but he simply wouldn't listen. But then, when he's caught them — when he's *tamed* them — he finds he no longer wants them. Poor Gabriel's fascinated by the unobtainable. He's inspired by the unobtainable. That's all women really are to him, something to inspire him. He adores us and he respects us — unlike a great many of his sex — but most of all he needs us to inspire him. But once he's put his wild little bird in a cage — once he's captured her — he loses interest. After he's pinioned her to the canvas he has to move on and find himself a new muse.'

Eva had to force herself to ask the question. 'Don't you mind?'

300

Sadie seemed to consider. 'I used to, but I don't think I do now.' She glanced around the untidy kitchen. 'I don't have to stay here, after all. I could go home to my mother. She's begged me to often enough.'

'Why don't you?'

'Oh, because of Gabriel, of course. I love him.' She sounded resigned. 'I often wish I didn't, but I do. Loving Gabriel's like an illness I can't shake off. And also because Mother would *crow* so. She'd try not to, but she wouldn't be able to help it. She's never liked Gabriel.' Sadie smiled. 'The funny thing is that I've become rather fond of some of the muses. I never expected to, but I have. I know that other people find that rather odd. Not Nerissa, of course, I could never be fond of someone so self-centred. But some of the others. Very fond, in fact.' She raised her eyes to Eva. 'And I wouldn't want them to be hurt. I wouldn't want them to waste their lives on a man who'll always put his art before everything else.'

This time the silence seemed to Eva to last forever. Then there was a cry from upstairs, and Sadie said exasperatedly as she left the room, '*Rowan*. That child will be twenty-one before he sleeps through the night, I'm sure of it.'

Eva went home two days later. At Mrs Wilde's house there was a telegram waiting for her. 'It arrived an hour ago.' Mrs Wilde glanced at it fearfully. 'The nasty thing.'

The telegram told Eva that Great-aunt Hannah had died in her sleep. Eva cabled home and looked out her blacks for the funeral. On the train to Sheffield, staring unseeing out of the window, she remembered all the times she had taken Great-aunt Hannah to the shops, or pushed her down the hill in the park, the bath chair sailing down the asphalt path like a ship through the sea. And she thought of Sadie sitting at the kitchen table at Greenstones, saying: *I love him. I often wish I didn't,*

301

but I do. And just then she felt only an immense emptiness, as if she had been hollowed out inside.

★ ★ ★

After the funeral they cleared out Great-aunt Hannah's rooms together. Iris paired up black woollen stockings, Clemency and Eva folded and wrapped in tissue paper dresses of creaking black bombazine and grosgrain, fringed shawls and mantles, vast pantalettes and petticoats. There were whalebone and calico stays three times the width of Iris's tiny waist, pelisses and tippets and a white fur muff, and a pair of pale blue silk dancing slippers embroidered with forget-me-nots. There was a Moroccan leather writing case stuffed with letters, the ink a faded brown, the paper fragile with age. Great-aunt Hannah's perfume, a mixture of camphor and violet cachous, lingered in her rooms among the stern daguerrotypes and watercolour landscapes.

They laid Great-aunt Hannah's jewellery out on the bed. Brooches, bracelets, necklaces and lockets. 'What shall we send to Marianne?' asked Clemency.

'*Not* the elephant hair bracelet.' Iris shuddered.

There was a pearl and amethyst ring. The prettiest thing by far, in Clemency's opinion. She picked it up and held it up to the light, and thought of Marianne, thousands of miles away in a strange land. 'This,' she said.

★ ★ ★

There was a half-finished painting on the easel in Gabriel's studio: Eva recognized Ruby Bailey's wild, windswept hair and the long, pale column of her throat.

When she told him why she had come, he looked stricken.

'You're leaving me? Eva, you can't.'

'I must.'

'Is it because of Nerissa?'

She shook her head. 'Not really. A little bit, perhaps. And a little bit because of *her*.' She glanced at the painting on the easel. 'And because of Sadie, of course. But most of all I'm leaving you because of me. Because being with you isn't making me happy any more, Gabriel. It used to — it still does, sometimes — but not enough, I find. Not enough.'

Before she left, she said, 'There's just one more thing I want of you, Gabriel.'

'Anything.'

'I want you to tell me whether I'm good enough to become a professional artist. I know you'll be honest with me.'

She saw that his gaze was already drifting back to the half-completed painting. But he said, 'You could be an illustrator, perhaps — or there's always interior decoration . . .'

'But not a painter.' Her voice was flat.

'It's a hell of a way to earn a living, Eva. Hard for the best of us. I'm sorry.'

'Thank you for telling me the truth.' She turned to go.

'Eva!' His voice followed her as she ran downstairs. 'Eva!'

But she did not turn back.

10

In the afternoons Marianne liked to sit beneath the banyan tree in the bungalow garden. When one of the thick, leathery leaves fell, it struck the ground with an audible thump. Barbets and orioles perched in the branches of the banyan: every now and then, looking up, she would catch a flicker of gold or green. In those peaceful hours in the garden she felt as though something that had been broken had begun to mend at last.

The voyage from Southampton to Colombo on board the P&O steamer SS *Pelagia* had taken four weeks. The grey, choppy sea of the English Channel had given way first to the blue of the Mediterranean and then to the intense, airless heat of the Red Sea. There had been days spent steaming across the Indian Ocean and nights beneath stars of diamond brightness, nights when the ship's wake sparkled with phosphorescence. And then, at last, Marianne had caught her first sight of the island, the highest peaks of the mountains lost in cloud. As they neared the port, she had seen brown-skinned men in outrigger canoes, and palm trees and sandy beaches fringing the coastline.

They had stayed for three nights in the Grand Oriental Hotel in Colombo. Lucas had business in the city; a fellow English-woman, who had also travelled to Ceylon on board the *Pelagia*, showed Marianne round. Rickshaws and bullock carts jostled with motor cars in the busy streets; an elephant hauled a load of logs through the entrance to a sawmill. Skinny cattle and yellow, feral dogs shared the roads and alleyways with slight, golden-skinned Sinhalese, Tamils, Burghers, Afghans, Malays and Europeans. Open-fronted shops displayed bracelets and necklaces set with moonstones, star sapphires, cat's eyes and rubies. There were bales of gorgeously coloured silks and cottons, and palm-leaf baskets heaped with spices and fruits. In the Pettah, the market in the native quarter, barbers shaved their customers in the street and snake-charmers played brass flutes to sleepy-eyed cobras coiled in baskets. Little brown babies, clad only in bead necklaces, played close to their mothers.

By the time she returned to the hotel, Marianne's white dress was pink with red dust from the streets and the scent of Ceylon, a mixture of spice and heat and sweetly scented blossom and bustling humanity, lingered in her nostrils. The air was thick and heavy; a languor seemed to seize her limbs and something inside her, tightly sprung for such a long time, began to unwind. At night, in that space between waking and sleeping that had since Arthur's death been populated only by grief and horror, different images now flickered behind her eyes: a black-haired boy bathing in a river; a Catholic church hung about with red flags; and the Sinhalese script on the shop signs, a script that seemed to her, with its graceful loops and curlicues, to sum up the strange beauty of the place.

Three days later they travelled by train from Colombo to Kandy in the centre of the island. Marianne had brought with her a novel to pass the journey, but did not open it. What she saw through the carriage window absorbed her. In the lush, flat plains of the hinterland beyond Colombo, the emerald-green paddy fields were busy with sari'd women, ankle-deep in water. White egrets stalked the bunds between the paddy fields, and bee-eaters, jewelled fragments of blue and green, perched on the bushes. Several times she caught the sapphire flash of a kingfisher darting along the course of a river. Buffalo waded in the marshland and cranes and ibis curled their long necks. Cascades of pink and purple bougainvillaea and white datura lilies lined the roads; lotus blossoms raised their exquisite heads from olive-green water, and a monitor lizard, five foot in length, hauled its mottled black body out of a stream. Once she saw a tall acacia tree that seemed to be hung with great dark rags. 'They're flying foxes,' Lucas told her. 'They roost in the trees by day. They're not foxes at all, of course, but bats with a wingspan of — ' He held his hands a yard apart.

A boat with a curved prow glided down a river and, in the shady rubber plantations, natives tapped the trunks of the trees. Green pods hung from cocoa bushes, and king coconuts the colour of the sun clustered in palm tops. As the train climbed higher and higher into the hills, Marianne had her first sight of a tea estate. The rows of bushes on the distant slopes had the appearance of a bolt of ribbed, dark green corduroy. She sensed an alteration in Lucas, a tautness, an impatience.

They stayed only one night in Kandy, where trees and elegant red-roofed buildings surrounded a rectangular blue lake. There was an island in the middle of the lake, shaded by palm trees — the King of Kandy had once kept his wives there, Lucas told her. Travelling from Kandy to Nuwara Eliya the following morning, Marianne saw waterfalls rushing over rocky precipices, and rumpled, green-sloped hills. From the dim, lichened conifer forests, shaggy bear monkeys stared wide-eyed at her, sheltered beneath the canopy of branches. Clouds clung to the ferns and mosses, and, in the valley below, the Nanu Oya river rushed and spilled through narrow chasms.

Nuwara Eliya meant City of Light. Here the air was sharp and cool and bright. Marianne felt dizzy from lack of oxygen and from the continual assault of unfamiliar sights, sounds and scents. More than six thousand feet up in the mountains of Ceylon, the roads of Nuwara Eliya were lined with bungalows whose neat gardens were planted with pansies, geraniums and red-hot pokers. They stayed overnight at the Grand Hotel; Marianne did a little shopping at Cargill's department store.

The next day they took the train through the mountains once more. They were met at the railway station by turbaned grooms dressed in white uniforms with yellow sashes. They had with them a horse for Lucas and a bullock cart for Marianne to take them on the final stage of their journey. As the road led out of the small town, with its bazaar and string of shacks, the tea fields spread out to either side, and Lucas leaned forward in his seat, light in his eyes.

'Blackwater,' he said softly. 'This is Blackwater.'

The road narrowed into a dirt track, barely wider than the wheelbase of the cart, which clung to the mountainside. Marianne saw that to one side of her the hillside fell away, steep and precipitous, thousands of feet down into the valley. The stony track snaked round slopes in a series of switchbacks and hairpin bends, and the cart rattled across log bridges that perched precariously over chasms. Beside the streams that cascaded over the rocks Marianne noticed bunches of flowers and odd-shaped stones tied around with coloured ribbons. 'Offerings to the gods,' said Lucas when she questioned him. 'The gods of the Tamil coolies who work on the tea estates.'

They must have travelled for two miles or so, skirting the mountains, rock to one side of them, emptiness to the other. Had the cart lost a wheel, or had there been a rockfall, then there would have been nothing to prevent them falling to their deaths. Yet Marianne was not afraid. She knew that she would survive, that she must survive. Because, with the passing days, and with the steady transformation of hope into certainty, she knew that she was pregnant.

Such a long journey; they should have begun to know each other better. Yet she felt that she knew Lucas Melrose little more by the time they reached Blackwater than she had when they had first boarded the steamship at Southampton.

Some things she discovered. He was a man of routine, rising early each day and taking exercise before breakfast. On board ship, and at the hotel in Colombo, he dined at the same hour, retired at the same hour. Marianne had noticed in London that he had an air of authority, a knack of getting what he wanted. Servants hurried at his click of the fingers and some of their fellow passengers, less certain of themselves than he, were deferential to him. He was exacting — he had his collars sent back to the laundry when they were not stiffened just so, and he was sharp when the driver of the rickshaw who carried their cases from Colombo docks to the hotel dropped a suitcase. Marianne put his anger down to weariness from the long journey.

On the voyage they did not talk as she and Arthur had talked, of unimportant, inconsequential things. Lucas was polite and informative, answering her questions, making sure her needs were attended to, but there was not that sharing of small interests and pleasures. He carried within him something suppressed, coiled like a spring, which tightened as they neared Blackwater. She guessed that he was homesick, impatient to see his house and estate after so long an absence.

Sometimes, returning to him after they had been apart for a few hours, she would catch a look of surprise in his eyes, as if he had momentarily forgotten she was there. Quick and decisive by nature, he rarely sought her opinion. He was used to command, of course, and to solitariness. They would come to know each other gradually, she reasoned. Their courtship and marriage had been rushed, and it was understandable that after so many years of living alone the sharing of everyday life did not come easily to him. And she herself was not looking for intimacy, only for companionship.

When she was sure, she told him about the baby.

'Are you certain?' he asked her.

It was evening; they were sitting on the bungalow veranda. 'Quite certain.' She laughed at his expression. 'Lucas, I haven't been able to eat my breakfast for weeks. And there are other signs, too. I'm perfectly sure.'

'Good,' he said. 'That's good. When will he be born?'

'March, I think. But it could be a girl, of course.'

He shook his head. 'Melroses only have sons. And I need a son — ' he stared out at the moonlit garden — 'for *this*.'

From that night he no longer shared a bed with her, but slept in a room on the other side of the bungalow. She felt a measure of relief; when he made love to her she had felt little of the delight that she had experienced with Arthur. How considerate of him, she thought, to put her comfort before his own pleasure and to endure abstinence for the sake of her health.

★ ★ ★

She kept her part of the bargain, quickly learning to run the bungalow with smooth efficiency. The Blackwater bungalow was large and light and airy, with four bedrooms, a dining room, sitting room and bathroom, and the pleasant, open, seven-sided vestibule at the front of the house. The kitchen and servants' quarters were at the back. All the principal rooms had fireplaces because the nights in the hill country could be chilly.

The boy, Nadeshan, woke Marianne at dawn with a tray of tea and fresh fruit, and then, after breakfast, she checked the storeroom, discussed menus and gave out supplies to the Sinhalese cook. Orders for provisions were written in the 'Beef Book' and sent out for. Then she supervised the cleaning and dusting of the house, picked flowers and arranged them in vases.

Lucas came home at midday for tiffin, a light lunch. Afterwards, in the hottest part of the day, Marianne retired to her room. Pregnancy seemed to have given her a great appetite for sleep. It was as though she was making up for all the broken nights and dawn wakings that had followed Arthur's death. After her siesta she wrote letters, and then she was free to amuse herself in the garden until teatime.

The Blackwater bungalow perched on a hill top. Three wide, terraced lawns led down from the veranda. The borders, with their shrub roses and perennials were, Marianne noticed, sadly overgrown. A path ran round the perimeter of the garden, and only a few feet beyond the path, the hillside fell steeply down into a valley. Caught within the boundaries were lawns, paths, flower beds and woodland. The initial similarity of the Blackwater garden to the gardens and woodland of England was deceptive, a second glance, and she felt herself seduced, almost overwhelmed by its strange opulence and luxuriance. The trees were not the oaks and beeches of English parkland, but eucalyptus, orange-flowered flamboyant trees, and turpentines with tall, pale trunks and feathery leaves. Wild bees swarmed around curiously shaped hives that hung from the branches; a ficus wound up the trunk of a cedar, smothering it in sinuous snaking fronds. Here the bird calls seemed louder and more insistent than in England, and clouds of white butterflies floated across the grass like a hundred blossoms blown by the wind. Columns of fat-bodied ants marched their armies through the undergrowth and, in a dark corner shaded by tall trees, Marianne came across a tiny shrine. Little more than a

310

triangle of sticks, it nestled inside the roots of a tree. Someone had placed flowers inside the house of sticks; from the branches of the nearby trees white streamers flapped.

At the far end of the garden was a small summerhouse roofed in palm leaves, built on a wooden platform that cantilevered out from the hillside. From the summerhouse, she looked down onto clouds. On a fine day she could see the ranges of hills, one behind the other, which crumpled and buckled the landscape as far as the eye could see. The hills were punctuated every now and then by the silver gleam of a lake or the emerald of a paddy field, which at that distance resembled a scrap of bright material in a patchwork. In her little wooden perch jutting out from the mountainside, she had a sense of precariousness, of fragility.

The young assistant managers often came to the bungalow for tea; occasionally another planter and his wife, or perhaps Dr Scott or the padre, would call in at the estate. Sitting in long cane chairs on the veranda, the men would talk shop while Marianne watched the hills become bluer and bluer as they melted into the horizon. The early evening sunsets, short-lived because Ceylon was so near the equator, were a brief, glorious flare of bronze and gold.

Then the letters arrived and there was time to glance through them before dressing for dinner. They dined at eight o'clock and afterwards sat by the drawing-room fire. At night, lying in bed, Marianne had the same sense of floating above the world, free and untethered, that she had in the summerhouse.

She must have fallen pregnant, she realized, during the first weeks of her marriage to Lucas. She felt a fleeting resentment that the same miracle had not happened in her marriage to Arthur, but any bitterness was soon subsumed by her longing for the baby. After the first three months her morning sickness vanished and her appetite returned. Her body changed, her waist expanding and her breasts becoming fuller. The first time she felt the child quicken in her womb, she experienced an emotion she had almost forgotten, a mixture of excitement and anticipation and delight that took her a moment or two to identify as happiness.

★   ★   ★

In the autumn of 1912 George Lansbury, the Labour Member of Parliament for Bow and Bromley, resigned his seat in an attempt to draw attention to the plight of suffragette prisoners. In the subsequent by-election Lansbury stood as the Women's Suffrage and Socialist candidate. His election headquarters in Bow Road rubbed shoulders with the headquarters of the Pankhursts' WSPU, Millicent Fawcett's NUWSS, the Votes for Women Fellowship, the Men's Political Union for Women's Emancipation, the National League for Opposing Women's Emancipation, and the Unionists' committee rooms. Mrs Emmeline Pankhurst herself addressed no less than three public meetings in Bow on the day before the election, meetings at which, Eva told Iris, the audience was comprised almost entirely of women, a great many of whom had brought their babies with them. The babies howled and chortled at regular intervals throughout Mrs Pankhurst's speech, sometimes rendering her inaudible. In the evening the suffrage societies assembled outside Bow church. A brass band played the Marseillaise, and the procession then marched through the constituency bearing banners and lanterns.

A visit to Bow wasn't how Iris would necessarily have chosen to spend one of her two precious days off that month, especially in a blustery November downpour, but she allowed herself to be persuaded by Ash. And there was, in spite of the awful weather, an untypically carnival atmosphere about the dingy East End streets. Flags — the purple, green and white of the WSPU and the green, yellow and white of the Women's Freedom League — streamed from motor cars and vans, and children's choirs sang election songs. Suffrage women stood outside polling booths; Eva, shepherding voters into one of the booths, had forgotten her umbrella. By the time Iris and Ash reached her, she was drenched to the skin.

Iris gave Eva her umbrella and shared Ash's. As they walked through the streets, Iris noticed how many people greeted Ash affectionately. Men in cloth caps paused to speak to him as they passed, women in shabby coats with rosettes pinned to their lapels waved to him, and children ran after him, begging for humbugs or boiled sweets from his pocket.

A dark-haired young woman hailed him from across the street, calling out to him as she dashed between the traffic. 'I've been looking for you, Ash! I've only just been able to leave the shop. I wanted to shut up early so I could get away, but Dad wouldn't . . . ' She broke off, catching sight of Iris, beneath Ash's umbrella.

'Thelma,' said Ash, 'let me introduce you to Miss Iris Maclise. Iris, this is Miss Thelma Voss.'

'Pleased to meet you, Miss Maclise, I'm sure.'

'Thelma and I delivered pamphlets for the election,' explained Ash. 'Five hundred of them, wasn't it?'

'Near enough.'

'I couldn't have managed without Thelma.'

Thelma went crimson. 'It wasn't any trouble.'

'It sounds utterly exhausting,' said Iris. 'Do you live nearby, Miss Voss?'

'Not far. Just off the Commercial Road.'

'Then we're almost neighbours. I work at the Mandeville Hospital.'

'My Dad went there when he hurt his leg.' Thelma

313

Voss's gaze slid over Iris, taking in her wide-brimmed hat with cerise chiffon trim and her new velvet-collared coat, which Iris had bought in Harrods. 'I didn't stop to change,' she muttered. Beneath her mackintosh Thelma was wearing a brown overall over her dress, and she had wrapped a scarf round her hair. She said suddenly, 'Some of the other women are looking so *smart*. The WSPU women.' She tugged at her overalls and jabbed a strand of hair beneath the scarf. 'I didn't think to bother.'

Iris said, 'The last time I saw my sister Eva she had a newspaper over her head to keep off the rain. Hardly a fashion plate. I don't think you need worry, Miss Voss. Do you belong to the WSPU?'

'Not me,' said Thelma scornfully. 'The WSPU isn't for women like me — it's not for *working* women.'

'What of Annie Kenney?' asked Ash. 'She was a mill girl, wasn't she?'

Thelma shrugged. 'Annie Kenney's the Pankhursts' *pet*, everyone knows that.'

'I was going to see whether they needed any help at the polling station,' said Ash. 'You'll come, won't you, Thelma? And then let me buy you supper. A thank you for all those leaflets.'

'Supper?' Thelma's face brightened. 'Well, I — '

'Iris and I were going to get fish and chips. You could join us.'

The sullen expression returned to Thelma's eyes. 'I can't,' she muttered. 'I promised Nancy Smith I'd help her with the teas. And then I must get my dad's supper.'

Without saying goodbye, she headed off. When Thelma was out of earshot, Iris said, 'She seems very fond of you, Ash.'

'Thelma?' He looked surprised. 'She's just a friend.'

She opened her mouth to argue with him, to say, *No, Ash, she's in love with you*, and then she shut it again. Thelma Voss's turbaned head had disappeared into the crowds. *For an intelligent man,* thought Iris, as she took Ash's arm and they continued down the pavement, *you really can be surprisingly dense.*

⋆   ⋆   ⋆

George Lansbury lost the Bow and Bromley by-election by seven hundred and fifty-one votes. The greatest irony, Ash thought gloomily, was that because of an error in the parliamentary register a lone woman, Mrs Unity Dawkins, had been able to vote in the election. Mrs Pankhurst herself had visited Mrs Dawkins to try to persuade her to cast her vote for George Lansbury; one of the suffrage societies had offered her a lift to the polling booth in a motor car. But in the end Mrs Dawkins had voted for Reginald Blair, the Conservative and anti-suffrage candidate. Ash himself had glimpsed her, proudly displaying a blue card proclaiming her support for Mr Blair.

Ash called on Thelma at her father's shop one evening after work. She was going through a box of apples, picking out the rotten ones. Her face brightened when she saw him.

Ash said, 'I wanted to thank you for all your help with the election. All those pamphlets in the rain.'

'Didn't do much good, though, did it?'

He watched her shine the apples with a cloth. 'I knew we might lose — it was always a risky thing, making women's suffrage the only issue — but I didn't think the margin would be that big.'

Thelma shrugged. 'I expect some of the men took against all those smart ladies barging into places they wouldn't normally be seen dead in and telling them what to do.'

'I suppose so. But the *Tories* — why vote for them? What have they ever done for the East End?'

'They're respectable, aren't they? That's all people

315

round here want. To be thought respectable. You can lecture them about socialism and all the rest of it till you're blue in the face, but all most of them want is to get another step up the ladder. The ones who put newspaper on their table want to be able to afford a cloth. Girls who've only got a shawl want to buy a coat. That's as far as their ambitions go.'

'Is that as far as your ambitions go, Thelma?'

She did not answer his question, but put down the cloth and said, 'Would you like to have tea with us? I was going to shut up shop anyway.'

'That would be splendid. If it's not too much trouble.'

Thelma turned the sign on the door and pulled down the blind. As they left the shop she whispered to Ash, 'Don't talk about politics or anything like that in front of Dad. It makes him nervous.'

The Vosses' shop was on the corner of the street; their house, at the end of a terraced row, was slightly larger than those of their neighbours. The parlour, which was behind the shop, had a small bow window facing out into the side street. Thelma's father was sitting in a chair beside the fire; he tried to rise as Ash came into the room. Thelma said, 'Don't get up, Dad, Ash won't mind. Dad, this is my friend, Ash. Remember I told you about him before. I've asked him to stay to tea.'

Ash talked to Thelma's father while Thelma put out the tea things. Though he could see a physical resemblance between father and daughter — the high, wide cheekbones and straight brows — Mr Voss had none of Thelma's liveliness and strong-mindedness. He was stooped and drawn, answering many of Ash's attempts at conversation with a monosyllable and his nervous gaze continually darted towards the kitchen, as though he felt ill at ease when Thelma was out of sight.

Tea consisted of tinned salmon sandwiches, fruit cake and jelly. They spoke about Ash's work, the changes in the street since the Vosses had first moved in twenty-five years ago and the rainy weather. When her father began to look tired, Thelma helped him back into his armchair and Ash thanked them and took his leave.

Thelma showed Ash back through the shop. Closing the parlour door behind her, she said quietly, 'That's why I'm not ambitious. That's why I don't do anything clever or useful, like some other girls.'

'I'm sorry,' he said. 'How long has your father been like that?'

'Six years. Since his accident.'

'What happened?'

'He was knocked down by a brewer's dray. They did their best up at the Mandeville, but his leg's never been right since.' Her voice lowered. 'His leg's the least of it, though. You saw what he's like. Mum died just two months before Dad had his accident. She had pneumonia. I suppose it was the two things happening so close together. Dad never really recovered. The doctor told me he'd had a nervous breakdown. He gets jumpy about the least thing. Loud noises especially — lorries coming past the shop, thunder, anything. And he's always afraid something bad will happen to me. If I'm ever late home he gets himself into a terrible state. When he's really bad, he hates me to go out of his sight for five minutes.' She stared at Ash fiercely. 'This isn't what I'd have chosen. I'd have liked to have gone to college. Or to be a nurse like your friend.'

'Iris?'

'Yes.' Her gaze, which had the directness and ferocity, he thought, of a hawk, did not leave him. 'I'd not seen her round here before, Ash. Is she an old friend of yours?'

'I've known her for years. Iris comes from Sheffield.' He smiled. 'That was where I first met her. She was cycling down a hill and the hem of her skirt caught in the front wheel, and she fell off the bike and almost

317

landed at my feet.' He added, 'We lost touch for a couple of years. We had an argument, a stupid argument. It was my fault.' He remembered the party at Summerleigh: Iris, whirling round the ballroom in the arms of one man after another. And he remembered the anger, and something else — jealousy, surely? — that he had felt, watching her. 'When I found out she'd become a nurse it was a shock. Iris never seemed interested in that sort of thing. She didn't seem the sort of girl who'd go in for nursing. Her friend, Charlotte — yes. But Iris . . . ' He had thought once, with an arrogance that now made him wince, that Iris was empty-headed and frivolous. That there was nothing behind the golden curls, the baby-blue eyes.

Thelma said flatly, 'It's because she's so pretty. You didn't think she'd want to be a nurse because she's so pretty. That outfit she had on . . . so smart.' There was a wistful look in Thelma's eye.

He said vaguely, 'Did you think so?'

Shortly after leaving the shop he heard footsteps, running to catch up with him. Thelma was holding something out to him.

'Take it,' she said. 'People round here won't eat them, they think they're poisonous or something. But I always ask Dad to get in one or two. I like them, don't you? I like to think of the places they've come from.'

It was a pomegranate. He thanked her and she gave him one of her rare smiles. Then she ran home.

★　★　★

For different reasons, Clemency was worried about all of her brothers. Though Philip seemed to have settled down at school, little things, which would hardly have troubled most people — a harsh word, Eva's cat killing a bird — seemed to hurt him deeply. It was as though he lacked a layer of skin, as though he had no armour against the world. If he had been a girl, Clemency sometimes thought, it might not have mattered so much. Sensitivity was prized in a girl but despised in a boy.

It was in the Christmas holidays, over a game of Ludo, that at last Philip confided in her. 'When I leave school,' he said, 'I want to train to be a priest.'

She shook the dice. 'You mean, a vicar.'

'No. A priest.' His dark blue eyes met hers; she could see how serious he was. 'If they'll take me, that is. I know it can be more difficult as a convert.'

She stared at him. 'You mean — you want to become a Roman Catholic?'

'Yes. I've been talking to a priest. We're allowed out on our own on Sunday afternoons now, and I was walking round the village, and he was weeding his garden and I offered to help. He's quite old, you see. And I've thought a lot about it, and I know it's what I want to do.' A small, resigned smile. 'I know Father won't like it. I know he's always expected me to go into the business. And he doesn't think much of Roman Catholics, does he? In his eyes, they're almost as bad as Communists. But I have to do this, Clem. I know it's the right thing for me. I've never been so sure of anything as I am of this.'

With a little coaxing, Philip agreed to wait until he was eighteen before taking any irrevocable step or speaking to Father. 'But I won't change my mind, Clem,' he said, and she found herself believing him.

As for James and Aidan, it was only that winter that Clemency began to understand just how much Aidan disliked James. They had never got on — none of the three brothers really *got on*, each was completely different in personality, and their separate orbits, which turned around the noisy, dominant sphere of Father, hardly touched. But since Aidan had started to work for J. Maclise & Sons he was necessarily in closer contact with James. Because James and Aidan were more than ten years apart in age, Clemency had never previously thought of them as rivals — if, indeed, they could be considered so, when all the rivalry was on Aidan's part. Good-humoured, artless James was incapable of the jealousy that was a necessary part of rivalry.

Aidan's nature was more complex. Often, Clemency sympathized with Aidan — she, the plainest of the Maclise sisters, knew what it was not to be noticed. Aidan's inability to show affection, and his odd looks — the reddish hair, the pale blue, darting eyes and slight build that had, in younger days, led his elder brother and sisters to nickname him the Weasel — made him hard to warm to. Yet of all the Maclise children, Aidan was the cleverest. He could work out sums instantly, sums that would have tangled up Clemency for hours. He had a natural quickness, and an ability to think logically and unemotionally that the rest of them lacked.

It must have been hard for Aidan that theirs was not a family which valued cleverness. Or, rather, Father did not value cleverness, because Father's was the only opinion Aidan cared about. Aidan's quietness and reserve translated in Joshua's mind as sneakiness or craftiness. It never seemed to occur to Joshua to hide his prejudices. Though Clemency adored her father utterly, she had lately come to recognize his faults. He had a way of stoking up Aidan's resentment of James without ever meaning to, a way of announcing James's successes with pride and Aidan's with a more grudging acknowledgement. It upset Clemency to catch the gloating expression in Aidan's eyes when Joshua and James quarrelled. It upset her to see how Aidan fuelled the fires, reminding Father of James's failings — his frequent absences in London, his refusal to find himself a wife and settle down to produce the next generation of Maclises — at the most inopportune moments.

Even James seemed less cheerful recently. Often, catching sight of him when he didn't know she was looking, Clemency saw a worried look in his eyes. That James — carefree, happy-go-lucky James — should be worried, jolted her.

One evening she was in the drawing room, feeding coal onto the fire, when James came into the room. 'I say, Clemmie, you couldn't lend me a bit of cash, could you?'

She stared at him, startled. He reddened. 'I know I shouldn't ask — '

'I don't mind.'

'It's only — well, I'm a bit short.'

'There's my Great-aunt Hannah money,' she said. Great-aunt Hannah had left each of her unmarried great-nieces a small legacy.

'I couldn't possibly take that. It's for your bottom drawer.'

'I don't mind giving it to you, James.'

He made a quick, impatient gesture. 'I feel such a heel, asking you. But I'm rather hard pushed just now. I'd ask Father, but you know what he's like.'

'Perhaps if you explained to him why you needed it.'

'I can't do that.'

'Why not?'

'Because — ' He broke off, and gave a short laugh. 'You know I'm not in his good books at the moment. He wants me to marry Louisa Palmer. He just won't let up.'

'I know.' Father was never subtle in his machinations. 'But you don't want to marry Louisa?'

'I can't.' His voice was flat.

'Don't you like her?'

'Oh, Louie's a sport. Not like Alice.'

'But you don't like her enough,' she guessed, thinking of Ivor. 'You don't long for the next time you see her.'

'Something like that.'

She said gently, 'Is anything wrong, James?'

'Actually — ' his face was troubled — 'actually, Clem, I'm in a bit of a mess.'

The door opened. Aidan came into the room. 'Edith said to tell you it's dinnertime.'

When they were alone again, Clemency said, '*James. Tell me what's the matter.*'

'Nothing.' James gave her an unconvincing smile. 'Nothing at all.'

★   ★   ★

Marianne had fallen in love with the Blackwater garden. She began to cut back the creepers that had wound themselves around the roses, to free the perennials of the weeds that choked them. She discovered treasures hidden in the undergrowth: scarlet geraniums, tiny blue pansies. Someone had loved this garden once, she realized; someone had created it, nurtured it.

The bungalow ran smoothly with little interference from her. The servants were numerous and efficient, and there was really very little for her to do. The servants included Rani, the ayah, who maided for Marianne, Nadeshan, the page boy, the cook and his assistant, the kitchen coolie, and the tappul or letter coolie. Other natives called at the bungalow: the dhobi, who washed the clothes and linen, pounding them on stones in the stream; itinerant pedlars from India, who spread out bundles of silks, lace and gold and silver embroideries for Marianne to choose from; and the tailor, who, squatting on the floor with his ancient sewing machine, ran up curtains and shirts and gowns. And then there was Mr da Silva, the Sinhalese who managed the transportation of the tea to Colombo. Mr da Silva, whose black hair had begun to grey at the temples, was pleasant and kindly, and when he visited once a month or so he always brought Marianne a gift

— a posy of flowers, a little cake with green and pink icing, or a paper windmill, to keep the birds, he said, from her beautiful garden.

On the tea estate itself there were the two assistant managers, Mr Salter and Mr Cooper, and numerous field officers, factory officers and clerks. The assistant managers lived in their own modest bungalows a quarter of a mile or so from the Blackwater bungalow, and the Tamil coolies, eight hundred of them, who had come to Ceylon from southern India, lived in the lines, the rows of shacks built among the tea fields. At six in the morning, drums sounded, calling the coolies to muster. They were counted, divided into gangs overseen by kanganies, or gang masters, and sent to different parts of the estate to pluck, weed or prune. Marianne learned that the women, with their small, thin, careful fingers, made the best pluckers, and that, for the best quality tea, they took only the top bud and two leaves from the plant. The Tamil men did the heavy work on the estate, pruning the tea bushes and planting new ones, as well as acting as servants and clerks.

The whole Blackwater estate revolved around tea, was devoted to tea. In the factory the air was perfumed with tea; outside, in the fields, the scent lingered, though more faintly. On the mountainsides reddish-brown paths traced squares and circles through the ridged dark green fields of tea plants. Women in brightly coloured saris, burdened by the large palm baskets they carried on their backs, dotted the plantations. Several times a day the baskets of leaves were emptied out, and the tea was sorted through to remove unsuitable leaves and twigs and then weighed, before being taken to the factory.

Mr Salter, the red-faced and raw-limbed assistant manager, showed Marianne round the factory. 'This is the withering rack,' Mr Salter explained. They were in the upper floor. 'The leaves are spread out here. We leave them there for about a day, depending on the weather conditions.'

They went downstairs. Pulleys, belts and flywheels clattered and groaned. 'And this is the roller,' shouted Mr Salter over the din. 'It bruises the leaf. The tea has to ferment. There's no alcohol involved, of course, but the juices in the leaves have to oxydize. The leaves are rolled four or five times. You have to stop at just the right moment. Then the roll breaker sifts the leaf through a mesh. Breaking up the leaves gives the flavour to tea.'

In the fermenting room the leaves were spread out on a glass table. Mr Salter mopped his perspiring forehead and glanced at Marianne. 'I say, I'm not boring you, am I, Mrs Melrose? This must all seem terribly dull.'

'Not at all,' she said. 'How do you know when it's ready?'

'By the colour. It has to be the right colour.'

He led the way into another room. 'These are the drying ovens. They blow a current of hot air over the tea. Makes the leaves dry and brittle, you see. Then the leaves are sorted and graded and then the tea is ready to be transported to our brokers in Colombo to be auctioned at the tea markets. And from there it's shipped all over the world.' Mr Salter pulled at his collar, showing a sprinkling of scarlet boils on his neck. 'Climate and elevation influence the taste of the tea. If it rains at the wrong time — or doesn't rain at the right time — that makes a difference to the taste, which in turn, of course, affects the price. Tea production's an art, Mrs Melrose. It's all about taste and colour and getting everything just right.'

'And Blackwater tea is just right?'

'Blackwater tea's the best in the world. Mr Melrose is very particular. And jolly good for him, that's what I say. Tea cultivation's a competitive business. Let your standards slip, and you'll soon see your profits gone and your estate snapped up by one of the big companies. That's why Mr Melrose has bought the Glencoe land, I daresay.'

'Glencoe?'

'The adjacent estate.' Mr Salter waved a vague hand westwards. 'Went bankrupt six months ago. Chap who owned it went a bit doolally. Between you and me, Mrs Melrose, he was rather too fond of the bottle. Everyone likes a nip now and then, but when you're drinking arrack for breakfast, well, it doesn't do, does it? Anyway, someone said that Lipton's were showing interest, so Mr Melrose had to get in quick. The land's been pretty neglected, though, and there's a lot of work to do. The jungle comes back, you see, given the least chance.' His gaze darted through the window, and he muttered, 'That's the trouble with this country — pretty as pie to look at, and when you first come here, you'd almost think you were in England. But you're not, of course.' He looked fretful. 'You can't seem to keep things *out*. The place presses in on you — it won't leave you alone. Turn your back, and you've got snakes in the kitchen and ants in your rice sacks and damned creepers pulling the zinc off your roof.' He wiped his face again. 'Excuse my language, Mrs Melrose. I'm not quite the thing today, I'm afraid. A touch of fever.'

★   ★   ★

One Saturday they went to the Planters' Club in the small town with the bazaar and the railway station. Lucas rode and one of the grooms drove Marianne in a bullock cart along the mountain track.

The planters and their wives and families met in a long, rectangular building. The men congregated at one end of the building near the bar, while the women sat around tables at the other. There were framed photographs on the walls of white-clad cricket teams and moustachioed men with rifles.

When she walked into the club, Marianne felt an almost tangible flicker of curiosity. Eyes turned towards her, neighbour murmured to neighbour. Congratulations were offered; someone signalled to the club boy, a white-haired, brown-skinned old man in a white tunic with brass buttons, for drinks to toast the newly married couple.

A succession of planters and their wives shook Marianne's hand. There was a hierarchy, she noticed: planter proprietors and senior managers were introduced to her first, before the junior and assistant managers. The hierarchies kept themselves separate, occupying different tables.

She was introduced to Ralph Armitage and the Rawlinsons. Armitage was tall and bulky and hook-nosed. His eyes raked over Marianne briefly before he bore Lucas away to drink at the men's end of the clubhouse. Mr Rawlinson, the Club secretary, was gaunt and white-haired, wraithlike beside his broad, solid wife. Anne Rawlinson had the coarsened, high-coloured complexion of someone who has been in the sun too long.

'So you're the girl who's caught our Lucas at last,' Mrs Rawlinson boomed. 'Let me have a look at you. Why, you're just a young thing. How old are you? Nineteen? Twenty?'

'I'm twenty-four.'

'*Twenty-four.* I wouldn't have thought it. You're very pale, my dear. You'll have to be careful here — the sun plays havoc with pale skins. How are you finding Ceylon? It's a good-sized bungalow, Blackwater. Lucas has found you reliable servants, I hope?'

'They seem very competent.'

'Keep a close eye on your ayah, that's my advice. Mine would be off with my jewellery if I gave her half a chance.' Mrs Rawlinson took a drink from the tray.

'They haven't much of an idea of right and wrong, these people. Like children, I always say.'

Marianne declined a drink. Mrs Rawlinson's eyes gleamed. Leaning forward, she said in a theatrical whisper, 'Is there going to be a Happy Event? I can always tell. Something about the face. There, don't mind me, Mrs Melrose. You'll soon get used to me — everyone knows I like to be direct. I'm right, aren't I? When are you due?'

'The middle of March, Dr Scott says.'

'And you were married at the end of June?' Mrs Rawlinson's eyes narrowed as she calculated quickly. 'My, Lucas was in a hurry, wasn't he? But then, he was never laggardly about that sort of thing.'

'What do you mean?'

'Nothing, my dear.' Mrs Rawlinson had almost finished her gin and tonic. 'Nothing at all.' She patted Marianne's hand. 'If you want to know anything, anything whatsoever, you must just ask me. I know the ropes — I've lived up here in the hill country for simply donkey's years.'

A fair-haired young woman came to join them. Mrs Rawlinson introduced her to Marianne as Mrs Barlow. 'Let me show you our tennis court, Mrs Melrose,' Mrs Barlow suggested. 'We're very proud of our tennis court.' As they went outside, Mrs Barlow lowered her voice. 'I thought I'd better rescue you.'

Marianne said furiously, 'So inquisitive — so *patronizing* — '

'The first time Anne Rawlinson called on me she snooped around the bungalow, poking her nose into everything. I thought she was going to start going through my wardrobe to check the lace on my petticoats was up to scratch.'

Marianne laughed. 'Thank you for coming to my aid, Mrs Barlow.'

'Clare. Please call me Clare.'

'And I'm Marianne.'

'I overheard you say that you're expecting a baby. It must be something in the air. I had my first nine months after I arrived here. And the second a year after that. There they are.' Clare Barlow pointed to two pigtailed little girls, playing on the swing.

'They're beautiful. How old are they?'

'Hilda's seven and Joan's six. They must go to boarding school in England soon. I don't know how I shall bear it. I've been putting it off as long as possible. I'll be so lonely without them. I suppose I could have another baby. Johnnie wants a boy, of course, for the wretched estate, but I don't know . . . I've been so happy with my girls.' Clare grimaced. 'And as we hardly manage to exchange a civil word these days, let alone share a bed, a son doesn't seem very likely.' She looked down at the glass in her hand and frowned. 'I'm sorry. I've had a couple of drinks — I don't usually drink in the daytime and it's gone to my head. And Johnny and I are just going through a bad patch. We had a frightful quarrel before we came out, which is why I'm drinking, of course.' Her eyes had clouded. 'Marriage isn't altogether easy here,' she said suddenly. 'I think we're too thrown in on each other. Too many long evenings spent in the bungalow, alone except for the children and the servants and nothing to do except write letters and read or play cards and drink too much. And the men are so used to having their own way, they expect *us* to jump when they snap their fingers, just like the coolies. I always tell Johnny he's like a little god on the estate. His word is law. They can do as they like, the men, and there's no one to stop them. It goes to their heads, I'm afraid.'

Then she called out, 'Hilda! You must give Joan a turn!' She smiled at Marianne. 'I shall call on you soon, if I may. I have a feeling we're going to be good friends. I'm sure we've a great deal in common — not least a mutual dislike of Anne Rawlinson.'

★ ★ ★

Lucas was clearing the Glencoe land, hacking away dense undergrowth, felling trees and moving rocks and debris. When he returned to the bungalow each midday his clothes were dyed red-brown by the earth, his face streaked with dust and sweat.

One night, walking back to her bedroom after visiting the bathroom, Marianne heard a noise, a rustle of movement in the darkness. She held up her candle, illuminating the corners of the corridor, afraid that a snake had found its way into the house. Then she heard a peal of laughter, quickly muffled, and then footsteps and a door closing.

She went quickly into the drawing room and moved aside a curtain. Looking out, she saw at first only the black tropical night and the dense darkness of the trees and creepers that surrounded the bungalow garden. Then her eye was caught by a flicker of bright colour. A blink and it was gone, swallowed up by the undergrowth.

The same thing happened a few nights later. Marianne realized that she (and she was certain their night visitor was a she from the lithe grace of her step and the bright cotton of a sari, pulled over long black hair) was heading towards the coolie lines.

She broached her problem to Clare, who was visiting one afternoon. 'If I was in England,' she explained, 'then I'd have any servant who brought followers into the house dismissed immediately, of course. But here I'm not sure what to do. I'm not even sure whether this sort of thing is thought of as normal. And whether I'd just cause a frightful fuss trying to find out what's going on. I don't want to ask Lucas. He's made it clear that he doesn't want to be bothered with the running of the house. And anyway, I should be able to manage by myself.'

They were sitting in the little summerhouse on the hillside. Clare lit a cigarette. 'Do you know who this girl is coming to see?'

Marianne sighed. 'I tried speaking to Rani, but she just clammed up. And I feel too embarrassed to talk to the menservants. I suppose I must, though.'

Clare frowned. 'Darling, you are sure that she's visiting one of the servants?'

'Who else?' Marianne stared at her. '*Lucas?* You surely don't mean Lucas?'

'Plenty of the men have a Tamil mistress or two. Johnnie does. There's a girl he's known a lot longer than he's known me. And half a dozen coffee-coloured children down in the lines.'

'But don't you mind?'

Clare drew on her cigarette. 'I did at first, terribly. But now . . . You must remember that Lucas lived here on his own for simply ages. You could hardly blame him if he needed company. No, if she is visiting Lucas, then best to turn a blind eye, I'd say.' Clare's gaze roamed discontentedly from the hills to the garden and the bungalow. 'I've heard that some of the planters end up becoming intimate with their dogs. Now I would draw the line at *that*.'

★ ★ ★

The diphtheria epidemic began in the New Year. The symptoms of the disease were fever and a sore throat. In the worst cases a pale grey membrane clung to the walls of the throat, covering the larynx and suffocating the patient. Because of the narrowness of their throats, children under the age of five were most at risk. The only treatment was a tracheotomy, the insertion of a breathing tube into the neck to bypass the blocked airway.

Within a fortnight a full-scale epidemic was raging through the East End. Weakened by malnourishment, children who had been playing in the street one day were dead by the end of the next. Some died on the journey to hospital, others in the admittance wards. Iris was reassigned to a children's ward, where she and Rose Dennison dashed from cot to cot, checking the babies had not coughed out their tracheotomy tubes, while the probationer changed nappies and bedclothes. Every so often a child would die. A blueing of the skin, a rattle in the throat and then stillness. Because she had always been quick with her needle, Iris sewed the shrouds while Rose laid the infants out. Many of the deaths took place just before dawn, as if, in the bleakest, coldest part of the night, the infants had simply abandoned the struggle for life. Some of the babies died from suffocation, but others' hearts gave out, exhausted by the struggle. There was a moment when they seemed to realize that they were beaten, a heaviness of the limbs and a lessening of the breath. Sometimes Iris cradled them in her arms as they died, stroking their sunken cheeks and murmuring to them. She could never afterwards quite separate the sight of her needle threading in and out of the white cloth from the hoarse rattle of the babies' breath.

Whenever she had half an hour or so, she escaped from the hospital. She became adept at slipping out of the nurses' home without home sister noticing. She would look in the shops, or browse the shelves of the penny library, anything to get away from the dark, claustrophobic atmosphere of the wards. Sometimes she went to see Ash. They would eat fish and chips from a newspaper as they walked through the chill, sleety streets; once he took her to the cinema, where she fell asleep, her head on his shoulder, as soon as the lights went out and he had to wake her when the show had finished. When she did not see him for a day or two, she missed him.

After the worst night, because they were short-staffed she had to work through most of the following day as well. Off duty at last, she should have returned to the nurses' home, to have tea and then rest, but instead, after she had changed, she went to see Ash.

Inside his kitchen a dog with a matted grey-brown coat snored in one corner, and a canary trilled in a wicker cage. Iris frowned. 'That dog — '

'Someone brought him here.'

'And the canary?'

'The Turners were doing a moonlight flit. They were behind with their rent. So I said I'd look after the canary until they were settled again.'

'And the *sink*.' She stared at the overflowing pots and pans. 'Oh dear, I sound like one of the ward sisters at the Mandeville. I'll be checking your hospital corners next. But really, Ash, you should find yourself a cleaning woman.'

'I have a cleaning woman.'

'Let me guess . . . you chose the most poverty-stricken, crippled, ancient cleaning woman you could find because you felt sorry for her.'

'I'm afraid she hasn't been able to do a great deal of cleaning recently. She has bad feet.' He glanced at Iris. 'Do you want to talk about it, or would you rather not?'

She gave her head a quick shake and blinked rapidly as she stared down at the floor. He put his arms around her and hugged her. Iris closed her eyes, enjoying the warmth of his body, and the feeling that here, at last, was someone to lean on, someone to take some of the horror of the last few weeks from her. There was the temptation to let her head drop against his shoulder, to sleep, enclosed in his arms.

And another temptation, one she had not anticipated. A need for him to go on touching her, for his hand, for instance, which was now patting her back, to caress her neck, her face. For his mouth, that every now and then brushed against her hair, to search out her lips . . .

She pulled away from him and said brusquely, 'There were twenty-five infants admitted to the ward last night. Twelve of them died. When it's like this, I can't think what I'm doing here. When it's like this, I hate nursing.' She clutched a fold of her dress. 'I think I must smell of it. That awful hospital smell.'

'Nonsense,' he said. 'You smell lovely, as always.'

She managed a smile. 'I'd like you to take my mind off it, Ash.'

'What do you want to do? I could take you out to supper.'

'I should like to go dancing,' she said. 'If you don't mind dancing with me. We have danced before, of course. At Summerleigh. Do you remember?'

'I remember being rather drunk and very cross and quite badly behaved,' he said. 'I promise to do better this time.'

From his wardrobe, she picked him out some passable clothes. 'I shall have to take you shopping. Your cuffs are fraying through.' Her voice seemed to hang in the air, light and glittering and glassy.

They went to an afternoon tea dance in a small hotel in Shoreditch. There was tea and sandwiches and cakes and a three-piece band, the hiss of kid shoes on polished floorboards and the smell of cigarettes and cheap perfume. Clerks in starched collars partnered their typists and shop girls on the small dance floor, and the jagged, raucous new rhythms of ragtime filled the room, hypnotizing the dancers, defying them not to dance, speaking of excitement, of alteration, of the coming of change.

Towards the end of the dance Iris went to the ladies'

cloakroom. Whey-faced girls were powdering their faces; one was pinning up a fallen hem. A girl in a pink taffeta frock was leaning against the washbasin, weeping. 'He says he loves me but I know it ain't true,' she was saying to her friend, over and over again.

Iris studied her own reflection in the mirror. Her face was pale and there were dark shadows round her eyes. Images from the last day and night flickered through her tired mind. Herself picking out a jacket from Ash's wardrobe. A three-month-old baby, whose hair had stuck out from his scalp like a bottlebrush, dying in her arms. Her needle running through white calico.

It seemed to her that in her shadowed eyes she glimpsed despair. She did not know whether the despair was for the babies or for herself, for what she had discovered that day. How foolish, she thought, to fall in love with a man who had years ago made it clear to her that he did not want her. How foolish to fall in love with a man who had broken her heart once already. How foolish to fall in love with Ash.

11

Once, watching from the drawing-room window as Lucas's night visitor ran from the bungalow, Marianne turned, hearing a sound behind her. Rani, her ayah, was standing in the doorway.

Marianne let fall the curtain. 'What is her name?' she asked. Rani did not answer.

'Rani, what's her name?'

A flicker of fear in the dark eyes. A whisper, disturbing the night. 'Her name is Parvati, Dorasanie.'

'Does she come here to see the Peria Dorai?'

Rani's fingertips touched her forehead. 'Lady should go back to bed. Lady is not wearing her shawl. She will catch cold.'

Driving through the estate, Marianne saw the babies sleeping in cloth hammocks suspended from the branches of trees at the side of the road as their mothers worked in the fields. When the children stared at her as she passed, she stared back, searching for a lighter skin, for those whose eyes were not black, but green or gold or grey. Her gaze sought out and fastened on the clusters of young women, looking for a red sari and the jangle of gold bracelets. Looking for a girl called Parvati, who shared her husband's bed when she did not.

The rhythm of the estate continued, the plucking and processing of tea, the pattern of daily life in the bungalow. The great swathes of tea fields, draped over the hills like a blanket, contained thousands and thousands of bushes: *camellia siniensis*, the plant whose cultivation dictated the course of all their lives.

At each new moon from the coolie lines Marianne heard the sound of drumming, and at night she saw orange fires burning bright against the ink-black sky. Flags and streamers hung from the tin-roofed shacks and blossoms were left as offerings at the roadside shrines. Once, after the rain, they found a snake on the veranda, a coiled brown creature, sleeping in the sun. Lucas fetched the gun and shot it in the head. The report echoed against the trees.

They stayed for two nights with the Barlows on their estate forty miles away. In the evenings Lucas and Johnny Barlow drank and exchanged anecdotes while Marianne and Clare sat by the drawing-room fire. A few weeks later Ralph Armitage called at Blackwater. At dinner Armitage's loud voice filled the room and his large body sprawled, legs akimbo, in the chair, as he ate and drank copiously. He rarely spoke to Marianne; she sensed that he thought her insignificant, unworthy of his notice. She left the room as soon as the meal was over. Throughout the remainder of the evening, the men's voices echoed through the bungalow. Every now and then Marianne heard the sound of Nadeshan's quick, light feet, hurrying to fetch the men another bottle of arrack. She had just fallen asleep when she was woken by gunfire. Rifle shots cracked in the garden. The following morning she found a Brahminy kite, its tawny feathers dulling and bloodied, near the roots of the banyan tree.

At the club Anne Rawlinson's inquisitive eyes studied the curve of Marianne's belly. 'You must be more than six months gone, dear. Are you well?'

They were sitting on the clubhouse veranda. There was a tennis tournament: the click of racket and ball and the cry of *out!* punctured the afternoon.

'I'm very well, thank you, Anne.'

'Dr Scott is looking after you, isn't he? He's a good man, one of the best. We all depend on Dr Scott.'

Dr Scott had hot, damp hands and smelt of pipe tobacco. When he visited Blackwater he always stayed for the evening, drinking with Lucas. Changing the subject, Marianne said, 'I've been pruning the roses in my garden. They're rather neglected and very leggy.'

'I remember when Blackwater's roses were the best in the province. Lucas's mother planted them, of course. Sarah was a marvellous gardener. So green-fingered. You wouldn't have thought it to look at her.'

There were no photographs or paintings of Sarah Melrose in the Blackwater bungalow. Marianne wanted to know more about the woman who had made the garden. 'What was she like?'

Mrs Rawlinson lit a cigarette. 'Yellow hair and blue eyes. The sort of woman men go silly over. Wound 'em round her little finger and they could never see it, the fools.'

'It must have been very hard for Lucas's father when she died.'

'Died?' Mrs Rawlinson's match scraped against tinder. 'Sarah didn't die. She ran off with a timber merchant from Colombo.'

'But Lucas said — ' Marianne broke off. What had Lucas said? She struggled to remember his exact words. *I lost my mother a long time ago.*

Mrs Rawlinson's expression was avid, disapproving. 'Not at all out of the top drawer, Sarah Melrose's beau. And between you and me, more than a touch of the tar brush. Didn't last, of course, she was off again in six months. I felt sorry for the child, though. Lucas was only four. And George Melrose was never an easy man. Too fond of a drink. There were stories — '

A shadow had fallen over them. The sentence hung in the air, unfinished. 'Lucas, dearest,' said Anne Rawlinson, looking up with a trill of laughter, 'aren't you playing tennis? I thought you were playing tennis.'

'You know that I don't, Anne.'

They left the clubhouse shortly afterwards. Lucas rode and the groom drove Marianne in the bullock cart.

They had ridden out of the town and started along the mountain track when Lucas said, 'What was that woman saying to you? Mrs Rawlinson — what was she saying to you?'

Something treacherous in his voice made her say, 'We were talking about the baby, that's all. And about the garden at Blackwater.'

He nudged his horse alongside the bullock cart. He seemed to Marianne to be treading along the edge of the precipice. 'I meant, Marianne, what was she saying about my mother?'

'It was nothing important, Lucas.'

'Tell me.'

'It's only that I realized I'd made a stupid mistake. I thought your mother died when you were young.'

'And that interfering bitch told you otherwise?'

She gasped. She glanced at the groom; his eyes were impassive, fixed on the curve of the track.

'What else did she tell you?'

'Nothing. What she said — I didn't believe her.'

He was silent for a moment. Then he said, 'I suppose she told you that my mother cut and ran, leaving me at Blackwater with *him*. Why must women gossip? Yap, yap, yap, like little dogs, sticking their noses into other people's business.' He spurred his horse and galloped ahead, disappearing around a rocky promontory in a cloud of red dust.

At dinner that evening only a slight fluidity about Lucas's movements and the smallest slur in his voice told Marianne that he had been drinking. The silence persisted, interrupted by the clink of plates and glasses. Neither of them ate much.

Nadeshan was clearing away the plates when Lucas said, 'If you want to know, my mother died nine months ago. That was why I went back to England. I'd heard she was ill and I thought the silly bitch might have left me something. But she didn't. Not a penny.' The grey, unfocused gaze slid towards Marianne. 'I needed the money to buy the land, you see. But the stupid whore let me down again. Even in death.'

He rose from his seat. As he left the room, he looked back at her. 'I don't think you should go to the club any more,' he said coldly. 'Not in your condition. That track is so stony and uneven. The cart might lose a wheel. I wouldn't want anything to happen to the baby.'

Marianne went to her room. Sitting on the bed, she could see herself shaking. In her entire life no man had ever spoken to her as Lucas had just spoken to her. Neither her father nor her brothers nor Arthur would ever have used the sort of words that Lucas had just used in front of a woman. Nor would they have used that tone of voice.

She was suddenly aware of the darkness of the night and of the alien nature of this land. And of the immense distance between herself and the people she loved. When she thought of her sisters she felt a pang of almost physical pain. Her gaze came to rest on her writing desk. On Saturday evenings she usually wrote to Iris, Eva and Clemency. What should she say? *I'm afraid I have made a dreadful mistake. I'm afraid I do not know my husband at all*. The paper and envelopes remained untouched.

But in the morning her fears seemed out of proportion, even slightly hysterical. How dreadful to lose your mother at such an early age. And how unforgivable, to abandon your own child. No wonder Lucas hated to hear gossip about his mother. And fatherhood would bring out the best in him, she was sure that it would. As for his drinking, many men drank too much and many were unpleasant when they drank. She had been fortunate that the men she had known until now could hold their drink. She must be patient: Lucas was working long hours and he was exhausted. They had not yet had the chance to discover the companionship that was the most she had hoped for from this marriage. When the Glencoe land was cleared, they would have time to know each other better.

The weeks passed. Any reservations about her marriage were more than compensated for by the beauty of the landscape and, of course, by the coming child. She did not mind that she no longer went to the club. She had always felt ill at ease among strangers, preferring the company of a few close friends. The artificiality of polite society persisted even here, in Ceylon, among the planters and their wives; she preferred the Blackwater garden, her sanctuary, her paradise.

★   ★   ★

The satisfaction that nursing had once given Iris seemed over the last few months to have diminished. She put it down to Sister Dickens, on whose ward she had been working since the end of February. Iris did not see eye to eye with Sister Dickens, who was a stickler for neatness, cleanliness and discipline. All the ward sisters at the Mandeville were sticklers for neatness, cleanliness and discipline, but there was a coldness about Sister Dickens that Iris disliked and a lack of sympathy with the patients. There were several nurses like Sister Dickens at the hospital, nurses who had worked at the Mandeville for years and years, and who, though brisk and efficient, seemed to feel little for the patients. Nothing touched them. Death, loss and grief all seemed to slide off them, like rain from a laurel leaf.

Sometimes Iris was afraid that she might end up the same. She still dreamed about the diphtheria epidemic, that she was running from cot to cot, and the babies were coughing out their tracheotomy tubes and she couldn't put them back in quickly enough. Since the epidemic it was as though a piece of her had hardened, as though she had only been capable of a certain amount of feeling and that feeling had been spent. Part of her knew that she was just tired, that her work at the Mandeville was demanding and that no one could go on and on at such a pitch. Part of her knew that the answer was to go somewhere new, try something different. Of her set, only a handful of nurses now remained at the Mandeville. The others had left for different hospitals or had become private nurses. On the notice board in the nurses' home were pinned letters and advertisements for private nurses; sometimes she found herself scanning them.

She never applied for the posts, though. She knew why she did not, knew that it was because of Ash. With Ash she did not lack feeling; instead, her emotions were an exhausting see-saw of hope and despair. She hid them well, though — if she had never been in love before, enough men had been in love with her for her to know the symptoms and to avoid displaying them. It crossed her mind that she should try to make him love her — she had not forgotten how to play that game: a particular smile, a brush of the fingertips. But something in her shrank from that.

She had never felt so unsure of a man before. She could not decide whether he was attracted to her or whether she was just a friend, one of his many, many friends. And, if so, whether she could be content with that. Sometimes she thought that she could. Friendship had been enough for her before, so why shouldn't it be so now?

Though she longed to be with him by herself, they were hardly ever alone. There was nowhere they could be alone. Male visitors, apart from brothers and fathers, were not, of course, permitted in the nurses' home, and friends flowed through Ash's house like waves over sand, eating at his table, sleeping on his sofa, forever knocking on his door. Thelma Voss was a frequent visitor. Every now and then Iris would catch Thelma's fierce, dark eyes upon her and would glimpse in them a challenge.

She treasured the moments they spent together — an hour in the Piccadilly cinema, or a walk through Whitechapel with an edgy spring wind stinging her face. A quick lunch in a café or, best of all, an afternoon tea dance in the shabby hotel, his arms around her and her face turned away from his, so that he would not guess at her happiness. Yet she found herself wondering how long she could go on. The deception that she constantly practised wore her down. Never let him know, never let him guess. She had humiliated herself in front of him once before; she would not risk that happening again. But she wanted to touch him, to thread her fingers into his hair, to brush her lips against his. She wanted him to take her in his arms and kiss her. The intensity of her desire took her by surprise.

Sometimes she hated that she had fallen in love with him. She would rather have remained the other Iris, the Iris who always had the upper hand, who always made the running. If this was love, she thought, then she didn't think much of it.

★　★　★

As her pregnancy progressed, Marianne's belly swelled like a ripe fruit and her limbs became rounded and heavy. The baby shifted and coiled beneath her skin. The heat exhausted her and she moved from veranda to banyan tree to summerhouse in search of shade. The bungalow and garden had become her whole world; she no longer ventured out into the estate or to the town. Four weeks before the baby was due her hands and feet became puffy and her rings no longer fitted her fingers. Even the walk to the summerhouse tired her — six thousand feet up, the air was thin and lacking in

342

oxygen. The baby pressed against her ribs and stomach, making it hard to eat and breathe. At night, in bed, she was unable to find a comfortable position, and her body felt bloated and unfamiliar, weighed down by the child. Lying awake in the small hours, the mosquito net blurred the dart of a green gecko across her bedroom ceiling and she heard from outside a rustle of movement in the jungle, a beat of wings and footsteps in the darkness.

It had been dry for many weeks. One morning Marianne was woken by the crackle of thunder. Great jagged tongues of lightning splintered the sky, but though the clouds darkened and swelled there was no rain. They were breakfasting on the veranda when Mr Salter rode up to the bungalow to tell Lucas that lightning had struck the Glencoe land, and that the undergrowth was on fire. Grabbing his hat and whip, Lucas called for his horse to be saddled.

Marianne felt restless throughout the day, unable to settle to anything. Lightning continued to fork from a hard, dry sky. There was a vibration in the hot, still air, as if something momentous was about to happen. When Lucas returned to the bungalow in the early evening his clothes and skin were blackened. Through the dirt and sweat his pale eyes glittered.

Marianne met him on the veranda. 'Did you put the fire out?'

He nodded and called for Nadeshan, who ran out to the veranda. Lucas gave the boy his topee and sat down so that Nadeshan could pull his boots off. 'Get me a drink, for God's sake,' he said curtly. 'And hurry.'

Nadeshan ran back into the house. 'We lost half the new bushes,' Lucas said.

'From the land you'd just cleared? I'm sorry, Lucas.'

'All that work. Just gone up in smoke.' He went to the veranda rail; his fist struck it hard. 'The ground's like tinder. We must have rain.'

Nadeshan reappeared with a tray. Hurrying to Lucas, he tripped on a rough edge of the planking and, as the bottle and glass flew from the tray to shatter on the wooden veranda, Lucas snarled an oath and struck him hard on the side of his head, sending him sprawling.

Another servant ran out with a fresh glass and bottle of gin. A dark red mark covered the side of Nadeshan's face and his fingers were cut and bleeding as he quickly gathered up the broken glass. As the servants retreated into the house, Lucas looked up at Marianne.

'What is it?'

'Lucas — ' She could hardly speak for shock.

His eyes narrowed. 'Answer me, Marianne.'

'You struck him. You struck Nadeshan.'

A bark of laughter. 'Dear God. You're not going to lecture me about *that*, are you?'

'Lucas, he's only a child!'

'He's a servant,' said Lucas harshly. 'A clumsy, slipshod servant.'

'You shouldn't strike servants. It's wrong to strike servants.'

'*Jesus*. Everyone strikes their servants now and then.'

'Arthur would never, ever have struck a servant!'

His eyes darkened. 'Your precious Arthur. How tired I am of the saintly Arthur.' He reached down again for the bottle. His lip curled. 'How it wearied me when I was in England, listening to dull tales of your perfect husband.' He threw back the contents of the glass. 'Just as well he died when he did before you had time to grow sick of each other.'

'That's a wicked thing to say!' she cried. 'A wicked, wicked thing! You're exhausted. Or drunk. I won't listen to this.'

But he grabbed her wrist to stop her leaving the veranda. 'Don't go. I don't want you to go. I was enjoying our conversation.'

She tried to pull away; he stood up in one swift, fluid

movement. 'I told you that I didn't want you to go, Marianne. It's impolite to walk away in the middle of a conversation, didn't you know that? What were we talking about? Oh, yes, *Arthur*. Your sainted husband.'

She could feel the heat of his breath. 'Let go of me.' Her voice trembled. 'Let go of me, Lucas.'

'Why can't we talk about Arthur? We spoke of him endlessly in England. Speak to me, Marianne.'

His fingers crushed her wrist. There were tears of pain in her eyes but she did not let them fall. 'No.'

'Why not?' His grip tightened.

'Because I — ' She faltered.

'Because you loved him?'

'Yes.' She made herself meet those hard, light eyes. 'Because I loved him.'

He let her go. She was shaking and had to grip the edge of the veranda for support. Picking up his glass, Lucas sat down again, staring out at the twilit garden. 'The trouble with you, Marianne,' he said softly, 'is that you still want to believe in fairy stories. *Love*. Don't you know that there's no such thing?'

She said angrily, 'Of course there is.'

He shook his head. 'What you felt for your saintly husband was lust, not love.'

'That's not true — '

'Oh, it is. There are only lust and self-interest. Nothing else. They are what drive us all.'

'No — '

'No?' The word was a sudden snarl. 'Then answer me another question, Marianne. Did you marry me for *love*?'

She was caught by those grey, glittering eyes, hypnotized like a rabbit by a snake. Again he laughed. 'Of course you didn't,' he said lightly. 'You didn't care for me at all. You married me because you're the sort of woman who is too weak to manage on her own, who must have a man to live off. Well, know this, Marianne.

I didn't love you either. I never loved you at. All those sweet words I had to mouth to you before you accepted me — ' his features contorted into a mask of disgust — 'God, it was all I could do to get them out. Sometimes I had to get myself drunk to be able to bleat them out to you.'

She felt as though something inside her was crumbling, breaking apart. But she managed to say, 'Then why did you marry me?'

'Why do you think?'

'Was it for my money?'

'Of course. What else?'

She said, 'Then we're a match for each other, aren't we?'

'*You*, a match for *me*?' He laughed again. 'Have a good look at yourself next time you glance at a mirror. See yourself as you truly are.' He stooped to refill his glass. Then he said sharply, 'Now leave me. You bore me.'

★ ★ ★

She went to her room. She knew that she had made a terrible mistake; she had married a cruel, unloving man. She would leave Blackwater in the morning. Grabbing a bag, she began to throw clothes into it.

Yet a wave of faintness and exhaustion washed over her and she had to sit down on the bed, trembling. She would pack tomorrow, she whispered to herself. Yes, she would pack tomorrow.

Her wrist throbbed where Lucas had gripped it. She became aware of another pain, a dull, intermittent ache in the small of her back, that had been with her through much of the day and had now suddenly worsened. She pressed her hand against her spine. *There are only lust and self-interest.* It wasn't true. Lucas might be incapable of love, but Arthur had loved her, and she had loved him. Nothing could change that.

She lay down on the bed. Unexpectedly, worn out with shock and distress, she dozed off. The sound of the dinner gong woke her. While she slept the pain had worsened so that now it wrapped itself like a vice around her abdomen. She remained lying on the bed, propped up on the pillows. There was a tap on the door; Rani came in.

'It is dinnertime, Dorasanie.'

'I'm not hungry.' That pain again. She gasped and said fearfully, 'I think there's something wrong with me, Rani!'

Rani came to the bedside. She put her thin, brown hand on Marianne's belly. 'Nothing wrong, Dorasanie. Baby coming, that's all.'

'The baby?'

'See, Dorasanie.' She took Marianne's hand in hers and placed it on her belly. As the pain intensified, her distended abdomen hardened. 'Baby born soon. Tonight maybe.'

She made to leave the room. Marianne grabbed her hand. 'Don't leave me, Rani!'

'I tell Master. He fetch doctor.' Rani smiled at her. 'Then I come back.'

She was left alone. Her memory of the quarrel faded, overtaken by the relentless rhythm of her labour pains. Soon afterwards she heard horse's hooves, heading out into the night. Rani came back into the room. She rubbed Marianne's back and gave her something bitter-tasting to drink, and the pain seemed to ease for a while. The rain, which began as darkness fell, drummed harder and harder on the tin roof of the veranda as the night wore on. Eventually she heard horses' hooves again, and then footsteps and voices — Lucas's and the doctor's — as they headed into the house.

And then there was Dr Scott, poking and probing, doing unspeakable things to her, hurting her, so that she

347

tried to push him away. 'There, there, Mrs Melrose,' he said, in that unctuous voice of his, 'you must calm down.' She lost track of time and was aware only of the relentless rhythm of the pain and the drum roll of the downpour on the veranda roof. They had sent Rani away, though she had wanted her to stay, and in some momentary easing of the rain, she heard Dr Scott say quietly, to Lucas presumably, 'She seems tired. If she doesn't progress, I shall have to give her chloroform.' And, in the middle of all the pain and exhaustion, a rediscovery of the cold, hard steel that had been inside her since Arthur's death, and she made to herself a silent vow that she would see her child born, that she would be there, helping him, at every moment of his journey into the world.

Her son was born at daybreak the following morning. A fierce contraction made her scream aloud and then he squirmed and his body parted from hers. And then a cry.

She insisted they put him into her arms, even though she was almost too weak to hold him. Love at first sight: the second time she had known it. Dark blue eyes fleetingly met hers and she was bound to him for life.

It was still raining. When, just before she fell asleep, she looked out through the window to the veranda, she saw Lucas with his son in his arms. Saw him put out a hand to the rain and touch his fingertips to the baby's forehead, as if anointing him with a little piece of Ceylon.

★　★　★

In a chill, windswept May, Ash fell ill. His appearance — pale and thin, with darkly shadowed eyes — alarmed Iris. 'Bit of a cough,' he explained, when she called at his house. 'It's a nuisance.'

'Have you seen a doctor?'

348

'It's only bronchitis. I've had it before.'

'You should look after yourself better. Bronchitis is a serious illness. People die of it, you know.'

'I've no intention of doing that.'

'I'm pleased to hear it. But *honestly*.' She glanced at him sharply. 'Have you been eating?' She began to open kitchen cupboards and found a stub of bread, an ounce of hardening cheese.

'I haven't been very hungry.'

'You won't get better if you don't eat.'

'Don't be cross, *please*, dear Iris. You don't know how terrifying you are when you're cross.'

'I'm not cross.' She made an effort. 'Just worried about you.'

'Thelma's been marvellous. She's taken the dog for a walk every day.'

Iris poked at the fire, where a few pink embers smouldered among a heap of ash. 'It's freezing in here.'

'I'm afraid I've run out of coal.'

She sighed. 'I suppose you gave it away to someone.'

'Mark Collins's wife has just given birth to twins. Mark's been ill so he hasn't been in work, so — ' He began to cough again.

She got him a glass of water. 'Sit down. Drink that. Be quiet.'

'Bully,' he croaked.

Iris cleaned out the grate and walked to the coal merchant's, where she cajoled a workman into carrying a sack of coal back to the house for her. When the fire was lit, she went to the shops and bought stewing beef, a chicken and vegetables.

Ash came into the kitchen. 'What are you making?'

'Vegetable soup. And beef tea. Why are you smiling?'

'Iris Maclise, *cooking*.'

'I know,' she said. 'Not so long ago I hardly knew what a stove was for. But it's really quite soothing.' And it was: Ash's was a pleasant house in spite of its messiness. There were books and a piano and some attractive old furniture and rugs. Odd how something so ordinary could seem quite perfect. And so lovely to be by themselves — for once, none of Ash's hordes of friends were around.

Dangerous ground, Iris, she scolded herself, *you are treading on dangerous ground*. 'When I first started at the Mandeville,' she said lightly, 'the sister told me to make the patients' beef tea. I hadn't a clue, so I just threw the meat into some water and boiled it for hours. It was completely inedible, of course. Sister was furious with me.'

'Why did you do it?'

'Ruin the beef tea?'

'I meant, take up nursing, of course.'

'Because I couldn't think what else to do.' She found that it was a relief to admit the truth. 'And I couldn't bear that Marianne was getting married before me. *I* was the eldest, *I* was the prettiest, so *I* should have married first. And then Father agreed that Eva could go to art school and I could see what would happen.'

'Your mother — '

'Exactly. I would have been the daughter left at home, looking after Mother. So you see, it wasn't a noble ambition at all. There, Ash, are you disappointed in me?'

'Should I be?' He peered in the saucepan. 'It seems to be *singeing* rather. Should I do something?'

'Here. Just give it a stir.' She handed him a wooden spoon. Then she said, 'There was a time when you thought me rather — well, rather shallow.'

'Did I? How obnoxious of me.'

'You implied that I was merely decorative.'

'Well, so you are. But not merely.'

'Of course,' she said with a sigh, 'you were right. All I wanted then was a splendid marriage to my rich, handsome prince, who'd ride up on his white charger to sweep me away.'

He was leaning against the stove, watching her. 'And you never met him? You never met your handsome prince?'

I met him four years ago. I fell at his feet and he picked me up and tied up my cut hand with his handkerchief. The words hovered on the tip of her tongue: she could almost have said them and be damned to the consequences.

But she remembered the wound he had inflicted on her before in the garden at Summerleigh, after the party, and knew that she could not bear to endure that again, so she said instead, 'You know me, Ash. I'm very fussy.'

'Good grief, yes. And as stubborn as a mule — '

'The cheek of it. You're hardly the easiest person in the world yourself.'

'Me? I'm no trouble at all.'

'You're every bit as picky as me.'

'You're forever accusing me of not being fussy enough. Even my clothes — '

'You have no dress sense whatsoever.'

'And my food — '

'You don't have to live on bread and cheese.'

He began to cough again. When he could speak, he said, 'I do appreciate all this, Iris. I know how little spare time you have. It's very decent of you.'

She said severely, 'I'm only helping you because men on their own never seem able to look after themselves.'

'And there was I hoping it was because you were fond of me.'

In the silence an electricity hung in the air. He started to speak again; there was a knock at the door. Unsure whether she was relieved or angry at the interruption, Iris went to answer it.

Thelma Voss was standing on the doorstep. Seeing

Iris, her smile faded and she said, 'Oh, it's you.' Her gaze swept over Iris, measuring, assessing her enemy. She said, 'I've come to walk the dog. But perhaps you — '

'Oh no.' *You're welcome to the horrid, smelly animal*, thought Iris spitefully. 'He's all yours.' She let Thelma into the house.

★ ★ ★

For the last six months Eva had worked for a small publishing imprint near Red Lion Square. The Calliope Press was owned by a woman called Paula Muller. Paula was slight and dark and elegant; her parents were both dead and she had sole care of her twelve-year-old sister, Ida. The Calliope Press specialized in memoirs, travelogues and poetry written by women. The books were beautifully produced, hand-printed, elegantly bound and ornamented with small lithographs. Paula oversaw the printing and illustration while Eva was responsible for almost everything else: book-keeping, copy-editing, proof-reading and stock-taking, as well as answering the telephone and dealing with correspondence from authors, suppliers and bookshops.

Every now and then Paula offered Eva some illustration work, but she always refused. She had not painted since she had parted from Gabriel. Whatever source had prompted her to paint in the first place seemed to have dried up. She had begun to fear that she might never paint again.

She had left Mrs Wilde's house and now rented a top-floor flat in a terraced red-brick house a few streets away from the Calliope Press. There were three small rooms and a tiny roof garden. She decorated the flat, ripping off the smoke-stained paper and emulsioning the walls in shades of terracotta, soft jade and a delicate pinkish-violet. She made curtains and cushions and bedspreads and searched the street markets for treasures — a Moroccan brass lamp inlaid with squares of coloured glass, and cupboards and side tables which she sanded down and repainted. She bought a recipe book and invited her friends to supper, experimenting with dishes that were sometimes delicious and sometimes inedible. She was truly independent at last and she took a quiet pleasure in it.

Every now and then one of the booksellers or salesmen she worked with offered to treat her to supper or to take her to a show. She always refused them politely. They were nice enough and it wasn't their fault, she often thought, that compared with Gabriel they seemed shallow and one-dimensional.

Since the beginning of the year, following the collapse of another Franchise Bill, which would have given a limited number of women the vote, the WSPU had intensified its campaign of violence against property. Pillar boxes were set alight, and parcels containing phosphorus were sent through the post, sometimes bursting into flames at post office sorting offices. There was a series of attacks on buildings, golf courses and railway trains.

And then, on 19 February, a bomb exploded at the new house that was being built for David Lloyd George, the Chancellor. No one was injured, but the direct attack on the property of a prominent member of the cabinet outraged the government. In response, they pushed through parliament the Prisoners' (Temporary Discharge for Ill-Health) Act. The Act, which quickly became known as the Cat and Mouse Act, permitted the release from prison of hunger strikers on licence. As soon as a woman's health recovered sufficiently from starvation, she was returned to prison. In the summer of 1913 suffragettes' lives became an unending cycle of imprisonment, starvation, force-feeding, liberty and then reimprisonment.

One evening Eva invited Lydia, May Jackson and another suffragette, Catherine Sutherland, to supper. Not long before, Catherine had visited Sylvia Pankhurst, the second Pankhurst sister and a friend of George Lansbury and Keir Hardie, shortly after she had been released from prison. 'I hardly recognized her!' she cried. 'Her gums were bleeding from that terrible steel thing they put in her mouth, and her throat was ulcerated from the tube they forced down. And her eyes were all bloodshot, and she was so thin! So terribly thin!'

Eva knew that Catherine and May sometimes threw stones and smashed windows; once Catherine had poured petrol into a letter box and set it alight. Occasionally Lydia had gone with them, but only occasionally because, Eva knew, Lydia had a dread of imprisonment. So far Eva had not accompanied them. Sometimes for practical reasons — both Catherine and May had private incomes and therefore had no need, as Eva and Lydia had, to work, and so could break windows or pelt Members of Parliament with eggs on a weekday afternoon. But Eva was uncomfortably aware that her reluctance had a deeper source. It was not that she was afraid of imprisonment like Lydia — though she would have hated it, she thought that she would have been able to bear it. Something else stopped her from taking part in active protest.

Recently Catherine had begun to notice and comment on her absence. 'When peaceful protest achieves nothing,' she said coldly to Eva, 'how do you oppose tyranny except by rising up and fighting?' Then she quoted Christabel Pankhurst: 'Women will never get the vote except by creating an intolerable situation for all the selfish and apathetic people who stand in their way.'

Was she selfish and apathetic? Eva wondered. Perhaps worse, was she cowardly? She was rather afraid that she might be. Physical violence had always sickened her. She had a mortifying habit of fainting at the sight of blood. But could she continue to stand back, primly hiding from horrors while other women suffered imprisonment and torture for a cause she believed in every bit as much as they did? Her position felt increasingly unjustifiable.

Catherine wrote Eva a note suggesting they meet at Catherine's flat in the West End on Saturday afternoon. The wording of the note was pointed. *If you care as much about the cause as you say you do, then perhaps you should put your words into actions.*

By Saturday morning Eva was still undecided. And then, shopping in Oxford Street, she saw Gabriel, a tall, unmistakable figure in his black overcoat, scarf and fedora, on the far side of the road. Since the evening they had parted, she had been careful to avoid the places where he went, and now her heart squeezed and her gaze fixed on him hungrily. She was painfully aware of the bleak emptiness of her life without Gabriel. She could remedy that: all she had to do was to cross the road to him. He would not reject her, he wasn't the sort to push her away, to hold a grudge. And if they could not be lovers, then why should they not be friends? She teetered on the edge of the pavement, waiting for a gap in the traffic.

But as she watched another figure ran towards him, a flicker of emerald green and black, threading through the Saturday crowds. Gabriel waved and called out to Ruby Bailey, then held out his arms to her, catching her up and whirling her round. When they kissed, Eva turned away, overcome by a mixture of shame, rage and hatred. The rage predominated: she wanted to slap Ruby Bailey's smooth, laughing face.

Instead, she walked quickly to the tube station. Lydia and May were already at Catherine's Charles Street flat by the time Eva appeared. Catherine greeted her arrival

355

with a crisp, 'Good. I wasn't sure whether you'd turn up,' and gave Eva a handful of pebbles for her coat pockets. Eva's heart hammered uncomfortably as they made their way to Regent Street. She was certain that everyone could hear the clink of the pebbles in her pockets. And they gave such an odd line to her coat — surely someone would notice? And what if she let the others down? What if none of her stones hit their target? She had no confidence at all that they would. And what if she was arrested? What on earth would Father say?

And then they were in Regent Street and Catherine was saying to her in that same crisp, cold voice, 'You are to break that window in Liberty's, Eva, when I give the signal. And when you've done, you must run as fast as you can and not trouble about any of the rest of us. As fast as you can, remember.' And then Catherine was calling out, '*Now!*', and Eva was fumbling in her pocket for the pebbles with cold, nervous fingers and drawing back her arm and throwing the stones at the window. Most of them missed, skating along the pavement, scattering passers-by. There was a yell of protest; several women shrieked. Eva thought of Gabriel: the delight on his face when he had caught sight of Ruby Bailey, and she scooped up more pebbles and hurled them hard. This time there was a loud crash, and then cracks rushed through the pane of glass, spreading out in a star shape from the point of impact, until the window display — plates, clocks, a Japanese vase — fragmented, its coloured, lacquered surfaces cut into pieces, like a mosaic.

For a moment she stood transfixed, staring at the broken window. Then a policeman's whistle snapped her out of her trance and she began to run, weaving through the crowds. Someone grabbed her arm; she flung him off. Someone else shouted curses at her. When she looked quickly back over her shoulder, she saw a policeman's helmet, bobbing through the crowd, drawing closer to her. Darting down a side road, she found herself in a row of smaller shops. She was tiring quickly and the rage and courage that had fired her were fast dissipating as reaction set in. When she looked back again the policeman was only fifty yards away.

There was a dress shop nearby; she ducked inside it. The shop assistant looked up from the counter. Her eyes swept over Eva, taking in her dishevelled appearance and the green, purple and white ribbon on her lapel. The policeman's whistle sounded very loud. For a long, awful moment Eva thought the assistant was going to throw her out of the shop, but then she beckoned to Eva to approach the counter. 'Take your coat off,' whispered the girl. 'Quick.' Eva pulled off her coat and it was bundled under the counter. 'He's coming in,' the assistant muttered. '*Here.*' She tugged Eva's arm, dragging her behind the counter. As the door opened and the policeman came into the shop, the girl said loudly to Eva, 'And you must sort out those laces, Miss Smith! Terrible state that drawer was in last time I looked!' The policeman peered around, then touched his helmet in a quick salute before leaving the shop. The door swung shut behind him.

Eva was trembling so much she had to sit down on the high wooden stool behind the counter. She muttered, 'I don't know how I can thank you, Miss — '

'Price. Florence Price. And I enjoyed giving them a poke in the eye. Here, borrow these — ' Miss Price picked out a jacket and hat — 'they won't know you in them. You can come back for your things in a day or two.'

Eva went home. Though she lit a fire, she could not seem to get warm. She felt no pride in what she had done, only the beginnings of a deep distaste. She remembered how a vase in Liberty's window, a lovely thing of blue and green and gold, had tipped and shattered. She remembered the fear on the faces of the women on the pavement, how they had cried out in alarm and drawn their children to them. She remembered a little girl, six years old perhaps, sobbing in terror, pressing her face into her mother's skirts. She found herself standing at the sink, scrubbing her hands clean as if to eradicate the squalor of the afternoon's events.

Her doorbell rang and she went downstairs to open it. May Jackson was outside.

'I just called to see how you were. Whether you'd managed to get away.'

'I'm fine. Where are Catherine and Lydia?'

'They were both arrested.'

'Oh God — '

'Lydia tried to run away, but a passer-by tripped her and she fell.'

'What will happen to them?'

'Catherine will certainly be sent to prison. It isn't her first offence. And she'll go on hunger strike, of course.'

'And Lydia?'

'If she agrees to be bound over to keep the peace, she may escape prison. It depends on the magistrate.'

'She will agree, won't she?'

'I hope so.'

'The gallery — '

'I'll keep an eye on the gallery,' said May briskly. 'I don't know the least thing about art, but I'll have a jolly good try.'

As she returned upstairs, Eva thought of Lydia, bright, elegant Lydia with her loathing of confined spaces. The flat seemed very quiet, very empty. Her thoughts drifted to Gabriel — not that she ever stopped thinking about Gabriel; he was always there, not far from the forefront of her mind. Now, when she looked back on their love affair, she felt a sense of shame and a growing conviction that she had sold herself short. She could not quite pinpoint where she had let herself down so badly, yet she knew that she had. Somehow she had confused freedom with acquiescence, and in doing so she had cheapened herself.

She had risked so much for Gabriel. It had been only through sheer luck that she had not brought into the world an illegitimate child, a child she would have been unable to care for properly, a child who would have brought disgrace on her and her family. Loving Gabriel had meant unending deceit, it had meant lying to her family, it had meant betraying Sadie and neglecting her talent. Could you ever justify deceit? And could you ever justify violence? She no longer knew.

She had lost her way and she wasn't sure, just then, whether she would ever find it again. All she could do was try to be true to her own beliefs, whatever anyone else might think of them. It was a bleak conclusion, and, sitting alone in her flat, her convictions seemed to amount to little, to be a poor consolation for what she had lost, and there was just the ache in her heart, which had been there for months now and might not, she suspected, ever quite go away.

★　★　★

It was August, a time of year Iris always disliked. In late summer the cramped streets and small, high-walled courtyards of the East End magnified the heat. Even the air seemed foul, the warm weather intensifying the thick, heavy stench that always lingered around the docks. Where the mud showed beside the piers, the viscid, grey-brown water was thick with refuse and debris.

The heat made everyone tired and irritable. Shopping in the market during her morning break, Iris saw two women fighting in the street, their faces contorted in anger as they squabbled over a cheap market-stall blouse that both had seen at once. As they cursed and scratched and pulled each other's hair, the crowd

359

roared, urging them on.

The atmosphere in the nurses' home seemed almost as poisonous as that in the surrounding streets, a serpent's nest of petty jealousies and squabbles, the epitome of everything Iris had always loathed about living among a large group of women. Two close probationer friends had fallen out, and their acquaintances had divided into whispering, offended factions. Iris kept herself apart from them. Though she tried to escape to the nurses' garden, the lawn was yellowed and scorched and a film of dust greyed the leaves of the roses, and she found herself moving continually from seat to seat to escape the sun.

Then an epidemic of German measles broke out among the nurses. The sick nurses were sent to a south London fever hospital to recover. Because they were short-staffed, Iris often had to work an extra half-shift to fill in for an absent colleague. As the weeks wore on a grinding exhaustion overtook her. She seemed to have a headache all the time and, because of the heat, she slept badly at night. She veered from a tearfulness and irritability which she felt ashamed of to a feeling of detachment from her work, mechanically carrying out the duties she now knew so well in a thoughtless stupor. She longed for — she was unsure what she longed for. For something to change. For this weather to break. For cool woods and green fields and for a way out of the torpor that imprisoned her. For Ash to tell her that she was not just one of his many friends. For Ash to tell her that he cared more for her than he did for Thelma Voss.

⋆ ⋆ ⋆

Ash was on his way home from work when he heard a voice calling out to him. 'Mister! Mister!' A small figure darted through the traffic and a grubby hand pulled at his sleeve. 'Mister!'

360

'What is it, Eddie?'

'It's our Janie! She's poorly or summat. She won't get up. You got to come, Mister!'

Ash followed Eddie down a side street. Eddie Lowman — seven or eight years old, Ash guessed, perpetually undernourished, and with the wizened, stunted appearance of so many East End children — was one of nine brothers and sisters. The Lowmans were on the bottom rung of society, the poorest of the poor. Bert Lowman, Eddie's father, was a casual labourer; Eddie's mother could sometimes be seen scouring the streets for scraps of wood to sell as bundles of kindling. The family lived in a two-up, two-down terrace in one of the roughest areas of Whitechapel.

The Lowmans' house shocked even Ash, who had thought himself accustomed to East End poverty. The few sticks of furniture were, presumably, too old and battered even for the pawn shop. There were no rugs on the floor, no curtains in the windows. A stale, heavy smell, of the sort Ash had come to associate with vermin and cockroaches, pervaded the house. Flies buzzed against the dirty window panes.

A small girl in a ragged pinafore stood in the front room, her thumb in her mouth, staring wide-eyed at Ash. In a corner a baby lay on a stained blanket on the floor. Urine seeped from the soggy mass of rags around the infant's middle; in the hot, unventilated room the stench made Ash's stomach turn.

'Where's Janie?' he asked Eddie.

'Upstairs.'

In the bedroom a young girl, fifteen or sixteen, perhaps, lay on the stained mattress. Eddie whispered, 'Is she dead, Mister?'

Ash put his fingers against Janie's neck: a pulse beat, fast and erratic. 'No, she's not dead.'

There was a bottle of cheap gin by the girl's side and a packet of pills. He guessed what they were even before he read the label on the packet: *Dr Patterson's Famous Pills — the great remedy for irregularities of every description.* An abortifacient, a concoction of ergot or lead, commonly used by women in the East End to rid themselves of an unwanted pregnancy. He rolled Janie onto her side in case she vomited and choked, and she gave a little snore.

Downstairs a door slammed, a voice roared and then loud footsteps pounded up the stairs. 'It's me Dad,' whispered Eddie and dived under a heap of dirty blankets.

Ash knew Bert Lowman by reputation. A great bull of a man, a drinker, a fighter, a man you wouldn't want to cross. The door was hurled open; Bert Lowman stood on the threshhold. He stared at Ash, swaying slightly.

'What the bloody hell are you doing here?'

'Eddie thought there was something wrong with your daughter.'

'Our Janie?' Lowman lurched across the room; Ash could smell the alcohol on his breath. 'Have you been messing around with our Janie?'

'No, Mr Lowman, I — '

'I know your sort.' Lowman's fists were clenched. 'You keep your filthy hands off my Janie or I'll keep them off for you — '

A blow landed hard on Ash's jaw. Ash saw stars, staggered, and fell. As Lowman swayed, rocked off his balance by the force of his own fist, Ash managed to scramble to his feet and stumble out of the room, down the stairs and out of the house.

He tasted blood; he clamped his handkerchief over the side of his face and made for home as quickly as possible. People stared at him in the street; his legs felt treacherously unsteady. In the sanctuary of his kitchen, he put his head under the cold tap. He heard the front door open and Thelma call out, 'Ash? Are you there?'

'In the kitchen.' It was a struggle to enunciate the words clearly.

Thelma came in. 'Mrs Clark's sitting with Dad, so I thought I'd take Sam for a walk — ' She stared at him.

'It's not as bad as it looks.'

'Well, I'm glad of that,' she said tartly. 'What happened?'

'Bert Lowman's fist happened.'

'You were in a *fight?*'

'If you could call it that.' He groped in a drawer for a bit of rag to stem the bleeding. 'He hit me because he thought I had designs on his daughter, then he fell over because he was drunk, so I ran away.'

'His daughter?'

'Janie. Stringy hair and funny teeth.'

'You should keep out of the Lowmans' way. Everyone knows they're trouble.'

'I didn't intend — ' He broke off, glanced at his watch. 'Iris,' he said. 'I'm supposed to be meeting Iris.'

'Your face, Ash. Sit down.'

'I can't — I'm late already — '

'Miss Maclise won't want to see you looking like that.'

His shaving mirror was on the mantelpiece; he squinted at it and groaned. 'No, I suppose not.'

'Let me tidy you up a bit.' She pushed him into a chair.

There was lint and disinfectant under the sink. Thelma dabbed at his face; he winced. She said, 'You're fond of Miss Maclise aren't you, Ash?'

'Yes. Yes, I am.'

She frowned. 'It's not too bad. Just a little cut. But you'll have a black eye. Are you and Miss Maclise just friends, or have you an understanding?'

He was suddenly glad that Thelma was here, glad that he had someone, at last, to give him advice. He'd been wondering what to do about Iris for ages, trying to summon up the nerve to speak to her. 'Years ago,' he said, 'I had a chance with Iris, but I messed it up.'

'And you're sorry about that now?'

'Yes. Dear God, yes.'

'Have you told her so?'

He shook his head, regretted it immediately. 'I don't know what she thinks about me now. It's so hard to tell. Sometimes I think she likes me. Sometimes I think she's changed her mind, but then . . . '

'Changed her mind?'

'A while ago Iris told me that she was glad that we'd never be anything more than friends.'

Thelma said, 'A girl like that must have men running after her all the time. My schoolfriend Lily Watson was ever such a pretty girl and she said she got fed up with all the men bothering her. Wished they'd just leave her alone.'

He remembered Iris at the party at Summerleigh, men clustering about her like bees round a flower. *It's just a game, Ash*, she had said to him. Love had always been a game to Iris Maclise. Perhaps it was still nothing more than a game. He said doubtfully, 'I thought I should speak to her. Tell her what I feel. See what she says.'

'I shouldn't, if I were you, Ash. You might drive her away. Then you wouldn't see her again. Is that what you want?'

'No,' he said. He felt his heart sink. 'No, of course not.'

'Better to wait till you're sure.' Thelma stood back. 'There. All done. You don't look too bad at all.'

★   ★   ★

Iris stood on the hospital steps, waiting for Ash. When, after a quarter of an hour, there was no sign of him, she walked to his house. His front door was ajar; she stepped inside. She heard Thelma Voss's peal of laughter from the kitchen.

'Iris,' said Ash, catching sight of her.

Horrified, she said, 'Your *face.*'

'It's nothing much, Miss Maclise.' Thelma Voss was putting away lint and disinfectant.

'Let me see.' Iris ran her fingertips over Ash's face, feeling for broken bones.

'See? I cleaned him up. That awful Bert Lowman. I told you to keep away from him, didn't I?' Thelma's hand rested proprietorially on Ash's shoulder.

Shortly afterwards, Ash's friends began to arrive — Harry and Fred and Nathaniel and Tom and red-haired, snub-nosed Charlie. Thelma Voss sat in a corner of the room, stroking the dog's matted coat. They talked about politics. Every now and then a phrase caught Iris's attention. *Britain's afraid that Germany will threaten her trade routes. Must protect the empire, mustn't we . . . Austria — Hungary and Serbia are flexing their muscles, that's all. Remember that game schoolchildren play, daring each other to blink first? . . . Germany is building a great many very large battleships. We prefer to have all the battleships to ourselves . . .*

'A short, sharp war might be fun.' Charlie rubbed his hands together.

'What a dreadful thing to say,' said Thelma.

Charlie raised his glass in a toast. 'King and country,' he said. 'Won't you drink with me?'

'Oh, put a sock in it, Charlie!'

'Temper, temper — '

Thelma grabbed the dog's lead and then, the mongrel at her heels, left the house, slamming the door behind her.

'Bit of a temper, our Thelma,' said Charlie and winked at Iris. 'Have you got a temper, Miss Maclise?'

'A perfectly foul one.' She looked at him coldly.

'Especially with insolent young men.'

Half a dozen Polish labourers arrived at the house, bottles of vodka in hand. An out-of-work bricklayer turned up, looking for a bed for the night, his drawn, anxious face brightening when Ash offered him the sofa. Iris watched Ash for a while, as the Polish labourers sang songs in their beautiful, incomprehensible language, and then she gathered up some empty glasses and took them into the kitchen.

Thelma Voss had returned to the house and was at the sink, washing up. 'I thought I'd better get on with it,' she said angrily, 'or they'll leave it all to him. They eat him out of house and home! They always do! I try to bring him odds and ends from the shop, but my dad would notice if I took too much.' She swung round to Iris. 'Some of them don't even care about him! They only use him!'

Thelma's eyes issued a challenge. Iris said, 'But you care about him, don't you, Miss Voss?'

'Yes, I do. He's one of the best, Ash. I don't want anything of him, you see. I don't expect anything of him. Not like some of this lot. They'll bleed him dry, they will. When they've finished here, they'll move on to the next place that'll give them a free meal and a bed for the night.'

Iris dried a plate. 'Perhaps Ash likes to be needed.'

'Perhaps.' Thelma's scornful glare settled on Iris. 'And you, Miss Maclise? What do you need from him?'

'Ash and I are just old friends.' Yet she felt herself redden.

Thelma's wet hands dripped soap; her gaze did not leave Iris. 'The thing with Ash is that he can't bear to let anyone down. I tell him not to be so foolish, but he doesn't listen to me. You can't give everyone what they want. Sometimes people want things you can't give.'

There was a silence. Then Iris said, 'What are you

trying to tell me, Miss Voss?'

'That he doesn't love you. That he won't ever love you.'

Iris's breath seemed to catch in her throat. She whispered, 'You can't know that.'

'I know him. And I know he feels sorry for you. That's the only reason he goes on seeing you.'

'No — '

'It's true. He told me. He feels sorry for you, just as he feels sorry for all the others who want a piece of him.'

Thelma's words stabbed her. 'I don't believe you.'

'He doesn't want to hurt your feelings, you see.' Thelma's voice was low and hypnotic. 'He told me there was once something between you. And then he gave you the push. I'm right, aren't I, Miss Maclise?'

That Ash should have shared her humiliation with Thelma Voss made Iris feel sick with shock. It took all her courage, all her powers of self-possession to say to Thelma, 'What are you really telling me? That Ash loves you?'

Thelma gave a bitter laugh. 'You don't know him at all, do you? Of course he doesn't love *me*. Not yet, anyhow. He loves *them*.' She made a gesture towards the adjacent room. 'He loves the tramps who eat his food and the scroungers who take away his coal in their pockets. Don't you see that he'll always put them before either of us — before me, who'd do anything for him, and before you, with your pretty face? Don't you see that?'

And yes, she did, she saw it quite clearly and realized that she must have been blind not to see it before.

Thelma turned back to the sink. 'You have a choice, Miss Maclise. It's up to you. You can stay here having your piece of him, just like everyone else, if that's what you prefer. Or you can cut your losses and start again. Don't leave it too long, that's my advice. That's what I'd do, if I had a face and figure like yours, if I could afford dresses like you. I'd forget about him and find someone else.'

Drying her hands, Thelma threw down the cloth onto the draining board and went back into the sitting room. The Polish labourers had begun to sing again; the music drifted in from the adjacent room, some low, mournful song of love and loss.

He'll never love you. He feels sorry for you. Such a terrible thing, to be an object of pity. Iris would have liked to have slipped out of the house without Ash seeing her, but he caught sight of her at the door and insisted on walking her home. All the way back to the nurses' home she talked, her words fast and bright and brittle, staving off his attempts at conversation. At the entrance to the hospital she gave him a peck on the cheek and walked quickly away. The hurt in his eyes followed her as she made her way through the nurses' garden.

She hardly slept that night. On the ward the next day she was jumpy and distracted. She was coming out of the kitchen when she heard Sister Dickens scolding one of the patients for having spilt a cup of tea on his clean sheets. 'Oh, for heaven's sake,' she heard herself snap. 'It's only a few drops of tea!'

The entire ward fell silent. Everyone stared at her. The expression on Sister Dickens's face, a mixture of outrage and surprise, almost made Iris want to laugh. Almost. Nurses never answered back and they never ever questioned a senior nurse's judgement. Nurses said *Yes, Sister* or *No, Sister*, whichever was appropriate.

The summons to matron's office came at the end of the afternoon. Walking through the hospital corridors, Iris lurched between rebelliousness and despair. She had been right to speak out because Sister Dickens was a monster. She didn't care if they sacked her; she'd had enough of the hospital anyway. Yet the ignominy, the sense of failure, coming on top of Thelma's revelations of the previous night would be unendurable.

Miss Stanley answered her knock. Standing in her office, Iris waited, watching the swift movement of the pen across the paper. Then Miss Stanley said, 'I hear from Sister Dickens that you've been impertinent, nurse.'

Iris muttered, 'I'm sorry, Matron.'

Miss Stanley put down her pen. Her cold blue eyes focused on Iris. 'I generally dismiss nurses for impertinence.'

'It won't happen again, Matron.'

'What sort of example does behaviour like that set the probationers?'

'But Sister Dickens is so unkind to the patients! Poor Mr Knowles — he can't help it if his hand shakes!'

Miss Stanley's mouth tightened. 'And is it your duty to reprimand a sister, nurse?'

Her fleeting defiance dissolved. Iris looked down at the floor. 'No, of course not, Matron.'

'I'm very disappointed in you, Nurse Maclise.'

All these years of work, she thought drearily, all she had endured, all the humiliation and exhaustion, only to be summarily dismissed because, like a silly probationer, she had spoken out of turn.

Miss Stanley was still speaking. 'I recognize that my senior nurses have recently been under a great deal of strain. This wretched epidemic.' She looked at Iris sharply. 'You're not sickening yourself, are you, nurse? You look quite pale and tired.'

'No, Matron. I've had German measles.'

Again, the cool blue eyes studied her. 'Tell me, are you quite happy here, nurse?'

Suddenly, she felt close to tears. She whispered, 'I don't know. I *was* happy.'

'If you've come to feel differently, perhaps you should reconsider your position with us.'

369

'You're dismissing me?' Her voice shook.

'I'll give you a good reference. I don't doubt that today's incident was due to exhaustion and strain. It need not be mentioned again.'

Iris hardly heard Miss Stanley's last words. She blurted out, 'But this is my *home*!'

'A hospital is a place of work,' said Miss Stanley crisply. 'If a nurse becomes unsuitable then she has no further place with us.' Her tone softened slightly. 'When you first came to the Mandeville, Maclise, some of my staff questioned your suitability. But I always had faith in you. I sensed that you had the grit one needs for nursing. But I think you need to move on. You have outgrown us, perhaps. It's not so much a question of ability, more one of type, of personality. Hospital nursing suits some nurses more than others. Our less conventional nurses may find themselves happier in a different sphere.' Miss Stanley picked up her fountain pen. 'You may go now.'

She couldn't bear to return to the nurses' home; she had to escape the hospital. But when she ran down the front steps she saw that Ash was waiting for her. She felt suddenly bitterly angry with him: for telling Thelma Voss what happened between them; for not loving her. She said sharply, 'You will just turn up.'

He blinked. 'Last night — '

She dashed across the road; brakes screeched. He ran after her. He said, '*Iris*. Listen to me. I wanted to apologize for yesterday. All those people — I didn't know they were coming.'

The market was closing down for the day. Litter and rotten fruit clogged the gutters, and the stalls had a tawdry, seedy look. She wondered what she was doing here in this miserable place, she who had always loved pretty things. She said coldly, 'You could have sent them away, Ash.'

'Yes. I suppose I could.'

She could see him searching for words — searching for the words, she thought, that would make poor, pitiable Iris Maclise feel better. 'It doesn't matter,' she said. 'It's only that it was rather a waste of an evening for me.' She gave a harsh laugh. 'You know I find politics so *dull*, Ash. I'd have gone somewhere else if I'd known I was going to have to endure that.'

'Somewhere else?'

'The theatre . . . dancing . . . ' Thelma Voss's voice echoed: *He doesn't love you; he won't ever love you.* And she knew suddenly what she must do. She must excise the cause of her unhappiness, she must cut it out and cast it ruthlessly away.

She spun round to him. 'How do you imagine I occupy my time when you're busy, Ash? Do you think I sit in my room pining for you?'

He flushed. 'Of course not.'

'Because I don't.'

'Iris, I didn't mean to imply — '

'I have plenty of friends.'

'I never thought otherwise.'

'And I've never exactly found it hard to find someone to take me dancing.'

His eyes became cold. 'No, I shouldn't think you would.'

There was a silence. 'That place — ' she glanced back across the road to the hospital and a mixture of affection, loss and resentment flooded over her — 'I'll be glad to see the back of it.' She stuck out her chin. 'I've decided to leave the Mandeville.'

His expression hardened. 'Is this a sudden decision?'

'Not at all. I've been thinking about it for ages.'

'You didn't say.'

'Didn't I?' They were walking between the stalls; she pretended to examine a bale of sprigged cotton. 'It must have slipped my mind.'

'What will you do?'

371

'I might go home for a while.' She shrugged. 'Or I might do some private nursing. So much easier than slaving away on the wards.' The look in his eyes almost made her falter, but she persisted pitilessly, 'Really, Ash, I can't stay here forever. The same old places . . . the same old people . . . You know me. I hate to be bored.'

'And I hate to be a bore,' he said curtly. 'You've made yourself perfectly clear, Iris. I hope you'll be happy. Whatever you do, I hope you'll be happy.'

Then he walked away. There was a moment when she might have run after him, but she did not let herself. Instead, she returned to the nurses' home, where she lay on her bed, her eyes closed, listening to the sound of her heart breaking.

12

George had white-blond hair, dark blue eyes and a gurgle of infectious laughter. Everything made him laugh — a chameleon darting along a branch, the gold braid on Rani's sari, the blue trumpet of a morning glory. On the rare occasions that he cried Marianne would pick him up in her arms and sing him his favourite song ('To market, to market, to buy a fat pig, Home again, home again, jiggety-jig') and he would laugh, the tears shining ribbons down his cheeks.

At six months old he could sit unaided, and at seven months he began to pull himself across the floor with his forearms. Something would catch his eye — the green jewel of a gecko pasted on the skirting board, or a brass lamp glinting in the sunlight — and he would be off, excitement in his eyes, a wide smile on his face. When, a month later, he began to crawl properly nothing was safe. They had been in thrall to him since the day he was born, Marianne and Rani, and now they dashed round the house and garden in his wake, anticipating the crash of a broken vase, or the disaster of a poisonous leaf stuffed greedily into that smiling mouth. Marianne became aware of dangers everywhere: the steep incline of the terraces in the garden, the hot coals in the fire, or a snake, swooping across the lawn, forked tongue reaching out to a soft, plump limb.

He was, of course, the most beautiful and clever baby ever born. It was only by great exercise of tact that Marianne forbore to point this out to the other ladies who called at the bungalow, but, privately, she thought they couldn't help but realize it anyway. Though she politely complimented her visitors on their offspring, she knew that none was a patch on George. When

George was six months old, they visited Nuwara Eliya and had his photograph taken. Marianne dressed him in a white lace gown, but left his head bare, so that his white-gold locks stood out in a cloud around his head. She sent photographs to her sisters in England, who, writing back to her, only confirmed what she knew already: that George was perfect.

Each day she took him round the garden, her paradise, his domain. She showed him the banyan tree and let him stroke the leaves, which were bigger than his own head, with his fat little fingers. He reached out to the bananas growing in the palms and the flowers in the borders, and he rolled on the thick green grass as Marianne kept a wary eye out for ants and other stinging insects. Holding him in her arms, she walked along the narrow, winding paths that threaded through the trees. At the call of a bird George's eyes widened, and he turned and stared. Far above, sunlight glittered black and white through the mesh of high branches. Marianne kept well away from the wild bees that swarmed round the high, globular hives and clutched George tightly whenever she heard a rustle in the undergrowth. *I shall always keep you safe*, she whispered to him. *My darling boy, I shall always keep you safe.*

Her decision to leave Lucas had faltered in the aftermath of George's birth. Where could she go? To Clare, perhaps, but she could not have imposed on her for more than a few weeks. And after that? She could only return to England. The thought of the long, difficult journey from Blackwater to Colombo, and the far longer journey from Colombo to Southampton, on her own, and with a new baby, was impossibly daunting. The thought of the disgrace and stigma of divorce was even worse. A woman was defined by her relationship to a man: she was a daughter, a sweetheart, a wife. If she left Lucas she would be nothing. Much worse, her disgrace would reflect upon George as well. Though she might be able to bear being ostracized by society, how would she feel when George, too, was shunned? Better, she decided, to make the best of it.

She reminded herself that marriage to Lucas had given her George. For George's sake, she would tolerate Lucas's occasional bursts of anger and bad language. In her letters to her sisters she told amusing anecdotes about bungalow life and described George's beauty and cleverness. She had always been adept at hiding what was in her heart. She told no one that Lucas had said to her: *I never loved you at all.*

She thought that she could manage. They had their spheres, she and Lucas. She had the garden and the nursery; he had the factory and the estate. They shared the bungalow in an uneasy truce. Six weeks after George's birth, Lucas came to her bedroom. Now his touch repelled her; once, leaving her bed, she caught him looking at her, a measuring look in his eyes. Shortly afterwards she heard once more the footsteps in the night, and glimpsed a flash of scarlet, running down to the coolie lines. She felt a mixture of relief and guilt; she knew that she was evading the duties of a wife, but those pale grey eyes, which she had once thought arresting, even angelic, had begun to frighten her.

She knew that her marriage was shoddy and second-rate, but knew also that she must make the best of it, for George's sake. Lucas was George's father. They had something to unite them now, she told herself, a common bond. And Lucas loved his son; she saw the hunger in his eyes when he bent over the cradle. She learned to be careful with him, to recognize the flashpoints that goaded the demons in him, and to avoid him when he drank. Better to weigh her words carefully before speaking to him, better to keep out of his sight when she glimpsed in his eyes that gleam, that darkness.

Yet curiosity gnawed at her. She remembered Mrs

Rawlinson saying, *I felt sorry for the child . . . George Melrose was never an easy man.* What had she meant? Marianne imagined Lucas, just four years old, left alone in the bungalow with his father and the servants after his mother had run away. She imagined the mark that desertion must have made on him. What sort of man had Lucas's father been? Moody and hard-drinking, surely, absent much of the time, attending to the affairs of the estate. A cold man, a man who, bruised by his wife's unfaithfulness, had been unable to show affection.

One Sunday afternoon the Rawlinsons called at Blackwater. While the men were drinking and talking after lunch and George was having his nap, Marianne showed Mrs Rawlinson round the garden. The cosmos were in flower, the pink and white daisy heads surrounded by a cloud of lacy green leaves. 'Clare Barlow gave me some seeds last year,' Marianne explained. 'I'm rather proud of them.'

'And the roses.' Mrs Rawlinson stooped to sniff a bloom. 'Quite a picture.'

Marianne glanced quickly back to the veranda. Lucas and Mr Rawlinson were out of earshot. She said, 'I remember you telling me that Lucas's mother planted the roses, Anne.'

'Every one of them.'

'And the rest of the garden?'

'It was scrub and jungle before Sarah came here. I'll give her that. She transformed this place.'

'Did you know her well?'

Anne Rawlinson's lips pursed. 'No, I wouldn't say any of us knew Sarah *well*. She was only here for a few years, remember. And she never fitted in. She was a frivolous woman — and an incorrigible flirt.'

'And her husband, Lucas's father. Do you remember him?'

'George?' They walked on, further away from the

veranda. 'After Sarah left, George kept himself to himself. He hardly ever came to the club — not that the club was much in those days, just a hut with a dirt floor. Life was harder then — often you didn't see another white face for weeks.'

'What sort of man was he?'

Mrs Rawlinson peered critically, plucked a leaf and rubbed it between finger and thumb. 'Your Gloire de Dijon has mildew, I'm afraid, Marianne.'

'Was he short-tempered?'

The crumpled leaf dropped to the path. Mrs Rawlinson said, 'George Melrose was one of the old school. He and his father made Blackwater out of nothing. They worked day and night. There was nothing they wouldn't do. I admire that. George had grit. Not enough of that around now. These boys that the tea companies send out, half of 'em run back to England in six months. Can't take the climate or the loneliness — or the hard work.'

'But Lucas's father wasn't like that?'

'George stuck it out.' Anne paused to inspect another rose. Her voice lowered, became confiding. 'He was never the same after Sarah went, though. He adored Sarah. Worshipped the ground she walked on. He built this house for her, let her make the garden. He had the roses shipped over from England. And all sorts of other nonsense — linen and glassware and gowns from Paris. George gave her everything she wanted. I suppose he could never believe his luck in catching her. I suppose he was always afraid that she'd cut and run. He spoiled her, you see, spoiled her ridiculously.'

Marianne glanced quickly back over her shoulder at the veranda. 'It must have been dreadful for Lucas's father when Sarah left.'

'He cut himself off from the rest of us. People tried to keep in touch, but it wasn't easy. The estates are so far apart and George wasn't welcoming. He had a way of making it clear when he didn't want company.' They had reached the far end of the garden, where the hillside fell almost vertically to the valley far below. In spite of their distance from the veranda, Mrs Rawlinson's voice dropped to a whisper. 'George Melrose once singed Davey Scott's ear when Davey came to Blackwater and George wasn't feeling sociable. Shot at him with his rifle.'

'He *shot* someone?'

'George Melrose was a good shot. That bullet went where he meant it to. The next shot would have done more damage, I daresay. Davey got the message and kept away. So did the rest of us.'

'And Lucas?'

'As I say, we kept away. But there were rumours.'

'What sort of rumours?'

Mrs Rawlinson's gaze darted quickly back to the house. 'That George Melrose beat the child.'

'*Beat* him?'

'Yes.' Horrified, Marianne thought she saw a flicker of sympathy in Mrs Rawlinson's faded blue eyes.

'Of course, boys need disciplining. When they were little my three felt the back of my hand more than once. But George Melrose went too far. He didn't believe in sparing the rod. That wasn't his way. He despised weakness. Even in his own child.' Mrs Rawlinson tugged at a length of creeper that had wound itself around a branch. 'You should have this ficus cut back, Marianne, or it will get out of hand. The weeds will smother your garden if you give them half the chance.' She frowned. 'I think that after she'd gone George despised himself for falling for Sarah. He was a strong man and he saw it as his only weakness, the chink in his armour.'

'*Loving* isn't a weakness!'

'Isn't it? Remember that George had devoted his entire life to controlling — to *governing* — the estate. He couldn't afford to drop his guard. Make that mistake and your servants and coolies will take advantage of you, and the jungle will steal back your fields. It must have been a shock to George to discover that he couldn't govern his own heart.' Mrs Rawlinson dropped the length of creeper over the hillside, brushed her hands together and said slowly, 'There's a pattern in the Melrose family. Lucas's father, George, was an only child, like Lucas himself. His mother died young, from a fever, I believe — there was a great deal of malaria in the hills in those days. So George was brought up by his father, just as Lucas was.'

Marianne thought: *if that should happen to my George. If I should not be here to protect him. My George, whom my husband named after the father who beat him.* Her heart seemed to still. She said, 'Did no one try to stop him hurting Lucas?'

'Best not to interfere,' said Mrs Rawlinson crisply. 'Never come between a man and his wife or a parent and child, that's what I say.'

'But surely someone — '

'We stick together out here. It's how we survive. George was one of us. And as I said, it was only rumour. Who knows how much truth there was in it?'

The men had risen from their seats and were crossing the lawn to them. Mrs Rawlinson said softly to Marianne, 'I called on George a few weeks after Sarah had gone. He'd lit a bonfire in the garden. When I went to speak to him, I saw what he was throwing onto the fire. All Sarah's things. Her clothes, her French lace, her soap and perfume. Every photograph and painting of her. Her letters and books — even her gardening tools. It was as though he wanted to burn every trace of her, so that there was nothing left. Perhaps that's why he took it out on the child, because he could see her in him.'

Then she raised her voice. 'I hope you put plenty of

horse manure on your roses, Mrs Melrose. Horse manure is by far the best thing for roses. If you're short, I can arrange to send you some.'

★ ★ ★

One Sunday evening James failed to come home. Father lurched between anger and anxiety; Clemency slept badly, imagining railway accidents and sudden fevers. Breakfast on Monday was a taut, gloomy affair, with Father reading the newspaper in a charged manner and Aidan smugly noting aloud that James would be late for work.

James turned up eventually at midday. He looked, Clemency thought, exhausted. Usually immaculately dressed, his shirt and jacket were crumpled. As Edith served the soup, he slid into his seat. There was a moment's silence, in which Clemency started to hope that James might come up with an acceptable explanation, and then Father said, 'And what time of day do you call this, then, James?'

'Sorry, Father. I was delayed.'

'*Delayed.*' Joshua repeated the word slowly. Everyone applied themselves to their soup, avoiding Father's eye. Then Joshua said with ponderous politeness, 'And may we know what delayed you?'

James mumbled, 'Nothing important. The trains — '

'So you allow *nothing important* to keep you from your family and make you late for work?'

James flushed. 'I didn't mean — '

'What was so unimportant? A night out at a restaurant, I suppose? Or a game of cards?'

James's face became set. 'I wasn't gambling, if that's what you mean.'

'Your mother was worried sick.'

'I'm sorry. I didn't mean to worry Mother. If we only had a telephone — '

380

'You are proposing that we furnish our house to suit your irregular habits?'

'No, Father.' James stared at his soup. 'I promise it won't happen again.'

Aidan said, 'Louisa Palmer asked for you at church yesterday, James.'

Joshua shook salt into his soup. 'If you leave it too long, someone else'll snap her up, and I can't say I'd blame her.'

James looked hard at Joshua. 'Father, I've no intention of marrying Louisa Palmer. I've told you that before.'

The two men glared at each other, Joshua's eyes resentful, James's defiant. 'It's high time you settled down,' said Joshua. 'What are you waiting for?'

James's gaze fell, and he looked away. 'Nothing. It's just — I'll make my own choice of wife when it comes to it.'

No one wanted a second serving of soup, so Clemency sent Edith to fetch the main course. Joshua was slicing the mutton and they were all helping themselves to vegetables when Aidan said, 'Rickett's are charging us two shillings more in the hundredweight for coal, Father.'

Joshua stabbed a slice of meat. 'You should have told me, James. I asked you to keep an eye on coal prices.'

'I meant to. I forgot.'

'*Forgot?*' Joshua looked furious. 'You know how close run things are this year. We'll be lucky if we break even, let alone make more than a few pence profit!'

'I've been talking to some other coal merchants, Father,' said Aidan. 'Earle's might give us a better price if we place a big enough order.'

'I'll stay late tonight at the office,' said James tightly, 'and make up the hours I've missed.'

Joshua's gaze slid over his eldest son, taking in his pale face and the dark shadows beneath his eyes. 'Stay

381

late at the office?' he said scornfully. 'You look like you'd fall asleep if you weren't propped up. Doesn't do you any good burning the candle at both ends.'

'No, Father.'

'You're the eldest. It'll all go to you when I'm gone! You want to remember you have responsibilities, James!'

James's temper snapped. 'I do remember! I always remember! Don't accuse me of neglecting my responsibilities!'

Joshua's fist thumped the table, and the plates jumped. 'Don't you raise your voice to me, my lad! Too bloody idle to turn up at work at the proper time! What sort of example does that set the men?'

'I said I was sorry.' James's sudden burst of anger faded, and his voice was low and strained. 'And it wasn't idleness.'

'What was it, then?'

'That's my business.'

'Mine, when you live under my roof!'

James stood up. The colour had drained from his face. 'Yes,' he said quietly. 'Then perhaps it's time I stopped living under your roof. I can't think why I've put it off for so long.'

He left the room. Clemency ran after him. 'James, you mustn't go! Father didn't mean it! James!'

Leaning against the wall, he closed his eyes. Then he shook his head. 'I've had enough, Clem.'

She was nearly in tears. 'James, please — '

A brief, brilliant smile. 'It'll be better this way. Better for you, too, Clemency. You must be sick of us always being at each other's throats.'

'But where will you go?'

'I'll find lodgings.'

'James, Father didn't mean this to happen.' She was crying openly now. 'He's just cross because he was worried about you.'

'He doesn't think much of me and that's the truth.

I'm a disappointment to him.' James's voice was bitter.

'No. He thinks the world of you! That's why he's like this — that's why he says those things — '

'Perhaps he has every right to be disappointed in me,' James muttered as he turned away. 'Some of the things I've done — well, I'm not proud of them.'

By the time Clemency returned to the dining room, it was empty apart from Aidan. Three plates of food cooled untouched.

'Father's gone to his study,' said Aidan. 'He said he didn't want any pudding.'

Clemency said suddenly, waspishly, 'And you don't help! Stirring things up when they're difficult enough already!'

She saw him flinch. Then he said softly, 'I'm better than James. Better at the job.' In his eyes she glimpsed a rare passion. 'James doesn't care about it like I do, only Father never sees that.'

Without James, the house seemed quieter, duller. At Ivor's concert on Wednesday afternoon, Clemency waited for the music to have its usual soothing effect on her. Yet her spirits did not lift and, for the first time, the harpsichord's tinkling trills and arpeggios seemed an irritation rather than a balm. When the recital was over, she did not go to Ivor straight away, but watched him as he sat surrounded by his admirers, beaming and accepting their offers of cake.

Later they walked to the café. A sleety rain pounded the pavements. Ivor shivered. 'So ghastly. And to think there's *months* more of winter. I do so loathe the north.'

She took his hand; his fingers were cold. 'We would never have met if you hadn't come to live here.'

'Of course.' He smiled at her. 'Even the direst situation has its compensations.'

In the café, Ivor ordered tea and cake. Clemency had noticed that Ivor had become a little plump around the middle recently; all that cake, she supposed.

He stared glumly out of the window. 'But do look at it.' The houses and trees were shades of grey and brown. 'Honestly, when one thinks of the places one could live. I do so long for London.' He sighed. 'If it wasn't for Rosalie . . .'

'At least you have lived somewhere different.'

'But to be dragged away . . . ' he said earnestly. 'Having something and then losing it makes one long for what one's missed.'

Clemency put the teapot down with a crash. 'I expect I'll stay in Sheffield all my life. I don't mind that — it's my home — but what I do mind is watching them all go away. All my sisters have gone and Philip is away at school and now James has left home too. And I daresay Aidan will marry some rich girl soon — I'm sure that's what he means to do, he only ever seems to speak to heiresses — and then *he'll* be gone. And then I'll be quite alone.'

'Clemency,' Ivor said. He was staring at her, horrified. 'You poor, poor thing.' He fished in his pocket and gave her his handkerchief.

'And I'll never have any children, and I do so love babies! That's the worst of it, Ivor! That I won't ever have any babies!'

'Well, I wouldn't give up on that just yet,' he said kindly. 'How old are you, Clemmie?'

A sniff. 'Almost twenty-one.'

'*Well*. Plenty of time, isn't there?'

His brown eyes were full of sympathy. She blew her nose. 'Do you mind not having any children, Ivor?'

'Oh no.' He lit two of the little black cigarettes that he liked to smoke, and gave one to her. 'I can't bear children. Bad enough teaching them. They clutter the house so.'

'Oh,' she said. Clemency had always assumed that it had been Rosalie's illness that had prevented her and

384

Ivor having children. Her favourite dream, the dream of herself and Ivor living in a cottage with their children, wobbled.

'And besides,' he went on, 'children are so expensive. School fees and doctors' bills.' He sighed. 'Things are rather a struggle just now. Rosalie's wretched uncle does hang on so — not that I'd wish the poor man dead, of course, but really, when one is so ill, one can't quite see the point . . . ' He squeezed her hand. 'Please cheer up, darling Clemency. I can't bear to see you look sad. You're usually so jolly.'

'Oh yes, a good sport,' she said, with a sudden savage bitterness. 'Most of the time I don't think anyone notices whether I'm there or not! They think that houses just look after themselves! If only I did something that counted, Ivor, like you!'

'Oh, much better not,' he murmured. 'Talent is such a *torment*.'

A few days later James came back to Summerleigh. It was quite easy once Clemency put her mind to it: she simply went to Father and James separately and told each that the other was missing him dreadfully. There was a truce for a while, with Father making great efforts to be tactful with James and James trying not to annoy Father.

At the recital the following month, Clemency arrived at the house to find all the ladies in a huddle in the drawing room. There was no sign of Ivor, or the harpsichord.

From the low, shocked conversation, she picked out strands.

'Just went in the night — '

'Didn't have time to call the doctor — '

'Poor boy, how will he manage?'

Mrs Braybrooke crossed the room to her. 'Clemency,' she said. 'Have you heard? The saddest thing. Poor Rosalie Godwin is dead. She died last night.'

Six weeks after Rosalie Godwin's death Clemency borrowed Father's car and drove out into the Peaks. She had never driven so far before: she had a map folded open on the front seat beside her and a glorious sense of freedom as she left the city behind. Mist clung to the highest hills and she peered through the greyness, concentrating fiercely.

Stopping for directions in Hathersage, she took a narrow, winding road that led up the hillside. Ivor's house was large and stone-built; a dark cypress shadowed the entrance.

'Clemency!' he exclaimed, opening the door to her. He was in his shirtsleeves; he looked, she thought, rather dishevelled. 'Such a surprise! How marvellous of you to trek out all this way. I'm afraid I'm in rather a state,' he added as she followed him along a gloomy corridor.

The sitting room was strewn with pieces of paper. 'I've been trying to find the coal bill,' he explained. 'I received a letter from my coal merchant's this morning — a rather terse letter, I'm afraid — and they suggest that last quarter's bill was not paid. But I'm sure Rosalie would have paid it. She was always most *conscientious* about that sort of thing.'

'I was so sorry to hear about Rosalie, Ivor.'

'Kind of you.' He was thumbing through a wad of papers. 'But really, poor old Ro, it was so ghastly at the end, I think it was a relief for her as well.'

'So terrible for you. Did you get my note?'

'It was very much appreciated, Clem.'

Her eye was caught by a piece of paper on an armchair; she gave it to Ivor. 'Is this what you're looking for?'

'Oh yes.' He beamed. 'So clever of you.'

She said, 'I thought you might write.'

386

He looked slightly hunted. 'I've been so busy. So many ghastly things one has to do. All the duty letters and calls.'

'Yes, of course. It's just that I was worried about you.'

'It's all been quite hideous, I'm afraid. The funeral — '

'Did it go well?'

'Oh yes. But so terribly cold in the church. I was afraid I'd come down with a chill.'

'Poor Ivor.' She squeezed his hand and he flashed her a grateful smile.

'And then Rosalie used to deal with the bills and the housekeeping.' He looked fretful. 'A woman from the village cooks and cleans for me, but she refuses to come in the afternoons. Apparently she has an aged mother. I mean, really, of course one understands, but sometimes one longs for a cup of tea . . . '

'Shall *I* make you a cup of tea, Ivor?'

'*Would* you? Or — ' he fished a bottle out of a cupboard — 'perhaps you'd prefer sherry. I've rather taken to sherry since Rosalie died. One doesn't have to fuss around with kettles and stoves.'

He poured out two glasses of sherry. When Clemency had finished her glass he refilled it. She felt rather light-headed and happy; she wasn't sure whether it was the sherry or whether it was the pleasure of being here, in Ivor's house, just the two of them.

They were sitting on the sofa, the only space uncluttered by letters and folders. He was holding her hand; when she nestled up to him, he put his arm around her and she rested her head on his shoulder. 'We've never had so much time together, do you realize that, Ivor? We've never had more than an hour by ourselves.'

'Haven't we? I hadn't thought. How splendid, then.'

She felt blurred and elated. Twisting in his arms, she kissed his cheek. He said, 'Sit on my knee. Rosalie

387

always liked to sit on my knee.'

Though she tried to be careful (he was rather slight, she had always been well built), the sherry made her clumsy and he gave a little gasp as she lurched into his lap. Then he kissed her again, the fleeting little brushes of mouth against mouth that she had always enjoyed, and then he began to unbutton her blouse. 'You don't mind?' he said, suddenly looking anxious, and she shook her head. He stroked and kissed her breasts very gently. While he was kissing her, his other hand ran up her leg, beneath her skirt. His fingers crept beneath the hem of her navy-blue gym knickers; he looked anxious again — 'You're sure you don't mind?' — and speechless, unsure what he wanted, she shook her head. He was breathing rather heavily and his chin scraped against her cheek as he kissed her — it had rather the consistency of a nutmeg grater, she found herself thinking. Then, quite suddenly, he slid from beneath her and sat beside her for a moment, running his fingers through his hair, looking wild-eyed.

'You must tell me if you don't want to, Clem,' he said. 'It's just that it's been so long — Rosalie couldn't be much of a wife to me — her illness, you know . . . '

She didn't know what he was talking about, but she held out her arms to him. 'I only want you to be happy, Ivor. You know how much I love you.'

'Dear Clemency.' Then he somehow leapt on top of her, buried his face in her breasts, pulled down her knickers, and pushed himself inside her. She gave a little scream, which he seemed not to hear. Then he gave a louder scream and, looking down, she saw that his face was contorted — in ecstasy, or in pain, she was not sure.

Very soon he rolled off her and she surreptitiously adjusted her clothing as he lit two of his little black cigarettes and handed one to her. '*Thank you*,' he said. 'So sweet of you, darling Clem. You have cheered me up tremendously.'

They remained on the sofa for a while, smoking in silence. She said, 'Will you move away, Ivor?'

He looked startled. 'Move away?'

'I thought you might go back to London.'

'Well, perhaps.' His lips pursed. 'The most vexing thing, though. Do you remember me telling you about Rosalie's uncle?'

'The wealthy one from Hertfordshire?'

'Yes. I had a letter from his solicitor this morning, telling me that he has just died.'

Another death in the family, she thought, poor Ivor. 'How awful!'

'Isn't it?' He tapped the ash from his cigarette into a saucer. 'So infuriating. If only Rosalie had hung on for another six weeks.'

She stared at him blankly. 'What do you mean?'

'All his money's gone to Rosalie's wretched cousin, not to *me*. *I'm* not a blood relative, am I, and that's what counts. All those years of waiting and then she goes and dies just a few weeks too soon!'

She found herself looking at him, studying his familiar, handsome face, and wondering what name she could put to the emotion in those dark brown eyes. Anger, perhaps. Resentment, even. No, neither of those. Just peevishness.

She realized that the buttons of her blouse were still undone. She fastened them quickly. Her head ached and something warm and wet clung unpleasantly to the insides of her thighs. In Ivor's bathroom she washed and adjusted her clothing and pulled a comb through her hair. After a while she found herself wondering whether what they had just done had been what married couples did on their wedding night and, if so, why so many girls were so desperate to be married.

She went downstairs. Ivor said, 'And I haven't even given you anything to eat! Would you like some cake, Clemency?'

She shook her head. 'I think I should go home.'

'I'll start the recitals again after Christmas. I know it's rather soon, but dear Mrs Braybrooke thought it might help. So sweet of her to be concerned.'

'I thought you'd write your concerto, Ivor, now that you have the time.'

He sighed. 'I'm afraid my concentration isn't what it should be. Such dark thoughts . . . And this time of year . . . I can never work at this time of year. So cold. So inclement.'

She kissed his cheek. 'Goodbye, dear Ivor.'

'Dearest Clemency.' He looked at her fondly. 'And do be careful on the road. The hills . . . so steep . . . '

Driving back to Sheffield, she stopped on the high road over the moors, where huge boulders like a giant's game of marbles spilled across the landscape. Of course, she thought, even had she still wanted to, she could never have married Ivor. Because of Mother, of course, and for many other reasons. Who would look after Father if she was not there? Who would make sure he had hot tea waiting for him when he came home from work? And who would tell the maid to light the fire in his study, so that, after dinner, he could smoke undisturbed? And who would make peace when there were family quarrels? Who would write the grocer's order and the butcher's and fishmonger's orders, and who would make sure that the laundry starched Father's collars properly? She was part of the fabric of the Maclise household, inextricably threaded through it, like a coloured weave in a length of cloth. Unpick that thread and everything would fray and rend. Though she might be the least important Maclise, though she would never be beautiful or clever or splendid or heroic, she was, at least, *necessary*.

As for Ivor, she saw now that something that had been of immense significance to her had been rather less so to him. That she had been a part of his life, quite a small part, instead of the shining beacon in it. Yet, whatever his faults, she could not dislike him, could not even regret what they had done that afternoon. It had been because of Ivor that she had begun to understand her own situation better. Affection, guilt and duty had tied Ivor to Rosalie just as they still tied her to her mother. But that Ivor had liked her, even if he had never really loved her, had allowed her to regain her confidence in herself, and that she had loved him, even if her love, she now saw, had lacked passion, had reminded her that she was capable of deep feeling, and of the need for love.

★ ★ ★

Lucas began to clear the highest and most inaccessible parts of the new land, where the hillside rose in an almost perpendicular peak to pierce the clouds. Returning to the bungalow at midday, sweat darkened his pale hair, and the red-brown earth that stained his skin was indistinguishable from his tan.

He liked to have Marianne bring George to him as he sat on the veranda, drinking and smoking. 'How is he today?'

'He's a little bit grizzly. There's probably a tooth coming through.'

'Come here, George.' Lucas beckoned to his son.

George had recently begun to walk; he tottered across the veranda to his father. Lucas's pistol, that he carried with him in case of snakes or tigers, lay on the table beside him. George reached out to touch the shiny mother-of-pearl handle.

'No,' said Lucas. 'Don't touch.'

George stuck out his lip and moved a step or two away. Nadeshan came to the veranda with tales of some disaster in the kitchen. Marianne went indoors to speak to the kitchen boy: fruit would do perfectly well for dessert if the blancmange had failed to set, she said — there were some ripe mangoes in the pantry. As she returned to the veranda, she heard Lucas say sharply, 'I said, don't touch!' and saw him smack George hard on the backs of his legs. George's eyes first widened in surprise, then he sat down suddenly on his bottom and began to cry great, gulping sobs. Marianne swept him up in her arms; the servants melted back into the dark interior of the bungalow.

She rounded on Lucas. 'You hit him!'

'He has to learn to do as he's told.'

'Dear God, Lucas, he's only eleven months old!'

'He needs to be disciplined now.' Lucas clipped the end from his cigar. 'Leave it till he's older and it will only be harder for him to learn obedience.'

She stared at him, unable to speak for rage. Lucas's composure seemed unruffled. 'You should put him to bed,' he said calmly. 'This temper — he needs to learn that it won't get him what he wants.'

In the nursery she cradled George, rocking him gently, murmuring to him until his taut limbs relaxed and his sobs reduced to intermittent quivering shudders. When she was sure he was asleep, she laid him in his cot. There were red marks on the backs of his legs from where Lucas had slapped him.

Mechanically tidying her dress and hair, Marianne went into the dining room. They had lunched, and she had dismissed the servants, when she said, her voice low and tremulous with anger, 'If you ever strike George again, Lucas, then I will leave you. I promise you that. I will not let you hurt him. Touch him once more and I'll leave for England, taking him with me. And, as God is my witness, you will never see him again.'

A few days later Ralph Armitage called at the bungalow. In the evening at dinner, he and Lucas talked of estate matters. By the time they had finished the soup and main course, the conversation had drifted from the price of tea to the problems with the new land.

'There's still almost a hundred acres to be cleared. It's taking longer than I expected.' Lucas refilled their glasses.

Armitage belched. 'You won't let it get the better of you, Melrose.'

'Of course I won't let it get the better of me. I don't let anything — or anyone — get the better of me. But it's difficult land.' A small smile. 'You could say that was my wife's marriage portion. Three hundred and fifty acres of difficult land. For that, I endured months of boredom in dear old England. Did I ever tell you about my visit to the mother country, Armitage? The interminable tea parties I attended, listening to over-indulged, over-fed women pronounce on the ills of the nation — the dull-as-ditchwater dinner tables I was forced to share with twenty vapid idlers — '

Something inside Marianne snapped. 'How sour you can be, Lucas! How critical of everyone except yourself!'

He smiled wolfishly. 'But surely that's something we have in common, Marianne. Our cold, critical eye. That house where we first met, the Merediths' estate, Rawdon Hall. Admit it, you loathed it. I saw it on your face. That was why I first noticed you. I knew you were the only one in the room who thought as I did.' He smiled and, turning to Ralph Armitage, said, 'Touching, don't you think? Tales of lovers meeting.'

'Very,' Armitage mumbled, as he snapped his fingers to the boy for more rice and stewed fruit.

'I can't tell you how relieved I was to come home.' Lucas looked under his lids at Marianne. 'Though perhaps you pine for England, my dear?'

She said tightly, 'I do miss it sometimes, yes.'

'Why?'

'Because I love it. I love my country.'

'How fascinating.' Lucas's eyes glittered. 'Tell me,

393

Marianne, which aspect of the national character do you most admire? The Englishman's sense of superiority over the subject races, perhaps?'

'Of course not! No right-thinking person — '

'Or his greed? His penchant for taking whatever pleases his eye? Or did you think the British *bought* the hill country of Ceylon from the Kandyan peasants who once farmed it? If you did, my dear, then you were mistaken, because we took it from them by force and then sold it off to the highest bidder.'

She thought: *He is trying to undermine me, he is trying to make me lose belief in the things I care about. Fight back. Don't let him have it all his own way.* She said, 'Even if that's true, we've given Ceylon a great deal in return. The roads, the railways — '

'True enough, Melrose,' said Ralph Armitage. He was shovelling up the last of his pudding. If she had not been there, Marianne thought, revolted, he would have licked out the bowl with his tongue. When he had finished, he sprawled back in his chair, his legs apart, his jacket open to reveal a stomach that sagged over his waistband. He wagged his finger at Lucas. 'The British civilized this damned place, remember.'

'The Sinhalese were civilized when our ancestors were still squabbling pagan tribes. There are the remains of cities in the north of this country which have gardens and fountains and irrigation systems, cities that were built when your ancestors, Marianne, were still scrabbling around for a living in ruined villas deserted by the Romans and mine were painting themselves blue and wearing animal skins.' Lucas sat back in his seat, a smile on his face. 'Your belief in the matchless nobility of your country is touching, but I'm afraid it's misplaced. Not that I would have it any other way, of course. There must always be a winning side and a losing side, and I intend to belong to the winning. And the empire has allowed me to profit, of course. Had my grandfather stayed in Scotland, I would have been nothing more than an impoverished sheep farmer.' He called for Nadeshan to refill their glasses. 'Of course, that's something I have in common with your former husband, isn't it, Marianne? The colonies also permitted the Leightons to make their fortune.' A puzzled frown. 'Only — correct me if I'm wrong — the Leightons' wealth had rather more sordid origins, didn't it?'

She stared at him. 'I don't know what you mean.'

'Would you say that your beloved Arthur was a good man, Marianne?'

'Of course he was!'

'The Leightons' business — remind me — '

'Shipping,' she said curtly.

'And before that?'

'They were in sugar. But I can't see — '

'Sugar,' he said slowly. 'In other words, the Leightons made their money through slavery.'

'No — '

His eyes opened wide. 'Surely you'd realized?'

Yet she had not. It was not, if she was honest with herself, something she had previously considered. 'I hadn't thought — '

'No,' he murmured. 'Perhaps that's a habit of yours. But who do you think worked the sugar plantations? Black slaves, of course, taken by force from their homes in Africa and transported across the Atlantic in some hellhole of a ship. Didn't Arthur see fit to mention that?'

'No,' she whispered.

'Shall I tell you what the sugar planters did to their slaves? How they raped the women? How they strung them up and beat them?'

'I say, Melrose,' murmured Ralph Armitage. His watery blue eyes flickered. 'Steady on.'

There was a short silence. Then Lucas laughed. 'I beg

your pardon. I meant to make a philosophical point, that was all. Can a man profit from other people's sufferings and still be considered good?'

She hissed, 'None of us chooses our forebears, do we, Lucas?' and she saw his eyes darken. She felt a flare of triumph, knowing her words had touched him.

Ralph Armitage said vaguely, 'All that's the way of the world, isn't it? Us and the blacks, I mean. One lot always has to come out on top, and it may as well be us, ha ha!'

'I don't see why anyone has to come out on top. Why one race must have dominance over another — '

'Dear God, Marianne, what Sunday school claptrap. I wouldn't have expected it even of you!' Lucas's mouth twisted in a sneer. 'Of course Ralph is right. If we didn't have the upper hand, then you wouldn't be sitting here. It's as simple as that. Or would you rather be living in the coolie lines? Would you, Marianne?'

She thought of the tin-roofed, wooden shacks, and how the Tamil women washed themselves, their clothes and their children in the stream. The endless, awful lack of privacy and comfort. 'No,' she muttered.

'I didn't think so.' He smiled. 'If we are not brutal, then we are weak. All of us — me, Ralph, even your sainted Arthur — have something of the brute inside us.'

'No.' Yet she found herself remembering the postcards she had found in Arthur's drawer, those plump, naked girls with their vacant, stupid faces.

Lucas raised his glass. 'We should drink a toast. To my wife. To thank her for buying me the Glencoe estate.'

Glasses clinked. 'Won't you drink, Mrs Leighton?' asked Ralph Armitage. Marianne shook her head.

Lucas said, 'My wife doesn't believe in overindulging herself. She is very proper, aren't you, Marianne? Even out here in the jungle. Still, I had the best of the bargain, don't you think, Ralph?'

'What?' Armitage looked confused.

'The marriage for the land,' said Lucas smoothly.

'Oh. Yes. No doubt.' Ralph Armitage's slightly bewildered gaze settled on Marianne. 'You're a lucky dog, Melrose.'

'You find my wife attractive?'

'Any red-blooded man would. A damned lucky dog.' Armitage leaned towards Marianne, his broad face flushed scarlet, his smile one of leering, drunken admiration; she felt herself shrinking back.

'She has just one fault.' Marianne half-rose; Lucas's gaze darted to her. 'Don't go, Marianne. Sit down. Our guest is still eating.'

There was a warning in his voice; she found herself sinking back into her seat. When he turned to her, she saw the night in his eyes.

He said, 'My wife is cold. Have I mentioned that to you before, Armitage?'

'Eh? What?' Ralph Armitage's blurred blue gaze jerked up. He gave an embarrassed laugh. 'Hardly my business, old chap.'

'It's almost a year since the child was born. Long enough, don't you think?'

Her heart pounding, Marianne glanced wildly round. 'Lucas, the *servants* — '

With a wave of his hand, he dismissed them. A mistake, she realized — when they were gone, she felt even more alone. Her skin was ice cold, every nerve ending jangled.

Lucas murmured, 'You don't mind me talking our little problems over with an old friend, do you, Marianne? I thought Ralph might have some suggestion to make. Or even — what a marvellous idea — an offer of practical help. After all, you don't seem to find *me* pleasing. Perhaps you prefer Armitage.'

Marianne's mind seemed to freeze. Ralph Armitage's

eyes widened; he licked his lips. A smile curled round the corners of Lucas's mouth. 'You did say you thought she was attractive, Ralph.'

'Good God.' Armitage's expression had shifted from shock to greed.

He would not do *that* — she was hardly able to formulate the thought. She whispered, 'Please, Lucas. Please stop. *Please.*'

In the silence she heard the whine of a mosquito and, from outside, a bird's call. Then Lucas laughed, breaking the tension. 'Lord, whatever are you both thinking of? I'm careful with my possessions, you know that. I'd have to be very, very angry with you, Marianne, to share you with anyone else. Now, run along, why don't you, and leave us in peace.'

Her hands were shaking almost too much to turn the handle of her bedroom door. Inside, she sank to the floor. Then, suddenly reaching up, she scrabbled with the key and locked the door.

That night every creak of the floorboard, every rattle of a window pane, made her eyes start open and her heart race. For the first time, the Ceylonese night frightened her. There was a threat in the beat of a wing, the menace in the cry of an animal, the chaos of the jungle seeping into her room. What had Mr Salter said? *The place presses in on you — it won't leave you alone.*

Eventually, at dawn, she fell into a fitful sleep. When at last she rose, Lucas was standing on the veranda. She looked round for Ralph Armitage, but he was nowhere in sight.

'He's gone. I sent him packing,' Lucas said. 'He's a fool. A tiresome fool.' His voice was dry and flat. He looked, she thought, as fatigued as she. Then he said slowly, 'You threatened me, Marianne. I dislike being threatened.'

She bowed her head, not trusting herself to speak.

'We'll get along perfectly well so long as we keep out

398

of each other's way. You do see that, don't you?'

She managed to whisper, 'Yes, Lucas.'

'So no more talk of leaving me. And no more talk — *ever* — of taking George away from me.'

She nodded mutely. He smiled. 'Now, where is my son?'

13

Ash often had the feeling in that winter of 1913–14 that events were moving too fast, speeding out of control, threatening to fall apart and disintegrate before his gaze. There was the rush towards civil war in Ireland as the two private armies of Sir Edward Carson's Unionists and the Irish Volunteers, under the leadership of Eoin MacNeill, squared up to fight. A military confrontation seemed inevitable. Arms and ammunition found their way to both sides; in March a brigade of the British army stationed in Ulster refused to act against their fellow countrymen.

The protests of the suffragettes became ever more bitter. Emmeline Pankhurst was arrested when rioting broke out after she had given a speech in Glasgow. Shortly afterwards, the suffragette Mary Richardson slashed the *Rokeby Venus* in the National Gallery in retaliation. There was some justice in it, thought Ash: the smooth, naked body of the odalisque, female perfection imagined by a man, desecrated by a woman who wanted something different, something new.

Throughout it all, like far-off thunder, could be heard rumblings of other, more troubling, discontents. Serbia's desire for autonomy, the struggles of the ageing Austro-Hungarian empire to hold itself together, Germany's increasing strength and militarism, France's old hatred of her powerful neighbour and Britain's fear for her empire, the empire that was needed to soak up the products of Lancashire cotton mills and Yorkshire steelworks, her touchiness at anything that might threaten the trade routes to India, the Jewel in the Crown. A bad mix, Ash thought uneasily: a mixture of volatile chemicals that only needed a spark, a carelessly dropped match, for something terrible to ignite.

He had other, more immediate troubles. There was Iris, of course. She could not have made it more clear that he meant nothing to her. Throughout the first part of the winter he was aware of a dark, consuming anger whenever he thought of her. Some of his anger was with himself for being stupid enough to think she might feel something for him. Some was mixed with jealousy, jealousy of whichever thick-headed, besotted man she now had under her spell.

In November his guardian fell ill. Ash took the train to Cambridge each Friday evening to be with Emlyn at the weekends. As the months passed, he began to feel as though he was taking part in a complicated juggling act, the sort of thing one might see at the Hippodrome, plates spinning, coloured hoops hurling into the air, something bound to fall. His job, Emlyn, his political and educational societies — he could not have managed, he often thought, without Thelma. Thelma walked the dog when he was out of London at the weekends, Thelma helped him deliver pamphlets on cold, rainy evenings and turned up every now and then with boxes of fruit and vegetables when he had forgotten to shop.

Emlyn died in the April of 1914. After the funeral there was a lunch at Emlyn's Grantchester house for the mourners and then, one by one, they drifted away. Ash told the housekeeper and the maid to take the rest of the day off. When everyone had gone, he walked in the garden. The air was sharp, the daffodils shaking their bright yellow heads, the leaves of the evergreen shrubs ruffled by the breeze.

He went down to the river bank, where the wind whipped up wavelets and the weeping willows trailed their long, thin fingers in the dark water. He remembered the first time he had come here. He had been a small boy of eight, orphaned following the deaths of his parents. He had not mourned his mother and father because he had hardly known them; they had been travellers and his had been a childhood of nurses and nannies. He had not been in the least afraid of the momentous change in his life and he had thought the train journey to Cambridge, the cab ride to Grantchester, and his arrival at the large, rambling house a great adventure. Yet in spite of his solitariness, he had been happy. Emlyn's tolerance and patience had been limitless. Such an extraordinary thing, such generosity, for a bachelor already in his forties to take in a child because of a remembered affection for an old friend. He dashed his fingertips along his eyelids and they came away wet with tears.

It seemed to him, looking back, that as a small boy he had been afraid of very little. More than once he had half-drowned in the Granta; he had broken an arm falling from the summerhouse roof, an ankle tumbling from a brick wall. Even the ghosts which, as a child, he had been certain haunted the house, had failed to frighten him. Yet, in the weeks since he had known that Emlyn was dying, he had felt fear settle over him. Inside the house, wandering from room to room, he was unable to shake off a profound sense of loneliness. The twilight revealed dark shadows pooled in corners, a patch of mould on the wallpaper, the threadbare arm of a chair. Now there were ghosts: in some distant corridor a door slammed, startling him. Something was missing; the emptiness oppressed him.

He went back to London, picked up the threads. His work, his meetings and his friends filled the days and evenings so that he did not have time to think. Yet he found that he had to drink to be able to sleep at night and sometimes, waking early in the morning, when there was only the clip-clop of the milkman's horse in the street outside, there it was again, that fear that he could not put a name to.

Thelma called one evening. 'Are you on your own, Ash?'

'Fred and Charlie came, but I sent them away.'

She looked suddenly doubtful. 'Would you like me to go too?'

He shook his head. 'Of course not.'

She followed him into the kitchen. 'Next door's sitting with Dad. They're doing a jigsaw. I hate jigsaws. What's the point of taking something apart only to put it together again?'

He offered her tea. She said, 'I'd rather have some of that.' There was a bottle of Scotch on the table.

He poured her a measure. He noticed that she had put on powder and lipstick and that, beneath her coat, she was wearing a green dress that brought out the colour of her eyes.

She said, 'Will you have to go back to Cambridge?'

'Soon. There's a lot to be sorted out.'

'It's a miserable job going through a place after someone's died. I remember sorting out my mum's things — I felt as though I was throwing pieces of her away.'

'That's just about it. I meant to do more after the funeral, but the house was so damned lonely. I should go back this weekend.'

'Doesn't anyone else live there?'

'Only the housekeeper.'

'What will happen to it?'

'Oh, it's mine now. Emlyn left it to me. I suppose I'll have to think what to do with it.'

She was looking at him closely. 'Will you go and live there? In Cambridge?'

'I haven't made up my mind yet. I might.'

'Is it a nice house?'

'It's a lovely house. Very peaceful. By the river.'

'Is it big?'

He nodded. 'Pretty big.'

She burst out, 'I don't know how you can think twice, if you've the chance of living in a place like that!'

'I'm sorry.' He felt suddenly ashamed, seeing the patch on the elbow of Thelma's coat, and the way her shoes, though well polished, were scuffed at the toes. 'I didn't mean to sound . . . spoilt.'

She was standing at the sink, her back to him, looking out of the window at the smoke-stained walls of the houses beyond. After a silence, she said, 'No, I'm the one who should be sorry. I shouldn't be scolding you when you've had such a rotten time.' She looked back at him and smiled. 'It's just that I'd hate you to go, Ash.'

'If I did, I'd miss this place.'

'I'd miss you.' And then she kissed him. Her lips brushed his cheek, then his mouth. She said softly, 'Wouldn't you miss me just a little bit?'

His mouth had gone dry. It seemed such a long, long time since he had kissed a woman, held a woman. The winter had been tainted by illness and death; he needed to be with someone young and vital, someone who could make him feel alive again. At the back of his mind, something whispered a warning, but she had nestled herself into him, and there was the soft fullness of her breasts pressing against him, and the scent of her skin and hair. She ran her fingertips the length of his spine and he shivered. He whispered, 'Course I'd miss you.'

'Show me. Show me how much you'd miss me, Ash. Kiss me properly. Just once.' She smiled. 'You owe me, Ash. All those bloody leaflets.'

Her lips were soft and yielding, her tongue flickered at the inside of his mouth. She wriggled and her coat fell to the floor. Then she began to undo the buttons on the front of her dress. 'Your face!' she said, and gave a gasp of laughter. 'It's all right, I've done it before. Me and Charlie were going to get married, you know.'

The green dress joined the coat on the floor. He saw

404

the ripe swell of her breasts and hips, the narrow curve of her waist, the inch of white flesh between knickers and black stockings. 'I like you a lot, you see, Ash,' she said, and there it was again, her familiar defiant glare. 'I suppose I shouldn't say that. A girl isn't meant to tell a bloke how much she likes him. But I don't care. And you mustn't worry. I'm not in love with you or anything like that. I only want some fun.' Her expression softened and she held out her arms to him. 'Go on. You do the rest of it. You know you want to.'

And he did. His need for her pushed out every other thought. At first his fingers fumbled as he began the complicated process of unfastening and unlacing petticoats, camisole and corsets. But then instinct and desire took over, and he knew just what he wanted and, parting her thighs, entering her, his only thought was to assuage his hunger.

★   ★   ★

He slept soundly that night; in the morning, waking, remembering, he felt a sense of disbelief. He remembered the green dress falling to the floor, that inch of white skin between stocking and knickers. After she had dressed and tidied herself up, Thelma had said, 'I'd better get home or my dad will worry.' Then she had left the house.

A couple of days later he was at home in the evening, when there was a knock at the door. A man wearing a shabby overcoat stood on the doorstep. He touched his cap to Ash. 'Sorry to trouble you, Mister, but someone told me you might be able to spare me a bite to eat.'

'It'll have to be bread and cheese, Mr . . . ?'

'Hargrave. Frank Hargrave. I'd be grateful for anything you can spare.' He shivered. 'Would you let me come in for a minute or two, Mister? I've been sleeping rough the last few nights and I'm chilled to the bone.'

Ash showed Hargrave into the front room, and left him standing by the fire as he wrapped bread and cheese in greaseproof paper in the kitchen. 'Here.' He gave Hargrave the parcel.

'Thank you kindly, sir.' Hargrave tipped his cap and made for the front door.

'I'll give you the address of a couple of hostels.' Ash looked round for pen and paper. 'They're not exactly the Ritz, but — '

There was the sound of the front door closing; Hargrave had gone. Ash blinked, and ran his eyes over the surface of his desk. His pen should have been there; he had been sitting at the desk, working, when there had been the knock at the door. It had rolled off the desk, perhaps; he stooped, searching for it. When he stood up, he noticed that the pen was not the only thing that was missing. The jar on the mantelpiece was now empty of the loose change he always kept there. The photograph of Emlyn on the bookshelves had been taken, for its silver frame, presumably. His jacket was slung over the back of a chair; quickly, he jammed his hand into the pocket, and found that his wallet, too, had gone.

And his camera was absent from its usual place in the corner of the room. The bastard had taken his camera. He felt a surge of rage and dashed out into the street. In the distance, he could see Hargrave, the camera over his shoulder, heading up Aldgate High Street. He began to run.

Hargrave turned, hearing his footsteps. 'Give me back my things,' said Ash.

A smile. 'Sorry. Don't think so.' The pleading nasal whine was gone, so was the submissive attitude.

'I said, *give* them to me.'

Hargrave seemed to consider. 'You can have this. Too bloody heavy. Can't be bothered lugging it round the pawn shops. Here, catch.'

406

He threw the camera deliberately wide: as it struck the pavement, Ash heard glass shatter, saw metal buckle.

'You bastard.'

Hargrave spat. 'Do you want the other stuff? Come on, take it from me.' There was the glint of a knife. Hargrave took a step towards him. 'They said you had some nice things.' The knife danced. 'They said you were a soft touch.'

He hadn't the smallest doubt that Hargrave would use the knife, would *enjoy* using the knife. He saw that he was alone, that around them doors had closed and passers-by had melted away. A shiver of fear mixed with his rage and made him say, 'Keep the bloody stuff.' Hargrave's scornful laughter echoed as Ash stooped and carefully gathered up the broken pieces of camera.

For the first time since he had moved into his house, he locked the door from the inside. Then he poured himself a large glass of Scotch. *They said you were a soft touch*: Hargrave's words mocked him as he inspected the damaged camera.

He found himself remembering the day he had shown Iris how to use it. He remembered the blossom floating from the trees in Summerleigh's orchard, the girls' white dresses and coloured sashes. Afterwards he had taken a photograph of the four sisters. He remembered the challenge in Iris's eyes, which had seemed then to dare him to capture her, to do justice to her.

And he remembered his first sight of her, speeding towards him down the hill on her bicycle. Her frock had billowed out in a pink cloud and her golden hair had framed her face like a halo. He had thought, seeing her that first time, that she was the most beautiful girl he had ever seen. Nothing that had happened since had altered his opinion.

He groaned and sat down, his head in his hands. He wondered whether Iris had sensed a detachment in him, the detachment of the orphaned and those who lack brothers and sisters, the detachment of those who have had to teach themselves to manage on their own. Were they truly his friends, those people with whom he filled his house? Or did he only use them to block out the silence? Unpractised at closeness, had he avoided intimacy, preferring safer, less risky demands? He would be thirty later in the year, and he had neither wife nor child, parent nor siblings. He knew that the melancholy that had haunted him since Emlyn's death was born of a fear that in ten or twenty years' time he might look round and find himself quite alone.

As for Thelma, he felt bitter regret and a dislike of himself for letting things go so far. He had used her too. It was one thing to let her walk his dog, he thought grimly, quite another to take her into his bed. He did not love her; he had never loved her. He loved Iris, he missed Iris, he longed to see Iris. He needed to take a risk, to tell her the truth, that he loved her, wanted her. He needed to fight for her. He needed to find out whether he'd left it too late.

★   ★   ★

At night Marianne locked her bedroom door. Just in case.

But he did not come to her. Sometimes she thought she must have imagined it, the not-so-veiled threat. Sometimes she thought she must have made a mistake, or misinterpreted what Lucas had said. She seemed to feel muddled a lot of the time. There were things she had once believed in utterly — her country, Arthur's goodness, her own integrity — that she now found herself questioning.

Clare Barlow called. They sat in the garden under the banyan tree, watching the children play. It was a bright, perfect day, the blue sky flawless, the trees and flowers seeming to glitter in the light. 'I'm going back to England,' Clare said. 'I've been putting off sending the girls to boarding school for ages, but I really can't delay it any longer. And I've decided to stay in England with them. That's what I wanted to tell you, Marianne. That I won't be coming back.'

Sunlight shone through the branches of the banyan, making shifting patterns on Clare's face. 'I haven't said a word to anyone else,' she added. 'Not even to the girls — they'd be bound to blab. But I know you'll be discreet.' She looked suddenly sad. 'I won't say that I don't care about my marriage because it wouldn't be true. But I hope that this way, if I simply don't return to Ceylon and Johnny doesn't kick up too much of a fuss, then it won't be too awful. Johnny may insist on a divorce, of course. I hope I can persuade him not to, for the girls' sake. But if he does, then I shan't blame him. He's never been unkind to me and I daresay he doesn't deserve this. But I don't love him any more, Marianne, and that's the truth. The thought of being thousands of miles away from my girls is intolerable, but the thought of being thousands of miles away from Johnny is . . . well, I'm afraid I wouldn't mind too much at all.' She lit a cigarette and sat for a moment in silence, smoking. She looked around her. 'I shall miss all this,' she said softly. 'Days like this, you can't think why you would ever choose to leave, can you?'

Later, leaving, Clare hugged Marianne and then she stood back, looking at her. 'You'll be all right, won't you?'

Phrases formed in her head. For a fraction of a second she thought she might be able to voice them. *I am afraid of Lucas*, she might have said. *There is a side of his nature that is cruel and unpredictable and which frightens me.*

But then one of the girls called out, and Clare gave a quick smile and said, 'I know you'll be fine. You're a survivor, aren't you, Marianne?'

The bullock cart headed away, was lost in the curve of the road. As Marianne went back into the bungalow she made a promise to herself: if, by the time George was seven or eight and must go to boarding school, her marriage was no easier, then she would stay in England with him. She felt a measure of relief; she had seen an escape route, a limit to what she must endure.

★ ★ ★

Throughout the winter Iris had worked as a private nurse for a family living in the Hampshire countryside. Her patient, Mary Wynyard, was in the final stages of tuberculosis. Because of the infectious nature of the disease, and because fresh air was believed to be beneficial to tuberculosis sufferers, Mary spent the last few months of her life in a wooden hut at a safe distance from the house in which her husband and children lived. It broke Iris's heart to see Mary wrapped up in blankets, sitting on the veranda of the hut and watching her children play outside the house, longing in her eyes.

Mary died in the spring. Afterwards, Iris agreed to stay on at the house until Charles Wynyard, Mary's widower, could find a housekeeper to help look after the children.

They were in the kitchen one morning and Iris was helping the children make gingerbread men, when something caught her eye. She looked out of the window and saw Ash, walking up the Wynyards' gravel path.

Charles Wynyard's five-year-old daughter, Mary-Jane, said, 'There's a man.'

Charles peered out of the window. 'He doesn't *look* like a prospective housekeeper.'

'He isn't. He's Ash.' Iris's heart pounded against her ribs. 'I mean, he's a friend of mine.'

'You've forgotten the buttons!' cried Mary-Jane with a peal of laughter.

'Darling,' said Charles gently. Then, to Iris, 'You'd better go to your friend. Mary-Jane and I will clear up in here. And don't feel you have to introduce him to us just yet — the poor fellow may want a bit of a respite before confronting the Wynyards covered in flour.'

She went out to meet him. She only remembered her apron as she stepped out the front door, and then she whipped it off and bundled it up beneath the hall stand. She saw that he had seen her, standing in the doorway.

'Iris,' he said.

'Ash. What a surprise.' She kissed his cheek.

'Do you mind? Are you busy?'

'I was cooking.' He was looking hard at her. 'Have I flour on my nose?'

He shook his head. She filled the silence by saying gaily, 'We thought you were a housekeeper!'

'A housekeeper?'

'My employer, Mr Wynyard, has advertised for someone to help with the children. We've been interviewing them. They all wear black, though some of them relieve the black by pinning a bunch of artificial cherries to their hats.'

He put up his hand to his head. 'No cherries, I'm afraid.'

'No hat.' She smiled. 'They overheat the head and stop the brain working.'

'You remembered. My guardian, Emlyn, told me that.'

'How is he?'

'Emlyn died three weeks ago.'

She thought he looked rather drawn and tired. 'Oh, Ash, I'm so sorry. Was it very sudden?'

He told her about Emlyn's illness and death. She touched his arm. 'How did you find me?'

411

'I asked Eva. She told me that your patient had recently died.'

'Yes. So sad. Poor Mary. And so awful for Charles and the children.'

She wondered why he had come here. She remembered last summer: the heat, and Thelma Voss saying, *He doesn't love you; he won't ever love you.* Although, for some time now, she had found herself questioning Thelma's version of events, she still feared there was an essential truth in her words.

She said, 'Shall we go for a walk in the woods? They're glorious at this time of year.'

The path that led through the beech woods was bordered by bluebells, great rumpled acres of them. There was the cobalt blue of the flowers, the silver of the beech trunks and the pale silky green of the leaves.

He said, 'When you left London — it was so sudden — '

'Well, yes. For me too.'

He frowned. 'You told me you'd been thinking about it for a long time.'

'A teeny white lie. To save my pride.'

His frown deepened. 'I don't understand.'

'I was dismissed, Ash, from the Mandeville. For impertinence.'

His eyes widened, then he gave a snort of laughter. 'Good grief. What on earth did you do?'

She told him about Sister Dickens. 'I was tired of the hospital anyway,' she explained. 'And really, now I've had time to think about it, I know that matron was right. I'd no wish to spend the rest of my days there.' She made herself meet his eyes. 'But that day — that's partly why I was so foul.'

'Partly?' he said.

Yet she still found herself shying away from opening herself up to hurt once more. Changing the subject, she said, 'I'll have to leave here soon. I promised Charles I'd stay here until he finds someone suitable to help with the children, but then I'll go.'

There was a blackbird singing, high in the branches, and a longing for him to say — what? She had had plenty of time these last few months to imagine what she would have liked him to say to her. And mostly it boiled down to telling her that he loved her.

But he said only, 'What will you do after you leave?' and something in her died a little.

'I'm not sure,' she said lightly. 'Perhaps I'll go home for a while. Or perhaps I'll find another private nursing post. Or I might go to France, to stay with Charlotte. It would be good to have a real break from nursing.'

'I see.' He was staring into the distance, to where the mauve of the bluebells blurred into the brown of the forest floor.

She said, 'Ash, why did you come here?'

'To see how you were.'

'And that was all?' Her voice was small. There it was again, that crack in her heart, and she wanted to pummel her fists against his chest, angry with him for coming here and spoiling her precarious peace of mind.

But then he said, 'No, it's not all. There are some things I have to know. And that *you* have to know. All those idiots you always have running after you — they can't possibly care for you as much as I do. However rich and good-looking and all the rest of it they are, you'd be bored with them within the week, I know you would. And though I'm probably not what you had in mind as a lover, Iris, I do love you. I won't stop you going to France if that's what you really want to do, but I won't just give up on you either. In fact — '

She said faintly, 'What did you say?'

'That if you really want to go to France then I won't try to stop you, of course.'

'Not that bit. The other bit. About loving me.'

'Oh yes.' He frowned. 'Well, I do. Have done for ages.

413

And that's why I came here. To ask you whether there's any possibility, any possibility at all, that you might like me a little.'

'No,' she said seriously. 'I don't like you a little.'

'*Ah*.' Such misery in that small sigh that she found she did not want to tease him any more. 'Actually,' she said, 'I like you rather a lot, Ash. Which is rather disconcerting because you're not at all the sort of man I meant to fall in love with. You dress so badly and we don't think the same about things at all, and — '

'Hush,' he said, and stopped her speaking with a kiss.

★ ★ ★

Marianne was in the garden when she heard the sound of horse's hooves. Riding into the grounds in a cloud of red dust, Mr Salter threw the reins to the groom and slid from the saddle. 'Mrs Melrose!' he called out. 'There's been an accident up on the Glencoe land! Mr Melrose is hurt. They're bringing him back in the cart!'

He took her shock, she realized, for fear. The young wife afraid for her injured husband. He touched her arm. 'He'll be all right. You mustn't worry. He's as tough as they come. Only he looks a bit of a mess, so I thought I'd better warn you.'

'What happened?'

'There was a snake in the undergrowth and his horse reared. They were clearing the high ground. He must have hit his head on a rock when he fell.'

The treacherous thought came into her head: *If he is dead, I shall be free*, but she pushed it away. Mr Salter rode away to fetch Dr Scott. Marianne had the servants boil water while she tore a linen sheet into strips for bandages. There was the rumble of the cart on the path; she went outside to meet it.

A strip of bloodied cloth was wrapped round Lucas's head and a broken bone distorted the shape of his wrist.

The men carried him into his bedroom, where, with Radu's help, Marianne stripped him and tried to stem the bleeding from the head wound. By the time Dr Scott had arrived, he was beginning to stir, groaning, his eyes flickering open.

Dr Scott's short, stubby fingers explored the bones of Lucas's skull. 'I don't think it's broken. There'll be concussion, though.'

He stitched the gaping wound and bound up the broken arm. Afterwards, over curry and rice in the dining room, Dr Scott said, 'The arm will have mended in six weeks or so and there's some damage to the knee, I believe. But the head wound is the most serious injury, I'm afraid. Head wounds are nasty things, Mrs Melrose. It may take him a while to get over this. He'll have a fever, you know, bound to. Cold compresses should help and I'll leave a sedative. But he'll be right as rain in a while, you'll see.'

For much of the next week Lucas was delirious. Marianne sat beside the bed, bathing his hot skin as he twisted and turned and muttered under his breath. At the height of the fever he shivered convulsively; once, in the middle of the night, his eyes opened, wide and dark with fear, fixed on a corner of the room, as though he could see some horror invisible to Marianne. Nursing Lucas brought back to her that other bedside vigil. She found herself waiting for the telltale bruises beneath the skin, for the smell of gangrene. To lose the husband she had come to fear in the same manner as she had lost the husband she had loved.

But he did not die. Later, she thought that the stubbornness and tenacity that made him fight to tame the most inhospitable land had given him the strength to battle against fever and pain. Ten days after the accident Marianne went into his room to find him half-dressed, struggling to pull his shirt over his head.

'Lucas! What are you doing?'

415

'What does it look like? Trying to get this damned shirt on.'

'Dr Scott said — '

'Damn Dr Scott.' He glared at her. 'Why do you just stand there? Won't you help me, Marianne?'

'Your arm — I'll have to cut the sleeve.'

'Then hurry up and do so, for God's sake.' Standing up, he swayed.

She said sharply, 'If you're foolish, the fever will come back. Do you want that?'

'Dear God, woman — ' She heard the anger in his voice and took a step back. But he gave a crow of hoarse laughter and sat down on the edge of the bed. 'You needn't be afraid of me,' he muttered. 'I couldn't hurt a fly.' He closed his eyes tightly; his skin was grey beneath his tan. 'The estate — '

'Mr Cooper and Mr Salter are taking care of the estate.'

'Cooper is idle and Salter is an incompetent dreamer. I'll have blister on the leaves and the pruning will be neglected if those two are left in charge for long.' He shot an angry glance at the sling that cradled his arm. '*Damn* this run of bad luck! Some of the coolies believe the Glencoe land is cursed, did you know that, Marianne? Old Macready drank himself to death because of it, and since I bought it it's caused me nothing but trouble. The fire — and now this.' His lip curled. 'A curse . . . nonsense, of course, but once or twice I'm ashamed to admit I've found myself wondering whether they're right.' He fumbled left-handedly with his cigarette case. Marianne struck a match for him. 'I need to see the estate books — they're in my office.'

'I'll bring them to you.'

'This damned room,' he said suddenly. His gaze darted round. 'It's like a prison.'

'Shall I ask Velu and Radu to help you out to the

416

veranda? It may be cooler there.'

'And George.' There was longing in his eyes. 'I want to see George.'

A few days later he made himself walk in the garden, using a stick. His incapacity frustrated him. One day he dashed the bowl of soup that Nadeshan had brought him to the ground. 'Invalid's pap!' he said furiously. 'Bring me something tolerable to eat, for God's sake!' He insisted, though his face was beaded with sweat and the pain was visible in his set features, on sitting at the dining table at mealtimes instead of eating on the veranda. He had his assistant managers report to him three times a day. He sat on the veranda for hours, watching George play, with the same close attention that he gave to Mr Cooper's and Mr Salter's accounts of leaf yield and pruning schedules.

She was woken one night by a loud cry. Almost inhuman, like a wolf's howl, it seemed to slice open the night. She lit a candle and left her room. Another cry and the hairs on the back of her neck stood up.

Outside Lucas's room, she paused. It took all her courage to tap on the door, to say, 'Lucas, it's me, Marianne,' and to turn the handle.

She could not at first accustom her eyes to the darkness: the entire room seemed flooded in black. Then she saw him sitting on the bed. When he looked up at her she saw the terror in his eyes. 'He's there,' he said softly.

'Who? Who's there?'

'*Him.*' A fearful whisper. 'My *father.*'

He was staring into the darkness again. She felt a shiver of fear and stopped herself from turning to check, to search for the ghost in the shadows. But she said calmly, 'No, Lucas. He's not there.'

'I *heard* him.'

'You heard an animal in the garden, perhaps. Or one of the servants.' She lit the oil lamp on the bed stand.

She saw him blink and give himself a little shake. Then he glanced at the clock. 'Four in the morning,' he muttered. 'The Devil's hour. That's when he comes to me.'

'You should go back to bed, Lucas. It was just a nightmare.'

He pressed his fingertips against his forehead. 'My *head* — why does it hurt so?'

'Shall I get you some of your pills?'

'No,' he said sharply. 'They make me dream. Get me something to drink.'

There was a bottle of arrack in the dining room. She saw how his hand shook when he put the glass to his mouth. Then he stared at her. '*You.* You're still here. Why do you stay?'

'Because I thought . . . ' She faltered.

'You thought I needed company?'

'Yes,' she whispered.

'Well, I don't. Neither your company, nor anyone else's.' His veiled eyes watched her. 'Haven't you learned yet, Marianne?'

'Learned what?'

'That it's a weakness to need other people. That it's needing them that makes you weak.' He drained the glass.

★   ★   ★

Thelma came to see Ash. Opening the door to her, he felt a flicker of guilt for avoiding her since that night.

'Hello, Ash.' She moved around the front room, her gaze lighting on a heap of books, a picture on the wall. He thought she looked nervous and that her skin had an unhealthy pallor. She said, 'I haven't seen you for a while.'

'I've been away rather a lot.'

'Sorting out your guardian's house?'

418

He knew that he must not lie to her. He said, 'I've had to do all that, yes. But I spent the weekend with Iris.'

'Miss Maclise?' A frown and an edge to her voice.

'We'd lost touch.' She was watching him narrowly. He said as kindly as he could, 'Thelma, you asked me once whether Iris and I had an understanding. Well, we didn't then, but we do now.'

To his surprise, she gave a high-pitched laugh. 'That could make things rather awkward.'

'What do you mean?' He added, hating himself, 'I hope you didn't think — I hope I didn't give any wrong impression — '

When she turned to him, he saw the fury in her eyes. And then it was gone, leaving him wondering whether he had imagined it. 'I'm sorry,' he said feebly.

'Are you, Ash?' Her voice was hard. 'It's a bit late for that unfortunately.'

'What do you mean?'

She paused, frowning, as if making her mind up about something. Then she said, 'Because there's a bit of a problem, I'm afraid.'

★　★　★

Odd how everything could fall into place at last. Odd how love should just slip into her cupped hands and transform everything. When, a month ago, Ash had told her that he loved her, it had been as though a magic lantern had been turned on, and since then everything had become glorious and full of colour.

Iris had left the Wynyards' house and returned to Summerleigh. Ash visited at the weekends; during the week Iris helped Clemency and read to Mother. Sometimes she just sat in the garden, a novel and a heap of sewing neglected on the grass beside her. It seemed an extraordinarily long time since she had done nothing. When she looked back, she saw that after Ash had turned down her proposal of marriage (in this garden: the smell of rain on new-mown grass) she had been running, filling her days so that she did not have to think too much. Not that she regretted anything that had happened. She knew that her years at the Mandeville had woken her up, had changed her. But just for a while it was nice to sit in a deckchair and feel the sun on her face and do nothing.

Ash came back to Summerleigh on Friday evening. Iris saw a flicker of blue striped dress as Clemency pointed out to him where she was sitting. She ran to him and kissed him. 'Ash. How lovely that you're early. I've loads of things to tell you. Did you get my letter? I thought we could go to the theatre tonight — we may have to take Clem, or Father will growl about propriety again, but you don't mind, do you?'

He said, 'Iris, I have to talk to you.'

His grim expression, something dead in his eyes. She felt suddenly alarmed. 'Ash, what is it?'

He glanced round. Edith was unpegging the washing from the line; Clemency was batting a tennis ball against the wall. 'Is there anywhere private?'

They went to the orchard. The blossom had been blown from the trees several days before by a storm and lay on the grass, the pink petals turning to brown. 'Ash,' she said, 'you're frightening me.'

His face twisted. 'I wish — I wish that anything but this had happened.'

'Anything but what?'

'I was going to ask you to marry me. I was going to ask you today.'

And in spite of the warmth of the day, there was a coldness inside her. 'You were *going* to?'

'Yes.'

'And now you're not.'

'And now I *can't*.' His voice was flat, heavy.

And then he was telling her why he could not marry her, but must marry Thelma Voss instead. Because Thelma was carrying his child. Iris seemed to stand apart from herself, as though she had split into pieces, watching herself from a distance, noting how at first she simply didn't believe him, noting the shame in his eyes, and (a click of the switch) making that inevitable connection: that he had shared a bed with Thelma Voss. That Thelma had won.

Eventually she heard him walk away. When he had gone, she sat down on a fallen tree trunk. Sometime later Clemency came and sat down beside her. Clemency's hand curled into hers, and though Iris closed her eyes very tightly, she could not stem the tears.

★　★　★

Though the head wound healed, leaving a livid scar that snaked down the side of his face, the headaches persisted — of such blinding intensity that Lucas would shut himself in his room with a bottle of arrack and drink the pain away. Yet he went back to work, returning to the bungalow at midday, exhausted and white-lipped from the jolting of the horse on the stony track.

If Marianne had hoped that Lucas's illness might soften him, might make him more understanding of other people's failings, then she had been badly mistaken. As if to prove to himself that he was as strong as ever, he drove himself and those who worked for him even harder than before. They cleared the last of the Glencoe land, ripping trees out from the hillside and using elephants to haul the logs to the lower ground. Marianne saw flames rising from the red-brown scars in the earth as they burned away the undergrowth.

His temper, always erratic, worsened, provoked perhaps by the lingering aftermath of the head injury.

421

Like wisps of smoke, tales drifted back to her — that one of the coolies had been burned while clearing the land and Lucas had refused to allow him to go back to the lines, insisting he work on. That, in a fit of anger, Lucas had struck Mr Cooper with his stick. Once, overhearing the servants talking among themselves, Marianne discovered that they now called Lucas by a different name: *Paitham dorai*. When she asked Rani what it meant, Rani's eyes dropped and she whispered, 'Mad master, Dorasanie. It means mad master.'

The headaches made him drink more to relieve the pain, and drink had always brought out the devil in him. Inside the bungalow it was as though they were waiting for a thunderstorm to break. The sound of Lucas's stick, clicking on the floor, made them fearful and clumsy. The servants fumbled as they served the food, spilling some on the tablecloth; after dinner, sitting in the drawing room in the dim light that Lucas preferred because it did not hurt his eyes, Marianne sewed, her needle making stitches that were too large, too uneven, her mouth dry, her heart beating too fast.

She began, almost without acknowledging to herself what she was doing, to keep back a few rupees from the housekeeping money and hide them in the back of a drawer. In her room, with the door safely locked, she spread out her jewellery on the bed. The diamond engagement ring that Arthur had brought her — she would never sell that; she put it away. Her moonstones, her sapphires, her bracelets and lockets. The pearl and amethyst ring that had once belonged to Great-aunt Hannah, which her sisters had sent to her. When she thought of her sisters now, something inside her hurt so badly she was afraid it might break.

She woke one morning with a headache nudging at the back of her eyes. She had slept poorly, her dreams vivid and disturbing. She had little appetite at breakfast, and, though she tried to do some gardening that morning with George playing beside her, she found that after a short time she felt exhausted and had to go back inside the house.

Lucas came home at midday. At tiffin the sight of the curried meat and vegetables nauseated Marianne. She felt him watching her. He drank steadily throughout the meal. The knife and fork slid in her hot hands; she lifted the glass and then put it down again, afraid she might drop it.

He said suddenly, 'Must you do that? Must you pick at your food like that?'

'I'm sorry.'

'I'm sorry,' he mimicked, his voice high-pitched. 'Dear God, Marianne, how you do bleat.'

She swallowed. Her throat hurt. 'I'm not very hungry.'

'Hear that, Nadeshan? I shall have to speak to the cook. The dorasanie doesn't care for the food he makes. Perhaps I should find a different cook.'

'I didn't mean to say — there's nothing wrong with the food — '

'Then eat it.' He had risen from his seat. He came to stand beside her, one hand on the back of her chair, his body overshadowing her. He said softly, 'Eat it, Marianne.'

'I can't.'

He seized her fork, stabbed it into the food. 'Eat it.'

'Please, Lucas — ' She could feel the tears in her eyes.

'I said, *eat* it.'

Somehow she managed to swallow the forkful of rice. 'Go on,' he said softly.

Out of the corner of her eyes, she could see Nadeshan, his eyes wide and dark with fear. She knew that they were standing on the edge of a precipice and that if she moved or said the wrong thing something unspeakable would happen. She began to eat. Once or

423

twice her gullet rose, and it was all she could do to choke down the food, grain by grain.

When her plate was empty, Lucas straightened and walked away from her. 'Good,' he said lazily. 'Such a fuss, Marianne, over a few mouthfuls of food.'

He left the room. She remained sitting at the table until she heard the sound of his horse's hooves heading away from the bungalow. Then, very slowly, she stood up. She had to hold the table for support.

She took a carpet bag from the box room. Taking it to her own room, she put it on the bed and opened it. She slid Arthur's ring onto her finger and put the rest of her jewellery inside the bag. Then stockings, underwear, skirts and blouses. A warm cardigan and jacket: it might be cold in England. The roll of money from the back of her drawer; she sat on the bed, trying to count it. Her fingers fumbled, the numbers muddling in her head. Was a rupee worth more than a shilling or less? How much would a train ticket to Colombo cost? How long had it taken them to travel from Colombo to Blackwater when she had first come to Ceylon? Three days, she thought — too long, far too long. She must be faster. He would follow her — and what would he do to her if he caught up with her? She shuddered.

She went to the nursery. George was having his afternoon nap. He was still asleep; she watched him for a few moments, seeing the shadow of his lashes on the curved pink cheek, and the way his arms were flung above his head in an attitude of abandon. Then she began to open drawers, to take out rompers, coats, cardigans. She would need nappies. How many should she take? A dozen . . . two dozen? She did not know. Rani always changed George's nappies.

She heard a sound behind her and turned, her heart hammering with fear. Rani was standing in the doorway. Her dark eyes took in the bundle of clothes in Marianne's arms.

'Dorasanie . . . ' she faltered.

'Shut the door.'

Rani did so. 'I'm going away,' Marianne whispered. 'I'm going back to England.' Rani's eyes widened. 'I have to go. I've got George's clothes, but I need nappies. Where are the nappies?'

Rani opened a hamper and took out a bundle of white cloths. 'You will need food, Dorasanie.'

'Yes. Of course.'

'I get you some.' Rani left the room. Marianne took the baby clothes back to the bedroom and packed them into the bag. She felt curiously light-headed and she felt herself sway, as though the floor was shifting beneath her.

When Rani came back, she was carrying a bundle wrapped up in a length of cloth. Marianne said, 'Tell Nadeshan to ask the grooms to bring round the bullock cart. And wake and dress George, please, Rani.'

Her hat and her parasol. The sun was strong today. She called Nadeshan and told him to carry the carpet bag to the veranda. Rani reappeared with George. Marianne went to stand on the veranda. It would have been easier, she thought, if only she had not felt so tired. She couldn't think why she felt so tired.

The bullock cart was brought round to the front of the house. The groom dismounted and bowed to her. Then he saw the child and the bag. Something flickered in his eyes; he took a step back, and spoke to Marianne. Though she had learned some Tamil during her time at Blackwater, she could not follow the fast flow of words. The groom was shaking his head, pointing at the cart. Marianne looked round wildly. 'Nadeshan — Rani — what is he saying?'

'He say wheel is broken — he say cart cannot be used today. He very sorry.'

She stared at it. 'The wheel doesn't *look* broken — '

Yet, to her horror, the groom was climbing back into

425

the cart and driving away from the bungalow. 'No!' she cried out. 'Come back!' The cart continued on around the curve of the path. She stood for a moment watching, despairing, and then she grabbed George from Rani and swept up the bag. Running after the cart, she was hampered by the weight of the child and the bag. By the time she reached the stables, the groom was unyoking the animals. Then he disappeared into the darkness of the stables.

She began to walk. She knew the way, had often driven along the hill track, travelling to the bazaar or the club. It could not be more than two miles to the road; if she hurried, there would be enough time for her to reach the railway station before Lucas returned to the bungalow for his evening meal.

The path from Blackwater clung to the side of the mountain, heading for the town in a series of hairpins and loops. Tea plants, great acres of them, covered the slopes as far as the eye could see. Dotted among the fields were women; they stared at Marianne as she passed. She found herself clinging to the inside of the path, afraid of the precipice, afraid that Lucas might be there, in the fields, that he might catch sight of her fleeing from him.

She abandoned the parasol, unable to carry it as well as George and the bag. She held George closely, shadowing him with her body, afraid of sunstroke. If only she had learned to ride a horse, she thought. Arthur had offered to teach her often enough. Yet she had never done so, daunted by the height and strength of the beasts. Now she cursed herself for her cowardice.

Stones dug into the thin soles of her shoes. She crossed a log bridge; a chasm fell away beneath it, glancing down, she felt a wave of dizziness and swayed. She was aware as never before of the unfamiliarity of this country. She was aware of the dangers that surrounded her, the snakes, the ticks and leeches, the heat. Of the fear that she might lose her way, become lost, and never find the right path again.

In her arms, George began to whimper. Sitting on a rock at the side of the road, she fed him some of the sugar water Rani had packed and gave him a biscuit to chew on. When she began to walk again, the bag seemed heavier than ever. Every now and then she felt an odd shift in reality and she would find herself wondering whether she was dreaming, whether this was a nightmare and she would open her eyes and find herself back at the bungalow. She never wanted to see the bungalow again. She knew that she should have left long ago, when Lucas was ill and unable to follow her.

She walked on. An eagle circled overhead. On a small patch of grass at a kink in the path a skinny cow grazed, chained to a tree. She passed a roadside shrine, set beside a stream. White ribbons trailed around the shrine. Rani had told her that the white ribbons signified there had been a death in the coolie lines. She shivered and, averting her eyes, walked on. The path continued to unfold beneath her feet; she felt as if she had been walking forever. The weight of the bag dragged at her arm, the handles dug into her fingers. Kneeling at the side of the road, she splashed cold water from a stream onto her face. She wanted to lie down, to close her eyes and sleep. But if she did that, George might wander away and fall down the mountainside. Instead, she unclasped the bag and took from it her jewellery and money and some of George's clothes, stuffing them into the cloth bundle Rani had made for her. Then, leaving the bag at the side of the road, she walked on. To one side of her the mountain rose up, shadowing her, to the other the cliff fell dizzily away. Once she found herself drifting towards the edge, almost tempted by it. But then George wriggled in her arms and, with a gasp of horror, she moved back to the inside of the track.

She saw that she had reached the place where the Blackwater track joined the road. She stood for a moment, struggling to remember which way to turn. Lights glittered on the folds and waves of the tea fields, shifting like the sea.

There was the sound of a bullock cart heading towards her. *Lucas*, she thought with a stab of terror. But Lucas always rode a horse; Lucas was contemptuous of those who travelled in bullock carts.

The cart slowed. Mrs Rawlinson looked out. 'Why, Mrs Melrose. Whatever are you doing here?' She climbed down. 'My dear girl, you look quite done in. Let me help you with your little boy.'

George slid into Mrs Rawlinson's arms. Marianne whispered, 'Would you take me to the railway station?'

'The railway station?'

'I have to catch a train. *Please.*'

'Whatever you like, my dear.'

Mrs Rawlinson helped her into the cart. The cart began to move; Marianne's head lolled against the canopy supports and her eyes closed. Every now and then her lids flickered open and she saw the wide blue of the sky, the green of the tea fields. 'Are we at the station yet?' she asked, and Mrs Rawlinson said, 'Soon, my dear. We'll be there very soon.'

Eventually, the bullock cart came to a halt. Marianne opened her eyes. She saw the banyan tree, the rose garden, the Blackwater bungalow. 'No — no — you promised me — ' Her voice rose in a hoarse croak.

Mrs Rawlinson called out, 'Lucas! Are you there? Now, my dear, don't distress yourself. Lucas! You there, boy! Run and fetch your master. Quickly now. Tell him that he must come home, that his wife has a fever and is very unwell.'

She tried to run from the cart, stumbling across the lawn. But her legs gave way and her fingers clawed into the grass. Her last clear thought before she slipped into unconsciousness was that she had left it too late, and that now she would never escape him.

★ ★ ★

Ash went through the business of arranging the wedding with a dogged determination: having made such an unholy mess of everything else, he would do the right thing by Thelma and by his child, at least. They were to be married as soon as the banns had been called.

Then Thelma sent a note to his office, asking him to call by the shop one lunchtime. She was standing on a stool on the pavement, tacking strings of onions to the awning, when he arrived. 'There you are,' she said.

'You wanted to speak to me, Thelma?'

'Yes.' She climbed off the stool. 'I've decided that I don't want to marry you after all, Ash.'

He stared at her. 'But the baby — '

'Is Charlie's.'

He blinked. 'I don't understand.'

'It's quite simple.' A quick glance into the shop, to check that they would not be overheard. 'I knew I was pregnant before I went with you.'

A silence, while her words sunk in. He said slowly, 'You mean, you *deliberately* — '

'Yes. In a way. It was a sort of insurance policy, I suppose. And besides, I wanted you to love me. But then, afterwards, I didn't think I could go through with it. But when you told me you'd been with *her* — '

He looked at her blankly.

'With Miss Maclise,' she said impatiently. 'You made me so *angry*. If it had been anyone else but her. She's got everything, hasn't she? Looks . . . money . . . a good family. Why should she have you as well? And why shouldn't *I* have something decent for once? A decent bloke with a nice house that Dad could be comfortable

429

in, and money enough so that I didn't have to go on working in a place like this.' With a sharp stab of her finger, Thelma opened up the cash register. 'After we were married, when the baby was born, I was going to say that it was a seven months' child.' She gave a short laugh. 'Of course, if it has red hair, like Charlie, I'd have had some explaining to do.' She looked straight at him. 'That's what I was going to do, Ash. Not very nice, was it?'

'But you changed your mind.'

She seemed to falter. 'I couldn't do it. I thought I could, but I can't. I know you don't care for me. I can see it in your eyes.'

He wondered whether she expected his sympathy; just now, he despised her. 'So it was for the house, the money — '

'Oh, don't be so stupid! It was for you.'

'But you said — you said you didn't love me — '

'Did I? Well, I always was a good liar.' A bitter smile. 'Just as I always told myself it didn't bother me that I wasn't pretty. But I'd have liked to have been pretty enough for *you*, Ash.' She was counting out change; she slid the sixpences into a cloth bag. 'So I've decided that I'll marry Charlie. He'll do, just about.' She looked suddenly stricken, and she muttered, 'The trouble is that I love you too much. I want you to be happy. Even if it means giving you to her. You can hate me if you wish, Ash, I know I deserve it.'

A few weeks later, walking through Whitechapel, Ash paused, reading the headlines on the news-stands. The Archduke Franz Ferdinand, heir to the Austro-Hungarian throne, had been assassinated by a nineteen-year-old Bosnian Serb nationalist, Gavril Princip. He was aware of a feeling of dread, a sudden certainty that his optimism, his belief in improvement and progress, had been misplaced. He remembered Iris saying to him, *It always seems to me that it's impossible to change other people's lives.* He had disagreed with her then; would he disagree with her now? What had he achieved in his years in the East End? *Nothing,* he thought, *almost nothing.* Once he had wanted to make a difference, yet he had made hardly any difference at all even to the small square of deprivation in which he lived. The poverty and injustice he witnessed daily were of such magnitude that it would take an event of cataclysmic proportions — a revolution, perhaps, or a great fire, razing the grimy, verminous terraces — to bring about any change at all.

Yet all that seemed, just then, of far less importance than that he had, through his own stupidity, lost the woman he loved. 'Cheer up, guv, can't be as bad as all that,' said the newsvendor, annoyingly, chirpily, breaking into his thoughts, and, fumbling in his pocket for change, he bought a paper and headed home.

★   ★   ★

Marianne was ill for six weeks. When, at last, the fever left her, her arms and legs were like sticks. She held her hand up to the light and saw the shape of the bones pressing through her skin.

The next day she managed to get out of bed. The few steps to the dressing table exhausted her. Looking at her reflection in the mirror, she saw that they had cut off her hair. Her stick fingers made feeble jabs at the short, dark tufts. She looked like a ghost, she thought, the ghost of the old Marianne.

When Rani next came into her room, she said, 'George. I must see George. Would you bring him to me, Rani?'

Rani came back, alone, a few minutes later. 'Where's George?' Marianne felt the beginnings of a terrible fear. 'Is he ill, too?'

431

'No, no,' said Rani. 'He very well.' But her eyes evaded Marianne's.

'What is it, Rani? Tell me!'

'He with his ayah.'

'His ayah? *You're* his ayah!'

Another shake of the head. 'New ayah come. She come when you sick, Dorasanie.'

Lucas came to her room that evening. 'George,' she whispered.

He frowned. 'I didn't think you'd disobey me. I didn't think you had it in you.'

'Let me see George.'

'Ama will bring him to you.'

'Ama?'

'George's new nurse. I engaged her when you were ill. Rani wasn't trustworthy enough.' He shook his head. 'Running away . . . that was a very stupid thing to do, Marianne. You do see that it changes everything, don't you? Now I know I can't trust you. So Ama will look after George now.'

Her fingers clawed at the sheet. She tried to rise but fell back on the pillow. 'Don't take him away from me, Lucas! Please don't . . . I'll do whatever you want — I'll do anything — '

'You'll still be able to see him if you behave yourself.' He went to the door. 'Or you can leave, if you choose. Whether you go or stay is of no consequence to me now.'

She whispered, 'And George?'

'I won't let you take my son away from me.' He came once more to stand by the bed. His pale eyes were expressionless as he said, 'You see, if you took him from me then I'd follow you to the ends of the earth. Wherever you went, I'd find you. If you returned to England, I'd follow you there. I'd watch your family, your friends. And the first time you turned your back, I'd take him. And then you'd never see him again.'

He left the room, closing the door behind him. It was twilight; she felt the night wash in, falling quickly as it did in the tropics, sweeping shadows into the room, filling the alcoves and corners with darkness. And, burying her head into her pillow, she wept, knowing that she had lost George.

14

Eva remembered a game they had played when they were children. One winter evening the sisters had gathered together in the attic at Summerleigh. They had collected all the sets of dominoes the Maclise family possessed — dominoes in battered, dog-eared boxes, with pieces missing, dominoes so old the colours had worn from the dots — and had arranged them in great lines and swirls. Marianne, the most patient of the sisters, had placed the pieces. Eva remembered the dark chilliness of the attic and that Marianne's fingers had been white with cold as she had put each domino just the right distance apart, so that when one fell it would topple the next. Iris, the eldest, had insisted she overturn the first piece. Eva had watched the dominoes collapse in a black ripple that had widened through the attic until all the pieces had fallen.

As the summer and autumn of 1914 passed, she seemed to hear an echo of that long-ago evening. At the end of July Austria — Hungary declared war on Serbia, using as a pretext the assassination of Franz Ferdinand. Shortly afterwards the Russian army was mobilized. Germany then presented neutral Belgium with an ultimatum, demanding that their army be allowed to march through its territory. Britain, France's ally, then issued its own ultimatum: that Germany respect Belgian neutrality. This ultimatum was disregarded and Britain declared war on Germany on 4 August and on Germany's ally, Austria — Hungary, just over a week later. The British Expeditionary Force crossed the Channel in an attempt to halt the German advance. But the German army swept through both Belgium and northern France, driving the British, on the left flank of the French, almost to the outskirts of Paris. Within a short time the two armies were facing each other at Mons, then at the Marne. By the end of the year, with no quick resolution to the conflict in sight, both armies had dug trenches from the Swiss border through northern France to the Channel. As the ripples spread, fighting with Russia broke out on Germany's Eastern Front.

Eva watched with disbelief and a growing dread as war blotted the face of Europe, its dark stain seeping further and further from the original flashpoint. She felt, at first, along with an abhorrence that her country should have involved itself with war at all, a profound reluctance to let the war change *her*. The sight of the great crowds that gathered in Trafalgar Square and Pall Mall, waving Union Jacks and French tricolours, and the posters exhorting the women of England to send their husbands, brothers and sons to war, revolted her. She disdained to take part in the overt expressions of patriotism that swept through the country and resolutely bought only what food she needed each day, while others swept the shelves of grocery stores clean in an epidemic of panic buying.

Her conviction that she could stand apart from the war lasted an even shorter time than the country's belief that it would all be over by Christmas. At the outbreak of war the government had introduced the Aliens Registration Act, requiring all those of enemy nationality to register at a police station. One night, fired up by newspaper stories of German atrocities, the offices of the Calliope Press were ransacked by a mob. Paula Muller, who owned the press, was of German birth, though she had come to England with her parents as a young girl. The next morning Eva swept up broken glass and helped Paula rescue as many damaged books and manuscripts as possible. A few days later Paula received an anonymous letter threatening both her and her younger sister, Ida, if they remained in England. Paula closed up the press and went back to Germany. Lydia offered Eva part-time work in the gallery. Eva accepted, though privately she suspected that soon the gallery, too, would close because art and beauty seemed to have little place in the new world that war was making.

The war began to work its dark alchemy on her family, too, in strange, unpredictable ways. Iris had spent the summer in France with Charlotte Catherwood. On returning to London, she had taken a nursing post at an army hospital. And then the oddest thing — Clemency wrote to tell Eva that one morning Mother had got up, dressed, breakfasted with the family, and announced that she intended to organize first aid and home nursing classes. Mother had added that Mrs Catherwood had told her that Mrs Hutchinson intended to run classes, which was quite ridiculous, as Mrs Hutchinson knew nothing whatsoever about either subject, whereas she, Lilian Maclise, had, during her years as an invalid, learned a great deal about nursing. As though, Eva thought, finding something better to do had enabled Mother at last to recover. As though illness had once interested Mother, but now did not. *And then*, wrote Clemency, *I asked Mother how she was feeling, and she said that she had never felt better in her life! Do you think she is really well again, Eva? Is it possible?*

★ ★ ★

Ama will look after George now. Ama was half-Scottish, half-Sinhalese. Her father had been a soldier, Rani whispered to Marianne, and her mother had been the daughter of a Kandyan shopkeeper. The one had deserted her, the other had died. Rani did not say how Lucas had found Ama. Marianne supposed that he had

436

caught sight of her in some back street in Kandy, and, recognizing her exceptional beauty in much the same way that he knew just the right moment to pluck a particular field of tea, he had bought her. Ama's skin was light gold and her small, lithe body moved with a sinuous grace. Her greenish-gold, almond-shaped eyes surveyed everything — the bungalow, the servants and Marianne — with an expression of scorn.

Ama never left Marianne alone with George. Ama bathed and fed George and slept in his room at night. When Marianne sat George on her knee, Ama sat cross-legged, watching, the bright silk of her sari covering her head to keep off the sun. Wherever Marianne went with George, Ama followed her. There would be no sound, but when Marianne glanced back over her shoulder, there would be Ama, her bare feet silent on the path. Marianne sensed that Ama despised her. Ama, who had used her wit and beauty to find her way out of the gutter, was contemptuous of a woman who had been born with everything, but had been too foolish to hold on to it. In the shade of the veranda, Ama's small, pointed, ringed fingers stroked the gold-embroidered border of her sari. Only then did Marianne see Ama smile, when she raised her slender arms and watched the gold bangles rain down her wrists.

Ama will look after George now: quickly, Marianne learned what that meant. She was not allowed to get her son up in the morning or to put him to bed at night. She was allowed to see George for two hours in the morning and another two in the afternoon, and to read him a story before bedtime. 'That should be time enough for you to teach him his letters and his numbers,' Lucas said to her. 'And teach him his manners, Marianne — I'll not have him grow up to be uncivil.' She did not protest, knowing that if she did Lucas might stop her seeing George at all. It seared her heart to see Ama sitting with George in the nursery, Ama — not much more than a child herself — who did not love him at all. Those tiny, tapered fingers could be rough and careless, buttoning George into his jacket, brushing his hair. That soft voice could be sharp when he wriggled and the ringed hand was quick to smack when he cried. After a while George stopped crying, sensing, perhaps, Ama's lack of concern. Now, when he came to Marianne, he burrowed his head into her bosom, his small hands clutching the folds of her dress. He had never been a clingy child before. Now he smiled less.

She remained weak long after the fever had left her. Weeks after she had first risen from her bed, the short walk from the bungalow to the palm-roofed summer-house still exhausted her. 'Enteric fever,' explained Dr Scott, testing her pulse, checking her temperature. 'You were unfortunate, Mrs Melrose — we rarely see such severe cases in the hills these days.' He recommended that Marianne rest and prescribed drops to help her sleep at night.

Sometimes she felt as though she had fallen asleep and woken to a different world. So much had changed. In her months of illness the garden had become overgrown once more. Creepers wound round the roses and weeds grew in the flower beds. She let them grow, lacking the strength or will to cut them back. She imagined camellias and bougainvillaea and hibiscus bursting through the lawn, crawling over the metal roof of the bungalow. One year — five — ten — and the forest would have taken back Blackwater.

While she slept, on the far side of the world, a war had broken out. *My family*, she thought, *my brothers and sisters!* Resting in her bedroom one afternoon, the Rawlinsons' voices drifted through the open window from the veranda, speaking of battles and blockades.

And *she* had changed. She was bone-thin, her hair a

short, dark crop, her eyes violet-blue pools in a gaunt, pale face. Worse, something had altered inside her: she knew herself beaten now, the fight gone out of her. Her memory of her flight from the bungalow was fragmentary and nightmarish, of an endless path and the hillside falling away to one side of her. It was some time before she thought of her jewellery. Then she searched her bedroom, opening every drawer, her desperate fingers scrabbling in the backs of cupboards. There was nothing, not a necklace, not a bracelet. Not long afterwards, taking George from Ama, she noticed on Ama's slender finger the little pearl and amethyst ring that her sisters had sent her, the ring that had once belonged to Great-aunt Hannah.

After that some last glimmer of hope was snuffed out. With no money and her jewellery taken from her, what could she do? She sank into the shadows, shamed by her degradation. She knew that she had been the author of her own humiliation. Looking back, she saw clearly now that Lucas, his hopes of inheriting money from his mother dashed, had chosen her. He had chosen her because of her wealth and because she had been young enough to give him the son he needed to inherit the Blackwater estate. Their meeting in London had not been by chance: he must have discovered her London address from the Merediths or their friends. He had played on her weaknesses and on her need to fill the void left by Arthur's death. The understanding, sympathetic face he had shown to her in London had been entirely false, designed to deceive. Iris had warned her, but she had not listened. Once in Ceylon, once he had used her money to buy the Glencoe land, and once she had given birth to his son, she guessed that Lucas had supposed that he could largely disregard her. She had been duped, played for a fool. She had given him everything he wanted; he had taken everything of importance from her.

She ate little, had no appetite. She seemed to live in a dark dream, her fingers too clumsy to sew, her head too blurred to read. When visitors called at the bungalow — more and more rarely, rebuffed by Lucas's increasingly erratic behaviour — she often hid inside, pleading her poor health, her altered appearance. Looking in the mirror, she thought: *You would not love me now, Arthur.* The night provided her only escape, the taste of Dr Scott's drops on her tongue and the bliss of the slide into darkness.

In the sanctuary of her bedroom, with the curtains drawn, she wrote to her father. The words sprawled across the paper, uneven, desperate. *I fear for my son . . . My marriage is a sham . . . I have no money . . . you must come for me, you must take me home.* When she was sure that neither Ama nor Lucas would see her, she gave her letter to the letter coolie, slipping him a few cents. A week later, she wrote another letter, just in case. And one more, for luck. A week for her letter to reach Colombo, she guessed, four weeks for the ship to take it to England. Longer, perhaps, because of the war. She counted off the days.

Weeks passed, then months. Whenever the letter coolie arrived back from the bazaar, she found herself staring at him, her heart pounding, dizzy with hope.

One day she saw that Lucas was watching her.

'What is it, Marianne? What are you looking for?'

'Nothing.' A shiver of fear. 'Nothing at all.'

'Liar.' He left the room and was back in a moment or two, something clutched in his hand. He said, 'You were waiting for an answer to these, weren't you?' He moved quickly, seizing her by her hair, thrusting the papers that he held into her face. She saw, with horror, that they were the letters she had written to her father.

He said, 'You insult me, Marianne, to think me so stupid. My servants are obedient to me, even though my wife is not.' He threw the letters onto the floor. Then he dragged her over to the writing bureau, took out a piece of paper, and thrust the pen into her hand. 'Now. *Write*.'

'No,' she whispered.

'No? Think very carefully before you say that, Marianne. Perhaps you believe that if you don't write, then your father and brothers will come for you? My poor, silly wife. England is at war, don't you remember? I doubt if your family thinks often of you now. They have other, more pressing, concerns. Don't you know how many Englishmen have died already? Your brothers may already be dead. Your father will be grieving for them, not thinking of you.'

Tears were rolling down her face. He said, 'And don't think to run bleating of mistreatment to any of our acquaintances, either. They'll not listen to you. They already think you — *unstable*, shall we say. I've made sure of that.' He put his hand on her shoulder; she shuddered. As his thumb stroked her neck, he said softly, 'Now, you'll write a letter to your father, Marianne, telling him that you've been unwell but are now recovered. And that you are happy and that the child thrives. Something like that.' His hand slid slowly down from her shoulder, inside her blouse, until it rested on her breast. She sat, rigid with horror. 'If you don't write, Marianne, then I may choose to remember the duties you neglect to carry out. Your duties as a wife.'

She wrote the letter. The next day Ama did not bring George to her. From the garden Marianne watched him playing on the veranda. She heard him cry and saw Ama slap him sharply. She wanted to run across the garden and pull George away, to hit Ama hard, to throw her violently to the ground. She had to force herself to continue walking round the perimeter of the garden, her knuckles pressed against her teeth until they bled.

In the heavy shade of the trees she sat down,

exhausted by her anger. There was a rustle in the undergrowth behind her and, looking back, she saw Rani. Rani stooped behind her and took her hand.

'You have this now, Dorasanie.' Marianne's clenched hand was opened; something slid into it. 'I take it from you when you ill. I keep it safe for you.' Then Rani was gone, twisting through the paths back to the servants' quarters.

Marianne uncurled her hand. Her diamond ring lay in her palm, the ring that Arthur had given her in the conservatory at Summerleigh.

She heard his voice. *I will love you always and forever. Beyond death, if need be.* His voice was so clear, as though he was here, in this place of nightmares, beside her. She looked round, half-expecting to see him beneath the flame tree and eucalyptus. The leaves shivered, as though someone had walked by.

She sat there for a long time, the ring in her hand, remembering. She unhooked the silver chain she wore round her neck and slid the ring onto it, tucking it carefully beneath the folds of her blouse. Then she went back to the garden. She felt stiff and old beyond her years as she knelt in front of a flower bed. But she began, slowly at first, to pull out the weeds, to thin out the new seedlings and, with unsteady hands, to unwind the creepers from the stems of the roses.

★   ★   ★

One midday in October James met Eva after she had finished work at the gallery. They had lunch in the Cottage Tea Rooms in the Strand. James was walking Eva back to her flat when he said, 'There's something I have to talk to you about.'

They were passing a small, iron-railed park; they went inside and sat down on a bench. James lit two cigarettes and handed one to Eva. He said, 'I've been trying to

442

pluck up the nerve to say something to someone for ages, but I've always funked it. But now I *have* to. I've decided to join up, you see.'

Her heart seemed to jolt. '*James*. No. Please.'

'Of course I must go. All my friends have gone. Anyway, I *want* to. I'd have enlisted weeks ago if it hadn't been for . . . ' He broke off. 'Eva, I can't just stand by and watch everyone else go off to France while I sit around in an office. So I've signed the papers. I'm leaving for training camp at the end of next week.'

First Paula, now James, she thought with a stab of grief. *Who next?* But she said, 'Have you told Father?'

He shook his head. 'Not yet.'

She recalled Joshua's simple, uncomplicated patriotism, and she said slowly, 'I don't suppose he'll be angry with you. I expect he'll be proud.'

'For volunteering? Oh, I don't think he'll mind about *that*. It wasn't hard making up my mind about that. It's the other thing.'

'What other thing?'

James was taking something from his pocket. 'This. I can't tell him about this. And I must tell someone now.'

He held out to her a photograph. Eva looked down at the portrait of a young woman and a small child. 'Who are they?'

'That's Emily, my wife. And this is Violet, my daughter.'

Another glance at the pretty, blonde woman and the little girl in a white lace dress. She whispered, 'I don't understand, James.'

'I married Emily in March 1911. Violet was born in the October of that year.'

She stared at him, disbelieving. 'You've been married since *1911*?'

'Yes.' His mouth was set in a grim line.

'For *three and a half years*? Without telling any of us?'

443

James nodded.

Eva had a sudden snapshot of memory. She squinted at the photograph once more. 'I saw you with her,' she exclaimed. 'Ages ago. You were coming out of a music hall in Whitechapel.'

'I met Emmie at a music hall. She loves the theatre.'

'But — ' she struggled to take it in — '*James*. Why on earth didn't you tell us?'

He groaned and put his head in his hands. 'I wanted to, but I couldn't. I kept trying to come clean, but then I always funked it. I couldn't face it. I couldn't face telling Father.' He looked up at her. 'But now you know. Do you despise me, Eva?'

She squeezed his hand. 'Of course not. Why should I despise you?'

'For being so deceitful. All those years.' He looked at her anxiously. 'You really don't hate me?' He sat back on the bench and gave a huge sigh. 'You don't know what a relief it is to tell someone at last.'

'Do you love her? Do you love Emily?'

'I adore her.' He smiled. 'When I first saw her, I thought she was the sweetest thing. She's so unaffected — she has none of the airs and graces so many girls have. She doesn't try to trip a chap up, make him say things he didn't mean to.'

She thought: *Three and a half years*. And the child was born in the October of 1911 . . . She said, 'You married Emily because she was expecting a baby?'

'Yes.' He flushed. 'But it wasn't only because of that — I knew straight away she was the girl for me.'

'But I still don't understand, James. Father would have been angry at first, of course, but then — '

'Emily was a milliner's assistant before I married her. She was born in Stepney. Not exactly what Father had in mind for his eldest son, the heir to the family business, is it, Eva?'

'No. I suppose not.' She looked at her brother,

struggling to absorb the enormity of what he had just told her. 'How awful for you,' she said. 'To keep such a secret. How did you manage?'

'I almost didn't, sometimes. I rent a house for Emily and Violet in Twickenham. It's only a little place, but I like it there. When we were first married, I was so happy. It was fun — exciting. I rather liked having a secret from the family. You know what it's like at home with everyone poking their nose into everyone else's business. But then, after the baby was born, it got so damned complicated. And though I knew I should come clean, I kept putting it off, and the longer I put it off the harder it was to say anything. Can you imagine? *Oh, by the way, it completely slipped my mind to mention it, Father, but I have a wife and child.*' James shook his head. 'And then, when he started nagging me to marry Louisa Palmer . . .'

'So that's why you always spent the weekends in London?'

'To be with them, yes. Violet's three now. She's going to start asking questions soon, isn't she? Why her daddy isn't at home like other daddies, that sort of thing. And as for Emily — none of the neighbours will speak to her, Eva. Because we can't tell them the truth, of course. I know that they think she's my mistress. It makes her so unhappy.' His eyes had clouded. 'And there's always the fear that something will go wrong. Last year Violet caught scarlet fever. I was afraid that something frightful might happen, so I was late getting back to Summerleigh once and there was the most awful row. I almost did it, then, almost told Father, and be hanged to the consequences.' He looked despairing. 'But how would I have managed? If Father cut me off without a penny, what would happen to Emily and Violet?'

'You must tell him now.'

'No. I couldn't possibly. I've only told you because

someone has to know. If something should happen to me — if they send me to France — '

'James,' she said fiercely, 'you mustn't talk like that.'

'Promise me, Eva.' His gaze was intense, pleading. 'Promise me that if I don't come back, then you'll make sure Emmie and Violet are all right.'

She said reluctantly, 'Of course I will. If it's what you want.'

'This is their address.' He handed her a piece of paper.

'James.' She tried again. 'You really must tell Father.'

'I can't.' He looked away. 'I know it's not fair on you, Eva. I suppose I've just saddled you with *my* secret.'

She thought of her father and Katharine Carver. She seemed to hold her breath as she came to a decision. She said slowly, 'Father may not mind as much as you think.'

'How can you say that?'

'None of us is perfect, James. Perhaps Father will understand.'

'*Father's* perfect,' he said bitterly. 'Father would never have done anything like I've done. He'd never have got himself into such a mess.'

'No, that's not true. James, I'm going to tell you one of *my* secrets . . . '

Afterwards, looking back, it troubled her that he didn't take it quite in the way she had expected him to. She had thought that in telling James about her father and Katharine Carver, she would make him see that Father was not the saint that James seemed to think he was. But instead of being relieved, James was shocked. No, she thought afterwards, worse than that, he had been horrified and appalled, as though the discovery that Father, too, had sinned, had rocked him to his foundations.

Two days later Eva was about to leave her flat for the gallery when the doorbell rang. There was a telegram from Clemency. It read: FATHER ILL STOP PLEASE COME HOME.

★ ★ ★

Father had collapsed at the works the previous day, Clemency told Eva when she reached Summerleigh. Mr Foley had told the family that James had been with his father in his office and then, not long after James had left, Mr Foley had heard a sound and had gone into Father's office and had found Father semi-conscious on the floor. Dr Hazeldene had diagnosed heart strain. None of them had seen James since then, Clemency added, looking worried. He had not come home and Aidan had told her that he had not been in to work either.

In the evening Eva went to sit at her father's bedside. It cut her to the heart to see Joshua, who had always seemed to her such a massive, vital figure, so helpless and diminished.

'It's me, Father,' she said softly. 'It's Eva.'

'Eva, kitten.' His hand moved on the blanket; she took it in hers. Then he said fretfully, 'The business — it'll all go to rack and ruin — never missed a day before — '

'You mustn't worry about that now, Father. Aidan will see to everything.'

'No. Mustn't let Aidan . . . '

He was struggling to sit up; his lips were blue. Eva, frightened, said quickly, 'I'll go and speak to Mr Foley tomorrow, Father. He'll make sure that everything's all right, I promise.' Joshua sank back on the pillow, his eyes closed.

Eva cycled to J. Maclise & Sons the following morning. It had rained the previous night and puddles glazed the yard between the heaps of coal and used crucibles. As always, the air was full of noise: the

447

pounding of hammers, the whine of grinding wheels and the voices of men calling to each other.

Mr Foley rose from his desk when she came into the office.

'Miss Eva. How is your father?'

'Dr Hazeldene seemed to be pleased with him this morning. But it's so awful to see him like this!' He offered her a seat; she sat down. 'Father's worried about the business, Mr Foley. That's why I came to see you.'

'I can come round with the figures after work today, if that would help. Nothing too much, so that it doesn't tire him, but enough to put his mind at rest.'

'Thank you,' she said, relieved. She frowned. 'There's something else I need to talk to you about, Mr Foley. But not here . . . '

He looked at the clock. 'I often stop about this time for something to eat. I like to walk down to the canal and watch the barges. Would you like to walk with me?'

They were heading away from the factory when she said, 'Father seemed worried about Aidan. He was worried about Aidan running the business in his absence.'

'Your father and Mr Aidan don't see eye to eye about everything.'

'Business things?' she asked, and Mr Foley nodded.

'Mr Aidan has different ideas about how he'd like to run Maclise's. You might say that he's more . . . *hard-headed* . . . than your father.'

'Do you mean harsh, Mr Foley?'

He did not reply, but then he did not contradict her either. Unable to put it off any longer, she asked, 'Did they quarrel? Did James and my father quarrel?'

'I couldn't say, Miss Maclise — '

'You have to tell me the truth, Mr Foley!'

A short silence, then he said, 'Yes. There was an argument, I'm afraid.'

Her heart sank. 'A bad argument?'

'Pretty bad.'

She stopped suddenly, beside the tramway, and cried out, 'It was my fault, then!'

'No, that's nonsense. How could it possibly be your fault?'

'It is, Mr Foley, it is!'

'Your father and Mr James quarrelled, yes. I caught a few words — I couldn't help it. Half the yard heard, I should think.'

'What did you hear?'

'I'd rather not — '

'*Please.*'

'Very well.' They had reached the canal basin. They sat down on a heap of pallets among the stacks of iron bars and timber on the wharves. He said, 'Your father accused Mr James of bringing shame on the family.'

She cried out, 'But I thought he'd understand!'

'Understand what?'

She shook her head slowly. 'I can't tell you. But my family has a great many secrets, Mr Foley.'

Barges threaded their way through the jumble of craft on the canal. She wondered how they managed to keep their course through so many obstacles, why they didn't collide and sink under the slick, dark water.

He said, 'If it's any comfort, your family isn't the only one to have secrets. And I find it hard to believe that your family's secrets are quite as iniquitous as mine.'

'Do you?' she said bitterly. 'I'm not so sure.'

He took a waxed paper package from his pocket and opened it. 'Here. Have a sandwich.'

'I'm not hungry.'

'You must eat. You look cold.'

She took one. He said, 'I told you that my father gambled. He gambled away every penny he owned and considerably more besides. When he realized that he was on the verge of bankruptcy, he hanged himself.'

Her head jerked up to look at him. His gaze did not

flinch as he said, 'I tell you this not to shock or disgust you, but so, perhaps, you see your own family in a better light. Whatever your family has done, it can't have sunk to such depths.'

She whispered, 'James and Father quarrelled because of something I told James. Father's ill because of that!'

'I'm sure you had your reasons.'

'I thought it would help!'

'Some secrets can be kept and some can't. You should ask yourself which category your secrets come into.'

She thought hard. She said, 'A few days ago James came to see me. He told me he'd decided to join up.'

'A great many men have. We've lost some of our most skilled workers.'

'Then he told me something else. He had to because he'd enlisted. I do see that. And I really can't see how *that* can be kept secret — it's too big, too important. And I can't see, actually, Mr Foley, why it should be kept secret! James hasn't done anything wrong! Not really.' She paused; her voice was lowered. 'But then I told James something about Father. And I think perhaps I shouldn't have.' She threw a few crumbs onto the ground; a flock of sparrows pecked at them. 'Do you remember that day — oh, ages ago — when I lost my bicycle and you found it for me?'

'Of course I remember.'

'You must have thought me so silly. Wandering round a place like that on my own.'

He said, 'No, that wasn't what I thought at all,' and the expression in his eyes took her by surprise because it told her something she would never have imagined, and she had to hide the shock of her knowledge by saying quickly, 'I'd just found something out, you see. I was so upset. I was so ignorant, then — I didn't know anything.' She paused, now unable to meet his eyes, twisting her fingers together. Then she said slowly, 'I used to think it mattered so much. I was so angry with Father for years.'

'And now?'

'And now — ' she sighed — 'it doesn't seem so important after all. People make mistakes, don't they? *I've* made mistakes.' She had begun to recover her composure and she was able to turn to him and say, 'How terrible for you to lose your father in such a way.'

'My family's secrets couldn't be kept,' he said grimly. 'Within a few days of my father's death all Buxton knew. There are former friends of my mother's who haven't spoken to her since then. My elder sister was engaged to be married at the time and her fiancé broke off the engagement. Neither of my sisters has married. All I can do is try to limit the damage — to make sure that my family lives as comfortably as possible. And all you can do, Miss Eva, is to help your father get better. And try to reconcile him with your brother.'

★ ★ ★

She knew where James had gone, of course. The next day, she took the train back to London, to Twickenham.

James's house was one of a row of red-brick villas, not far from the Thames. Winter pansies were planted by the path that led through the small front garden to the door; a rose, with a flower or two still blooming, scrambled up a trellis.

James, in shirtsleeves and corduroy trousers, opened the door to her. 'Eva.' He kissed her. Then he said, 'I won't go back. If you've come here to persuade me to go back to Summerleigh, then I'm afraid you've wasted your time.'

'Father's ill, James.'

'Oh God.' He shut his eyes and leaned against the door jamb. At the end of the corridor someone moved, listening. Eva saw in the shadows a woman in a

451

violet-coloured dress, and the child in her arms.

James said, 'What happened?'

'It's his heart, Dr Hazeldene says.'

'How bad is it?'

'With rest and good nursing he should make a complete recovery.'

The woman came forward. She was slight and fair, with a cut-glass, finely drawn prettiness. The little girl she held was her miniature. She touched James's arm. 'James?'

'Emily.' He smiled at her. 'This is my sister, Eva.'

'Won't you come in, Miss Maclise? You mustn't stand on the doorstep on a cold day like this.' A soft London voice.

They went into the sitting room. Emily offered tea; Eva accepted. James followed his wife into the kitchen. Eva heard them talking, their voices lowered. Then James came back into the room. Eva said quickly, 'James, please come back with me to Summerleigh. Just for a short time. Just long enough to make it up with Father.'

'I can't. I'm sorry, Eva.'

'But *James* — '

'Not unless Father apologizes.'

'You know he won't apologize. He *never* apologizes.'

'Then I can't come back with you.' His face was set. 'I'm sorry Father's unwell. And I'm truly sorry if I was the cause of it.' James threw a quick glance into the back room to check his wife was out of earshot. 'But I can't forgive the things he said to me. The names he called Emily — I couldn't repeat them. Even Violet. I can't forgive that. You can't just patch up something like that. It's the hypocrisy I find so intolerable. That he should criticize me, when he's been carrying on with that creature . . . ' He was white-faced with anger. 'Father told me he'd disinherit me, did you know that? Aidan will be delighted, no doubt,' he added bitterly.

'He's always thought I stood in his way.' Emily came into the room with the tea things; he broke off.

After tea, while Emily was putting Violet to bed, James walked Eva back to the station. On the platform she began, 'James, you could write. Just a letter.'

He shook his head. 'No, Eva.'

She sighed. Then she said, 'You'll let me tell the others about Emily and Violet, though. Emily is our sister-in-law and Violet is our niece.'

'Yes. Yes, of course.'

She found that there were tears in her eyes. 'I can't bear that you're going away, James! This awful war — '

'Oh, I won't be *fighting* for ages.' He grinned at her. 'I'll be sitting in an army camp, reminding myself how to put a rifle together. It'll probably all be over long before I get a crack at it.'

The shriek of a whistle and a cloud of white smoke announced the coming train. Sitting in the carriage, Eva thought: *What a mess we make of things. We love the wrong people, we quarrel with them and insult them and are then too proud to draw the words back.*

And yet we also find love in the strangest places. In a crowded music hall, or sitting on a wharf by a canal. She thought how they had all misread Mr Foley these past years, believing him to be dour and dull. There was a heart beneath that still, dark exterior, a heart that had not yet recovered from the injuries of the past. She wondered whether she minded that Mr Foley loved her and found that she did not. She suspected that he would never speak of it to her and, besides, just now she needed a friend. Her treasured independence had faltered a little, she acknowledged, and it would be a relief to know that there was someone she could turn to.

★ ★ ★

Marianne made herself walk a little further each day. Once around the perimeter of the Blackwater garden, then twice, then three times, George in her arms and Ama's little feet padding on the path behind her. Though she never again heard Arthur's voice as clearly as she had that morning in the garden, she still sometimes felt his presence.

She made herself eat. Rice and meat and vegetables, swallow it, and never mind that your stomach rises. Her skirts and blouses did not hang quite so loosely from her now and her hair had begun to grow back. She no longer took the sleeping draught Dr Scott had prescribed for her. Her head felt clearer and she had fewer nightmares. She kept the drops, though, hiding them at the back of a drawer. Just in case.

She knew now that she must leave Blackwater, however she might and whatever the consequences. She must take George away from Lucas because if she did not then Lucas would corrupt George as his father had corrupted him. Returning to the bungalow in the evening, Lucas liked to give George a taste of wine. It amused him to watch the little boy stagger, amused him to see George, slightly tipsy, pummel Ama with his fists. 'Oh, don't make such a fuss,' Lucas drawled when Ama cursed the child angrily. 'Let him show a bit of spirit. I'll not have him grow up a milksop like his mother.'

It broke her heart to see the seeds of corruption already planted in her child. Sometimes George was imperious and high-handed, and Lucas laughed at his impudence to Ama, egging him on, encouraging him to act more and more outrageously. On other days Lucas was short-tempered and impatient, and smacked him, or shut him in his room. Alternately over-indulged and punished, George became sometimes silent and withdrawn, sometimes prone to violent tantrums.

She knew that if they remained at Blackwater, there were things that George must grow accustomed to. To

Lucas sitting on the veranda, Ama's slender arms wound round his neck, her red lips caressing him. To Lucas pushing Ama roughly aside when she wearied him. Marianne knew that some day Lucas would tire of Ama, just as he had tired of Parvati, just as he must have tired of Parvati's predecessors. Marianne suspected that Ama knew that too, which was why she counted her gold bracelets so carefully.

She understood what they would make of him, her only and deeply loved child. Five years, ten, and they would have ruined him. A few more years, and the sweet, affectionate boy would have gone, replaced by an unscrupulous and cynical young man. He would be beyond redemption. Often, she had to fight to contain her rage, to maintain the downtrodden, slavish exterior that made Lucas despise her and discount her as beaten. *That* was her only weapon, that he did not see her as a threat. At night, alone in her room, she clenched her hands and imagined dragging her nails down Lucas's face. Or snatching away the glass of wine that he was feeding to her child and dashing it to the floor. Or worse, far worse.

She felt herself changing once more, becoming colder, harder, less feeling, with only one desire left, to protect her child. She made herself look back and understand why her last attempt at escape had failed. Of course the groom had refused to drive her to the railway station — all the Blackwater servants were afraid of Lucas. And of course Mrs Rawlinson had driven her back to Blackwater. *We stick together out here*, Mrs Rawlinson had told her. *It's how we survive.* 'We' meant the Rawlinsons, Lucas, and all the rest of the Ceylon-born British community. Here, *she* was the outsider.

She saw she would never get away from Lucas if she were dependent on other people. She must be able to survive by herself. She had not even known how to care

455

for her own child; she had had to ask Rani what clothes and food to take for George. Now, she must manage on her own. For the rest of her life, she realized, she might have to manage on her own.

Once more she made lists. The things she would need for George: food and drink for the journey, a change of clothes, his sunhat, his favourite toy. When no one was looking, she took a little jacket that was drying outdoors on a bush and a hat discarded on the veranda, and hid them beneath the mattress on her bed. She watched Ama as carefully as Ama watched her, learning George's routine. Now two years old, he was out of nappies in the daytime, Ama's hand providing a swift corrective for any accidents. Soon, Marianne thought, George would be strong enough to walk part of the hill path himself. She encouraged him to be as active as possible, to build up his strength. The thought of herself and George, a white woman with a child, walking the long, winding path from Blackwater to the bazaar town, an object of interest and remark to anyone who cared to look, worried her, but she could see no alternative. She would have preferred to leave the estate at night, but Ama slept in the nursery and, even if she managed to take George when Ama was with Lucas, then Ama would raise the alarm as soon as she went back to the nursery. And there would not be time to reach the railway station before Lucas came for her.

What would she need? Money, of course. The engagement ring that Arthur had given her was the only item of value she still possessed; her decision to sell it was swift and unemotional. Who could she trust to sell it for her? She ran through the list of her acquaintances. Dr Scott and Ralph Armitage were in Lucas's thrall. Anne Rawlinson had betrayed her once already. Then there were the assistant managers, Mr Cooper and Mr Salter. Mr Cooper was lazy and dull-witted, always one to take the shortest cut. Mr Salter . . . once, she had thought that Mr Salter had a soft spot for her.

She began to watch Mr Salter too. She noticed that nowadays he often spent the evenings alone in his own bungalow instead of drinking with Lucas at Blackwater as he had once done. She guessed that Lucas, increasingly tyrannical on the estate as well as at Blackwater, had insulted Mr Salter once too often and had antagonized him, just as he had antagonized so many others.

Then there were the tradesmen who called at the bungalow. The dhobi and the pedlars, with their silks and laces. And Mr da Silva, who came to the factory each month to collect the tea and transport it to the station in bullock carts. Calling at the bungalow, Mr da Silva brought a posy for Marianne, a sweetmeat for George. She saw him nod to Ama on the veranda. His amber eyes studied Marianne kindly. 'You look thin, Mrs Melrose,' he said. 'Next time, I will bring you a cake, a big cake, and you must promise to eat it all.'

It would take at least two hours, she estimated, to reach the railway station and to catch a train. Her greatest difficulty, she knew, would be to find a time when neither Lucas nor Ama would notice their absence. Lucas, of course, was out on the estate for most of the day, but at those times Ama was always with George.

She thought of the Tamil festivals at every full moon. How the work of the estate halted as the coolies danced and feasted and made offerings to their gods. How, on those days, Lucas drank, more and more often to insensibility.

She began to take her Sunday afternoon walk past Mr Salter's bungalow, George holding her hand, Ama trailing sulkily behind, annoyed at being dragged from her favourite place on the veranda at the hottest time of day. Mr Salter waved to her from the garden; Marianne noticed how Mr Salter's eyes slid from her to Ama, and how his gaze followed her lithe, sari'd figure up the hill.

Once or twice, on her Sunday walk, Marianne stopped to pass the time of day with Mr Salter. Ama stood a few yards away, shaded from the sun by her parasol. 'We don't see you so often these days at the bungalow, Mr Salter,' Marianne said. Again, she saw that frequent flick of his eyes towards Ama, unable to help himself, hypnotized by her beauty. And she felt a sense of urgency when he added, mopping his brow, 'I may go home at the end of the year, Mrs Melrose. This place . . . I've never got used to the climate. I thought I would, but I can't. I prefer the cold. You wouldn't think you'd long for a winter day in Edinburgh, would you?'

Once he picked flowers for them, from his garden. A spray of bougainvillaea for Marianne and lilies for Ama, their white trumpets dusted with gold. She saw the sweat on his upper lip as his hand brushed against Ama's. And the simper at the corners of Ama's full, red mouth. 'We'll miss you if you go back to Scotland, Mr Salter,' said Marianne, thanking him. 'We are quite dull without you. Poor Ama finds the days in the bungalow very long, I'm afraid. I think she misses the towns and the shops. She loves pretty things.'

She counted the days to Mr da Silva's return. He kept his promise, bringing her an iced cake. A quick look back to the bungalow to make sure they were alone, and then, taking his hand to thank him, she slid her diamond ring into his palm. 'I need you to sell this for me,' she whispered. 'Please, Mr da Silva. And if . . .' Ama had come into the vestibule, George in her arms; Marianne thought the beating of her heart would choke her. But Mr da Silva said cheerfully, 'I shall bring something for the child next time, Mrs Melrose. Something pretty. No one shall know. It shall be our secret.' He went away. Kneeling by a flower bed, Marianne began blindly to pull out weeds from the garden. 'I had to, Arthur,' she whispered. 'You do understand, don't you? I had to.'

⋆ ⋆ ⋆

Since she and Ash had parted, Iris had spent three months touring France with Charlotte before returning to Summerleigh. On the outbreak of war she had left Sheffield to nurse at a military hospital in London. Throughout this time she had been aware of a deep unhappiness inside her, which had mostly realized itself as an absence of feeling. Though she had been able, intellectually, to appreciate the beauty of the French towns and chateaux which she and Charlotte had visited, privately all that opulence and loveliness had wearied her. Her numbness had made her able to bear her decision, made inevitable by the war, to return to hospital routine and discipline.

One evening, she met Eva at the Lyons Corner House in the Strand. Snowflakes clumped on the windows and slid down the glass. Iris, who had been on the ward all day, ordered tea, toast and muffins. While they were waiting for the food to arrive, Iris told Eva about the hospital she was now working in — 'I hope I never become a sister. Sisters are always so odd — Sister Leach insists the bedsteads are dusted three times a day. I know cleanliness is important, but *three times a day*?' Then, looking at Eva, she said, 'Go on. Tell me.'

'Tell you what?'

'Tell me what's bothering you.' Eva had always been easy to read. 'Is it Father?'

'Father's getting better. He's gone back to work. But he's changed, Iris.'

'Father's always been very strong, so any illness must come as a blow to him. Are you worried about James, then? Or his family?' The phrase sounded odd: Iris still

459

found it hard to think of James as a husband and father.

'Emily and Violet are very well. I had supper with them a few days ago. And I had a postcard from James. He seems to be all right.' The tea arrived; Iris poured. Eva said, 'It's Marianne.'

'Have you heard from her?'

'I had a letter a few days ago. And something's not right, Iris. I know it. She sounds funny.'

'Funny?'

'Odd. Not like Marianne. Not like the Marianne we know. Different. As though she doesn't really care what she's saying — and doesn't really care who she's writing to. Marianne was never like that. Marianne always cared. If anything, she felt things too much.'

'She hasn't been the same since Arthur died,' Iris pointed out. 'You can't expect her to be the same after something like that.'

'No. Of course not. But then I read through these.' Eva took a bundle of letters out of her bag. 'And Clemency let me see the letters Marianne's written to her. And they don't *say* anything, Iris. Just little things about George and the garden and chit-chat about the weather. Nothing that matters. Nothing about Marianne. Nothing about how she feels. Or whether she's happy.'

'What are you afraid of?'

'I don't know. I just don't know.'

Remembering Marianne's rushed marriage, Iris felt worried too. She said slowly, 'Perhaps the marriage isn't happy. Marianne has always kept her own counsel — she might not want to admit the marriage has been a failure.'

'Of course, there's nothing any of us can do at the moment. This awful war . . . ' Eva scowled, black-browed, at her tea. 'I hate it. Everything feels *wrong*. Even though I tell myself that beauty is even more important now because of the war, my work at the gallery feels trivial and self-indulgent. It makes me so angry that I should feel like that about something that was once everything to me. So I thought I'd train to be a nurse like you — don't you dare laugh, Iris — and I went to one of Mother's first-aid classes. But just the sight of the pretend blood made me feel ill, so how on earth would I manage if it was real?' She lit a cigarette, the match snapping angrily against the tinder; then she said, 'So I've decided to go home.'

'Eva.'

'I know.' The cigarette waved in the air. 'It will be intolerable. I'll hate it — I'll be longing to be back in London after a week. I was always so proud of myself for earning money, for wanting to be independent. I used to look down on you, Iris, because all you seemed to think about was dresses and hats, and I looked down on Marianne for getting married and on Clem for staying at home. But now it's me who's useless. This horrible war seems to have turned everything on its head.'

'What will you do?'

Eva sighed. 'I thought I could help Father with the business. I can type letters and write accounts and make telephone calls. Lydia taught me how and I did all those things when I was working for Paula. And with James gone and Father not really well yet, they need me, Iris. I can see that they do.' She attempted a smile. 'So hard to swallow my pride, though, and go back to the family after all these years managing on my own.'

'None of us are very good at swallowing our pride.'

'No.' Eva's eyes narrowed; she blew out a thin stream of smoke. Then she said, 'There's something else. I saw Ash.'

Iris's heart lurched, but she said coolly, 'Really? I hope he was well.'

461

'Perfectly well. He'd like to see you.'

Iris looked away. 'I don't think that would be a good idea.'

'He's not married, you know.'

A silence, in which Irish tried to absorb her shock, then she said, 'I can't see that that makes any difference to me.'

'Ash didn't tell me what happened and I didn't ask. But I think you have to assume that things weren't quite as you thought they were.'

A jumble of thoughts, angry, resentful and hurt. And, to Iris's dismay, through them, a thread of hope. Dismay because, if you hoped, then you laid yourself open to disappointment and pain again.

'Ash wants to see you, Iris. He asked me to ask you.'

'I can't.'

'Of course you can.'

'You don't understand — '

'Oh, I do. I understand that you and Ash have hurt each other dreadfully. But I also understand that you could be happy if you chose to be. If you could forgive.'

'I'm not sure that I can.'

'When I think of Father and James — when I see how unhappy they're making themselves because neither of them can forgive.' Eva leaned across the table to Iris. 'You love Ash and he loves you. It's as simple as that.'

'If only it was — '

'It is. He loves you. I can tell. I do know something of love, you see. I know how it feels. And I can tell Ash loves you by the way he speaks of you.' There were tears in Eva's eyes.

There was a silence, then Iris said, 'Who was he? The man you loved? I always wondered whether you might tell me, but you never did.'

Eva smiled through the tears. 'He was an artist — quite a famous artist. And he was married and he had children. I tried not to love him but I couldn't help myself. Everything we were always warned not to do — well, I did it. And, since we parted I've felt as though I've been cut in half.' She looked down at the table and added softly, 'But I don't regret it. I can't regret it, even though I know it was wrong, even though he hurt me so much. I still write to his wife. He's in France now. He wouldn't fight, but he's a stretcher bearer.' She met Iris's gaze. 'Sometimes, no matter how much you love someone, you know you can't ever be happy. But you two can be happy, Iris, and you'd be so foolish to pass up the chance. So very foolish.'

★   ★   ★

A cold, sleety evening and Ash was waiting for her outside the hospital. Iris stood for a moment, seeing him before he saw her, testing herself. He had changed: the close-cropped hair, the khaki. Eva hadn't warned her about that.

He turned and saw her. There was an awkward moment when neither of them seemed to know whether to kiss, which she smoothed by saying, 'Oh dear, home sister's watching us. Give me a kiss, Ash, a brotherly kiss, and I'll tell her you're James. She's as blind as a bat and you both have yellow hair. And then you can walk back with me to my lodgings.'

His lips brushed against her cheek and she thought — a flutter of relief, or perhaps it was despair? — that she felt nothing. They headed away from the hospital. She touched his sleeve. 'I never imagined you a soldier, Ash.'

A rueful smile. 'Neither did I.' He shrugged. 'But it seemed the thing to do. So many of the men I knew in the East End have joined up. The army feeds you and clothes you, you see. And as it's my lot who are running this show — well, I felt I had to go too.'

She knew what he meant by *my lot*. The men who

463

had been in the Officer Training Corps at their public schools, the men who were used to, and expected to, command.

'And you, Iris,' he said. 'Back in a hospital . . . never again, you said.'

'It's utterly dreadful.' She sighed. 'Back to bossy sisters and ridiculous rules and regulations. Though the men on my ward are very sweet. And so young, some of them. Sometimes I feel as though I'm their mother.'

'Some of the men in my battalion are only sixteen or seventeen years old. They lied about their age so that they could join up.'

'Where are you stationed, Ash?'

'I'm still at training camp.'

'So's James.' She thought of the wounded men on her ward. 'Thank goodness.'

A black cat darted across the path; half a dozen soldiers spilled out of a pub. He said, 'It was good of you to see me.'

She said bluntly, 'Eva told me you hadn't married.'

'No.'

'Why not?'

'It turned out that it was all a mistake.'

'And the child?'

'There was a child.' He looked grim. 'But it wasn't mine.'

She thought how much Thelma Voss must have wanted him, to try that old, old trick. 'Did you love her?'

'I liked her. I admired her. But I didn't love her.'

'But you went to bed with her?'

'Yes.'

'And — did you love me?'

'Yes.'

'Then I don't understand why you went to bed with Thelma.'

After a moment, he said, 'It's hard to know where to

start. To apologize would seem quite revoltingly inadequate. Even to *explain* — it seems presumptuous of me to assume you care enough to hear.'

'Satisfy my curiosity.'

He stopped beneath the dim flare of a gas lamp and said, 'I went to bed with Thelma because I was lonely. And because, at the time, I didn't think you loved me. And because I was angry with you. And because Thelma was there and you weren't.'

See, she thought, *it doesn't hurt at all*. She was still walking, talking — why, she could even manage a smile. She said, 'We never seem to time things very well, do we, Ash? We never seem to feel the same way about each other at the same time.'

'Or perhaps we never admit to feeling the same way at the same time.'

She felt his gaze and looked away. 'Why did you want to see me, Ash?' She touched his khaki sleeve again. 'Was it because of this?'

'In a way, I suppose. Not — not to play on your sympathy. 'Goodbye, Dolly, I must leave you', and all that. But there's a need to try to sort things out. Not to leave things unsaid.'

They were passing a café. He asked, 'Are you hungry?'

'Not really. But a cup of coffee, perhaps . . . '

They went inside. The warm air smelt of wet towels and steamed pudding; a tableful of factory girls, in headscarves and aprons, made eyes at some soldiers across the aisle.

Iris said, 'I used to think you were so good. So helpful — so generous — and everyone always liked you. And clever, too. All those books you'd read. I thought you were so much better than me. I was never good. Perhaps that was really why I became a nurse, to prove myself your equal.'

'Maybe it wasn't goodness. Maybe it was just a way of filling in the time. Or of avoiding being close to anyone in particular.'

'Maybe. But you set my life on a different course, Ash, whether you meant to or not. And I think — I think you came here to ask me whether I could still love you. And the honest answer is that I don't know. I truly don't. The only thing I do know, is that, even if I could, then it won't be the same as before.'

She saw him bow his head, accepting her words. Then he said, 'Even now, looking back, I can't tell you when I began to love you. Whether, even, we were in London or in Sheffield. Maybe it was the first time I saw you cycling down the hill. I simply don't know. So perhaps I'm not so clever, after all. But all I really wanted to say was that, whatever I've done, however it may appear, I do love you, Iris, and I know that I always will.'

There, she thought, *I haven't wept with joy or grief. See, it doesn't hurt at all.* But she realized that her hands were clenched into fists and, when she opened them, there they were, four treacherous red half-moons, dug into each palm.

'I had another reason for wanting to see you,' he said. 'I don't have many people to write to — or to write to me. No parents, brothers, sisters, cousins. Most of my friends have joined up. And I imagine that if I'm sent to France or wherever, that might seem rather . . . *bleak*. So I wanted to ask you whether, as my dearest friend, I could write to you, Iris?'

Only a moment's indecision and then she knew what she would say. Because he might not come back. Because her beautiful, strong, generous Ash might end up like one of the broken men she nursed on the ward. And she would mind that.

'Of course you can,' she said.

15

Marianne hid the money Mr da Silva had given her for the sale of her engagement ring behind a loose skirting board in her bedroom, tucked into a tobacco tin in case of insects or mice. Walking past Mr Salter's bungalow on a Sunday, she remarked on Ama's boredom, Ama's loneliness, Ama's love of pretty things. When she noticed new bangles on Ama's wrists and ankles, bangles that Ama took off before Lucas came back to the bungalow, she felt a flare of triumph.

Each day she walked for miles, round the perimeter of the garden or through the dusty red paths of the estate. She must grow strong, she told herself, so that the walk to the bazaar town did not tire her, and so that she could undertake a long journey. She stole whatever might be useful to her — a palm-leaf basket, a flask, a knife, a book of matches — taking them without a flicker of guilt, hiding them and keeping silent if a servant was blamed for their disappearance. She studied maps and railway timetables and unearthed old books from Blackwater's small library. A book on home nursing, so that she would know how to care for George when she was the sole person responsible for his survival, and a small pamphlet that one of Lucas's forebears, she guessed, must have brought with him to Blackwater, which told the reader how to light a fire, and how to recognize which snakes were deadly and which were harmless. She read them intently, learning them by heart.

She kept these things from Lucas, of course, but every now and then she caught him watching her, suspicion in his eyes. Once, as she passed him on the veranda, he grabbed at her hand and said, 'You look pleased with yourself, my dear wife. Like a cat with cream.' His thumb dug deep into her palm, but she did not let herself cry out. 'What do you plan? What do you plot?' he murmured. 'Whatever it is, it won't do, you know — you won't beat *me*.'

They went for a picnic in the hills with the Rawlinsons. A rutted track led into a mahogany grove. Wild bees hummed not far above and, in a clearing, a thousand white butterflies floated like petals over the grass, drawn on the breeze. The meadow rose to a headland that jutted out over the valley. Marianne looked down to where the green and silver handkerchieves of paddy field and lake were spread out on the valley far below. 'Don't they say that a young girl killed herself here, long ago?' asked Mrs Rawlinson, striding over the grass to the precipice. 'Threw herself over the cliff. For love, or something ridiculous.' The distant hills echoed in a ghostly reply.

That evening Marianne was in the summerhouse at the edge of the Blackwater garden, standing by the balcony watching the sunset, when she heard footsteps. She turned and saw Lucas. 'Such a view,' he said softly, coming to stand behind her. 'My grandfather chose this place to build his house because of the view. On a clear day, you can see the sea.'

She felt his outstretched fingers press against her back. 'It's a long way down, though.'

Rays of sun, vermilion and gold, flared across the folding hills. His fingertips were small pinpoints, charged as if with electricity. A slight increase in pressure; she swayed and, far below, the valley floor seemed to shiver.

'Such a touching story that Mrs Rawlinson told us this afternoon,' he murmured. 'Dying for love. Didn't you think so?'

She swung round. 'What will you do?' she hissed. 'Will you kill me, Lucas?'

'So histrionic. There's no need for that. I only thought to warn you.'

'To warn me?'

'To be careful. To be very, very careful. And to be obedient.'

'And if I'm not?'

'I'm sure you will be. After all, there's rather a lot at stake. And besides, you're obedient by nature, aren't you, Marianne? That's why I chose you. Because I knew you wouldn't cause me too much trouble.'

His hand slipped from her; he walked away. He was leaving the hut when she said harshly, 'What fools you men are. How simple you are.'

He paused, looked back at her. 'What do you mean?'

'To judge so on appearances. To mistake a lack of physical strength for a lack of every other strength.' She crossed the hut to him. 'Do you think that I'm weak, Lucas? I've lost the only man I'll ever love. I've forsaken my family and travelled halfway round the world. And I've given birth to a child. I've survived all that and you think that I'm weak?' She shook her head slowly. 'No, you're wrong. It's *you* who are weak.'

He gave a short laugh. 'Me?'

'You believe that love is a weakness — '

'So it is — '

'Yet you love George. I see it in your eyes, Lucas. In your own strange, twisted way, you love him. You might hurt him, but you still love him. You love him, but you can't bear to admit it. You don't know yourself. That's weakness.'

'What nonsense you talk, Marianne.' Yet she saw a flicker of uncertainty in his eyes. 'Love doesn't come into it.'

'I told you before, we're a match for each other. You married me for my money and I married you because I wanted a child. So I've got what I wanted.'

His mouth curled in a sneer. 'Oh, you're a hard,

deceitful bitch, I don't doubt it. All women are. I learned that a long time ago.'

'If I've become hard and deceitful, then it's you who has made me so.' Her hands were clenched into fists as she said softly, 'Understand this, Lucas, that I'll do anything to protect George. That I'll lie for him and I'll steal for him. And I would kill for him.'

He began to walk back up the path to the garden. Suddenly, he turned and said, 'And so would I, Marianne.' He gave a peal of laughter. 'So would I.'

Then he walked away, leaving her standing in the summer-house, dry-mouthed. His threat had been unambiguous. A memory came back to her, of Mrs Rawlinson in the Blackwater garden, saying, *There's a pattern in the Melrose family. Lucas's father, George, was an only child, like Lucas himself. His mother died young, from a fever . . . So George was brought up by his father, just as Lucas was.* If she should die, she thought, with a stab of terror. If she should die, and George should be left alone with Lucas . . .

★ ★ ★

The first person Eva knew who died in the war was Mrs Bradwell's grandson. Mrs Bradwell was Summerleigh's cook; Eva remembered Norman, who had been just a few years younger than herself, coming to the kitchen when he was a little boy. He had freckles and a snub nose, she recalled, and Mrs Bradwell had scolded him for scraping out the pudding basin with his fingers. Now Norman Bradwell was dead, killed at the second battle of Ypres in April 1915, just two days short of his nineteenth birthday. Afterwards, Eva thought it was as though a little piece of Mrs Bradwell had been rubbed out, leaving her faded and subdued.

The stalemate on the Western Front had shaken the country's complacent assumption of British military superiority. The losses in battle were followed by a series of other shocks in May — the formation of a coalition government, in which the new Ministry of Munitions was headed by Lloyd George, the sinking of the liner *Lusitania* by the German navy with the loss of 1,200 lives, and the bombing of London by Zeppelin airships. A cousin of Mrs Catherwood's was drowned when the *Lusitania* sank; an old schoolfriend of Lydia's, a regular soldier whom Eva had danced with once or twice at parties in Lydia's flat, died of dysentery at Gallipoli. Each day she dreaded to look at the newspaper. She caught herself glancing quickly at the headlines, praying that a day might pass without some new horror. She could feel the war coming closer. There was the constant fear that next time it might touch her, might touch the people she most loved.

That spring she had gone back to Summerleigh. The morning she left her London flat, she took a last look round the rooms. Her belongings had already been packed up and sent to Summerleigh, but she saw how the sunlight washed over the walls she had painted, and how the rays gleamed on the floor she had so painstakingly polished, and she felt a deep sense of loss.

At first going home was every bit as bad as she had feared. Countless times she found herself regretting her decision to leave London and return to Sheffield. She still found her mother infuriating — Mother's voluntary work, organizing first aid and home-nursing classes, now dominated Summerleigh just as Mother's illness had once done. Mealtimes were rearranged and rooms stripped of furniture so that Dr Hazeldene could lecture to the ladies of Mother's set, or Mother could instruct them in the bandaging of broken limbs or the care of a fevered patient. In the evenings Eva and Clemency knitted balaclavas and mufflers for the troops. Eva noticed that Mother did not knit, but spent her time writing letters and drawing up schedules.

Yet as the war continued, there was a gradual but noticeable relaxation of the restrictions that Eva had always found so irritating. So many young women were joining voluntary organizations to help the war effort that chaperonage was hardly practicable. It was becoming more acceptable for a well-brought-up young unmarried woman to travel alone. Nor were young women necessarily expected to be content with tennis parties and bridge afternoons. Instead they were encouraged to work as VADs in hospitals or to join the Women's Volunteer Reserve or the Women's Legion.

Clemency had become a member of the Women's Volunteer Reserve. Mother had looked vaguely at Clemency one morning, as if she had just remembered her existence, and had said, 'Clemency, don't you think you should *do* something?' And from that moment, thought Eva, Clemency had been free. These days they saw less of her. Clemency had paid her two pounds for her khaki WVR uniform and had learnt first aid and how to drill and march. Because she could drive, she had been asked to act as a chauffeur for a Mrs Coles, who ran the local branch of the WVR and had been a militant suffragette before the war. Clemency drove Mrs Coles to meetings and to fund-raising events in Sheffield and further afield. As well as being an officer in the WVR, Mrs Coles was also a member of the committee of the National Relief Fund, which tried to relieve the distress brought about by rapidly rising food prices by dispensing food and assistance to the hard up. So Clemency made cakes and biscuits for fund-raising teas and scoured Summerleigh's attics for unwanted items to sell at jumble sales.

The war had also brought changes to Sheffield's traditional industries. Many skilled men had enlisted, leaving large gaps in the workforce. A city battalion made up of volunteers from the university and from the professional classes left Sheffield for training camp in

May. So many carthorses had been requisitioned to work at the Front that one manufacturer now employed a circus elephant to haul its loads of castings through the city streets.

Because the saws, files and agricultural machine parts that J. Maclise & Sons manufactured were in even greater demand in wartime, the business had to increase its output. Returning home, Eva had marshalled her arguments before announcing to her father her intention to work for the family firm: the loss of skilled men to the Front, James's absence, Father's own ill health. But the anticipated battle was a hollow echo of what it once would have been. With surprising ease, Joshua gave way. To begin with, he insisted Eva work from home, deciphering his scrawled notes into typed-out letters, but quite soon he grudgingly acknowledged her usefulness and agreed to let her work in the office. At first there was a great deal of staring and whispering, but the passing of time made her less of an object of interest. And after all, though she might be a woman, she was also a Maclise.

In James's absence, Mr Foley had taken over Aidan's work, freeing up Aidan to run the new site in Corporation Street, while Eva managed her father's office in Mr Foley's place. Rob Foley showed her round the melting shops, forging shops, grinding shops, wood-handle-turning shops, packing shops and warehouses. He explained her father's filing methods, unchanged since the days of her grandfather. Eva filed and typed letters, wrote up receipts and payments in the books, arranged appointments with wholesalers and exporters, and chased up late payments and consignments of coal and steel that had gone astray. She dealt with salesmen and buyers, answered the telephone and kept her father supplied with tea and coffee.

Sometimes her head reeled. It was all so different from working for a publisher or art gallery. The noise,

473

the mud and smoke and coal dust assaulted the senses. Yet she soon found herself taking pleasure in her work. She loved to see the boxes of finished files and saws wrapped in waxed paper in the packaging rooms, and she loved to run alone through the industrial districts of Sheffield with messages or papers for Aidan. She noticed that the employees liked and respected her father, but feared Aidan, and that Aidan ran the Corporation Street workshops as his own private fiefdom. She noticed also, with a sinking heart, that Joshua no longer had the heart to stand up to his younger son. When Aidan sacked half a dozen men because he said they weren't pulling their weight — men who were old or chronically sick after years of exposure to lead baths or noxious fumes — Joshua's protests lacked conviction, as though he expected defeat. When Aidan changed working practices to make savings, cutting long-established perks, Joshua only said morosely, 'It's all James's fault. Letting me down like that. How can I be expected to manage without James?'

Some spark had gone out of Joshua, and it chilled Eva to see that he no longer had the drive to fight for the business he loved. His illness and the unresolved rift with James had taken the spring from his step. He lacked energy and spirit; for the first time, he had begun to look like an old man. Entering his office, Eva would sometimes catch sight of him staring into the distance, desolation in his eyes.

She tried to coax him into making his peace with James. 'James misses you, Father,' she said one day. 'I know he does.'

Joshua made a contemptuous sound. 'If he missed me, he'd write to me, wouldn't he? And I haven't had as much as a word. Writes to all the rest of you, doesn't he, but not to *me*.'

'If you'd only say sorry . . . '

'Why should I say sorry? It's he who deceived us all.

He who pulled the wool over our eyes for three and a half years! *Three and a half years!* I wouldn't have thought him capable of a trick like that! What sort of a son is he, to keep something like that from his father?'

'The only reason James didn't tell you was because he was afraid you'd be angry.'

He muttered, 'Damned right I am.'

'If you'd only meet Emily and Violet, Father, I know you'd love them.'

'Never! And I won't have their names mentioned in this house, do you hear me?'

Provoked by his intransigence, Eva cried out, 'I can't see why you are being so unreasonable! James only married someone! What's wrong with that?'

Joshua shouted back, 'He married his mistress, that's what's wrong with it! The folly of it, the utter folly!'

'But Father — '

'I've said my piece, my girl, and I won't hear another word about it! That's enough, do you hear?' He had gone purple-faced; Eva let the subject drop.

James's battalion was sent out to France in the middle of the year; Eva went to see him on his last leave. They went for a walk on the path beside the river. Violet ran ahead, Emily hurrying to keep up with her. Watching them, James smiled. Eva said, 'If you'd just write a little note to Father. Just a few words before you go.'

'No.' The smile disappeared. 'I can't.'

'But to leave England with a quarrel unresolved . . . '

'I might not ever be able to put it right? Is that what you were going to say, Eva?' He looked grim. 'Don't think I haven't thought about that. I have. But what can I do? I might wish I'd done things differently, but I can't regret anything. Emily's the best thing that ever happened to me.' His face lightened. He said softly, 'The first time I saw her, she was sitting in the row in front of me at the theatre, a few seats along. I couldn't stop looking at her. Hadn't a clue what was going on on stage.' He swung round to her. 'Can you imagine what it is to feel like that? That nothing else in the world matters except this one thing, this one person?'

She could not answer. These days she tried not to think about Gabriel. When she was busy at work she managed well enough. But even now, in moments of quietness, he would seep into her mind.

Brightly painted barges drifted by; on the prow of one, a black and white dog stood, barking. She asked James, 'Are you afraid?'

'Of going to France? No.' Violet had thrown her ball into the undergrowth beside the towpath; James broke off an elder switch and cut a swathe through the nettles to retrieve it for her. When he came back to Eva, he said, lowering his voice, 'I'm only afraid for them. Emily thinks she may be expecting another child. She had a bad time with Violet. I worry for her. You will keep an eye on them, won't you, Eva?'

'Of course I will.' She squeezed his hand.

'Perhaps the war will be over before the baby's born.' He looked wistful. 'Perhaps it'll be a boy this time. I'd love to have a son.'

★   ★   ★

'It was so lovely, wasn't it,' said Clemency to Iris, 'to find out that we had a sister-in-law and a niece. And Violet's so *sweet*.'

Iris nodded absently. They were in Gorringe's; Clemency had driven Mrs Coles to a meeting in London that morning. It was Iris's day off so they had arranged to meet for tea.

Clemency said, 'When you think that there's seven of us . . . and until we knew about James only one of us was married, and we had only one nephew whom none of us has ever seen. I sometimes think that we're a

476

rather barren lot, aren't we? I wonder why that is.'

'Because we're all horrified by the possibility of having seven children, perhaps?' suggested Iris flippantly. She looked down at her plate. 'Do you want my ham, Clem? I'm not as hungry as I thought I was.'

'Please.' They swapped plates. Clemency opened a case of little black cigarettes. 'Would you like one?'

'I didn't know you smoked.'

'It's a bad habit that a friend of mine taught me. But really — ' she frowned — 'Ellen Hutchinson has just had her third daughter. And Louie Palmer has married — and she'd only known her husband for six weeks, Iris. And yet, when you look at us — '

'Three spinsters?' Realizing that Clemency was serious, she said, 'You'll marry, I know you will. And you'll have dozens of children.'

Clemency shook her head. 'I won't ever marry.'

'Mother's better now. You don't have to sacrifice the rest of your life for her.'

'It isn't Mother. It's me. I know marriage wouldn't suit me.'

It occurred to Iris that they had always tended to notice what Clemency wasn't — that she wasn't pretty, or clever, or especially talented — when they should have noticed what she was. It had been Clemency who had kept the family together. Without Clemency's practicality and warmth there wouldn't have been much of a home to come to. Clemency had a strength and integrity that the rest of them, perhaps, lacked.

She said, 'You can't know that.'

'I can. I couldn't even have married Ivor and he was the sweetest man.'

Iris stared at her. 'Ivor?'

'He was a friend of mine. I suppose you could say that he was my lover.'

'Your *lover*?'

Clemency looked at Iris coolly. 'Men can love girls

477

who aren't pretty, Iris. And girls who aren't pretty can love.'

'I'm sorry. I didn't mean — '

'Yes, you did. I can see that you did. But it wasn't just a crush.'

Iris managed to gather her thoughts. 'What was he like?'

'Oh . . . he was very handsome and talented and kind. I adored him.'

'Do you still see him?' Clemency shook her head. 'What happened?'

'I realized he didn't care for me as much as I cared for him. And when he kissed me, he was so rough and bristly. And it just felt — oh, as though it didn't fit. Like putting on a dress that was much too small for you. It didn't *suit* me. I didn't like it.' She made an expression of distaste. 'And you have to, don't you, if you're going to have children?'

'I don't believe all women enjoy that side of marriage.'

'They should do, though, I think. Remember Marianne and Arthur, how they touched each other all the time. Marriage should be like that. I don't think you should marry someone if you'd really rather not touch them. So,' she said sadly, 'no babies for me. And I do so love babies.'

They parted shortly afterwards, Clemency to drive Mrs Coles back to Sheffield, Iris to wander round Selfridge's before meeting Ash at Victoria Station.

But the bales of silks and satins, and even the glories of the millinery department, did not give her as much pleasure as they usually did. There was an uncomfortable niggling thought in her head that she could not push to the back of her mind, no matter how hard she tried to distract herself with laces and pearl buttons, ribbons and silk flowers. Clemency's words echoed: *We're rather a barren lot, aren't we?* And she herself, thought Iris, was the most barren of them all. Marianne had married twice and had had a child. Eva had had a lover — a lover who had undoubtedly broken her heart, but a lover all the same. Even Clemency had loved. Only she had kept herself apart, untouched, avoiding the messiness and complexities of sharing her heart with someone else. She could not blame Ash solely for what had happened. Looking back, she saw that she had kept him at arms' length for years; she suspected that in doing so she had driven him into Thelma's embrace. She had not managed to make the leap of trust to tell him that she loved him until it was too late. She was twenty-nine years old and unless she overcame the hard, mistrustful part of herself that constantly warned her of the risks of love, she saw how she might end up. Walking between day hats made of felt and evening hats made of taffeta, she had a sudden horrible vision of herself, in ten or twenty years' time, an ageing beauty, still expecting men's admiration as her due, flirtatious and flippant even then because those were her defences.

She looked at her watch and saw that it was time to meet Ash. On the tube train she realized how frightened she felt. That was the root of it, of course: she, who had always secretly prided herself on her fearlessness, her lack of squeamishness, was held back by her fear of loving and losing.

That fear haunted her as she waited by the ticket barrier. Lost in the crowds, surrounded by billowing smoke and the hiss of steam, she was still unsure what she should say to him. She found herself taking a penny from her purse and tossing it into the air — *heads I'll love him, tails I'll wait till I'm sure* — but the train disgorged its passengers just then, and she fumbled the catch and the coin was lost in the armies of rushing feet.

Then she saw him, walking down the platform towards her. A warm smile and a kiss on the cheek and he said, 'So good of you to come, Iris,' and she heard herself make some light, non-committal response.

They ran down the steps to the underground station. The platform was crowded with jostling masses of office workers and khaki-clad soldiers. There was the distant rumble of a train, and she found herself suddenly terrified that if she did not find the words now she might never find them, and that they might remain, loving each other yet distant from each other, forever.

Then she realized that she did not need to find the words. Sometimes words separated, kept you apart. There was a rush of air as the train drew into the station; she felt Ash start to move forward. She put her hand on his arm, staying him. 'Iris?' he said. Standing on tiptoes, she kissed him. Hesitantly at first, but then, when she saw the light in his eyes and felt herself crushed in his embrace, and heard him whisper her name in a sort of groan, she threw caution to the wind at last and she closed her eyes, kissing him over and over again, as the crowds divided in a stream around them.

★　★　★

It was a question of gritting her teeth and waiting. Waiting for the right time. Waiting for certain things to coincide.

Lucas was teaching George to ride. He sat the little boy on the pony and led him up and down the path. George clutched the reins, his eyes wide with fear. When the pony, irritated by an insect, bridled, George began to cry. When, at his next lesson, George became hysterical, Lucas shut him in his room to punish him for his cowardice. Listening to George's howls of fear turn to sobs of despair, Marianne knew that she could wait no longer.

A few days later there was the full-moon festival. Work on the estate stopped. The Saami, the Tamil god, was taken from the temple and, mounted on a painted wooden peacock, paraded through the bazaar town. Drums pounded from the coolie lines, a monotonous throbbing that seemed to make the earth vibrate. The Blackwater garden was particularly beautiful that day, the air crystal clear, every leaf and petal sharply delineated. Beside the tiny shrine in the trees white ribbons fluttered. Did they, Marianne thought, mourn a death or did they predict one?

In the morning she played with George in the garden and then, when Ama took him from her for his lunch, she sat beneath the banyan tree. Though her book was open and though every now and then she turned a page, she did not read, but watched and listened. She saw, as Ama seemed not to, that Lucas's head was bad that day, knew it from the way he winced at the light and moved carefully, as if reluctant to disturb the pain that beat inside his skull. She saw that Ama was angry and resentful, that she was short-tempered with Lucas and imperious with the servants. Soon her alternate wheedling and sulking aggravated Lucas and he shook her roughly, saying, 'For God's sake, woman, will you stop your complaints! And that *noise*! If only they'd stop that damnable noise!'

Ama ran into the bungalow, her small feet pattering on the floor. Lucas drank steadily through the lunch hour, eating little. After tiffin he went back to the veranda. Smoke from his cigar curled in the still air. The wooden floor of the veranda seemed to shiver to the beat of the drumming. In the garden Ama moved disconsolately from one patch of shade to another, pausing every now and then to admire the rings on her fingers and the sleek fall of her long black hair.

Ten minutes later, Marianne left the veranda on the pretext of fetching a length of embroidery silk. In her bedroom, from the back of her drawer, she took out the sleeping drops Dr Scott had prescribed for her. She hid the small phial in the sleeve of her blouse. In the vestibule she stopped Nadeshan, coming from the kitchen quarters with a bottle of arrack and a glass on a tray. She took the tray from him. 'I'll take Master his drink. You may go to the festival, Nadeshan. And please tell the rest of the staff they are free to go out for the afternoon.'

Alone in the vestibule she poured out a measure of arrack, and then she slid the phial out of her sleeve, unstoppering it and, with shaking hands, emptying it into the glass. *If he sees me, then he will kill me*, she thought. Then she hid the empty phial and carried the tray onto the veranda.

She put the tray beside Lucas and sat down a short distance away from him. She picked up her embroidery and made herself sew. She must not watch him, she must do nothing out of the ordinary. She must not look up at him because then he would read the rage and rebellion in her eyes. The needle threaded in and out of the linen. A French knot here, a flower petal there. How much had he drunk? Enough, surely. How long would he sleep? For hours, perhaps.

There was the creak of the wicker rocking chair and the scent of cigar smoke. And it was some time, surely, since she had heard the clink of his glass. She looked up.

Lucas's eyes were closed. The empty glass was beside the chair. The butt of his cigar smouldered in the ashtray. She said his name, but he did not wake.

Slipping out of the bungalow by a side door, she ran down the path to Mr Salter's house. Mr Salter was sitting on his veranda, a glass in his hand. 'Poor Ama,' said Marianne. 'She wants to go to the bazaar but has no one to take her.'

He said, 'Mr Melrose — '

'Mr Melrose has a headache. He's asleep. I expect he'll sleep all through the afternoon.'

She ran back to the bungalow. In her bedroom she pulled down the blinds, drew the curtains and spread out on the bed a large silk shawl. Onto it, she placed George's clothes, her money and the odds and ends she had stolen. Then her brush, her comb, a change of linen and her photograph of Arthur.

She went to the kitchen. Pushing open the door, excuses hovered on her tongue. *I need a flask of weak tea for the baby . . . the Peria would like a few biscuits and some fruit . . .* But the kitchens were empty, the servants gone to the festival, and she was able to gather what she needed unimpeded.

Back in her room, she put the flask and the food with the rest of her belongings and tied up the bundle. There was a sound from behind her; she looked round and saw Lucas.

'You bitch,' he said. 'You little bitch.' He came a few paces into the room. Frozen with terror, Marianne registered the unsteadiness of his movements and the way his large frame swayed as he moved towards her. His eyes, flickering from her to the bundle on the bed, were glazed, the pupils black pinpoints in his pale irises.

Movement returned; she tried to run for the door. But he grabbed her, his fingers digging into her flesh. 'Leave me alone, would you? *Again?* I knew you were planning something, you bitch.' With a swift, hard sweep of his arm, he threw the bundle of food and clothing to the floor. 'I told you I wouldn't let you take him from me. *Never.* I'll see you dead, first.'

Then his hands were gripping her round the neck, his thumbs pressing against her windpipe. She could hear the sound of her own breath, rasping, panicking. There was a roaring in her ears, a darkness in the air. Blindly, she struck at his head with her fists. The impact on his throbbing skull must have shocked him because he gasped and the grip round her neck slackened. She twisted out of his grasp and he stumbled, losing his balance. As she gulped for air, one hand to her throat, the other clutching the bed for support, he fell, striking his head on the brass fire surround. Closing her eyes, retching, she leaned against the bed, fighting for consciousness. When she was able to look again, she saw that Lucas was attempting to struggle to his feet. His eyes were fixed on her, enveloping her in their agonized, enraged glare. She grabbed the first thing that came to hand — her sewing scissors — and struck at him.

After a while she realized that he wasn't moving any more. He was sprawled in the fireplace, his face down, his arms flung out over the hearth tiles. A dark stain spread slowly across his pale hair.

She whispered, 'Lucas?', but he did not move, did not speak. Her own limbs juddered.

Mechanically she began to pick up her things from the floor. She kept looking back at Lucas, half-expecting him to gather himself up and rise from the floor, her accuser, her nemesis. Yet he did not move.

Looking up, she saw Rani, in the doorway. Rani's wide dark eyes focused on Lucas. 'Master dead?' whispered Rani.

'I don't know, Rani.' Her voice was hoarse.

'Lady must go. Lady must go *now*.'

And she saw that she must. But her hands were shaking wildly, too much to tie the bundle. Rani took it from her and knotted it.

Lady must go. Lady must go now. As she closed the bedroom door, she seemed to be closing herself off from horror and madness. In the nursery she woke and dressed George. Rani came back, carrying a length of blue cloth.

'Lady must wear this.'

A sari. 'Yes,' she whispered. 'Of course.'

Rani helped her dress. Beads from the bazaar for her arms, and her dark hair parted in the centre and pushed behind her ears. Her head covered with a cloth, her feet bare.

'See, Dorasanie,' said Rani.

Marianne looked in the mirror. She saw dark blue eyes in a paper-white face. The red marks of his fingers on her throat.

A twitch of the cloth to shadow her features and then the old Marianne was gone, changed forever. Now, in the mirror, there was instead another woman, from another country.

She gathered up her child and her bundle. As she hurried away from Blackwater, she seemed to hear the sound of his footsteps, the whisper of his voice, pursuing her, but she did not look back.

★   ★   ★

James was in northern France on his way to the Front when the bombardment began. There was an initial thrill of excitement that now, at last, something was about to happen after days of marching over dusty white roads through sullen little French villages, and then, as the noise continued, for hours, for days, louder and louder as they neared the front line, it seemed to thread through him, making his head ache, setting his teeth on edge.

In the shelter of a haybarn, he wrote to Emily.

The condensed milk and candles you sent me are much appreciated. I was almost out. And the cake you and Violet made is such a treat. Tell Violet she's almost as good a cook as her mother. Some more cigarettes would come in handy next time you can manage it, darling, and some toffees, perhaps. The nights are cold here now, my love. Is it cold in London? You must make sure you wrap up well when you go out. Use the money I've left in the drawer if you need to buy yourself or Violet a new coat or gloves. You mustn't worry about money or stint yourself. I treasure the lucky charm you gave me. I keep it next to my heart.

And, in an action that had become habitual, he patted the pocket that contained the silver four-leafed clover that Emily had given him as a parting gift.

He often thought it ironic that he, who had once longed for adventure and the chance of heroism, should find himself here, now. Once he had railed at mundanity, but now all he wanted was the ordinariness of domestic life. He would have happily exchanged hardship and adventure for an afternoon in the park with Violet, or for a night holding Emily in his arms as she slept. All he wanted was to survive. He needed to live, for Emily and Violet and the unborn child.

When he had finished his letter, he went to stand in the doorway of the barn while he smoked a cigarette. He saw that there was a glow of light on the horizon, orange against the black of the night.

Waking in the morning, leaving the barn, he glimpsed, high against a brilliant blue sky, an aeroplane. Puffs of white smoke flowered round it and then dispersed. But the plane remained untouched and James watched it for a moment before rousing his men.

The evidence of battle accumulated as they marched that day. They passed the wreckage of carts and motorbikes, abandoned at the side of the road, and a horse, its belly ripped open, dead in a ditch. Soon they saw the walking wounded, cradling injured arms or holding field dressings to their heads as they made for a first-aid post. To begin with there was a trickle of wounded men and then, quite soon, the trickle became a river. Then twilight fell and James saw more brightly the coloured flashes of light that illuminated the flat land ahead. The men no longer talked or sang; there was only the squelch of boots in mud, the jangle of buckles and webbing, and the roar of the guns, deafening now.

As they neared the village of Loos, shell holes pocked the ground, slowing their pace. Every now and then shells flew overhead and they flopped onto the ground to save themselves. After a while their greatcoats were heavy with mud and the flaps banged against their legs, making it hard to walk. Over the hill, some way away, a thick cloud of grey smoke rolled just above the ground like a fog bank.

They saw the outline of the ruined village, lit up by shellfire, the jagged walls of the roofless houses like so many broken teeth and the shattered spire of a church jutting out from the rubble. Roofbeams and telegraph poles were scattered like matchwood, and James glimpsed signs that told him that people had once lived in this hellish place: a battered saucepan, a hen coop spewing straw, a stoppered wine bottle lying in the mud.

One of the men lit a cigarette and there was a sound like the whine of a wasp as a bullet buried itself in a nearby wall. As they dived for cover, there was another zzzz, and someone cried out. They sent the wounded man away from the village in search of first aid, and then James and his sergeant picked off the sniper, who was perched in the upper storey of the ruins of an estaminet. James didn't know whether it was his shot or his sergeant's that struck the sniper, but it gave his stomach a curious twist to see the man fall. It was an odd thing, he thought afterwards, not to know whether you had, for the first time in your life, killed a man.

They spent the night in a muddy trench at the bottom of the hill. They had been given orders to go over the top at dawn. Waking from a restless, intermittent dozing, James felt his guts twist with anticipation and he muttered a prayer. In the two-hundred yard dash to the German lines the first fifty yards or so were masked by the smoke bombs they had thrown. Then there was the rat-tat-tat of machine-gun fire and to begin with James thought that his men, frightened by the gunfire, had thrown themselves into the mud for cover. When he reached the German lines he discovered that the barbed-wire entanglements that surrounded the trenches had not, as he had been led to expect, been flattened by the British artillery. He was running along the lines of barbed wire, looking for a gap, when something stung his shoulder and he fell to the ground.

He found himself in a shell hole with his corporal, a short, squat man called Browning. When he looked back to the British lines, he saw that his men were not in a funk, as he had believed, but had been mown down by the machine-gun fire. He noticed other things, too. A bit of rag and bone to one side of the shell hole that he realized after a while were the remains of a man. A boy pinioned on the barbed wire, his outstretched arms in an attitude of crucifixion, his fair hair falling over his face. A man kneeling, as if he were praying, except that he lacked a head.

He and Browning didn't quite fit in the shell hole. Though they curled up against each other so that their heads and bodies were below the level of the ground, their legs remained outside the hole. Bullets rained in the mud. James heard Browning gasp when a bullet struck him in the thigh. When another line of British soldiers advanced with fixed bayonets, the machine guns felled them as soon as they left their trenches.

After a while the guns fell silent as the British admitted defeat, abandoning the attack. In the aching quiet that followed James saw men emerge from holes in the stricken landscape, mud-covered, grey-brown men who seemed to be made of mud. Slowly, the wounded crawled back to the British lines. His shoulder blades pricking, James hauled Corporal Browning back to the

British trenches through the two hundred yards of no-man's-land, but the German soldiers did not fire once.

★ ★ ★

The newspaper reports of the battle of Loos shifted from early assurances of glorious victory to a more sombre recounting of events. The columns listing the names of the dead ran down the front of *The Times* like a black scar.

Eva had acquired a host of superstitions. She shrank from single magpies, from walking under ladders and from wearing pearls and opals. Every knock at the door made her jump, her nerves taut. She hated to be at home, where the family's fears seemed to accumulate. She preferred to be at work, her head bent over her desk, typing letters, adding up columns of figures. At home she found herself going to the window over and over again. If she caught sight of the telegram boy coming down the street, her stomach squeezed and she looked away, holding her breath, until she guessed that it was safe to look again. As though, she thought, if she didn't look at *it*, then *it* might not notice her, and James would be all right.

There was an accident in the grinding shed towards the end of one Thursday afternoon. One of the girls, hurrying to finish her work so that she could go home, caught her hand in the belt of a grinding wheel. Joshua was in London, so Eva arranged for a cab to take the injured girl to hospital and saw her off the premises.

She managed to get back to the office before she fainted. A stifling heat swept over her, making her pull at the collar of her blouse, and she saw a greenish mist. The next thing she knew, someone was shaking her and saying her name. Opening her eyes, she saw Rob Foley. There was a knock at the door and one of the girls who

489

worked in the packing shed came in, a glass in her hand, and gave it to Rob.

'Here,' he said. 'Drink this.' He held it to Eva's lips.

It was brandy. Harsh and cheap, from the nearest pub, she guessed, but the dizziness lessened and she was able to sit up and say, 'I'm sorry. So silly of me, to faint.'

'I'll send for a cab to take you home.'

'No.' She pressed her knuckles against her eyes, trying to stem the tears at source. She said, 'How is she? The girl who was hurt.'

'She'll survive.'

'Her hand — '

'She's likely to lose a couple of fingers.'

'Oh — '

'They'll patch her up. You mustn't worry. She'll be looked after. And now you must let me call you a cab.'

'Please, Mr Foley,' she whispered, 'I don't want to go home. Not yet.'

'Rob,' he said roughly. 'For heaven's sake, won't you call me Rob?'

She sniffed. 'If you'll stop calling me *Miss* Eva. So Victorian.'

He helped her sit down on a chair. She found her handkerchief and blew her nose. She said, 'You seem to have a habit of coming to my rescue.'

He looked embarrassed. 'Won't you finish this?' He offered her the glass again.

'I hate brandy. You have it.'

'I don't drink.'

'Not at all?'

He shook his head. 'My father,' he explained. 'I know what drink can do.'

'I don't suppose you smoke?'

He took a cigarette case from his pocket, lit two and passed one to her. She puffed on it for a while, and then she said, 'I truly don't want to go home. I prefer to be here. It stops me worrying.'

490

'About your brother?'

She bit her lip. 'Except that I worry about James all the time.'

'If you haven't heard anything yet — '

She hissed, 'I don't dare think that! I'm afraid that if I allow myself to believe that he's all right, then something awful will happen!' Then the passion drained from her and she felt limp with exhaustion. 'Ridiculous, isn't it? Just superstition. As if anything I think or do can make any difference to James now.'

'My sister, Susan, holds seances. She believes that she speaks to the dead. Mothers who've lost their sons at the Front consult her. At least you haven't resorted to the rattle of the ouija board.'

'I can understand why people do, though, can't you? Even though it's such nonsense. I can't seem to take my mind off it when I'm at home. Nothing works.'

'What about your painting?'

'I haven't painted for years.'

'Why not?'

She shrugged. 'Because I found out that I wasn't good enough.'

'That's not true,' he said. 'That drawing you did of me, do you remember?'

'When you were so cross with me for going into the furnace room?'

'I kept it.'

'It was just a silly little sketch.'

'*I* liked it. Theresa, my sister, liked it too. She said you'd caught me exactly.'

'Oh, *likenesses*,' she said scornfully. 'Anyone can do likenesses.'

'I assure you, Eva, that if I tried to draw your likeness you'd probably end up resembling a turnip or a beetle.'

She smiled. 'Haven't you an artistic side?'

'I love music, but I can't play. I can lose myself in a picture, but I can't draw. And sometimes, when there's something I want to say, I can't find the words.' A short silence: she heard the workmen and women calling goodbyes to each other as they left the factory. 'But of course you can draw. And you shouldn't just abandon a talent like that. Who on earth told you that you weren't good enough?'

'Someone,' she said softly. 'Someone I knew well.'

'Perhaps they were wrong.'

'I don't think so. No, I'm sure he was right. I knew it myself, really. If I hadn't known, here, in my heart, I wouldn't have believed him, would I? No, I'm quite certain about that. If nothing much else, these days.'

He looked at her questioningly. 'No?'

'I used to think I knew everything. I knew I had to go to art school and I knew that I was going to be a great artist. And I knew that I wanted to live by myself and never, ever be tied to anyone else. And yet — ' she looked around the office — 'here I am. I never thought I'd end up here. I wish I was like you, Rob. So unwavering.'

'Unwavering? Or dull?'

'No. Not dull at all,' she said, and she glimpsed a spark in his eyes before he looked away from her.

'You used to think I was dull.'

'Only when I was a silly, ignorant little girl. Now I'm a mature woman I know better.'

He grinned. He said suddenly, 'Would it help take your mind off things to meet my family?'

'I'd be delighted to, but — '

'I go home on a Friday night. You could come to tea tomorrow. I'd see you back to Sheffield, of course.' A sudden frown. 'How stupid of me. You must have other arrangements, of course.'

She shook her head. 'No. I don't. I don't have any other arrangements at all. I'd love to come, Rob.'

★ ★ ★

If he was afraid, then it was not like any fear he had experienced before, thought James, not like that sinking feeling you had before taking an exam, and not like the dread he had felt, trying to pluck up the courage to tell Father about Emily. Most of the time, he just felt hungry and tired. Whenever he was not required to do something, he curled up and fell asleep in a minute or two. There never seemed to be enough food; he had finished the contents of the last parcel Emily had sent him, sharing it with his men, who, like himself, were hungry. After all the food had gone he found himself dreaming of Christmas dinners and picnics and suppers at the Savoy.

Whenever he had the chance, he wrote to Emily. He had never been much of a letter writer, but writing to Emily was much like talking to her and came easily. Often, he thought through the years he had known her. The day they had met, their courtship, the first time he had made love to her. When she told him she was expecting his child, she had cried because she had thought he would abandon her. Instead he had asked her to marry him. On their wedding day he had bought her a posy of white heather from a gypsy in the street. Afterwards he had taken her to the Twickenham house and had carried her over the threshold. She had been as light as a feather. Later, making love to her, he had run the palm of his hand over the small swell of her belly and had thought about the child, *his* child.

He knew, though, that he was no longer the man that Emily had married. Sometimes he thought that his letters were just another form of deception, much like the deception he had practised for years when he had hidden Emily and Violet from his family. Two days ago it had begun to rain and the guns had fallen silent at last. He still seemed to hear them in his head, a long echo, not quite drowned out by the sound of the rain. Sometimes he wondered whether they would ever really die away. Whenever he closed his eyes he saw, like a series of snapshots, images from the battle. Bodies and pieces of bodies. Bodies of horses and bodies of men. Men he had once known, men with whom he had once joked and laughed, whose heads had been shot away or whose limbs were now rotting in the mud. Could he ever go back to the person he had once been? In his heart, he knew that he could not. In dreams, in quiet moments, he would be haunted by what he had seen. He seemed to feel the taint of it clinging to him, more deeply ingrained than the mud of the trenches.

After he had finished writing the letter, he had to take out a wiring party to check the barbed wire around the trenches. It was a dark, murky night, the moon hidden by rain clouds and he was just a second too late in noticing the German patrol. There was a very bright light, and he thought for a split second that the bombardment had begun again because he seemed to hear the guns boom very loud. He tried to reach up his hand to touch his pocket where he kept his photograph of Emily and the silver clover leaf, but his arm would not obey him. His limbs felt suddenly cold and he could not see. He felt a surge of anger and longing for the life he would not have and a terrible loneliness, knowing that he would never see his wife and child again. And then something seemed to explode in his head and he felt himself falling, a long fall that seemed to have no end.

★　★　★

Joshua felt that he had been dying a little each day, ever since Katharine had told him that she no longer wanted to see him.

It had been in the October of 1914. An acquaintance they had in common, an ironfounder, had asked her to marry him and she had accepted, she told him. 'Do you love him?' he had shouted and she had answered quietly, 'He's a wealthy man, Joshua. He's a widower and is therefore free to marry. And I have two daughters whom I must, in these dreadful times, find husbands for.'

Two days later James had told him about his wife and child. Looking back, Joshua could see now that his fury had sprung from a variety of sources — from his pain at losing Katharine and from envy that James had been free to marry the woman he loved when he himself had not. From a consciousness that James's deceit seemed to echo his own, stirring his guilt, a guilt which, as was his way, he expressed as anger. And from a great hurt that James had not trusted him, his father, had not loved him enough to share his secret.

But anger was a combustible, dangerous emotion, fast-spreading and quick to catch fire. The shock had made him say some harsh, foolish things and James, enraged, had answered in kind. Then there had been another, even more awful shock, when he had realized the implications of the accusations that James had flung at him. *How you think you have the right to criticize me — you hypocrite, you, who've betrayed my mother for years.* Looking into his eldest son's hostile eyes, Joshua had realized that James knew. The discovery had stunned him, had made him bluster and shout. Put on the defensive, Joshua had tried to justify himself — it was one thing for a man to take a mistress, he had cried out pompously, quite another for him to marry her. But the contempt in James's eyes had only deepened.

Afterwards, after James had gone away, his anger had burned for weeks. How dare the boy accuse him of hypocrisy when he himself had behaved in such a shabby, underhand way? Why could he not see that in taking his light o' love — *a milliner's assistant*, for God's sake, a fortune hunter, surely, little better than a whore — for his wife, he had brought shame on the entire family? Why could he not see that he had, in one fatal step, ruined all Joshua's and his father's work and dragged the Maclises back into the gutter?

They had come from nothing, the Maclises, Joshua thought bitterly and, when he was gone, they'd like as not return to nothing. His children were a disappointment and a burden to him. No one could say that Clemency was a beauty, though Joshua himself had always thought her fetching, but his other daughters were, each in quite different ways, beautiful. And yet what had happened to them? Poor Marianne had lost her husband and then, heedless of her family's protests, had shackled herself to that snake-eyed fellow whom Joshua hadn't trusted one bit. She was always in his mind, a nagging anxiety. Not one of his other three daughters had married, or had even become engaged. When he thought of Iris and Eva, such lovely girls, wasting away their youth, exasperation mingled with the anger.

Then there were his sons. James was a liar and a fool and Philip was a weakling. For Aidan, Joshua felt a mixture of pity and distaste. He recognized Aidan's iron will, his intelligence, his snobbery, his intransigence, his love of money. He knew what Aidan would do, given the chance, to the business that Joshua and his father had spent their lives building up. After the quarrel with James, Joshua had found himself lacking the will to oppose Aidan, recognizing how power was slipping away from him. Aidan had youth and strength and he now had neither.

As for Lilian, when he looked at her he felt a sort of weariness, a resigned recognition of her limitations. Though he knew it to be wrong to compare Lilian to Katharine, he could not help remembering that Katharine had always been generous, kind, and concerned for him. She had noticed when he was tired or worried, had sensed when he had had a difficult day at work. Such things never intruded into Lilian's world, a world which was bounded only by herself.

And oh, Katharine, Katharine . . . She was always in his mind. He had not expected love so late in his life. Now his longing for her consumed him. He missed the nearness of her, the warmth of her, the sight of her.

His strongest emotions these days were regret and disillusion. As the battle of Loos raged and the truth about the conduct of the war began to leak out, he learned that the country he loved had been responsible for sending men with bayonets to fight against men with machine-guns, and for ordering the use of chlorine gas, gas which blew back in the faces of its own men. He knew — every iron-master knew — that the troops were not properly armed, that they were short of weapons and short of bullets. They were even short of food. They had rushed into a war for which they were not prepared, a war whose outcome politicians and generals had viewed with both complacency and a lack of urgency.

But his greatest disillusionment was with himself. For his pride and his lack of forgiveness. When, scanning the columns in the newspaper, he had realized that James's regiment was fighting in the battle of Loos, all his anger and resentment had in an instant been replaced by fear. He wrote to James that night, a stumbling, awkward letter because he had never been good at expressing himself on paper. He watched, as they all watched, for the telegram boy. He prayed that, if God was good and let James come home, he himself would live long enough to see him. He knew that his heart was failing. More and more often he felt its treacherous skip and dance and the deep, dark pain flooding through his chest and arm.

He was about to leave for work one morning when there was a knock at the door. Even before Edith opened it, he *knew*. The rest of them had gathered in the corridor at the sound of the door knocker: Eva,

Clemency, Aidan, Lilian. Joshua saw the fear in their faces, their hesitation and dread, and then he strode down the corridor and took the telegram from the boy himself.

★   ★   ★

Breathless and grey-complexioned, Joshua stumbled around the house, Aidan thought, like a great, wounded bull. There would be a memorial service for James, he announced, to which James's wife and child would be invited. The two of them would, of course, stay at Summerleigh. Mother protested; Joshua, paling, hissed, 'They'll stay here, I tell you! And you will welcome them! They're all that's left of him!'

Father insisted that Aidan travel to London to escort Emily and Violet to Sheffield. As far as Aidan could tell through the black mesh of her veil, Emily was pretty enough in a cheap way. When she spoke, which was only occasionally and in a soft, tremulous voice, it made him cringe to hear her miss her aitches or say 'somefink' for 'something'. He noticed that whenever she made a mistake, she quickly corrected herself.

Sitting with Emily and the child in the first-class railway carriage, Aidan distracted himself by going over in his mind his plans for the business. James had gone. Father was unwell and would surely soon retire. And then he himself would have a free hand at last. For a start, he would get rid of the dead wood — the sick, the old, the idle. Father's failing had always been his sentimentality — going through the books, Aidan had discovered a list of old workers Father had pensioned off to save them from going into the workhouse. Then there was the yearly celebration for Grandfather Maclise's birthday, when the foundries and workshops were awash with beer and hardly a stroke of work was done. And Eva had recently come up with some

498

nonsense about installing washbasins and a drinking-water tap for the women — with so many men absent because of the war they'd had to take on more female workers. A ridiculous waste of money; they could manage with the outside tap as they always had. These were all small measures, but they added up, ate into the profits. Then, in time, he'd float the business on the stock market. Father should have done so years ago; it would allow them to expand and diversify. The war had brought unlimited opportunities for engineering companies like J. Maclise & Sons; the war would allow them to make their fortunes.

Eventually, his mind wandered and he found himself thinking about Dorothy Hutchinson. Dorothy was the youngest of the five Hutchinson sisters. She was a pretty girl, dark-haired and dark-eyed and spirited, though not to the point of pertness. Aidan had danced with her at balls and suppers and had played tennis with her. Soon, he decided, he might ask her to marry him. The Hutchinsons were one of the best families in Sheffield; Aidan had often noticed that the Hutchinsons did things that little bit better than the Maclises — their house was more luxuriantly furnished, the family was more ordered, more aware of the importance of appearance. Even now, at social events, the Hutchinsons seemed to manage a white-gloved manservant or two, whereas the Maclises had to settle for slapdash Ruby, or Edith, forever complaining of her bad legs. Marrying Dorothy Hutchinson would be a step up the ladder of status and wealth that Aidan intended to climb. Father would approve of an alliance with the Hutchinsons; Aidan would please Father at last by making the prestigious marriage that James had so signally failed to do.

In the end, though, Joshua survived his eldest son by only six weeks. Two days after the memorial service Joshua's overburdened heart failed. He died at the works, collapsing into the coal dust and puddles of the courtyard, surrounded by the battering of hammers and the smoke from the furnaces. When they told him of his father's death, Aidan felt a dreadful chasm open up inside him. An emptiness, which he suspected might never be filled. It was as if some great, indestructible god had been felled.

He had them bring back his father's body to Summerleigh on a bier of black velvet, the horses plumed and caparisoned in black. The workers lined up in silence at the gates to pay their respects as the bier left the factory. The men doffed their caps and the women wept.

Another funeral. When, shortly afterwards, Mr Hancock, the family solicitor, read the will, Aidan discovered that Father had not, as he had believed, disinherited James. Instead, after James's death, Father had altered his will, leaving half to Aidan and putting half in trust for James's son (if Emily's child should prove to be a boy), the child's portion to be managed until he was of age by, of all people, Eva. Father had also left Emily an allowance, to care for James's children.

Aidan comforted himself by telling himself that the child would, like as not, be another girl. Yet the hurt remained, a deep, wounding sore, and for it he could find no solace. Father had not trusted him. Even after death Father's disapproval endured.

And when, the following month, the telegram arrived telling them of the birth of James's baby son, Aidan had to go to his room and fling himself on his bed, clawing at the coverlet in a paroxysm of rage and disappointment. Then, realizing how ridiculously he was behaving, he rose and washed and shaved and dressed in his best clothes. Black coat, black hat, black tie and muffler, for Father and James. He would go into town, he decided, and have a drink and a smoke in one of the better hotel saloon bars.

In the centre of town, he caught sight of Dorothy Hutchinson standing outside John Walsh's. He crossed the road to her. He had expected greetings, condolences, sympathy. But she said only, 'What, not in khaki yet, Aidan?' and pressed something into his hand. And when, after she had walked away, he opened it, he saw lying in his palm a white feather.

16

After James and Father died it seemed to Clemency that the spirit had gone out of the family. The Maclises had shrunk, had become duller, quieter, almost colourless. Every night in bed, recalling how James had taught her to drive or how Father had taken her to Ivor's concerts, she cried, weeping silently, her heart seeming to constrict, tears seeping from her eyes.

In the spring of 1916 the government introduced conscription. Posters were pasted up in the city streets reminding all unmarried men of military age that they were now required to enlist and join the Colours. In the Easter holidays, Philip told Clemency that he had decided to join up straight away and not wait until he had completed his school year. When Clemency protested, he said with a rueful smile, 'Did you think I would run away? I always used to, didn't I, but I won't this time.'

She burst out, 'But Phil, you'll *hate* it!'

'Oh, it'll be loathsome, I daresay. And it'll feel wrong all the time, I know it will. But Clem, so many Old Boys have been killed or wounded already. The headmaster reads out their names at morning prayers. Why should I be different? Why should I be spared? I know I won't be any good as a soldier. I've always been hopeless at OTC — I can't march in line, and I can never remember how to put my rifle together. But I'll do my best. You do understand, don't you?'

But the army medical board turned Philip down on health grounds. He still suffered from asthma and his short sight had worsened over the years. Clemency was immensely relieved, but she could see that, though Philip was relieved, too, he had also suffered yet another rejection. 'I wanted to be useful,' he told her. He sounded bewildered. 'All that nerving myself up to do the honourable thing and then they didn't want me after all.'

Then Eva had an inspiration. She wrote to a friend of hers, Sadie Bellamy, who lived on a farm in Wiltshire. Sadie wrote back by return of post, saying that she would be delighted for Philip to stay with her and help with the farm. Philip had always loved animals and the fresh air would be good for his asthma. Clemency and Eva saw him off on the train. Clemency watched until the white dot of Philip's handkerchief, waving from the open window, was lost in the curve of the track. *Another one gone*, she thought. Now, there were only three of them left. Not so long ago there had been ten. And there it was again, that tightening of the heart.

She and Eva lived for letters, snatching them from the postman's hand as soon as he knocked at the door. Letters from Philip at Greenstones, full of stories about the Bellamy children and the farm. Letters from Aidan, in an army training camp in the north of England. Letters from Iris, now nursing at a military hospital in Etaples in northern France.

But no letters from Marianne. Every day they rifled quickly through the envelopes the postman had delivered, searching for one addressed in Marianne's handwriting. Every day they were disappointed. They heard nothing at all, even after they wrote to tell Marianne of James's and Father's deaths, which took away their last hope that Marianne's lack of communication was due to anything less than some terrible change in her circumstances. Though they rarely spoke of it to each other, Clemency knew that they all now feared for Marianne's safety. One evening Eva wrote to the governor of Ceylon, asking for his help in finding out what had happened to Marianne. Clemency stood at Eva's shoulder, watching her write the letter. Losing Father and James had left them grey, cold and empty. But to lose a sister, she thought, would be to lose a part of herself.

They had all forgotten what it was to hear good news. There was none from the Front, where horror was increasingly heaped on horror. In January tens of thousands of Allied troops, largely from Australia and New Zealand, were evacuated from the Gallipoli peninsula, where they had been fighting since the spring of the previous year with huge loss of life. That defeat was followed, in May, by the naval battle of Jutland. For as long as Clemency could remember she had been brought up to believe the British navy was invincible: Britannia ruled the waves, it was an indisputable fact. Yet the Royal Navy's losses were far greater than those of the German Grand Fleet.

Then, at the beginning of June, Lord Kitchener, who had created the New Army of volunteers, which was even now being sent out to France, drowned when his ship was sunk by a mine. Clemency was shopping in Sheffield when she read the headlines on the newspaper billboards. There was a silence on the streets; in the eyes of passers-by she read her own numbness and incredulity.

Towards the end of June the British opened up an artillery bombardment on the Somme. The bombardment, which was intended to destroy the German defences, was so vast, so overwhelming, that the vibrations from the great guns could be felt in London. On the first day of July one hundred and twenty thousand men were sent into battle. To begin with the newspaper headlines were jubilant. Then the news of the casualties began to come through. Whole battalions, many made up of Kitchener's volunteers, had been obliterated. At the outset of the war British towns and cities had proudly raised their own Pals' battalions of local men; now, after the slaughter on the Somme, those

504

same towns and cities were plunged into mourning.

The Sheffield city battalion had been formed shortly after the outbreak of war. Ordered to capture the village of Serre, the battalion had found itself advancing into a hail of machine-gun fire. The dead were Sheffield men, who had worked in the city's foundries and factories and academic institutions. Some were from families Clemency had known for as long as she could remember. Oswald Hutchinson was dead; Alfred Palmer was missing. Ronnie Catherwood had suffered severe wounds when a rifle grenade had exploded beside him; the doctor had told his mother that he was unlikely to recover his sight.

Clemency went to visit Ronnie in the London hospital where they brought him as soon as he was well enough to be shipped home from France. A white bandage covered half his head; his right arm had been amputated just below the elbow. Sitting beside the quiet, pale figure in the bed, Clemency remembered how, years ago, when she was younger, there had been a party at Summerleigh and she had sneaked downstairs and peeked round the door and had seen Ronnie waltzing with Iris, a look of ecstasy in his eyes.

After that, she visited Ronnie once a fortnight. One day, travelling to London, Clemency had the compartment to herself until they reached Northampton station, when a young woman opened the door.

'Are these seats free?'

Clemency explained that they were, and the young woman came into the compartment. She was wearing a black dress and a black hat and veil. After she had sat down, she said to Clemency, 'I say, do you mind if I take my hat off?'

'Not at all.'

She began to extract hat pins. 'I always feel imprisoned by hats, don't you? Especially when it's so hot and one has to wear a veil.'

She took off the hat. Her thick, shining dark hair was coiled at the nape of her neck. Her slanting eyes were a light hazel brown and her complexion was a rich cream. Clemency thought she was one of the most beautiful girls she had ever seen.

The girl held out her hand to Clemency. 'My name's Ottilie Maitland.'

Clemency introduced herself. Then, '*Ottilie*,' she said. 'How lovely.'

'I'm rather fond of it. And Clemency's so pretty, too.' Ottilie put her head to one side, looking at Clemency, considering. 'Yes. It suits you. Would you like a cup of tea?' She took a Thermos flask out of her bag. 'Michael used to take a Thermos and a packet of ginger snaps whenever he travelled by train, and I caught the habit from him. He always said it saved queueing up for the dining car.'

'Michael?'

'He was my husband. He died of pneumonia in France four months ago. He was a captain in the Guards.'

Clemency offered her condolences. 'How long were you married?'

'Two years. I have a baby, a little boy, who's eight months old. Who are you in mourning for, Clemency?'

'My father, and my brother, James.' She said suddenly, 'I worry about my family all the time. I can't seem to escape from it,' and then she felt suddenly embarrassed. 'I'm so sorry — '

But Ottilie said, 'Do have a ginger snap,' and offered a packet of biscuits to Clemency. 'I live on biscuits and tins these days. It hardly seems worthwhile cooking just for oneself, does it? I suppose when the baby is older we can have nice little suppers for two, but at the moment he only eats bread and milk and stewed fruit.' Then she looked at Clemency thoughtfully and said, 'If you need to escape, you could always come and visit me.'

Clemency couldn't help but stare at her. Ottilie gave a throaty laugh and said, 'My nanny always tells me off for being too forward. But I always know whether I'm going to like someone as soon as I meet them, and I know that I'm going to like you, Clemency. So why prevaricate? And you'll adore my house, I know you will. Everyone does. It's rather falling apart, but that doesn't matter, does it? And I should love you to meet my little boy. One needs friends in these awful times, and Archie and I do rattle about rather.'

★　★　★

Ottilie lived in Leicestershire, in a small manor house set in a remote countryside of gently undulating woods and meadows. The house was a nest of crooked-walled rooms and twisting, turning stairs and corridors that had a way of spitting you out in an unexpected place. The furniture was of old, carved oak, beeswax-polished for centuries and upholstered with worn velvets or mildewed damasks. There were ghosts at Hadfield, of course, Ottilie flung casually over her shoulder to Clemency as she ran down a flight of dark, narrow stairs. 'But I always think ghosts are like spiders — they won't disturb you if you don't disturb them. And I think that, like spiders, they keep the place tidy, somehow.'

Outside, there were overgrown shrubberies and parterres. 'The only bits of garden that are *kempt*, you might say,' said Ottilie, 'are the vegetable patch and the soft-fruit cages. I'm planning to plant lots and lots of potatoes this autumn. And then, if the Germans sink all our ships, at least Archie and I won't starve.' Archie was Ottilie's plump, energetic baby son. Ottilie kissed him and looked fierce. 'And if this wretched war isn't over by the time Archie is a man, then I shall hide him away in an attic. I've quite made up my mind. The army shan't have him.'

507

The house was, as Ottilie had told Clemency, in a state of disrepair. Storms dislodged tiles from the roofs, and doors and windows wedged themselves into their frames, never to be opened again. Ottilie's only servant was a very old woman called Mrs Forbes, who had once been Ottilie's nanny, and who now helped care for Archie. Ottilie and Mrs Forbes existed in a state of largely affectionate warfare, with Mrs Forbes insisting that Archie be kept to a rigid routine and Ottilie utterly careless of bedtimes and the sinfulness of eating between meals. The servants who had staffed the house when Ottilie and Michael had first married had all been rather old, Ottilie explained, and had since died or retired and gone to live with their children. Somehow Ottilie had never got round to replacing them. Fiercely practical by nature, she patched up the worst of the decay herself, gardened with fanatical devotion, and cooked and cleaned when the mood took her. When rats nested in the compost heap, Ottilie shot them, leaning out of an upper window. She was a good shot and the courtyard was soon littered with little brown corpses.

Their friendship deepened as summer drifted into autumn. Quite often Clemency stayed the night at Hadfield, sleeping in a high four-poster bed, hung with faded crewel-work hunting scenes. In the day, she helped with Archie and the garden and got on with any tasks that needed doing in the house, climbing into the cold, dark attics to fix a roof tile, or clearing leaves from the gutters. Though Hadfield itself, with its lonely, dilapidated, fairytale beauty, was both an escape and a pleasure to visit, Clemency knew that she would have gone back time and again had Ottilie lived in a semi or even a slum terrace. It was Ottilie herself who drew Clemency to Hadfield. She thought that Ottilie was like an onion — not a very flattering or poetic comparison, but she couldn't think of a better one to describe the layers of fascination and magic that she seemed constantly to discover. Back at Summerleigh, or driving Mrs Coles to a meeting, Clemency would picture Ottilie, wearing her husband's old riding breeches and tweed jacket as she dug her garden, or sitting in the kitchen after she had had a bath, her damp hair spread out like a dark veil over her shoulders. And Clemency would feel a thrill of longing and joy that sometimes reminded her of how she had once felt about Ivor, though it lacked the insecurity and deference which, she now saw, had always been a part of her love for Ivor.

She noticed that Ottilie rarely spoke of her husband, Michael. The wound of Michael's death must still be too raw, she concluded, too painful. There was a photograph of Michael Maitland on the drawing-room mantelpiece. In spite of his army uniform, he was boyish in appearance, his round dark eyes like ebony buttons, his smile hesitant, eager to please.

Visiting Hadfield one afternoon, Clemency found Ottilie in the kitchen, kneeling on the floor in front of the stove. 'The wretched thing refuses to light,' she said crossly. 'I've gone through an entire box of matches.'

Clemency offered to try while Ottilie went to see to Archie, who had a cold. The stove was clogged up with soot, so Clemency spent an enjoyable couple of hours cleaning out ash pans and adjusting draughts. By the time the stove was lit, Clemency was covered in soot and had to boil up pans of water so that she could take a bath.

Afterwards, she sat in the kitchen, wrapped up in Ottilie's dressing gown, while Ottilie made cheese on toast. Then Ottilie said, 'It's Michael's birthday today. He would have been thirty-one, poor darling. We always used to climb the big oak tree in the garden on his birthday. We'd take up a bottle of claret and a couple of glasses and drink it up in the branches. Absolutely mad and tricky to find your way down when you were plastered, but rather fun. Of course, when we were little we took lemonade instead of claret, but it was still great fun.'

'You knew each other when you were little?'

'We were cousins. Distant cousins. We had the same grandmother. I'd known Michael for years by the time we got engaged. He was six years older than me and I'd always admired him tremendously. He was so tall and clever and handsome.'

'You must miss him dreadfully.'

'In some ways. Not in others.' She was making cocoa; she poured boiling milk into mugs. 'We should never have married. There, you're the first person I've admitted that to. There isn't anyone else I *can* admit it to. And I don't mean to shock you, Clemency, but it's the truth.'

'Didn't you love him?'

'I loved him very much. But as a friend or a sort of brother. Not as a husband.' She dashed brandy into the mugs and put one beside Clemency. 'Michael was very sweet and kind and we were great friends. When we were engaged he used to kiss me sometimes, at the end of an evening, and I hated it. I thought it would be different when we were married, that marriage would change the way I felt, but it didn't. When he kissed me I used to close my eyes and pretend I wasn't there. I tried not to show it, but I know that he knew. And I think that he felt the same. It must have been worse for him, I often think. Men are expected to take responsibility for that side of marriage, aren't they?' She frowned. 'Do tell me to pack it in if you don't want to hear all this, won't you? I'd quite understand.'

Clemency said, 'I don't mind at all.'

'More cocoa, then?'

'Please.'

'And a ciggie. I must have a ciggie.' Ottilie offered Clemency a cigarette. 'On our wedding night, neither of us had a clue what to do, so in the end we just hugged each other and went to sleep. But Michael thought that wasn't right, so he went to see a chap in Harley Street, who put him on the right track. And after that we just about managed to be properly married at last. And then, when we knew that little Archie was on his way, we stopped sharing a bedroom. And it was better then. Though we weren't *happy*. We knew we weren't like other couples, you see, and I think that made us . . . uneasy. Ashamed, almost.' She sighed. 'I think that Michael preferred the company of men. He didn't have any sisters and he went to a boys' school, of course, and then, after university, he joined the army. So I don't think he ever had the chance to get used to women. When I think back, I wonder whether he liked me because I was always rather a tomboy. We had lots of things in common — we both loved motor cars and hunting and sailing. And, of course, he had to marry because of Hadfield. My little Archie's the last of the Maitlands.'

'Why did you marry him, Ottilie?'

Ottilie smiled rather sadly. 'Not for the right reasons, I'm afraid. My friends were all getting married and I didn't want to be left out. And it started to worry me that I never met anyone I wanted to marry. I often think that Michael and I married each other because we each thought the other was the best of a bad lot. And because, if we got married, we wouldn't have to keep pretending we might be able to find someone else.'

Clemency said, 'Do you think you'll ever marry again?'

'Oh no. I've learnt my lesson.' Ottilie plunged the milk pan and dirty plates into the sink. 'I knew very early on in my marriage that I'd made a terrible mistake. I hated not having my own room. I hated Michael being in my bed. It felt . . . disgusting.'

Clemency thought of her tussle with Ivor on his sitting-room sofa, of her bewilderment — if *that* was marriage, then why on earth did people bother?

She heard Ottilie say, 'Let me comb out your hair for you,' and she closed her eyes, warm and blissful, as Ottilie stood behind her and combed.

Ottilie said, 'The only thing I regret is that I always knew, deep down, that it wasn't right. Do you remember me telling you that first day we met that I always know what I feel about people straight away?'

'Of course I do.'

'I knew I didn't really love Michael, yet I didn't listen to myself. After he died I promised myself I'd never make that mistake again. It wasn't fair to me and it certainly wasn't fair to Michael.'

The comb paused. Suddenly fearful, Clemency reached up and clasped Ottilie's hand. 'Do you ever change your mind? About liking people, I mean.'

'Never. I'll never change my mind about you, my darling Clemency. I love you. I've known *that* for ages.' And Ottilie stooped and kissed the top of Clemency's head.

★   ★   ★

Since the beginning of the year Iris had been nursing in a British military hospital in Etaples, near the coast of northern France. Towards the end of June they were ordered to clear out the convalescents from the beds and to ready the wards for a new influx of casualties. Over the next few days an air of apprehension hung over the hospital. Then the first wounded men began to arrive from the Somme, convoyed by train. The casualties covered the floor of the admittance wards in a mass of muddy khaki. They were wrapped in brown blankets, their broken limbs bound to splints or their heads smothered in bloodied bandages. A quick flick of her eyes round the room, to check that *he* wasn't one of them, and then Iris followed the same procedures over and over again. Take off the muddied, bloody clothing, peel back the bandage that had been applied at the casualty clearing station, wash the wound and cover it with a sterilized dressing and bandage, all the while murmuring words of comfort. Take temperatures and pulses, send the VAD for bedpans and water. The patients were quickly sorted into groups: those to be taken for X-ray, those for immediate surgery, those in danger of haemorrhaging. When all the beds were full, Iris had to direct the orderlies to move the less seriously wounded onto the floor to make room for the new convoys of critically injured.

In the autumn, during a lull in the fighting, she received a note from Ash, telling her that he was on army business in nearby Le Touquet, but would be free the following day. Matron granted her a long-overdue day's leave. Meeting Ash the following morning, seeing him for the first time, Iris found herself wanting to run her hands over his limbs, as if to check they were still whole. Reading her mind, he grinned and said, 'All in one piece. I've always been a lucky devil.'

'Stay lucky, Ash.'

He kissed her. 'What shall we do? I thought perhaps a walk along the beach.'

They followed the coastline to Paris-Plage. A breeze ruffled the grass on the sand dunes and filled the sails of the fishing-boats out to sea. There was the salt smell of the waves and his arm around her as he said, 'I've often wished I was a bit faster off the mark. Just think, if we'd married when you asked me, years ago, after your party — '

'I didn't *quite* ask you to marry me.'

'Near as makes no difference.' He peered at her. 'You're blushing.'

'Nonsense. It's just a healthy glow from the sea air.'

'Anyway, if we'd married then, we could have had half a dozen children by now.'

'Not *half a dozen* — '

'It would have been perfectly feasible. Three sets of twins.'

'Good Lord . . . We'd need an enormous house.'

'I have an enormous house.'

She remembered that Ash had inherited his guardian's Cambridgeshire home. 'Of course you do.'

He said, 'If we get through this — '

'*Ash*. We shouldn't make plans. You know it's bad luck.'

'I'm afraid I have been making plans. I bought you this.' He took something from his pocket. When she opened the small box she saw that inside there was a ring, an old-fashioned design of pearls and tiny rubies. 'I found it in Le Touquet,' he said. 'If you don't like it, I'll buy you something more splendid when we're next in London.'

There was a lump in her throat, but she managed to say, 'I love it. It's beautiful.'

'I'm damn well going to do this properly this time,' he said and knelt down in the sand. The surf licked at his ankles and she had to clamp her hands over her mouth to stop herself giggling.

Then he said, 'Will you marry me, Iris?' and suddenly she didn't want to laugh at all.

She whispered, 'Of course I will.'

★　★　★

He took her to lunch in Le Touquet. Over a bottle of champagne and shellfish served over bowls of ice, they had a long, rambling conversation about anything except the war. Their wedding, where they would live, what they would do. He said, 'I've been thinking of opening a school. Emlyn's house would make a marvellous school. The trouble with the law is that you end up trying to clear up the messes people have made

514

of their lives. Better to get in at the beginning, when you can still make a difference.' He threaded his fingers through Iris's. 'If you don't mind a houseful of children, that is. You might prefer a bit of peace and quiet after all this.'

'I might.' She lifted his hand to her lips and kissed it. 'Dear Ash. Still trying to change the world. How do you manage to keep the faith?'

'Sometimes I don't,' he said.

She caught the expression in his eyes. 'You've had an awful time, haven't you?'

'Pretty rotten.' He refilled her glass. 'But I can't imagine that you've been sitting around twiddling your thumbs. So let's not talk about it. Let's have a day off from the war.' He smiled. 'Tell me about your family. I'm marrying you for your family, of course, Iris. I always wanted a large family.'

'You'll make up the numbers a bit. It seems so odd that there's only six of us now.' She paused. 'Or five, perhaps.'

He was prising something out of a shell; he looked up at her. 'Five?'

She told him about Marianne. 'I truly think that something dreadful has happened to her, Ash.' She added bluntly, 'Actually, I believe that she's dead. I haven't said that to Eva because I know it would only make her cross, but I've thought so for some time. She wouldn't have just forgotten us, I know she wouldn't. Something awful has happened to her, I know it.'

'But her husband . . . and the child . . . '

'I never trusted Lucas Melrose. You couldn't *like* him, Ash. He was very handsome and clever and rich, I suppose, but I couldn't make myself like him. And Eva felt the same.' Iris sighed. 'Eva has written to the governor of Ceylon. But we haven't heard anything yet and there have been so many ships sunk in the

Mediterranean we've no idea whether her letters have got through.'

He squeezed her hand. 'You shouldn't give up. Until you know for certain, there's always hope.'

She managed to smile.

He said, 'Here, have this,' and she said dubiously, 'It looks like a snail.'

'I believe it *is* a snail.'

'You have it.'

'Better than army rations. How's Eva?'

'She writes me terribly dull letters about orders from the Ministry and rates for piecework. And different sorts of steel and things going wrong with machinery. Half the time I haven't a clue what she's talking about. It's so strange, to think of *Eva* running Father's factory.' She said sadly, 'Poor Eva. She misses Father so much. We all do, of course, but I think that Eva misses him most of all.'

He poured the last of the champagne into her glass. 'Now, drink up,' he said. 'I'm going to take you dancing.'

⋆ ⋆ ⋆

Ash had a friend, David Richardson, who owned a portable gramophone. On the part of the beach between the dunes and the sea, where the glistening, impacted sand was studded with pink and yellow shells, they danced. Lieutenant Richardson had brought two records, a song from *Hullo, Ragtime!* and the waltz from *Gaiety Girl*. Iris danced with each man alternately. There was the sound of the gulls and the hiss of the waves and the soft warmth of the autumn sun. She forgot the war, shutting it out of her mind as she danced.

She was dancing with Lieutenant Richardson when she caught sight of Ash, sitting hunched in the lee of the dunes, staring out to sea. He took her hand when she came to sit beside him. He said, 'I wonder if it would have been better not to have seen this. I wonder if it would have been easier.' Above the sound of the waves and the whisper of the breeze in the marram grass she had to strain to hear his voice. 'When I'm there, in the trenches, I tell myself that that is all there is. That there's nothing else. Then you don't waste time longing for what you can't have. Such unimaginable ugliness. As far as you can see there's just mud and craters. Perhaps there might be a telegraph pole or a tree stump sticking out of the mud. Or a cross to mark where a man has died. And then there's all the *rubbish* that the war makes — the shell cases and spades and kitbags and rusty old tins and wrappings from chocolate or cigarettes. But the only living things are us and the rats and the lice. Nothing else is alive, nothing at all.'

He danced with her one last time. The music was almost lost as the wind got up and the sky darkened. She thought: *Whatever happens, I will always remember this. I will always remember my head pressed into the hollow of his shoulder and his arms around me and his cheek against mine. And the water lapping over my feet as the tide comes in and he kisses me.*

She whispered, 'Stay lucky, Ash. Promise me you'll look after yourself. Promise me.'

★   ★   ★

There was a phrase they used rather a lot: *I'll just have to get on with it.*

Getting on with it meant anything from making stews out of cat meat to going back to work the day after you had received the letter telling you that your son had died. Because there was no body to bury, no funeral to arrange.

Getting on with it meant, for Eva, dragging herself

out of bed in the early morning seven days a week, when every tired bone in her body pleaded with her to be allowed to sleep another hour, so that she could be in her office at Maclise's before the workforce arrived, just as Father had always been. It meant staying at the works until late in the evening to finish an order for the Ministry of Munitions when her head ached and the rows of figures danced in front of her eyes. It meant gritting her teeth when, after Ruby, the housemaid, left Summerleigh to work in a munitions factory and only the increasingly frail and elderly Edith and Mrs Bradwell were left to run the house, Mother complained of the food and the cold.

As the German submarine blockade bit in early 1917, sinking huge tonnages of merchant shipping, there began to be a real risk that the country might starve. They were exhorted to eat less bread because of the severe shortage of grain. Parks and playing fields were dug up and planted with vegetables; King George V announced that he would replace the roses and geraniums in the royal parks with potatoes and cabbages. Clemency had dug up Summerleigh's borders and, in any spare moment, Eva weeded the seedlings she had planted. Then, in February, Clemency joined the newly formed Women's Land Army and was sent to work on a farm near Market Harborough.

Though food at Summerleigh was dull, plain and limited, Eva knew they were fortunate. Tales drifted to them from impoverished rural areas and from the worst slums, of infants starving to death from malnutrition. Slum children, hollow-faced and clothed in rags, gathered outside the city's factories, begging leftovers from the employees' packed lunches.

Eva knew that she was fortunate in other ways, too. Though they had lost both James and Father, James's wife and children remained well, supported by the allowance Father had bequeathed them in his will.

Aidan had come through the bloodbath of the Somme and was now relatively safe, stationed at a military headquarters some way from the Front. And Philip was happy at Greenstones. *I couldn't manage without him,* wrote Sadie. *He's a treasure — so hard-working, so marvellously patient with the children, and he never, ever complains.*

So many of their friends and acquaintances were suffering far, far more. Fathers, husbands and sons had died in battle or of pneumonia or dysentery. Or had survived, permanently maimed, like Ronnie Catherwood, or with their nerves shot to pieces so that the least sound — the turn of a page, the wind in the trees — made them shake with terror. There were men working at Maclise's who had lost two, three, even four sons. There were young women working at Maclise's who had lost their father, their husband and their brothers. There were women who, receiving the telegram or letter telling them that their husband or son was missing, continued to hope, a hope that shrunk as the months and years passed and there was no word, until they were forced at last to accept that their loved one was dead, his body unclaimed, his final resting place never to be known.

Eva worried constantly about Marianne. So dreadful, not to know. Walking home from work, or stooped in the garden, picking slugs from the cabbage seedlings, she would puzzle over the mystery of Marianne's silence. Perhaps, as Iris had suggested, the marriage had broken down and Marianne had left Lucas. But if so, why did she not write? Surely she could not believe that her sisters would judge her — her sisters, who had, by and large, made such a hash of love themselves? Or perhaps Marianne had simply cut and run. Perhaps, discovering that she had chosen the wrong life, she had taken her son and made a new start somewhere else.

What Eva could not believe, refused point-blank to

believe, was that Marianne was dead and they would never see her again. She knew that Iris thought so. It made her angry that Iris should just give up on Marianne. It seemed to Eva — a superstition that she never voiced because she knew it to be irrational — that Marianne needed their belief.

At the factory, as at home, she *got on* with it. War had changed Maclise's, too. They now manufactured bayonets and tin helmets as well as edge tools. It made her smile sometimes to wonder what Father would have thought of the rows of overalled women in the workshops, women who now successfully carried out complex engineering tasks that once only men had been thought capable of. It made her smile, too, to buy her tram ticket from a woman conductress or, visiting a friend in hospital, to see women doctors working on the wards. Women were changing, just as the Maclise sisters themselves had changed. As some of the old restrictions and frustrations were stripped away, women displayed talents and qualities never allowed to shine before. All this Eva had hoped for, fought for. She felt a quiet pleasure, but not triumph, knowing the price they had paid and were still paying.

★   ★   ★

Someone gently ruffled her hair; Eva woke up. She had fallen asleep over a sheaf of invoices; she felt them pressed against her cheek.

Rob Foley said, 'You should go home. It's probably more comfortable than sleeping in the office.'

'Just about.' Eva rubbed her eyes. 'Though Mother tells me off if I fall asleep in the drawing room — she says she has little enough company without her daughter dozing through the evening. And it's so cold at home — we never seem to have enough coal to heat such a big house. I have thought of sleeping in the office overnight, Rob. Just think of all the time I waste going to and from Summerleigh. But it wouldn't do, would it?'

'Not at all, I'm afraid. Here, I brought you some coffee.' He put a cup and saucer in front of her. Then he said, 'Eva, I have to tell you that I've decided to give in my notice.'

'Oh, don't be ridiculous, Rob — ' She stared at him, her mind still fuddled by sleep. A host of reasons — he had been offered more lucrative work elsewhere; he was tired of working for a woman — darted through her head and were immediately dismissed. Then suddenly, looking at him, she understood, and she said angrily, 'Rob, *no*. No. You mustn't. Not *you*.'

'Eva, I have to.'

'No, you don't.' She felt furious with him. 'Your work here is so important — and you have three dependants — you don't have to join the army, you know you don't — '

'Strictly speaking, no, I don't. But Eva, this war isn't going to end soon. Should I wait till they're scraping the bottom of the barrel? Should I wait till they're calling up the fifty-year-old men, the widowers with children? It's more dignified, don't you think, to go now, under my own steam.'

She cried out, 'But I *need* you!'

'For the business, you mean?'

'Yes,' she said harshly. 'For the business.'

There was a long silence; she drank her coffee. Too hot, it scalded her mouth. She felt unbearably upset; she wanted to cry, to shout at him, to make him see reason.

She heard him say, 'You'll manage, I know you will. You've been working here for two years now.'

'But not on my own, Rob! Not on my own!'

'You won't be on your own. You've got good foremen and craftsmen who know the job inside out. And it's not as if we have to go chasing after orders these days.

There's too much work, not too little.'

She said spitefully, 'If you know there's too much work then why are you deserting us just when we need you?'

'That's not fair. You know that's not fair.' He went to the door. 'I have to go. I'll be late for supper. Are you coming?'

He held open the door. Sulkily, she pulled on her coat and followed him. As they walked out of the gates, he said, 'You're good at the job, Eva. You'll be all right. You're your father's daughter,' but she did not reply.

It was bitterly cold. Icy flakes of snow darted against their faces as they walked to Rob's lodgings. Then, passing a church, they heard singing.

Rob paused. 'Shall we go in?'

'Your landlady . . . your supper . . . '

He said forcefully, 'Be damned to my supper,' which shocked her rather, because Rob Foley never used bad language.

The church was ice-cold, lit with candles. As they stood at the back, listening to the singing, some of Eva's rage melted. It struck her that the choir was made up largely of girls and women, the tenor and bass supplied by a handful of old men and supplemented by the organ. She felt tears sting behind her eyes. She knew that her anger was not with Rob, but for the waste of it all, and the loneliness she would feel when he had gone. 'But I need you,' she had said. 'For the business.' *Not true, Eva Maclise*, she thought, *not true. Not just for the business.*

But oh, the risks of love . . . The pain of being the less loved and the pain of losing love. The Maclise sisters, she thought grimly, could have written a book about it. Yet after a while, she curled her hand into his. He did not speak, did not even look at her, but she felt the answering pressure of his fingers.

The chorale finished; they left the church. As they

walked down the steps he said, 'I love you. I know I shouldn't, but I love you, Eva.'

'Why shouldn't you?' She felt angry once more. 'You're not going to come over all Victorian again, about *stations in life* and all that rot, are you?'

'Well, there is that. And then there's my father.'

They walked down the road. The snow fell gently, caught briefly in the dim light of the street lamps, before disappearing. She said, 'Your father killed himself. I took a married man for a lover. So I should think that makes us just about equal, shouldn't you?'

She watched for the shock in his eyes, listened for the revulsion in his voice. But he gave a flicker of a smile and said, 'Both equally degenerate, you mean?'

'I suppose so.'

They began to walk again. When they reached the corner of the street in which he lodged, he said, 'What happened to you — is it over with?'

'Oh yes. It was over a long time ago.'

'But what happened to me will never be over. Suicide is a sign of a deranged mind. Many doctors believe madness to be hereditary.'

She said heatedly, 'I've always thought that doctors talk a lot of nonsense. Look at all the doctors who tried and failed to cure my mother when all she needed was something interesting to do.'

'But you could never be sure, Eva. There would always be that possibility, that shadow.'

She shivered and put up the collar of her coat. 'I'm not sure that I even *want* to love anyone ever again. I'm not sure that I want to risk it. And I'm not sure whether I can have children anyway — it never happened when Gabriel and I were together and it could have, so easily.' She swung round to him and said fiercely, 'You can't be sure of anything, Rob. If I've learned anything, I've learned that.' Then she kissed his cheek before she walked away to catch the tram.

She hadn't meant to see him off at the station. She had always hated railway station goodbyes, the whole awful business of watching someone you loved being taken away from you. But she had business with the family lawyer in Fargate that morning and when she left his office, she saw, glancing at her watch, that if she hurried, she might be just in time to see Rob off.

The train was already standing by the platform. Through the crowds, Eva picked out first Rob's mother and then Susan Foley, in the flowing black garments she affected to wear since her career as a medium had, with the war, taken off. She saw Rob's face light up when he caught sight of her, and saw that transformation she had first noticed, such a long time ago — a plain face made beautiful by a smile.

She said, 'I was going to post this to you because I didn't think I'd complete it in time. But then I finished it last night.' She handed him a piece of paper. 'I didn't frame it because I thought it would be easier to put it in your kitbag like this.'

He unrolled her sketch of his mother and sisters. She said quickly, 'I had to do it from memory, of course. And I'm afraid I'm rather rusty.'

'It's perfect. Thank you so much.' There was a shriek of steam and he picked up his luggage. 'I thought you didn't draw any more?'

'I don't. You're very honoured, Rob.'

The guard blew his whistle, waved his flag, and Winifred Foley burst into tears.

'Now, Mother — '

'I shall pray for you, Rob — '

'And if anything should happen, remember there is only a shadowy veil between the Now and the Beyond.'

'*Susan!*' Winifred Foley wept louder.

Both women clung to him, sobbing. Eva stepped

back. Disentangling himself, Rob climbed into the carriage.

The train drew a few yards down the platform and then stopped. She saw him lean out of the compartment door and heard him call out her name. And then she was running down the platform to him.

He swept her up in his arms, kissing her over and over again. They were still clinging to each other when the engine started up once more and, when at last he let her go, she stood back on the platform as the train pulled out of the station, watching, too breathless to wave.

★   ★   ★

Because of the cold and the shortage of coal, Ottilie had taken to wearing her fur coat indoors. The coat was much the same dark colour as her hair, Clemency thought: they had the same bright animal gleam.

Once, visiting Hadfield on her day off, Clemency was in the garden with Ottilie and Archie when the great black cloud of a Zeppelin grew and grew on the horizon. They watched it, filled with awe, until its shadow fell over them, and then they ran indoors and huddled under the kitchen table until it passed.

That night they shared a bed for warmth. Ottilie's body curled into Clemency's and her soft hair drifted against Clemency's face. Outside the wind raged. Clemency stroked Ottilie's hair as she slept, and thought how strange it was, how very strange, that in spite of everything — James, Father, Marianne — she should feel happier than she ever had in her entire life.

★   ★   ★

By the February of 1917, when the German army fell back to the Hindenberg Line, Iris had been nursing at

Etaples for over a year. Promoted to charge sister shortly after her arrival at the hospital, she was now responsible for a medical ward. Throughout the winter the cold seemed to still the grass that covered the dunes and freeze to icicles the drips leaking through the seams of the wood and canvas hut where she slept.

On the ward she cared for men with pneumonia, men with septicaemia and trench fever. Many of the patients also suffered from shell shock; when she was on night duty, the cries of the shell-shocked men and the groans of the wounded punctuated the darkness. She knew, as the months went on, that something had switched off inside her, much as it had done during the diphtheria epidemic at the Mandeville. There was only so much one could endure and she had long ago reached her limit. Though she carried out her duties with expert efficiency, sometimes she caught in the eyes of the VAD who assisted her on the ward an expression that discomfited her. Once, when there was a 'push', she found herself snapping at the VAD, hurrying her in the laying out of a dead soldier. Quite often she seemed to hear the hollow echo of her own voice, murmuring words of comfort to a dying man, words which had, for her, long ago ceased to have any meaning.

She always felt dirty, always felt tired. She felt dirty because there never seemed to be, in that long, long winter, enough hot water to take a bath. Like many of her colleagues, she had caught a stomach bug, an intermittent, grumbling nausea that every now and then sent her off to the lavatory to vomit wearily. When they were very busy she once or twice found herself dropping off to sleep standing up; it frightened her that she did so, made her fearful that she might make a mistake, neglect her duty. When she was able to go to bed, she slept very deeply, a blank, dark emptiness that often, by day, she found herself longing for. When they wrote to each other, she and Ash no longer spoke of the end of the war. In her heart she had accepted that it would go on forever. She guessed that Ash felt the same, that he, like her, knew that there was nothing now but dirt and horror, nothing to hope for, nothing vile that could not happen. Now, when she looked at the ring he had given her and tried to conjure up the sands, the dance, his kiss, she could not really remember what it had felt like. This was the more real.

On Easter Sunday, after prayers, Iris was ordered to empty her ward and prepare it for an influx of surgical casualties. The patients were shipped off to other hospitals or to convalescent homes in England and France and the beds were made up with clean linen. The following day the convoys of wounded began to arrive. Iris slid back into the familiar routine, the routine that she could now carry out unthinkingly: take off the patient's clothing, remove the CCS dressing, wash the wound, assess the patient's condition, put on a clean dressing. Take round bedpans, boil kettles, check pulses and temperatures. And all the time listen to the trains shunting to and fro, bringing wounded men back from the front, taking newly arrived troops out in their place.

Late on Tuesday evening a fresh convoy of wounded was brought into Iris's ward. She was moving from one patient to another when she caught sight of the VAD, one hand holding a pair of scissors, her other hand clamped over her mouth as she stared at her patient. Iris saw that the wounded man's entire head was swathed in bandages; only his mouth and nostrils were uncovered to permit him to breathe. She took the scissors from the VAD. As she was about to begin to remove the bandages, she found herself thinking wildly: *This could be someone I know.* The man's uniform was caked in mud; she could not see the insignia of his regiment. It could be Ash, it could be Aidan. It could be any one of her old friends from Summerleigh: she might have danced with this man when she was a girl. The hand holding the scissors began to shake uncontrollably. Then the patient whispered, 'Bit of a mess, aren't I, nurse?' and she got hold of herself and began to take off the bandages. As she peeled off the layers, she heard him murmur in a frightened voice, 'It isn't too bad, is it, nurse?'

'Not too bad at all.' Yet she had to concentrate to keep the tremor out of her own voice. 'We'll give you something for the pain. We'll patch you up, don't you worry.'

All the old platitudes and yet, as she removed the last of the bandages, she saw that half of his face had been shot away. She did what she could for him, sent him off for surgery, and as soon as she could, snatched a few moments outside, where she smoked a cigarette, her fingers juddering as she struggled to light it.

After that the numbness that had protected her for months seemed to dissolve. She lost what little appetite she had and her fitful sleep was interrupted by nightmares, nightmares in which she peeled away bloodied bandages to reveal horrors. A skull, crawling with maggots. James, blinded and dumb. And once, worst of all, an emptiness, a blank space where a head should have been.

A few days later, she was accompanying a patient from the ward to theatre, when a VAD came rushing up to her.

'Sister Maclise, there's a soldier on my ward says he knows you.'

Ash, she thought, her heart suddenly rushing. She knew that Ash's regiment, the York and Lancaster, had been involved in the fighting at Arras. She ran quick, shaking hands over her hair, pulled off her dirty apron and shoved it into the nearest laundry bin, and followed the VAD to the ward.

But it wasn't Ash, it was Lieutenant Richardson,

Ash's friend with the gramophone. There was a cage beneath the bedclothes covering his wounded leg, and his face was almost as white as the pillow.

'David.' She stood at his bedside. 'How are you?'

'Not so bad.' A shadow of a smile. 'Won't be dancing any more, though. They've just told me they're going to take off my leg.'

'David, I'm so sorry.' She took his hand.

He said, 'There's something I have to tell you — don't want to — but I must. Have to say it now in case I don't come through the operation.'

Inside she felt suddenly cold. 'Ash?' she whispered. 'Do you know something about Ash?'

'He didn't make it. Posted missing, someone said. I asked around — a chap from another platoon told me that Lieutenant Wentworth died at Monchy-le-Preux. I'm sorry, Iris. I'm so sorry.'

★ ★ ★

Apart from writing to her sisters, she didn't tell anyone else about Ash. She hadn't told any of her colleagues at the hospital about her engagement, and she didn't tell any of them about his death. She put his ring away in the little box where she kept her treasures and she tied up his letters with a ribbon and put them at the bottom of her bag. She didn't even cry. She had wept for James and Father, but she did not weep for Ash, whom she had loved and had meant to marry. Instead she continued to carry out her work, applying tourniquets and splints, cleaning and bandaging wounds.

The convoys began to ease off as the heat of the battle ebbed. She was on duty one evening, washing out utensils in the sink, when she realized that some of her hair had come down. She unpinned her cap and started to roll up the long lock of hair. Then she noticed something moving, caught among the gold strands.

Picking it off with her fingertips, she realized that it was a louse.

She gave a weak laugh. She remembered herself, twenty-two years old, dressing for the party at Summerleigh. Putting on her ball gown, tucking ostrich feathers and a gardenia into her hair. Diamonds in her ears, a spray of perfume. How foolish she had been to think that silks and diamonds would last forever. *This* was how life really was: dirt ingrained into her hands and lice in her hair.

There was a pair of surgical scissors on the draining board. She pulled the remaining pins out of her hair and then she picked up the scissors and began to cut. There was a sound; she looked up and saw the VAD staring at her, open-mouthed.

Iris went on cutting. She heard the VAD run out of the hut. Hanks of golden hair fell to the floor. Cut, cut, cut, cutting away a past that would never return.

More footsteps. A voice said, 'Sister? What are you doing?'

Iris looked up. 'I'm cutting my hair, Matron,' she said calmly. 'I'm cutting my hair.'

★　★　★

After Rob had gone, she began to make mosaics. It pleased her to make pictures out of broken things, from tiny offcuts of metal from the workshops, from fragments of old cups and plates, fragments that she discovered hidden away in attics and outhouses because the Maclises had been brought up to be frugal, not to waste anything.

Her pictures were of the girls in the workshops or of children playing in the streets. She had always been able to see beauty in ordinary things. She made the mosaics in the evenings, after work, in the sliver of time between supper and falling asleep. She had cleared out one of the maids' rooms in the top storey of the house; it was cold and damp, but she wrapped her coat around herself and put a hot-water bottle beneath her feet. On the day that she received the letter from Iris telling her that Ash was dead, she sat among the splinters of china and porcelain and thought of Ash at the picnic, sitting in the rocks, eating strawberries, Ash with Iris on his arm, walking through the rainy Whitechapel streets, and Ash, his eyes shining as he told them of his hopes for the future.

Not long afterwards she caught a bad cold. 'You will persist in sitting in draughts,' said Mother. 'You know how careful I have to be — it's so thoughtless of you to bring infection into the house. And you must remember to order more coal, Eva. I felt chilled to the bone when I sat in the drawing room yesterday afternoon.' No matter how often Eva explained to Mother that they were short of coal because there wasn't enough coal to go round, just as they were short of food because food had to be queued for these days and often as not, by the time you had queued, there wasn't anything left in the shops, Mother still put their difficulties down to inefficiency on Eva's part.

Waking the next day, her head pounded and her throat rasped. She wanted to roll over in bed and pull the eiderdown over her head, but she forced herself to get up, wash and dress. At work, in her office, she seemed to lurch between peeling off her cardigan and jacket because of the heat, and throwing them all back on again because she was cold. She had a fever, she realized wearily; she must remember to buy aspirin at lunchtime. Her sinuses felt as though they were filled with cement, and it was an effort to resolve the simplest problems in a day that was beset with difficulties. Several of the staff were off sick, which meant that women had to be moved from one workshop to another to fill the gaps. They grumbled, separated from their

531

friends. There was a new order from the Ministry of Munitions which, because it had to be given priority, meant that other jobs, some of which were already late, had to be delayed. A consignment of steel had been lost at the docks; in the end Eva walked down to the wharves to chase it up herself. Weaving through the heaps of coal and timber, she thought miserably how much she missed Rob, and how nice it would be if he were here, to take some of the burden from her shoulders.

She spent her lunchtime queuing for groceries in the city centre. There wasn't anyone else who could queue, what with Clemency away and Edith's legs so bad and Mrs Bradwell just too old and too sad these days to be expected to stand around in a chilly wind. And the thought of Mother, in her by now curiously dated outfits of whalebone, crêpe de chine and lace, standing in a queue, was simply ridiculous.

It was raining by the time she left work that evening and then the tram was full. She decided to walk home instead, her umbrella in one hand, the bag of groceries in the other. Reaching Summerleigh at last, she opened the front door, put down the heavy bag and peeled off her wet coat and scarf.

She heard her mother call out querulously, 'Eva? Is that you, Eva?'

'Yes, Mother.'

Lilian was in the dining room, sitting at an empty table. Eva stared at her. 'Mother? What are you doing?'

'Waiting for my supper.' Lilian looked bewildered.

'You haven't had your supper yet?' Eva glanced at the fireplace. 'And the fire . . . you haven't lit the fire!'

'So cold — I'm quite faint with hunger. You really will have to see about replacing Edith, Eva, she is getting more and more unreliable — '

'Mother,' said Eva heatedly, 'it's Edith's day off and Mrs Bradwell had to go to the hospital. I *told* you.'

'Please don't be cross with me, Eva — '

'I *said* that Mrs Bradwell would leave you a plate in the larder. You only had to fetch it — you only had to put a match to the fire — '

'Please don't shout at me, Eva — my poor head — if only Clemency or Iris were here — so tired — how can I be expected to manage on my own?'

Lilian's voice quivered with tears and her face crumpled. Suddenly Eva felt bitterly ashamed of herself. She wanted to cry too, but managed instead to kiss her mother on the cheek and say more gently, 'Why don't you have an early night? I could bring something up for you on a tray.'

In the pantry, she found the plate of bread and ham and pickles that Mrs Bradwell had prepared earlier, cut a slice of cake and made a pot of tea and carried the tray up to her mother. Then she helped her mother out of her petticoats and stays and into a nightdress, found her a hot-water bottle and kissed her goodnight.

Back in the kitchen she was too tired to eat, so she drank the remains of the tea, now rather cold, and then cleared up. Then she put on her mackintosh and went out into the garden. There was a lacework of tiny holes in the cabbage seedlings Clemency had planted so carefully. She couldn't even defeat the slugs, she thought hopelessly. Back in the house, she made her packed lunch for the following day, ironed a blouse, washed out some stockings and laid the breakfast things. By the time she had finished it was eleven o'clock. Catching sight of herself in the hall mirror, she felt a wash of despair. Her hair had frizzed because of the rain and her nose was red and peeling. She was bundled up in jumpers and shawls because of the cold. *Once I was pretty*, she thought. *Once, I meant to be an artist, to have my own place, to live life my own way.*

In the drawing room, she got out her pen and paper, intending to write to her sisters. She sat in Great-aunt

Hannah's chair: she missed Great-aunt Hannah, she missed Winnie. It would have been lovely to have had Winnie sitting on her lap, lovely to have been able to stroke her. Then she wouldn't have felt so alone. The house echoed; she was aware of the many empty rooms, of the shadows in stairs and corridors and the stillness of the drapes and hangings. The thought came to her as she sat there, blowing her nose, that it might always be like this, that she might always be alone. That Rob might never come back. That Aidan and her sisters might never come back. She threw the pen and paper aside. The foolishness of writing to Marianne when they had not heard from her for so long!

Great-aunt Hannah's tartan rug was folded on the arm of the chair; she wrapped it round her. It was an awful old prickly thing, but it still smelt, reassuringly, of camphor and violet comfits. She knew that she should go to bed, yet now, for the first time that day, she felt comfortable. Her eyelids were heavy; she curled up in the chair, her head against the wing. She thought: *I must remember to ask Mr Garrett to check our supplies of brown paper and sacking . . . I must find out whether that wretched girl in the packing shed . . . what was her name, Sally something, ever intends to come into work again . . . I must remember . . .*

Eva slept. She dreamt that they were children again and they were playing on the beach. Marianne, her skirt tucked into her knickers, was collecting shells. Iris and Clemency were playing catch. Eva herself was making a castle. She was putting a paper flag on the topmost turret when she heard Iris say her name. Not wanting to be interrupted, she ignored her, but Iris said her name again, louder this time.

Eva opened her eyes. Iris, wearing a navy-blue coat and hat, was standing in front of her. Eva blinked, expecting the dream to dissolve. When it did not, she whispered, 'Iris? Is that really you?'

Iris nodded. 'I've come home, Eva.'

Eva flung her arms around her sister. 'Oh, *Iris*,' she said and burst into tears.

17

Ned Fraser fetched her the opals from White Cliffs. When she held them up to the light, she saw the twists of colour caught in the stone. 'The opal miners live in white caves under the ground,' he told her. 'I'll take you there, Annie, if you like.'

'Some day, Ned,' she said. 'Some day.'

She had been working at Redburn's Hotel for a year. When she and George had first arrived in Broken Hill, she had trudged from shop to hotel to pub to laundry, looking for work. Time and again she had been turned down — her slightness, she thought, her soft, quiet voice, so out of place here. And the child, of course. But Jean Redburn, the short, dumpy, no-nonsense widow who owned the hotel, had taken pity on her. 'There's a room at the back of the house you and the boy can have,' she told her. 'I'll take the rent out of your wages. And my three can keep an eye on George.' She chucked George under his chin. 'My Jenny will love you, little fellow. She'll think you're the bees' knees.'

At first Marianne cleaned and washed dishes, but then, after a few weeks, Jean offered her work in the saloon bar. 'You've a pretty face, Annie,' she said to Marianne one evening, 'if only you'd smile a bit more. My boys like to see a pretty face.'

Jean's boys were the miners who had made Broken Hill a boom town, the miners who prised silver and lead from the earth. Every Friday evening they poured into the hotel bar, some still wearing their filthy work clothes, others spruced up, dressed in their best. Redburn's bar echoed with their shouts, songs and laughter. Whenever there was a fight, Jean threw a bucket of cold water over them. If that didn't work, she ordered them out into the street. And if they didn't go quietly, then some of their colleagues were always happy to hurl them through the doors.

Marianne hadn't meant to stay so long in Broken Hill. She had meant to move on after a few months, as she had always done before. It was better that way, she reasoned, safer. Yet, in the end, she had stayed. After a while she realized that she probably wouldn't find anywhere safer than Broken Hill. Though she still had bad days — days when, walking down the busy main street, she'd catch sight of a man with a head of pale hair, a man with a certain attitude and stance, and she'd shudder — there began to be less bad days. Broken Hill, in the middle of tens of thousands of acres of wilderness, would not be easy to find.

She still had nightmares, though. Often, dreaming, she relived that last journey from Blackwater, stumbling along the mountain path, George in her arms, glancing back over her shoulder to see whether *he* was pursuing her. She relived the hustle and bustle of the bazaar as she threaded through the festival crowds to the railway station. Inside the third-class carriage, no one had stood aside for her, no one had murmured respectful greetings. She had sat in the only available space, perched on the end of a wooden bench. A beggar, sitting on the floor between the seats, had stretched out a clawed hand to her; pedlars had pushed through the crowded corridors, selling nuts and sweets. Her anonymity had protected her, had kept her safe.

In Colombo she had found a Dutch mail packet to take her as far as Singapore. From Singapore, she travelled on a series of steam ferries that skipped their way from one local port to another. Somewhere between Singapore and Surabaya, she had changed back into Western clothes and become Annie Leighton, a war widow with a small son. She became used to third-class cabins in the petrol-smelling depths of the hold, and to sleeping on deck on a hot, tropical night, George in her arms. She eked her money out as far as possible and never drew attention to herself.

Two months after she had left Blackwater she reached Sydney. By then, most of her money had gone, so she worked as a cleaner and seamstress, all the time plunging deeper and deeper into the fathomless red heart of Australia. As they travelled, she watched George shake off the fears and tantrums of his infancy and become once more the happy little boy he was meant to be. She made herself resist the impulse to coddle him, to watch him every moment of the day.

She discovered skills and aptitudes she had not known she possessed. She nursed George when he was sick, she made his clothes, she fed him and cared for him. She taught herself to cook, to light a fire, and to clean a floor so she could see her face in the tiles. She learned how to dispatch rattlesnakes, mad dogs and amorous miners.

She had other, darker talents. She had learned how to steal and how to lie. She had learned how to kill.

There was a price to be paid for freedom and that price, she feared, was to live alone for the rest of her life. She was neither free to love another man nor free to go home. If Lucas lived and she returned to England, then he would find her and take George from her. If he was dead, then she had killed him. Though she could, perhaps, have convinced a court of law that his death had been an accident (his head hitting the fire surround, her need to protect herself), she herself knew the truth. She had meant to kill him. She had wanted him to die. A strange state of being, she often thought, not to know whether she was a widow or a wife; only to know for certain that she was a murderess.

Yet, though it had been a long journey from Summerleigh to Broken Hill, she regretted none of it. She knew that with Arthur she had had a year of perfect happiness, longer than many people knew in a lifetime. And her marriage to Lucas had given her George. Love could be born out of hatred.

Sometimes, on her evenings off, she walked with Ned Fraser to the Menindee Lakes. Black-branched trees grew out of the pale water and wedge-tailed eagles circled overhead. Ned told her about his family, back in Scotland.

'Do you write to them?' she asked.

'I'm not much of a writer,' he said, 'but I send something home every now and again.'

'What do you send?'

'A photo, sometimes. Once I sent them opals from White Cliffs.' He threw a pebble into the lake. 'Reckon you've got to keep in touch. Reckon it wouldn't be much of a world if people didn't let their folks know they were thinking of them.'

News of the war reached even Broken Hill. She found herself thinking more and more about her family, wondering whether they had survived, or whether, with her silence, she added to their griefs.

Sometimes, Arthur had said to her the first time they had met, *you have to take a chance.* One day she asked Ned to buy her the opals. Three of them, one for each sister. She wrapped them in cotton wool and placed them in a box.

She had a photograph of herself and George taken, dressed in their Sunday best. She pressed flowers from the garden that she was making behind the hotel and chose one of George's drawings. She gave the package to one of the travelling salesmen who stayed at the hotel, who promised to find someone to post it for her, somewhere far, far away from Broken Hill. She would not yet let them know where she was. Not yet. One day maybe. When she was safe.

★ ★ ★

Iris explained to Eva that matron had sent her home. 'She said I needed a rest,' Iris told Eva, as she took off her hat. 'I think it was because of this. I think she thought I'd gone crackers.'

Eva stared, horrified. 'Your hair. Your beautiful hair.'

'I had lice,' said Iris. 'I must have caught them from one of the soldiers. I think I've got rid of them — they gave me some stuff to wash my hair with. But whenever I think about them, I scratch.'

She would not go back to France, Iris told her. She'd had enough; she was through with nursing. She was home for good. Eva thought how tired she looked, how thin.

They looked after each other, taking each other breakfast in bed so that they could take turns having a lie-in. Iris queued for food and helped with the house. Iris also discovered the address of an expensive little nursing home in Scarborough, and packed Mother off for rest and recuperation.

In the evenings they talked for hours. Eva learned that Ash had been posted missing. Eva said, 'Then you don't know for sure.'

'That's what Ash said to me the last time I saw him.'

'You mustn't give up hope, Iris.'

'I know what *missing* means. It means that he was blown to bits, that there wasn't even a body to bury.' There was despair in Iris's eyes.

Eva changed the subject, but in secret she wrote letters. Letters to the War Office, letters to Ash's commanding officer, and to military and Red Cross hospitals.

There was, at last, better news from the Front. The battle of Arras had been, if not an outright victory, at least a partial one — something to celebrate in a war where victories had been few and far between. That month, the Americans came into the war on the side of the Allies. Even though the American volunteer army would not be ready for battle for some time yet, it seemed to Eva that with American energy and American strength the conflict might one day come to a conclusion.

Iris had been home for three weeks, when, returning to Summerleigh one evening after work, Eva found her sitting at the kitchen table, crying.

She was clutching a letter in her hand. Eva's heart sank. She sat down beside her. 'Iris — '

'It's Ash.'

'I'm so sorry.'

Iris shook her head. 'He's alive.' There was joy beneath the tears. 'He's alive, Eva!'

★ ★ ★

There had been two Lieutenant Wentworths in Ash's battalion; it had been the other one, Alan Wentworth, who had been killed at Monchy-le-Preux. Ash had been badly wounded. Left for dead, he had eventually been picked up by stretcher bearers and taken to a casualty clearing station. From there he had been transported to a military hospital, where he had been unconscious for several days. After he had come round, he had written to Iris at Etaples. By the time his letter was returned to him, telling him that she had left Etaples, he had been moved to another hospital. He had not realized that Iris believed him dead until, in the London military hospital in which he was recovering from his wounds, he had received letters from both Eva and David Richardson.

Iris went to visit him. At the entrance to the ward, she paused, looking from bed to bed. She tried to ready herself, to steady her nerves. She knew that he would not be the same. They never were the same. She must not show him that she was upset, she told herself sternly. She must be gentle and undemanding; the last

541

thing an injured soldier wanted was his fiancée weeping over him.

Her resolution lasted as long as her first kiss and greeting. Then, looking at him, at the cuts and bruises and bandages, at the *mess* the war had made of him, she said with sudden passion, 'Oh, *Ash*. I *told* you to look after yourself! I *told* you!'

He took her in his arms. 'Don't cry. I'm here now, aren't I? Don't cry, my darling Iris, please don't cry.'

★　★　★

Iris and Ash were married in the July of 1917. Eva knew that it wasn't the grand wedding that Iris had once hoped for. But Iris looked beautiful in Mother's old white lace wedding gown, made to fit, and Ash was handsome in his army uniform, though he still had to lean on a stick. And the weather was fine and Clemency and Mother and Philip were there, and even Aidan had managed to get leave.

They held the reception at Summerleigh. They had hoarded food for the buffet and Aidan had brought back bottles of champagne with him from France. They decorated the table with pink and white roses from Summerleigh's garden, and Mrs Bradwell made a cake.

After the speeches, after the cake, they went outside. There was some talk of dancing, which never really came to anything, and then they began to trail off, in twos and threes, through the garden.

'My pills,' said Mother suddenly, putting her hand up to her head. 'I've forgotten to take my pills. My poor head. Eva, darling . . . '

Eva walked through the garden. She saw that Ash and Iris were in the orchard, sitting in the shade of the trees. Aidan was talking to Clemency. Philip seemed to be trying to persuade Clemency's friend, Ottilie, to keep pigs. 'So many people have completely the wrong idea about pigs. They're marvellous animals . . . so intelligent and clean . . . '

Eva fetched Mother's pills from her bedroom. She was running downstairs when there was a knock at the door.

The postman handed her a parcel. She thought at first it was another wedding present, but then, reading the inscription, her heart began to pound.

She took the parcel outside and called Iris and Clemency.

'A *parcel*,' said Iris.

Clemency said, 'Who's it for?'

'It's for us,' said Eva. 'It's for all of us. It's from Marianne.'

Eva cut through the string and sealing wax. As she unpeeled layers of tissue paper to reveal a gleam of opals, a child's drawing, a photograph, Clemency straightened out the brown-paper wrapping. She read what Marianne had written there.

To all my sisters.

Other titles published by
The House of Ulverscroft:

MIDDLEMERE

Judith Lennox

The Coles have lived in Middlemere, an isolated tenant farm, for half a century. When, in 1942, the family are threatened with eviction, Martha Cole and her small son, Jem, flee the house, while Martha's husband, Sam, and their eight-year-old daughter, Romy, barricade themselves inside Middlemere. When Sam brandishes a shotgun, the police are called in, and Romy sees her father shot dead. Years later, Martha Cole has remarried and she and her family are living in much-reduced circumstances. Romy, now almost nineteen, is quick, clever and single-minded. She has never forgotten — or forgiven — the violence and injustice of the Coles' eviction, and schemes to restore the family fortunes.

THE SHADOW CHILD

Judith Lennox

July 1914, the eve of the First World War, and fourteen-year-old Alix Gregory is holidaying in France with the wealthy Lanchbury family. She is looking after two-year-old Charlie Lanchbury when he disappears during a picnic and is never seen again. Alix is blamed for the tragedy and cannot escape from the resulting disintegration of the family. After the war, through her marriage and the birth of her son, Alix finds happiness. Yet she is haunted by the loss of her baby cousin. As the years pass, and as the world again descends into the horrors of war, the question remains: will Charlie Lanchbury ever be found?

THE WINTER HOUSE

Judith Lennox

Three girls growing up in the Fens between two world wars would meet, winter or summer, at an old wooden house by the waterside to confide all their secrets and heartaches. There was Robin, idealistic and clever, destined for Cambridge; Maia, beautiful and ambitious, looking for a rich husband; and quiet Helen, living under the seemingly benevolent tyranny of her widower father, the local vicar. Adulthood separates the three girls, and Robin, abandoning ideas of university, goes to London to work amongst the poor, meeting there her first great love. Maia's ideal marriage ends in tragedy, and Helen, meanwhile, has her very sanity threatened.

FOOTPRINTS ON THE SAND

Judith Lennox

The Mulgraves are a rootless, bohemian family who travel the continent, staying in crumbling Italian palazzos, Spanish villas, French vineyards, picking up friends and hangers-on as they go, and moving on when Ralph Mulgrave's latest enthusiasm dwindles. Faith, the eldest child of the family, longs for a proper home. But, in 1940, Germany invades France and the Mulgraves are forced to flee to England. In the dangerous landscape of wartime London, Faith finds work as an ambulance driver, and meets once again one of Ralph's retinue from those distant and, in retrospect, golden days of childhood . . .

WRITTEN ON GLASS

Judith Lennox

It is 1946 and the Temperleys and the Chancellors are old neighbours, living on the south coast of England. Marius Temperley has recently left the army and is struggling to fit into civilian life. His quick-tempered and passionate sister, Julia, has been running the family business since her father's death. When seventeen-year-old Topaz Brooke visits her cousins, Jack and Will Chancellor, for the first time since the outbreak of war, she finds that a great deal has changed. Both brothers are in love with Julia Temperley. As the years go by, family secrets are revealed, and the Temperleys and the Chancellors learn that passion can be both destructive and redemptive.

THE DARK-EYED GIRLS

Judith Lennox

Growing up through the 1970s, Liv, Rachel and Katherine have to come to terms with the harsh realities of life and relationships . . . Liv marries the man of her dreams, who turns out to be dangerously unstable. Katherine embarks upon a risky affair. And Rachel marries against her parents' will. Pregnant with her first child, Rachel suddenly calls her two friends in desperation, demanding that they come to her immediately. But Liv can think only of the man she loves and Katherine is preoccupied by her new life in London. They aren't there for Rachel when she needs them most, and the tragic consequences will haunt them . . .